Choices in Life

By

Karen Jamison

This book is a work of fiction. Places, events, and situations in this story are purely fictional. Any resemblance to actual persons, living or dead, is coincidental.

ISBN: 1-4140-1075-3 (e-book)
ISBN: 1-4140-1076-1 (Paperback)

This book is printed on acid free paper.

1st Books - rev. 11/17/03

Chapter one

Just your average day in a drug-infested, lower-class neighborhood in a big city. There are raggedy houses with the doors and windows boarded up, abandoned by the owners. Cars are parked on the streets that can't be driven because they are broken or probably stolen and abandoned. Teenagers hanging on street corners or in alleyways more than likely selling drugs. Little dirty and dingy looking children are running around with hardly any clothes on. There are a few adults sitting on their steps or porches gossiping. Every now and then a police car would pass by and the teenagers would scatter. But as soon as the police car is out of sight they resume their positions.

A few of the residents often complain about the drug dealings going on in their neighborhood, but to no avail. Most of them turn a blind eye to what happens in their own neighborhood and on their street, hoping and praying nothing will happen to them or their family members.

Twenty-year-old Darlene Carson has an aunt and cousins who live in such a neighborhood. She used to live in the same neighborhood when she was a child. Back then it was a safe and fun neighborhood. Over the years it changed. Her parents were killed in a car accident a couple of years ago and her aunt is her only close relative. Since her parents' death, she has lived with her aunt and cousins off and on for two years.

Darlene attends college in a nearby city. She lives on campus and will be a senior this year. She rarely has a reason to go home other than living with them for the summer. The only times she goes home to visit are on holidays or if there is a family emergency.

The summer has come and it was time for Darlene to go and live with her aunt, which is something she was not looking forward to. Darlene considered herself to be quite mature for her age. The death of her parents had catapulted her into adulthood at a rapid pace. She had to look out for herself and depend only on herself.

In the year that followed her parents' untimely death, she was forced to become independent. Sure she had her aunt, but she was very self-reliable. Besides, she really didn't like visiting her aunt's house that much.

Darlene's parents hadn't been highly educated people, but they obtained their high school diplomas. Her father had taken training classes and had been a certified electrician. Her mother had gone to nursing school and became a nurse. They earned a fairly good income between the two of them. They lived in a nice middle-class neighborhood and she was their only child.

Darlene has a good deal of money, which she saved from the insurance from her parents' death. They both had a ten thousand-dollar life insurance policy with a double indemnity pay-off for accidental death. She had received forty thousand dollars from their deaths. She spent ten thousand dollars for their funeral, put twenty thousand dollars in a mutual fund, and bought a slightly used car for seven thousand dollars cash. And the remaining three thousand dollars were put into a regular savings account. She had put all of her parents' furniture in storage and had given all of their clothing away. Some went to family and friends who wanted them and the rest went to charities. Darlene could have chosen not to live with her aunt and cousins, but she thought she could help them out financially. And even though she wasn't technically staying with them, she sent her aunt one hundred dollars every month. Her aunt had no idea how much money she had received from the insurance company or how she was able to send her money every month. She was just glad to take what had been offered.

There wasn't much for Darlene to spend money on. She is a very good student and was attending college on a full academic scholarship. Her only expenses were the food she bought off campus, clothing, school activities, socializing, car insurance, gas, and the storage of her parents' furniture, which she paid annually.

Darlene is pursuing a double major in accounting and finance. She also works for one of the local accounting firms. They usually solicited the help of the top students in accounting from the university to help out during the tax season. It was only part-time work that lasted from January to the end of the semester in May. Darlene has worked with them since her sophomore year. This year she was offered a summer internship with a bank in her home city. Her job doesn't start until June and that gave her two weeks to hang out with her cousin, Crystal. The two have always been close. They are first cousins because their mothers were sisters, but they are like day and night. Darlene's mother had always tried to better herself while Crystal's mother had always depended on a man. Darlene is a year older than Crystal, which was the same age difference between their mothers. Their characteristics seemed to have passed down a generation also because Darlene always went after what she wanted and Crystal always waited for it to be given to her. Darlene's other cousins, Robert and Darryl, are fifteen and seventeen years old respectively. Darlene is closer to Darryl because he has a good head on his shoulders and he did well in school. Robert only wanted to act like a common thug and had already been held back a year in school.

While on the road driving home this time, Darlene did a lot of thinking about her future for some reason. She only has a year left in college. She already has a few job offers from out-of-state banks and accounting firms lined up for after graduation. But she really didn't want to go too far away from what little family she had left. She liked her independence, but the knowledge that her family was always close by was comforting.

It is only a two-hour drive to get to her aunt's house from college, but she was in no hurry so it took her a little longer. When she was a few blocks away from her aunt's house, she noticed a group of boys hanging on the street corner. A white Mercedes Benz with dark tinted windows pulled up and all of the boys started gathering around the car. Normally she would have kept going, but she recognized one of her cousins among the boys so she pulled over and parked her black Volkswagen Jetta.

She noticed a few of the boys reaching their hand in then taking it out the car. She had a good idea about what was going on so she got out of her car and approached her cousin. He is the same height as her, but a bit husky and very light skinned.

"Robert," she said, startling him as he turned around to see who had called him. He looked as if he had been caught red-handed doing something he shouldn't be doing. "What are you doing?" she asked. "Let's go," she said not giving him a chance to answer.

A few of the other boys started laughing and teasing him. Robert didn't like the way Darlene was trying to embarrass him so he said, "I ain't ready to go," very indignantly.

Darlene shouldn't have said it the way she did so she tried another method. "I just got in town and wanted you to help me unpack. But if you don't want what I have for you . . ." She let the sentence trail off intentionally.

Every time she came home she brought Robert and Darryl something. She usually brought clothes for them. It helped her aunt out a lot and it gave her peace of mind to know they wouldn't have to steal them. At least Robert wouldn't, she thought.

"Yeah. I'll help you unpack."

The guy sitting in the car was checking her out and wondering who she was. He decided to speak up and said, “Say, Rob. Who’s that fine honey you talkin’ to?”

Darlene noticed that he had been looking at her from her head to her toe during her conversation with her cousin. She was wearing a pair of blue jean shorts, a white tank top, white tube socks, and white leather sneakers. Her shoulder-length, permed, black hair was pulled back from her round face into a ponytail that hung down her back. She is five feet, six inches tall with a medium figure and a medium brown, nutmeg complexion. But she doesn’t pay too much attention to the guy in the car. She knew his type and she didn’t want to be bothered. He was wearing dark shades so she really couldn’t see much of his face. Not that she cared to see it anyway.

“She just my cousin, man,” Robert answered as she started walking back to her car.

“What’s her name?” the guy from the car asked.

By then, Darlene was at her car and getting in it. She didn’t hear whether or not her cousin had told the guy her name. But she did notice that while Robert was talking with him, he was looking in her direction. She blew her horn impatiently and a few minutes later Robert came and got in the car. They rode the rest of the way home in silence.

When they arrived at her aunt’s house, she parked alongside the curb in front of the house. As they were getting out of the car, she saw Darryl walking up the street coming toward the house. He is six feet tall and very slim. He is just about the same shade of brown as she is and they look a little alike. He can easily pass as her brother. And he was always glad when she came home. Both boys helped to bring her things into the house.

Once Darlene got inside, she plopped down on the very comfortable gray sofa in the living room. She wondered where Crystal was because her cousin was always there when she got in town so she asked, "Where's Crystal?"

Everyone was silent for a few noticeable seconds. She looked around at each of them and noticed her aunt was looking a bit uncomfortable. "Auntie Betty?" she prompted.

"Have you talked to Crystal lately, Darlene?"

"No, not since Easter. Why?"

"She pregnant," Robert blurted out.

Everyone was silent, but Darlene still couldn't understand why that would cause this type of reaction. "And?" she asked, probing for a reason for their odd behavior.

Robert explained further and said, "My mama kept saying how you ain't got pregnant and that you doin' somethin' with yo'self. And that she oughta be like you. She just started cryin' and left."

Darlene was hoping nothing like that would happen. She could see that her aunt was feeling bad about what had happened. "Darryl and Robert, take my suitcases to Crystal's room," she said since they always shared a room when she visited. After they left the room, she talked to her aunt and tried to comfort her. "It's okay, Auntie Betty. She'll come back," she said, rubbing her aunt's shoulder.

"I know," Betty said. "It's just that she's gotten worse. I know I shouldn't have thrown what all you've done in her face. But she need to get her life together. I don't want her to end up like me."

Darlene was aware that her aunt had tried to do good for her children. She had lived a life she didn't want her children to have to live. Crystal, Darryl, and Robert all had different fathers. Crystal's father had just up and left them without a word when she was two years old. Him and Betty had never married. Robert's father had left because Betty had still been in love with Darryl's father, who had been killed and was the only man she had married.

"She'll be fine," Darlene said. "How long has she been gone?"

"About a month," her aunt answered.

"Do you know where she might be?"

"No. The boys might know," her aunt said then she called them back into the living room and questioned them about the whereabouts of Crystal and they had a few ideas.

The three of them got in her car and drove around. Darryl suggested a few places, but everyone they had talked to hadn't seen Crystal. Robert took them to some other places and they had a little luck. They came across the same white Mercedes Benz. Darlene pulled over at Robert's request. He got out and went over to the car and started talking to the guy inside. Darlene took the opportunity to talk to Darryl.

"So what's been going on in school?" she asked.

"Same old thing."

"How're your grades?"

"B's and C's mostly. With my usual A in art."

"I hope it's mostly B's."

"Yeah."

They continued to look out the window at Robert then she asked, "Who's that Robert talking to?" The driver-side window was rolled all the way down on the car so she was able to get a better look at the driver.

"That's Al. He hardly ever comes around. He usually sends one of his flunkies around."

"Oh. So he's the big man in charge, huh?"

"As far as I know."

"Do you and Robert mess with that stuff?"

"I don't. I can't speak for Robert though. All I do is smoke a cigarette now and then."

"You don't need to do that," she said just as Robert started walking back to the car. The guy in the car was looking in their direction. Robert came to the driver-side of the car and squatted down so he could talk to her.

"Big Al say he might know where Crystal is, but you have to ask him."

"What?" Darryl and Darlene asked in unison.

"He wanna talk to Darlene."

Darlene looked over in Al's direction then she turned her head and looked out the front windshield before she asked, "Did he give you any idea where Crystal might be?"

"No. Just go ask him, Darlene," Robert said, moving so she could get out of the car.

Darlene really didn't want to talk to this guy, but she wanted to find her cousin. She got out of her car and walked to where he was parked. He was waiting patiently for her, she noticed. She started to turn around and go back to her car, but she kept walking.

When she approached his car, he smiled and showed off his gold tooth. It was on the right side next to his front tooth and it had a dollar sign in it. He was also wearing a small diamond stud earring in his left ear. She noticed his skin color was almost the same shade of brown as hers. She couldn't tell much more than that from his position in the car.

"Do you know where my cousin is or not?" she asked impatiently. She wanted to make this conversation as short as possible.

"Maybe. Maybe not. That depends."

"On what?"

"On you."

"And how's that?" she asked, really beginning to get irritated. She stood with her arms folded, just below her breasts and her left leg supporting most of her weight while she impatiently tapped her right foot.

"Maybe if you ask me a little nicer, I can remember the last time I saw her," he said, looking directly at her face.

Darlene was silent for a moment while she weighed her options. She could be nice to him and probably find her cousin within minutes or walk off and not find her cousin for days. She wished she could look him in his eyes, but all she could see was her own reflection in his shades.

"Okay," she said after making her decision. She relaxed her body and stood in a less irritated stance. "Do you know where my cousin could be?" she asked in a nice and soft voice.

"I may have some idea," he said.

"Well, will you please tell me?" she asked. She could tell he was enjoying this. She decided she would walk off if he didn't tell her and to hell with it.

"She was over at Paula's house the last time I saw her."

"Paula?" Darlene frowned a little, trying to place a face to the name, but she couldn't.

Al noticed the confused look on her face and he asked, "You not from around here, huh?"

"I'm away a lot," she said. She didn't see a need to go into detail.

"Robert will know who I'm talking about."

"Thanks," she said and turned with the intentions of walking away.

"Hold up," he said, stopping her from leaving. "You busy tonight?"

"What?"

"I asked were you busy tonight. I thought maybe we could go out tonight."

"I don't think so."

"Why? What harm could it be? It's just dinner. You have to eat."

"I can eat at my house. And I'm busy tonight."

"How about tomorrow night then?"

"No," she said with finality and walked off. She heard him call her name, but she ignored him.

When she got back to her car, she told Robert the name of the woman and he directed her to the place. They ended up in a housing project a good distance from her aunt's house. Darryl stayed in the car while Robert and Darlene went to Paula's apartment.

Robert knocked on the door and a kid answered. He looked barely four years old, Darlene thought. Soon an older woman came to see who was at the door. She recognized Robert and let them in.

The living room was a mess from the ceiling to the floor. The plaster was peeling and there were cracks and stains all over the walls. Trash was spilling out of the garbage can in the kitchen and was all over the floor. There were empty beer and soda cans, fast food containers and bags, and dirty diapers scattered about. It made the house smell of old garbage and urine and as if it hadn't been cleaned in years. And the roaches seemed to have the run of the place.

Crystal came from one of the other rooms. Crystal is very dark skinned and a few inches taller than Darlene. Her permed hair stopped at her neck and was cut evenly. She wore it combed straight back, slicked to her head. Overall she was a nice-looking young woman. But from the expression on her face she was shocked to see Darlene.

"How did you find out where I was?" Crystal asked Darlene.

"Big Al told us," Robert answered.

"And you just couldn't wait to bring Darlene," she said and plopped down on the very dirty, torn, and worn down, green sofa.

Darlene wasn't about to sit down or touch one piece of furniture in the room. She wanted to just leave. But she wanted to leave with her cousin.

"Don't act like that, Crystal. Auntie Betty is worried about you. Why don't you come home," she said.

"Yeah, right. That way she can throw you in my face while you're here."

"If that's the way you feel, I'll move out so you won't have that excuse to not come home," she said, bluffing to see if her cousin would take the bait.

"Oh no you won't," Crystal said, getting up off of the sofa, taking the bait. "I don't wanna be the one to blame for you moving out. That'll just be one more thing for my mama to throw in my face. I'll get my stuff."

Robert and Darlene waited while Crystal got her things. Robert carried her bag and put it in the trunk of the car then they got inside.

Crystal rolled her eyes at her other brother and said, "I betchu glad Darlene's home, huh?" She knew Darryl wished deep down that Darlene was his sister instead of her. Crystal and Robert rode in the back while Darryl stayed up front. No one talked all the way home.

When they got home, Betty was standing in the door. She looked relieved when she saw Crystal. Betty cooked mustard greens, rice, corn bread, and fried chicken for dinner. Everyone ate silently until Darlene started a conversation.

"So, Robert, how's school?"

Both Crystal and Darryl started laughing.

Betty said, "He was suspended again. I keep telling him that he better stay in school. Maybe you can talk some sense into him."

Darlene looked back at Robert and asked, "What happened?"

"It's them teachers. They be trippin'. Talkin' 'bout my clothes 'n stuff like that."

"Uh-huh. What do they say about your clothes?" she asked.

"Stuff like they don't fit right."

She didn't care for seeing her cousins dress like some of those other kids. That was why she usually bought them clothes when she visited. And she always made sure the clothes wouldn't fit too big. Fitting loose and baggy was one thing. But when the clothes looked like another person could fit inside them also was too big, she thought. The clothing she got them were always name brands and they loved the gifts.

"Well, I hope what I got 'fit right'," she said as she got up from the table and went to Crystal's bedroom. She pulled out two basketball jerseys with matching shorts with her college logo on them. She brought them back with her to the kitchen. She usually bought them regular clothes, but this had a college name on it. They thanked her and went to their room. She usually gave Crystal her gift too, but she didn't this time because she didn't want to start another argument. Soon Crystal got up and went to her room. Darlene gave her aunt an envelope with three hundred dollars in it. Her aunt saw the money and got teary eyed. She usually sent her one hundred dollars a month, but since it was the summer and she would actually be staying there and working she gave her more. Her aunt was getting by okay financially. She worked as a housekeeper in a hotel and she also received a Social Security check for Darryl. But Darlene was sure the extra money she sent was helpful. She left and went to the room with Crystal. There were twin beds in the room. Crystal was lying across her bed and didn't bother turning when Darlene entered the room. She sat on her bed and looked at Crystal. She couldn't tell whether her cousin was asleep or not. She just wondered why it seemed as though her cousin resented her all of a sudden. They had been real close growing up. With hindsight she did sort of notice that their relationship started to taper off. It started when she first went away to college. But when she came home, she always hung out with Crystal. She decided not to dwell on it any longer. She reached into her suitcase and pulled out a T-shirt with the college logo on it and laid it on Crystal's bed before she walked back into the living room. She sat and talked with her aunt about her summer job and how much she was looking forward to it.

While they were talking, Crystal came into the living room holding the T-shirt Darlene had given her. Darlene braced herself for a scathing remark and was surprised when it didn't come.

"Thanks for the shirt, Darlene," Crystal said.

"Come and sit down with us," she said then patted the spot on the sofa.

Crystal slowly walked over and took a seat. The telephone started ringing and Betty left to go and answer it. That gave the cousins time to talk privately.

"I guess you already know I'm pregnant," Crystal said and Darlene nodded. "Well, it was an accident. I guess I got careless with my pills."

"Careless?"

"Yeah. I forgot to go to the clinic and get some more. I thought that since I had been taking them for a few years, I was still protected. Anyway, we used a condom but it broke."

"It broke?" Darlene repeated. She was finding all of this hard to believe. It was a sad fact that with free family planning clinics around young women and teenage girls were too lazy to go and get a yearly exam and free contraceptives.

"Yeah. It happens sometimes," Crystal said, giving a lame excuse.

"Who's the father?" she asked curiously.

"You don't know him. I met this guy at a club a few months ago. It was after you went back to school after Christmas."

"Does he know that you're pregnant?"

"Not yet."

"How far along are you?"

"Three months."

"Three months!" she exclaimed in a hushed tone because she didn't want her aunt to hear. "Why didn't you tell me sooner?" She was shocked that her cousin would keep something like that from her and for so long because they used to tell each other everything.

"I don't know. I guess it's hard trying to follow in your footsteps. You were always good at things. You had good grades all through school. Now you're in college and . . ."

"Aw, Crystal. Look at how we grew up. I lived with both my parents in a better neighborhood and went to better schools. You didn't. But you can still go to college."

"Not with my grades. I barely graduated from high school."

"What about those training schools they show on TV? It doesn't take long for those. I remember at one time you wanted to be a nurse like my mama. We can check on some of the courses and see what we could find out."

"I'll think about it," Crystal said not committing one way or the other.

Darlene was glad her cousin was considering it. But enough about that, she thought. It was a Saturday night and she wanted to go out and have fun. She didn't go out much while she was away at school. But when she came home, Crystal always knew where a party was going on or a good club to go to. They got dressed and went to a new club she wasn't familiar with.

Loud music greeted them once they entered. The dance floor wasn't that crowded. They both were dressed rather casual wearing blue jeans, a blouse, and flat shoes. Crystal saw a few of her friends and Darlene remembered a couple of them from previous visits. They joined them at their table. There were six women at one table. Men would approach the table and ask a few of the ladies to dance. On some of the fast songs, all the ladies got up and danced. They usually paired off with a man on the dance floor. When they returned to their seats, they usually ordered another round of drinks. The night went pretty much on the same pattern.

At around midnight, Darlene started getting tired and was ready to leave. On the way out, a group of men were entering. They seemed to be very popular with the ladies. One man in particular. Women seemed to swarm around him.

Crystal wanted to tell one of her friends something before they left so she went back to the table. Darlene started checking out the brother who was so popular. He was tall and good-looking. A little on the slim side, but he had a sturdy physique. He had on a pair of cream-colored slacks and a multi-colored, short-sleeved, silk shirt with black as the dominating color.

There was a woman standing next to him with her arm looped through the crook of his arm.

Crystal called Darlene's name and it drew his attention because he looked over at her. Their eyes locked for a few seconds then she turned her attention toward Crystal. A friend of Crystal's wanted to meet her. She talked with the guy for a few minutes, but she was really tired and wanted to leave. The guy handed her his phone number. She accepted it to be nice, but she didn't have any intentions of using it. As they were leaving, she took one more glance at the attractive man she had been looking at minutes ago. She was a little surprised to find him still looking at her. She turned her head and kept walking.

Chapter two

Two weeks later Darlene started work on a Monday morning. The day was beautiful and she was eager to get started. She was a little disappointed because she wasn't assigned too much work. She mainly assisted the other accountants with mundane work like filing papers. She started doing a little number crunching for some of them once they realized how good she was with numbers. She even pointed out a few of their mistakes. Most were grateful, but some were offended. She got along well with just about everyone in the department. The ones she didn't get along with didn't get along with any of the other workers.

After two weeks of working, she was really starting to enjoy her job. Marie Crawford is one of the ladies she worked more closely with. Marie is thirty years old, very tall, slim, and sleek. She is light skinned and has long, thick, black hair and she dresses very stylish. She looks like she could be a fashion model. She's having a pool party the coming Saturday at her house and she invited a few of the people she worked with to her party. Marie took a special liking to Darlene and invited her and a guest to the party. Darlene was practically the youngest person working at the bank. There was a couple of other college students there also. All the other workers ages ranged from twenty-five to forty-five.

When Darlene got home that evening, she told Crystal about the pool party. Crystal really didn't want to go because she didn't like hanging with Darlene's friends. When they would come across some of the people that Darlene went to college with, she noticed Crystal wouldn't say much to them. But she wanted to make an appearance since she had told Marie she would come. She even offered to buy Crystal a new swimsuit.

Darlene had to drive to the suburbs to get to Marie's house. It took her about forty-five minutes to get there from her aunt's house. Marie and her husband lived in a huge two-story house in a gated community. The house had five bedrooms, a living room, dining room, game room, den, breakfast room, kitchen, study, four and a half bathrooms with three of the bathrooms adjoined to bedrooms. There was a deck out back, a patio, and a built-in swimming pool and spa in the backyard. She didn't know what Marie's husband did for a living, but he had to make a lot of money to live in a house that big, she thought.

Marie walked to the door and met them after someone showed them in. Crystal's mouth hung open in amazement while she looked around the beautiful house. When Marie neared them, Darlene jabbed Crystal with her elbow causing her to close her mouth.

"Hi, Darlene. I'm so glad you made it," Marie said, smiling.

"I'm glad to be here. I just love your house. It's beautiful," she complimented as she admired the chandelier in the dining room and the beautifully framed artwork.

"Thank you. And who's this?" Marie asked, looking from Darlene to her guest.

"This is my cousin Crystal Jones. Crystal, this is Marie Crawford. I mostly work with her at the bank," she said and they shook hands.

"I'll show you where you can change. Everyone is almost here. They're all out back by the pool. You can eat or swim. Whatever you want to do is fine. Follow me."

Marie showed them where to change then she left. They both changed into their swimsuits. Since Crystal's pregnancy wasn't showing yet, she wore a basic black one-piece with a black net cover-up. Darlene wore a white, French-cut bikini. She had a nice figure and she enjoyed showing it off.

They walked out to the backyard and sat on a couple of lounge chairs near the pool. Somewhere a stereo was playing music. They had just sat down when Marie came by with a couple of sodas. She sat and talked with them for a while.

Later when most of the guests left the pool to get something to eat, Darlene took that opportunity to take a swim. The rectangular-shaped pool, which was thirty-five-feet long and twenty feet wide, ranged in depth from three to eight feet.

After swimming the width of the pool at the deep end a few times, she was ready to get out. She had left her towel on the chair near Crystal. While walking toward her chair, she noticed two rather handsome black men walking out onto the deck above. Both men seemed to be very popular with the guests. She didn't look at them too long. When she got to her seat, she was suddenly hungry. She and Crystal got up and they went and helped themselves to finger sandwiches, rolled meats, chicken drummettes, fruits, and vegetables that were set up buffet style.

They went back to their chairs to eat. Darlene noticed Marie walking toward them with the same two men she had seen earlier. Something was vaguely familiar about the shorter man, but she just couldn't put her finger on it. The trio stopped when someone approached them. One of the guests, a woman, stood next to the shorter man and touched his arm. Darlene instantly remembered the night at the club. He was the good-looking brother she had seen.

As soon as they were close enough, Marie made the introductions and said, "Darlene, I'd like you to meet my husband, Jeff. Jeff, this is Darlene Carson. She's the intern student who's working with me at the bank." Darlene shook hands with Marie's husband. "And this is my brother, Al." He smiled. Then it hit her that he is Big Al and she found herself staring at him.

Al saw the recollection on Darlene's face. He was surprised she hadn't recognized him sooner. He had recognized her immediately. He had been aware of her the night at the club. But then he was otherwise occupied. He had been watching her while she had been swimming. At first all he had noticed was a fine brown-skinned female body. Then when she had stepped out of the pool, he remembered her instantly. Her hair was slicked back off her face from the water. She had been dripping wet and he had let his eyes roam over her body. Her stomach was flat and her legs were muscular, especially her calves, but they still looked feminine. He took a special liking to her breasts, which were not too big and not too small. They were just right for him, he thought.

She extended her hand and said, "Please to meet you," lightly touching his hand.

"And this is her cousin, Crystal," Marie said and both men said hello.

They all sat near the pool and talked. Darlene was beginning to feel uncomfortable at Marie's house. During their talk she learned that Marie's husband owns a Mercedes and BMW car dealership and is involved in real estate and Al worked for him at the dealership. She was letting most of the conversation go in one ear and out the other because she was wondering if Marie and Jeff knew that Al was dealing drugs. She didn't want to be the one to tell them if they didn't already know. She noticed that Al kept looking at her. She was relieved when he finally left. She laid back on the lounge chair and closed her eyes. At least until her cousin started with the questions.

"You know Al?" she asked.

"No. Why?"

"He kept looking at you all hard and carryin' on."

"What are you talking about?" Darlene asked and sat up because she was beginning to get annoyed.

"I mean he was watching you close. I know a lot of women who would go crazy if he was to look at them like that."

Darlene ignored the comment and laid back down on her chair and closed her eyes, but Crystal continued talking.

"You just practically ignored him. I know that must be a first for him."

"Meaning?" she asked, opening her eyes a little more interested now.

"He's probably never had a woman give him a don't-wanna-be-bothered attitude like you just did. Some women I know be tryin' to throw themselves at him."

"I'm not about to," she said and closed her eyes again. Without anymore questions from Crystal, she managed to doze off.

When she opened her eyes again, Crystal had left the chair next to her. When she looked around for her, she saw Al approaching. She started to get up and leave, but decided to stay because she wasn't going to run from him.

Al walked up to her and asked, "Is this seat taken?"

"My cousin is sitting there."

"I'll get up when she comes back," he said and sat in the seat next to her.

She noticed he had changed clothes. He was now wearing a pair of stone washed jean shorts, a dark brown T-shirt, and a pair of casual brown leather shoes. It was a big change from the shirt, tie, and slacks he had on earlier. She was able to see more of his body. She noticed he was slightly bowlegged and she thought it made him look sexy.

"I was surprised to see you here," Al said, distracting her attention from admiring his body.

"Yeah, likewise."

"Why do I get the feeling you don't like me?" he asked, smiling. "I like you."

"I bet you say that to all the ladies you see in a swimsuit."

"Nope. It's something about you."

"But you don't even know me," she said, looking straight ahead and not at him.

"I think we can rectify that. Don't you?"

He was so sure of himself, she thought so she said, "Nope," just as sure of herself.

"Why you being like that with me?" he asked. He had never had a woman brush him off so quickly.

"I'm not being any way with you. I just don't see any reason for you to get to know me."

"Well . . . how about if you get to know me?"

She had to admit that he *was* persistent. She turned to look at him and saw that he was smiling. Her mouth gave a hint of a smile that she tried to suppress, but Al saw his opening and continued to talk.

"Let's see . . ." he pretended to think, "you already know my first name." He sat up straighter on the chair. "I'm Alvin Williams, but everybody calls me Al. I'm twenty-nine, in good health, and I have all my teeth. I'm six-feet tall and weigh about one hundred and seventy pounds." He extended his hand to her and she couldn't help but to laugh at his introduction of himself. She shook his hand while laughing and he continued talking.

"So I see you wasn't all that busy the other weekend," he stated.

"What are you talking about?"

"I saw you at that club. I could have taken you there. And to dinner."

"From what I saw, you had your hands full," she said, thinking about the woman she saw with him.

"Only because I couldn't be with you."

"You didn't know me or had never seen me until that day."

"True," he said, nodding his head. "But I liked what I saw. And I still do." There was a moment of silence. "So are you studying accounting in college?" he asked, changing the subject.

"Yes."

"You like it?"

"College or accounting?"

"Both."

"They're both all right."

"How old are you?"

"What?"

"Your age. I told you mine now tell me yours."

Darlene found him to be very entertaining so she said, "I'm twenty. Why?"

"Just making sure you are old enough to get married without parental consent."

"What are you talking about?"

"I wanna marry you. I would have told you that the first time I saw you, but you walked off. And the second time I didn't have a chance either."

"I see you must dip into your own stuff," she said. Something had to be wrong with him to make him think about marrying her or that she would marry him for that matter.

"And what's that supposed to mean?" Al asked. He knew what she was referring to, but he didn't want to let on.

"Figure it out. I have to go. Goodbye." She got up from the chair she was sitting on, leaving him sitting on the chair looking at her as she walked away. She went back into the house and found Crystal talking to some man. She was ready to leave, but she wanted to find Marie and tell her goodbye first. She walked back outside and saw Marie talking with other guests. As she was nearing Marie, she saw Al approaching from the other direction. They reached her at about the same time. Marie excused herself from the group she was talking with.

"Marie, I had a really nice time, but I'm about to leave," she said and looked at Al and saw that he was smiling.

"I'm glad you came," she responded.

"So am I," Al agreed. "I think I'm gonna like being married to you."

"*What?*" Marie screamed and soon started choking on her drink. Her husband came over and patted her on her back. After she recovered, she looked at her brother and said, "Run that by me again."

"Darlene's gonna be my wife."

All three of them looked at Darlene for confirmation. She couldn't believe what Al had said. She was so stunned that she didn't know what to say. All she was thinking that whatever kind of drug Al was on it must be good.

"She hasn't accepted it yet," Al said. "Give her time."

Marie looked at her again and asked, "Darlene, what is my brother talking about?"

"I don't know what he's talking about."

"Al?" Marie said, looking at him for an answer.

"You see it's like this," he said, looking at his sister. "You keep bugging me about when I'm gonna find a good woman and get married. And Jeff here always said that if I ever find a woman who is as smart and pretty like you I should go for it. And I think that woman is Darlene."

Darlene had heard about all she wanted to hear so she said, "I'm sorry to interrupt, but I'm leaving. Marie, I'll see you at work. Jeff, it was nice meeting you. And Alvin . . . you need help. Goodbye." She turned and walked away. She found Crystal in the house. They changed and headed to the car and left.

Al was still standing with a shocked sister and brother-in-law. His sister asked, "What made you say something like that, Al?"

"Like what?"

"You don't even know Darlene and I'm sure she doesn't know you."

"We've met before," he said to his sister.

"Just met?" she asked, wondering if there was something going on that she didn't know about.

"Something like that," Al answered

"But you still don't know her," Marie said.

"Your point?"

Marie looked at her husband for help.

"Listen, man," Jeff said. "You can't just tell a woman out of the blue you're gonna marry her. You have to get to know each other a while. And besides, you have enough women as it is."

"I think you and my sister knew each other for . . ." he thought a while, "what was it, two months before you were married?" They both were silent. "And you've been married for about five years now."

Marie spoke up and said, "But Jeff and I loved each other. You don't love Darlene. Hell, you don't even know her."

"In time. You'll see," Al said.

Marie walked off and left her husband and brother to talk. "Say, man, you have to know what you're doing if you plan on getting married," Jeff said as him and Al walked into the house and to the den. "Things change. You won't just have yourself to worry about. And you know what I'm talking about. Marie's my wife and we share just about everything. But certain things she's better off not knowing. She knows about most of it, but I keep her in the dark to protect her."

"Yeah, I see what you mean."

"So think about it. Find out about this broad and let me know what you decide."

"Okay. Check you later, Jeff," Al said and left his sister's house and headed home.

On the drive home, he thought about the things Jeff had said. He has come across a lot of women in his life. He has a lot now to choose from if he wanted. But he has never entertained the idea of marrying any of them. It was just something different about Darlene. Maybe it was because she didn't seem at all interested in him. He was so used to women all in his face and wanting him that it was strange to be ignored. And then there had been her little remark about him dipping into his stuff as she so delicately put it. Maybe that was it. Most women he associated with didn't mind that aspect of his life. They usually bragged about it. It seemed like the more Al thought about the things Darlene didn't like about him, the more he wanted to get to know her.

While Darlene was driving home, she thought about how glad she was that Crystal hadn't been around to hear what Al had said. She still couldn't believe the nerve of him. She was just starting to have fun talking with him until he started talking crazy. She didn't realize she was mumbling while she was driving.

"What did you say?" Crystal asked.

"Huh?"

"I thought you said something that's all."

"I was just thinking to myself."

"About Al?" Crystal asked.

"You can say that. What do you know about him?" She had to admit to the fact that she was a little curious about him. It wasn't everyday a man told a woman out of the blue that he wanted to marry her.

"All I know is what I hear. Everybody knows he deals drugs. He's not like the ones you see hanging on the streets. He hardly ever comes around. And he always have a different woman. He drives the cars from the dealership sometimes. But I think the white Benz is his."

"I've seen it."

"You mean to tell me you knew Al before today?" she asked, turning on an angle to face her.

"No, I don't know him. He told me you were at Paula's house."

"I thought he told Robert."

"Robert asked him, but he wanted to talk to me. So that's the only time I've really talked to him," she said. It was true. The second time she had only seen him.

"He must like you then," Crystal said, turning to sit correctly in her seat again. "He was watching every move you made. His sister and her husband seem nice. And they must be rolling in money. That was one bad house," Crystal said and Darlene just kept quiet and let her finish her praises of Marie's house on the way home.

Chapter three

The following Monday at work flowers were delivered for Darlene. It was a vase with a dozen red roses. She thought there must have been some kind of a mix-up, but there was a card and it had her name on it. The flowers were sitting on Marie's desk since that was whom she mainly worked with. Everybody noticed the roses. They were so beautiful it was hard to not notice them. When she read the card, she started laughing. Marie wanted to know what was so funny so Darlene handed her the card. The card read:

> Dear Darlene,
> Roses are red. Violets are blue.
> I want to marry you. I hope you want to marry me, too.
> Waiting for an answer,
> Al

She also laughed at her brother's unorthodox proposal. She didn't know whether her brother was serious or not. She handed the card back to Darlene and they went about doing business as usual.

Later that day, Marie received a call at her desk. It was for Darlene. She took the receiver from Marie and said, "Hello?"

"You liked the flowers?"

"They are very nice, Alvin. Thank you."

"Are you gonna marry me?"

"No."

"Why not?"

"Are you serious?"

"Yeah."

"How can you want to marry me and you don't know me?"

"Well, why don't you let me get to know you?"

"I . . . don't know about that," she replied nervously. She was actually starting to believe that he was serious.

"That's better than a flat no. How about if I take you out tonight?"

"No, Alvin."

"Why do you always call me Alvin? Everybody else calls me Al."

"That's because I'm not like everybody else."

"You're so right," he noted in a deep and sexy sounding voice. "And that's exactly why I wanna marry you."

"Will you quit with the marriage talk because that's all it is. Talk." What was she saying? Was she trying to call his bluff? She couldn't be doing anything that foolish. Could she?

"One way to find out. Name the date, time, and place and I'll be there."

"Give it a rest, Alvin."

"For you, anything. So how about lunch tomorrow?"

His persistency was really weakening her, but she wouldn't let him know it.

"I'll think about it. Goodbye, Alvin," she said and hung up the phone.

Marie had been sitting at her desk listening to the one-sided conversation. After Darlene hung up the telephone she said, "I can't believe my brother lets you call him Alvin."

"Why?"

"He never lets anyone call him Alvin. Our mother always called him Alvin. But nobody else that I know of. He must really like you," she said, shaking her head in amazement.

"I guess you know your brother better than anyone. Why is he doing this? Talking about marrying me I mean."

"You've got me there. Last he told me was that he wasn't never getting married. He said he couldn't find a woman he could trust. That all the women he's met so far were too materialistic and stupid."

"So why does he be with them?"

"I don't know."

"What makes him think I'm not like those other women?"

"Beats me," Marie said, hunching her shoulders. "Maybe it's because you have a brain. I've seen some of the dizzy women he messes with," she said and her and Darlene laughed.

The following morning some balloons were delivered attached to a bigger balloon with a stuffed teddy bear inside. It was sitting in the office on display on Marie's desk along with the roses from the day before. Marie thought it was funny. Darlene didn't because she was getting stares from some of the workers. The ladies thought it was nice. The men didn't. This time the card from Al only said he would see her at noon for lunch. She had only told him she would think about going to lunch with him. It was nothing definite. She decided she would leave before he got there to pick her up.

At about eleven-thirty, Marie's husband showed up. He noticed the balloons and roses sitting on his wife's desk. He knew he hadn't sent them and he was wondering who they were from.

"Whose balloons and roses?" he asked.

"Al sent them to Darlene."

"He what?" Jeff asked.

"Yesterday it was the roses and today it was the balloons. I've never known him to send a woman anything. Maybe he's serious."

"Could be. Where's Darlene anyway?"

"She'll be back in a few minutes. Al is supposed to meet her for lunch at noon, but she plans to leave a little early so she won't see him. I don't know," Marie said, shaking her head. "She doesn't seem to like him all that much. I think he should leave her alone."

"That's why he wants her. I've seen how women are with your brother. It's the same way it was when we first started going out. It's just that I didn't respond to the women like he does."

"Well, I guess we'll have to wait and see how this turns out," she said as she got up from behind her desk and they left.

As they were leaving, they saw Al entering the bank. "Is Darlene still upstairs?" he asked.

"Yeah. But she's about to leave for lunch," Marie said.

"I know. I'm taking her to lunch."

"But you weren't supposed to meet her until noon. It's only eleven-forty," Marie said after looking at her watch.

"I know that, too. I didn't want her tryin' to sneak out," he said, looking at Marie and Jeff and they all laughed. He sat on a wooden bench across from the elevators and waited for Darlene to come down.

While Darlene was sitting at Marie's desk, she debated on whether she should leave or wait until noon and meet Al. She decided to go with her first decision to leave and try to avoid him. It was eleven forty-five by the time she left the office. When she got off the elevator and headed for the doors, she stopped because she saw Al. He stood up and started walking towards her. She looked at her watch and it was ten minutes to twelve. She couldn't believe he was early.

"I thought you said noon," she said accusingly.

"I did. But I couldn't wait to see you again. Did you like the balloons?"

"Every woman in the office liked them."

"Too much?"

"Yes," she said and turned and walked to the doors.

"I'll have to send smaller gifts until you agree to marry me," he said, walking toward the bank doors with her.

"You don't have to send me anymore gifts, Alvin."

"Then you've agreed to marry me?" he asked surprised, thinking she had agreed to marry him.

"No," she said and walked out of the doors. Then she stopped just outside and turned to face him and said, "Tell me something, Alvin. Why do you want to marry me?" she asked. At that moment she realized she really wanted to know. She hadn't given his proposal much thought until that moment.

"Can it wait until we're having lunch?"

"I guess. Where are we going?" she asked, agreeing to have lunch with him.

"To this nice restaurant I know about."

"I'll follow you."

"Why not ride with me? I can start telling you why I wanna marry you," he said, trying to persuade her.

"Okay, Alvin."

They walked to the parking lot to his car, got in, and headed to the restaurant. Not long after they were in the car, Al put in a CD. It was some rapper. Darlene couldn't understand what was said other than a lot of swearing. Al looked at her sideways and asked, "You don't like rap?"

"Not really. So are you going to answer my question?"

He turned down the volume and said, "You don't waste time do you?"

"You should talk. I'm not the one ready and willing to marry someone I don't know and let alone love."

"Is that the problem? If I say I love you, would you marry me?"

"Stop playing and tell me why."

"All right," he said as if he was losing his patience. "When I first saw you, I liked you. I asked your cousin about you and he told me you were in college and only in town for the summer. So I thought my chances were real slim at meeting you. Then I see you again. I must tell you, you're not good for my ego. You were looking all pretty and sexy and you didn't wanna give a brother the time of day. Then I see you again at my sister's house. By the way, you looked some fine in that bikini. You're lucky I wasn't in the pool with you."

"Why is that?" she asked.

"Because I don't think I would have been able to keep my hands off you," he said, looking over at her sitting next to him. "Anyway," he said and concentrated on driving again, "I think it was destiny for us to meet and get married."

She had sat quietly and listened to what all Al had said. But he still hadn't answered her question.

"Alvin, that still doesn't answer my question. Why me?"

He thought for a while before answering then said, "It's just a feeling."

"Oh, that's just great. I wonder how often does this feeling hit you," she said just as he pulled into the restaurant's parking lot.

When he stopped the car, he didn't immediately turn off the engine. He turned in his seat and looked at her.

"Listen, Darlene. I don't know what you've heard about me as far as women. But I've never asked a woman to marry me. Maybe it's because you don't seem to want the things I can give you. I can't say that

I love you because I've never been in love. But I'm sure once we're married I'll start loving you. Besides, it's about time I was married. I need to be a family man."

"And what do I get out of it?" she said, meaning the question to be rhetorical. But he didn't receive it that way.

"Oh, so it's like that. What do you want? A car? A house? Money? Jewelry? Name it. I guess you're not so different after all," he said before getting out the car.

Darlene couldn't quite figure out why his comment hurt her a little. She didn't want to be placed into the same category as the other women he was associated with. She watched him as he walked around the front of the car to her door. Then he snatched the door open and said, "C'mon and get out. Let me treat you to a fancy lunch. Maybe I'll even surprise you with something from a jewelry store."

That remark went past the line for Darlene. She slowly stepped out of his car and he closed the door. She looked at him and very calmly said, "I don't think so. I think you should go and find someone else to treat to lunch and buy jewelry for." Then she walked off in a different direction from the restaurant. She saw a telephone mounted on the wall of a gas station foodmart across the street from the restaurant. She walked over to it and called a taxi. As she stood there angrily with her arms folded waiting for the taxi to come, she ignored Al when he quietly walked up. He didn't say anything to her and she wasn't about to say anything to him. He just stood there with her as the minutes ticked by. When the taxi pulled up, she got in and left him standing there.

Al stood there totally shocked. A woman had never walked out on him. He had walked out on women a few times. But he couldn't figure out what had set Darlene off. He didn't give it too much thought. He went back to his car and left.

When Darlene got back to work, she only had enough time to grab a salad from a fast food restaurant near the bank. When she walked into the office, Marie asked, "How was your lunch?"

"You don't want to know," she answered still pissed off.

"Another proposal?"

"I don't think I'll be getting any more proposals. I think your brother should stay with the women he already has."

"Uh-oh. It went that bad, huh?"

"Yes," she answered and was glad that Marie let the subject drop.

Al called later that evening, but Darlene didn't want to talk to him. That went on for the rest of the week. Everyday he would call twice a day. The calls seemed to stop by Thursday and she was somewhat relieved. She felt uncomfortable asking Marie to lie to her brother, but it hadn't seemed to bother her.

Friday when Darlene was just about to leave work for the day, the telephone on Marie's desk started ringing. Marie wasn't at her desk so she answered the telephone.

"Accounting, may I help you?" she answered very business like.

"May I speak to Darlene Carson?" Al asked. He didn't recognize the voice on the phone. He knew his sister usually answered her phone, but this voice wasn't familiar to him.

Darlene knew it was Al since no one else called for her. She didn't want to talk to him so she said, "She's unavailable at the moment. Would you like to leave a message?"

"Yeah. Tell her Al will see her later tonight."

"I'll make sure she gets the message."

"Thank you," he said and hung up.

Darlene was glad he hadn't recognized her voice. Now she was going to make sure she had plans for the night. By the time she got home from work, her aunt had just gotten home also. Her aunt looked so tired, she thought. Only Darryl was home. Robert and Crystal were out somewhere. Darlene suggested they go out to eat dinner. She only wanted to go out to eat because she didn't want to be home in case Al showed up. She changed out of her work clothes and put on a pair of jeans and a T-shirt. She watched TV while she waited for her aunt to change also. Robert came inside and let her know that someone wanted her outside. She didn't think anything of it. But as soon as she walked outside, she saw a white Mercedes parked at the curb right behind her car. She walked to the curb where it was parked.

"Hey, Darlene," Al said.

"Hi," she said pleasantly as she stood next to the car.

He leaned over toward the passenger side so he could see her better and said, "Get inside and sit down and talk to me."

"I can't."

"Why?"

"I'm about to leave in a few minutes."

"Where you going?"

"To dinner with my aunt and cousins."

"Didn't you get my message at work?"

"Yes," she answered truthfully. She just didn't confess to taking it herself.

"I made plans for us to go out to dinner tonight."

"I think we tried that once and it didn't work out."

"C'mon, Darlene, don't be like this."

She looked around when she heard the door opening to her aunt's house. Her aunt and cousins were coming out. She leaned over and said, "Look, Alvin, I have to go. But I'm sure you can find some willing woman to take out." She looked at her watch. "And some jewelry stores are still open if you hurry." She moved away from his car and walked back into the house to get her purse and keys. Her cousins got in the back seat of the car while she helped her aunt get in the front seat. She noticed that Al was still sitting in his car. She ignored him as she walked around the back of her car to the driver side door and got in. He was still parked at the curb when she pulled away.

Al watched Darlene get in her car and drive away. He didn't know why he thought about taking her out. He could tell she didn't seem to want anything from him. He decided to follow her to see where she was going. He saw the restaurant they went into and decided he would get something to eat also. But he had to go and get some feminine company first.

Betty was glad to be eating in a restaurant. It had been a long time since she has had the time to enjoy a meal in a restaurant. Darlene took her to a family owned soul food restaurant because she didn't want to go anywhere fancy. This place specialized in home cooked meals. Robert and Darryl ordered fried chicken and French fries meals. Betty ordered a smothered pork chop and baked macaroni meal. Darlene ordered a fried shrimp and French fries meal and a catfish and French fries meal to bring back for Crystal.

While they were eating, Robert noticed Al walking into the restaurant and he brought it to Darlene's attention. As soon as she looked around, she saw Al with a woman and he was looking directly at her. She turned her head and continued eating her meal. She was enjoying her dinner with her family and she didn't have time for Al.

When they finished their meals, she gestured to the waitress to pay the check. She was surprised to find out that someone had already paid the check. She wanted to know whom and the waitress pointed at Al. She was pissed off now. First, he accused her of wanting him to buy her stuff. Now he's paying for her and her family's meal. She decided to teach him a lesson.

On the way out, she handed Darryl the car keys so they could go out to the car. She lied about wanting to go back into the restaurant to use the restroom. She only went in there to count out the money for the bill. After that she headed straight towards Al. When she first walked back into the restaurant, the woman he was with started asking him something and he turned to answer her. He was still talking to her when she walked up and was standing at his table. He looked up at her and smiled. She couldn't deny that he had a sexy smile. Then she brought her mind back to the reason why she was standing there. She couldn't believe the nerve of him smiling in her face while he was sitting there with another woman. Then she had to wonder whether it could be jealousy that was making her so mad. But she cleared her head of those thoughts and pulled the money for the check out of her pocket. She carefully placed the money on the table in front of him. He looked from the money to her and asked, "What's that for?"

"I don't believe I asked you to pay for our meal," she said with her hands on her hips.

"Al, what's she talkin' about?" the other woman asked, speaking up.

Darlene decided to make this good so she said, "Oh, I see," rolling her neck and placing her hand on her chest very dramatically, "you want to marry me, but here you are out with somebody else. I'm glad I found out before I said yes."

"Whatchu mean he wanna marry you?" the woman asked with an attitude.

"Alvin, *honey*," she placed her hand on his shoulder, "aren't you going to enlighten your friend?"

"Are you saying yes?" he challenged.

"That depends," she said, looking from him to the other woman. "I don't share. Period."

"I can deal with that. So is it yes?" he asked again.

She looked at the woman at the table with Al. The poor woman looked ready to have a fit and he was totally ignoring her. "I'll say this. Try not to keep my *fiancé* out too late." She leaned over with every intention of placing a quick, unexpected kiss on Al's lips. But when she felt his tongue gently touch her lips it sent a shiver through her body. When she pulled back, she saw that Al was looking directly into her eyes with a serious stare. He placed the money back into her hands. She hadn't noticed when he had picked it up from the table. She straightened up and left. When she got in the car, it dawned on her that Al was probably going to take her serious. She shrugged off the thought and drove home.

Crystal had been upset because no one had told her they were going out to eat. Her anger vanished when she saw the plate of food they brought back for her.

That night Darlene had a little trouble going to sleep. She kept thinking about what had happened when she had gone back to confront Al. Now that she thought back to the scene, she realized how serious he had appeared to be. And that kiss. She really hadn't planned on it, but now she knew he had soft lips. But she wasn't going to waste her time thinking about that tonight. She only has a little over a month left of her summer vacation and she wasn't going to waste it thinking about Al.

Chapter four

Darlene didn't hear from Al the next week. She realized she was getting worried for nothing. Maybe his friend had changed his mind about wanting to marry her, she thought. She had never been proposed to and she was flattered to get a proposal from Al. A proposal period. Since she hadn't heard from him in over a week, she decided to put him and his proposal behind her.

Two weeks later, one of Crystal's friends was having a birthday party at one of the local clubs and her and Darlene were invited. Crystal had started eating like crazy and she couldn't fit any of her dressier clothes anymore so Darlene loaned her something to wear. They used to be the same size give or take a few pounds. Since Darlene always wore her pantsuits a little baggy, Crystal was still able to fit her clothes. Darlene wore a royal blue, short-sleeved, silk pantsuit with matching shoes. She loaned her cousin an almost identical lavender pantsuit.

They arrived at the club a little after ten o'clock that night. They saw a few friends they knew and sat at the adjoining table. She and Crystal started dancing soon afterwards. Darlene only drank virgin daiquiris. Crystal had a few alcoholic drinks then stopped after Darlene kept reminding her that she was pregnant.

While they were seated at their table, a waitress brought over a couple of drinks. Darlene knew she hadn't ordered any drinks and inquired. She was told a gentleman at the bar had sent the drinks and wanted to know if he could join them. Crystal immediately said yes before Darlene could answer.

A tall and handsome man came to their table and introduced himself. He was dark skinned, chocolate. It was obvious he worked out. His hair was cut real close to his head with a little on top in the front and a part on the upper left side.

"How are you ladies doin' tonight?"

"Fine," they answered in unison.

Taking a seat at the table with them he said, "My name's Vincent."

"I'm Crystal and this is my cousin Darlene."

"Nice to meet you two. Tell me. How come two fine sisters like you two are sittin' here all alone?"

"We're not anymore," Crystal replied, flirting just a little.

"Would you two mind if a friend of mine joined us?"

"No. Not at all," Darlene answered.

Another guy walked to their table. He wasn't as tall as Vincent. Maybe five feet, nine or ten inches tall. He was dark skinned also. His name was Thomas. He was a little too chubby for Darlene's taste. She liked guys on the slim side. More like Vincent. Crystal seemed to be interested in the other guy anyway. The four of them talked for a while. Darlene found out that Vincent worked in his uncle's paint and body shop. They went on the dance floor on a fast song. The place was very well air conditioned, but it was a bit hot on the dance floor. When a slow song came on, Vincent pulled her into his arms. They were dancing and enjoying the music. His cologne smelled good, she thought. She felt comfortable in his arms. He was moving his hands along her back in a soothing motion. Someone tapped him on his shoulder and caused him to stop. And when he stopped dancing, Darlene looked up to see Al.

"You mind letting my wife go?" Al said to Vincent.

Darlene was utterly shocked. All she could do was stand there wide-eyed, open-mouthed, and wonder where had he come from. Then he had a hell of a nerve not to talk to her for weeks then say she's his wife, she thought.

Vincent looked at the shocked then angry expression on Darlene's face. Not a caught-in-the-act expression at all. "I didn't realize she was married," he said calmly. "I didn't see any rings or ring mark on her finger."

By now, a few of the other couples had stopped dancing and were watching. Crystal and Vincent's friend, Thomas, gathered around them too. Thomas knew of Al and about his reputation and walked up and greeted him.

"What's up, Al?" he said. Al turned to see who had spoken to him. He had seen the guy before, but he didn't know his name. That wasn't unusual. A lot of people knew Al, but he didn't know half of them. Only their faces may be familiar to him.

"Nothin' much. Just trying to find out why this dude here is dancing with my wife." He and Vincent seemed to have entered into a staring contest. Neither broke eye contact.

Darlene couldn't believe all this was happening. And in a club of all places. She knew it would be all over the streets by the next day. She thought she'd better speak up before matters got out of hand.

"Uh, listen you two," she said interrupting. That seemed to break the staring at each other. They turned their eyes on her. She looked at Al and said, "Can you excuse us for a minute?" She didn't wait for a response. She pulled Vincent by his hand and said, "Can I talk to you for a minute in private?" He looked from her to Al. Then he agreed and put his arm around her waist and escorted her back to the table.

"I'll be waiting for you, *sweetheart*," Al said to their retreating backs.

When they got back to the table, Vincent asked point blank, "Are you his wife?"

"No."

"Then what's his problem? He's your man or something?"

"I think it would be safe to say we're something. Listen, I really had a good time tonight. Maybe I'll see you some other time. Bye, Vincent." She left the table to find Al and give him a piece of her mind. He was standing near the bar. She walked up to him and said, "What the hell was that all about?"

"I don't like sharing. Remember?"

Why was he throwing her words back at her? He's the one who hasn't been in touch with her. So why was she feeling guilty? "Look," Darlene said, trying to talk calmly. "I didn't see any reason for you to broadcast that big lie."

"What lie?"

"That I'm your wife."

"It's only a temporary lie. As I recall, you said we were engaged."

"Oh no I didn't," she said, shaking her head.

"I do believe that to be someone's fiancé is to be engaged to marry. And I'm ready to marry."

"We can't talk here."

"I fully agree. Take a ride with me."

"I have my own car. And the last ride I took with you wasn't such a good idea."

"I promise I'll be good. After all, we're engaged," he said and smiled.

"I don't see anything that proves that. Let me go and talk to my cousin," she said and walked off.

"I think I can do something about that," Al said more to himself when she left.

Crystal was still sitting at the table with Vincent and Thomas. She and his friend had been enlightening him on who Al was. So when Darlene neared them, Vincent looked up at her, but he didn't say anything. He just shook his head. He wouldn't have mind getting to know her better. She was pretty and fine, he thought. But if she preferred men like Al he didn't want to waste his time with her. He never knew what the attraction was for some women to men like that. He assumed it was the money.

Darlene thought about saying something to Vincent, but he looked as if he didn't want to be bothered. She gave Crystal her car keys so she could drive her car home since she would get a ride home with Al. She left and headed back to Al who was smiling almost ear to ear.

As they were walking out, he slipped his arm around her waist very possessively. When they were outside, he turned her to him and kissed her. He started rubbing all along her back going down to her butt. She was caught off guard and instinctively pushed him away.

"What's wrong with you?" he asked. It seemed like everything he usually did with women wasn't working with Darlene. Sending the flowers and balloons was something he had never done.

"Nothing's wrong with me. I just don't like to be attacked."

"I wasn't attacking you," he said, taking a few steps away from her.

"What would you call it? Your hands were all over me."

"It didn't seem to bother you when that other guy had his hands all over you."

"His hands weren't all over me, Alvin."

"That's not how it looked to me."

"Come here."

He walked back toward her and she raised her arms and put them around his neck. He put his arms around her waist and held her to him as close as he could. He leaned down and kissed her. When she broke the kiss, she was speechless because she had gotten more than she had bargained for from that kiss. That kiss was nothing like the other little kiss before. This one was head spinning. He didn't dominate. He gave and received. He didn't release his hold on her immediately. He looked at her for a moment then said, "Let's go." They got in his car and left. Her head was still spinning from the kiss and she didn't have any idea where they were going.

When they parked in the parking lot to an apartment complex, she figured this was where he lived. He got out and went around the car to help her out. They walked the short distance to his apartment. It was very nicely furnished with a black leather sectional sofa in the living room, tan carpeting throughout the apartment, oak and glass coffee and end tables, and an oak entertainment center with a TV, stereo, VCR, and DVD.

"Nice place," she commented.

"Wait until you see the bedroom."

"I'll pass. I'm sure enough women have seen it many times."

She was right about that, he thought. He has had numerous women in there. And for some reason he really didn't feel right about having her in the same bed he'd had all his other women in. He didn't know why, but he felt that way.

"Can we sit down and talk?" hc asked as he led her to the sofa. He offered her something to drink, but she declined. "Now am I to assume you've agreed to marry me?"

"It's not that simple, Alvin. I still don't know that much about you."

"Ask me whatever you wanna know. I'll answer you truthfully. Just make sure you really want to know the truth before you ask." He sat back on the sofa with one ankle resting on the opposite knee and spread his arms along the back of the sofa.

Darlene figured she might as well get it over with. "Okay. Do you have any children?" she asked. That was important to her because she didn't want to get involved with a man who had a lot of children. And she definitely didn't want to deal with any baby's mama.

"None that I'm aware of. But I sure would like to make some with you."

"Stop it, Alvin. I'm serious."

"Me, too," he said smiling. "But seriously I don't have any children."

"Am I to assume you're not seeing anyone now?"

"I'm only serious about you."

"That's not an answer."

"Okay. I haven't been seeing or sleeping with anyone since I saw you in that bikini."

"What about at the restaurant? That was afterwards."

"I just picked her up at the last minute. Nothing happened." She looked at him doubtful. "I swear."

"Well, you better let all your women friends know you're taken."

"So does that mean you'll marry me?"

"On one condition," she said.

"Anything," he said.

"Keep your other business away from me. I don't want it anywhere near me. I don't even want to know about it. And I hope it won't be nothing long-term."

Al didn't pretend to not know what she was talking about this time. "I can manage that. So when do we get married? Next week? Next month?"

"No. What's the hurry? I want to finish school first."

He removed his arms from off the back of the sofa and sat up. He then clasped his hands together and said, "You mean I'll have to wait another year?"

"Well . . ." she said and shrugged shyly.

"How about we compromise. We can get married over the Christmas break."

"I won't be able to plan a wedding that quickly. Oh wait. I do get a wedding don't I?" she asked jokingly

"Anything you want. How long will you be here before you have to go back to school?"

"The semester starts the second week in August. I have to be there to get my dorm room the first week in August."

"Why not stay in an apartment close to campus. I'll pay the bills."

"No, Alvin. I like staying on campus. I'll have my same roommate. Chris and I have become close over the years and we get along great."

"Who in the hell is Chris? You living with some boy?"

Darlene didn't realize he would assume Chris was male and not female. "Chris or shall I say Christine is not some boy. I didn't know you were so jealous, Alvin."

"I just like to keep what's mine, mine. And you will definitely be all mine. Until death do us part. Ain't that how it goes?"

"I guess."

"So do you have a date in mind?"

"Why don't you pick one," she said.

He got off the sofa to go and get a calendar. He came back with one and sat closer to her. "Let's see," he said, looking at the calendar. "When do you get out of school for Christmas break?" Darlene looked at the dates and told him. "How about the weekend before Christmas?"

"That sounds fine," she said in agreement.

"My sister knows a lot about weddings. She can help out a lot. So with the date set I guess we're officially engaged to be married."

"Looks like it," she said indifferently.

"Not quite. Hold on a minute." He got up and headed to his bedroom. When he came back, he was holding a box. "You have to wear your engagement ring." He sat down next to her on the sofa, opened the box, and showed her a one-carat total weight round diamond solitaire engagement ring. He had bought it for her the day they were supposed to have lunch together. He was hoping to persuade her to change her mind then.

"How do I know this ring wasn't meant for some other woman at one time?" she said, looking down at the ring.

Al let out an exasperated breath and said, "How many times do I have to tell you that I've never asked nobody to marry me? Wait a minute." He stood up and pulled out his wallet. He looked through it until he found what he was looking for. He handed her a yellow slip of paper. She saw that it was a credit card receipt from a jewelry store dated almost a month ago to the day. It was the day she left him at the restaurant.

She also noticed how much he paid for the ring. She looked up from the receipt to see him watching her. "You believe I bought it for you now?" he asked, sitting back down to the sofa.

"Yes," she whispered. She was really beginning to believe he wanted to marry her. He took the ring from the box and placed it on the proper finger and it fit perfectly. He pulled her to him and kissed her. She wrapped her arms around him and the kiss became heated. He stood with her intending to take her to his bedroom, but she stopped him and he looked at her questioning.

"Not in there. I just wouldn't feel right," she said then shivered as if to ward off the knowledge of all the women that might have been in there with him.

"Damn. Well, do you wanna go in the other bedroom? I gotta twin bed in there."

"Maybe we ought to just wait."

"Wait?" How could she expect him to wait? He had just proposed and she accepted. He even gave her a ring to seal the deal. And now she didn't want to have sex with him. Something was definitely wrong with this picture, he thought. "What do you mean wait? For how long?"

"I don't know about your sexual activities. Or that of the women you've been with."

"Are you trying to say I might have some disease or something?" She shrugged her shoulders not giving a verbal agreement. "Okay. If I get a clean bill of health from a doctor will that satisfy you?"

"That and another bed," she said and shyly looked away.

Al saw humor in her statement about the bed. He pulled her into his arms and said, "Tell you what. How about we go looking for a new bedroom set tomorrow? And I should have a doctor's note for you by next weekend."

"That fast?" she asked.

"I have connections. Is that okay with you?"

"Yes."

"Can we at least kiss and play touchy-feely on the sofa?" he asked teasingly.

"Now you know where that could lead, Alvin," she warned.

"I don't know about you, but I can control myself," he said arrogantly.

Darlene decided to call his bluff. "Okay. Let's see what you got."

"Huh?" he said stunned.

"I might as well see what I'm getting. Come on," she said, walking to the sofa.

He couldn't believe what she was implying. Nonetheless, he followed her back into the living room. "Do I get to see, too?" he asked hopefully.

"I do believe you wanted to marry me without knowing anything about me. So you'll just have to accept me as I am."

When she stood in front of him, he looked down at her and pulled her to him and she kissed him. She started rubbing him along his chest and back then stopped and admired his body.

"Want a better look?" He didn't give her a chance to answer. He pulled his shirt from his pants and started unbuttoning it. Darlene saw that his chest wasn't too hairy, just a small patch in the center that thinned as it trailed to the waistband of his pants. She splayed her hands across his chest and he closed his eyes. He grabbed her hands and guided them to the lower part of his body. She hesitated, but he firmly held her hands, helping her rub him.

When she started rubbing him on her own, he unfastened his belt and pants then unzipped them. He placed her hand inside his pants. She heard him moan when she started feeling his engorged sex through his briefs. He was getting very hard, very long, and very thick. Darlene slowly withdrew her hand and Al opened his eyes and looked at her. He was breathing hard and said, "You can't leave me like this. I need release."

She knew this would happen. She just wasn't ready. "I'm sorry, Alvin. We can't have sex tonight," she said, looking up at him.

"There are other ways you can give me release, Darlene," he said as if she were naive.

Darlene wondered if he was suggesting what she thought he was and said, "I know you don't mean what I think you mean."

"What's wrong with that? Everybody does it. We're getting married. So what's the big deal? You can't get pregnant that way."

"I think it's time you took me home." She should stop this farce of an engagement now, she thought. She took the ring off her finger and held it out to him.

Al looked down at the proffered ring and all of his pent-up sexual needs dissolved. "I'm sorry. I shouldn't have asked you to do that. I still wanna marry you though. Please put the ring back on." She didn't make any move to do so. She just let her arm relax at her side, still holding the ring. Al closed his pants. Then he tilted her face up and said, "I won't ask you to do that again. C'mon, I'll take you home." He started buttoning his shirt. "Are we still gonna go and buy that bed tomorrow?" She only nodded. "Are you still gonna marry me?"

"I said yes, Alvin."

"Just checking. Are you ready?" She nodded.

They walked to the door. But before he opened it he turned to look at her and said, "You know what? I might be falling in love with you. I think this is the first time I've wanted to have sex and was willing to wait." He hunched his shoulders. "Must be love." Darlene didn't respond and they left the apartment.

On the drive to her aunt's house Darlene was quiet. Al talked and she listened or answered when necessary, but she didn't initiate any conversation. When they parked near the house, Al didn't make any effort to get out. He turned and looked at her. He noticed she was still holding the ring in her hand. She sat quietly as he reached over and removed it from her hand and placed it back on her finger.

"Dee, listen," he said, taking it upon himself to shorten her name. "I said I was sorry. I didn't think. I still wanna marry you as much as I did before tonight. So is everything still on?"

"Yes, Alvin."

"Are you going to wear my ring all the time?"

"Why wouldn't I?"

"Just asking. How about if I pick you up at about two o'clock tomorrow afternoon?"

"Fine."

“Here. Take one of my cards. It has my home and cell phone numbers on it. Call me anytime.” She took the card. He got out and walked her to her door. “Do I get a goodnight kiss?” Darlene turned to face him. Al was expecting a quick smack on the lips, but she surprised him. She pressed her body against his and laid a kiss on him that made him a little dizzy. He pulled back and looked at her and asked, “What was that for?”

“Just in case you still need release and find it somewhere else, you can consider it a goodbye kiss.”

“The only release I’ll be getting is when we get that new bed. I love you, Dee. See ya tomorrow.”

Darlene went inside and he walked back to his car. She thought about what he had said and doubted if he meant it. How could he love her this fast? She went to her room and was glad Crystal was asleep. She knew she would have a lot of explaining to do in the morning.

Chapter five

Darlene was awakened by someone shaking her. At first, she thought she was dreaming, but the shaking became more persistent. She slowly opened her eyes and saw Crystal leaning over her, staring in her face.

"What?" she asked groggily.

"Did you and Al get married? Did y'all eloped last night?" Crystal asked curiously.

"What?" Darlene asked. Now she was confused because she hadn't married anyone.

"Al said you was his wife and now you're wearing a big diamond ring."

Darlene sat up in bed. She had completely forgotten that she had gone to sleep wearing the ring. "A gold band means you're married. This is just an engagement ring," she explained.

"You mean to tell me you're engaged to Al?" Crystal asked shocked.

"What if I am?"

"I just didn't think he was your type."

Darlene let that remark pass because her cousin didn't know her type. She was only guessing it wouldn't be anyone like Al.

"Then again. I didn't think you were his type either. So what happened? You told me you had never met him until you came home this time."

"That's true. He told me at Marie's pool party that he wanted to marry me."

Crystal jumped up off the bed, waving her hands around in excitement and said, "You can't be serious?"

"I am."

"For real?"

"Yes."

"So when y'all gettin' married?"

"I wanted to wait until I finish school—"

"Are you crazy?" Crystal asked, cutting her off before she could finish. "You better hurry up and marry him, girl. I know after what happened last night, all his women—I mean ex-women—will come out of the woodwork now. But why you wanna wait anyway?"

"As I was saying," Darlene continued, ignoring her cousin's comment about Al's other women. "I wanted to wait until I finish school, but we decided to get married the Saturday before Christmas."

"I like winter weddings. What colors are you going to have? Where are you having your reception? You know Al can afford some fancy stuff."

Darlene was amazed at how her cousin was more excited than she was.

At breakfast, Crystal couldn't wait to tell everyone Darlene's news. Robert was happy because he only saw it as being related to Big Al. Nothing more. Her aunt was happy if she was happy. Darryl didn't seem to care one way or the other and that bothered Darlene.

"When is the wedding?" Betty asked.

Crystal gave all the details she knew and Darryl finally spoke up. "So I guess you'll be moving for good now," he said, sounding sad.

"You know I'll be going back to school in August. And after I get married, I'll still go back to school when the semester starts again. I'm hoping to get a job at the bank I'm working at now after I graduate. That way I'll be living close and you can come by anytime," Darlene said and that seemed to satisfy him. "And one more thing. I want you to give me away."

Darryl's whole face seemed to light up when he asked, "I get to wear a tuxedo and stuff?"

"What about me?" Robert asked.

"Well, you can't give me away, but you can escort Auntie Betty," she said. "And you both get to wear a tuxedo."

"You'll have to tell me how many people you're inviting so I can get some people to help me cook for your reception," her aunt said.

"No way, Mama," Crystal said. "Al is probably having the reception somewhere fancy."

Darlene didn't like the fact that Crystal kept focusing on Al's money. Come to think of it, she had never thought about his money. She didn't dwell on it. She had a whole year before she had to worry about money.

"We haven't decided any of that yet, Auntie Betty, but I'll let you know in plenty enough time."

"You only have six months. What are you going to do about a wedding dress?"

"I don't know yet. But I'll have everything under control before I go back to school."

"Do I get to meet this boy?" her aunt asked.

Darlene would hardly call Al a boy. But it was only natural for her aunt to think he was closer to her age.

"He'll be here at about two o'clock today," Darlene said, rising from the table. "I need to go to the store. I'll be back soon."

While Darlene was getting ready to leave, Darryl wanted to go with her. On their way to the store, Darlene sensed that something was bothering him.

"Okay Darryl, what's up?"

"Nothin'," he answered.

"Come on, Darryl, this your favorite cousin. Tell me."

"It's just . . . why you wanna marry Al? You know he's a dope dealer."

Of course she knew that. She wasn't blind. "I know that Darryl. It just sort of happened. Besides, he's going to stop doing that soon. You don't like him or something?"

"Nah, it's nothin' like that. I really don't know him. I just hear a lot of stuff that's all."

"Maybe if you get to know him you'll like him."

"Maybe."

"Tell you what. We're going shopping for furniture later. Do you want to come?"

"Sure."

They rode the rest of the way listening to the radio. Darlene went to the store and picked up what she needed. She noticed she needed gas, too. They pulled into a gas station. Darryl filled up the car while she made a phone call. She called Al at home. He answered on the fourth ring.

"Hello?" He sounded as if he was sleeping.

"Alvin?" she said a little unsure. She hoped she dialed the right number.

Al knew who she was because no one else dared call him by his full first name. "Hey, Dee."

"How did you know it was me?" she asked.

"Because I let you call me Alvin. What do you need?"

"I don't need anything really. It's just that Crystal made a big deal about the ring and now my aunt wants to meet you and I sort of told my cousin he could come with us when we shop for the bedroom furniture. I hope you don't mind," she said then held her breath while she waited for his response.

"No, I don't mind. But I may have to come earlier. I have somewhere to be later this afternoon."

"Sure. When are you coming?"

"What time is it?"

"A little after eleven. Do you always sleep this late?"

"No. I had to do something after I left you."

"Release frustration?" she asked.

"C'mon now, Dee. It was business. I told you. You're all I want. How about if I come at noon?"

"I'll be ready. Bye." When she hung up, Darryl was driving her car to where she was standing. She didn't know he could drive. He got out and walked around to get in on the passenger side. "Since when have you been driving?" she asked as she got in behind the steering wheel.

"I've been driving," he said as if he'd been driving for years.

"Do you have a license?"

"Uh . . . no."

"Then you shouldn't be driving. I'll see if I can get off early one day and take you to get your license."

"For real, Darlene? You'll bring me to get my license?"

"Yeah. Now let's go. Alvin has to come by earlier."

"Alvin?" her cousin asked confused.

"Al."

"That's his name?" Darryl asked, trying to suppress a smile. "I thought it was plan ol' Al. And you call him Alvin?"

"Yes. Apparently I'm the only one who does. So don't say anything okay? Just call him Al like everybody else."

"You got it. Alvin," he said the name again then he just started laughing.

"Okay, keep it up. You won't get your driver's license." That stopped the laughing. He would giggle every so often, but nothing too loud.

When they got home, she let her aunt know that Al would be coming over earlier than planned. The three women waited in the living room. Robert and Darryl chose to wait outside. Darryl walked inside and let them know Al had just drove up. Robert walked in with Al.

"Good evening everyone," he said in general.

Darlene walked over to him and whispered in his ear, "I'm sorry for springing my family on you."

"Don't worry about it," he whispered back.

She introduced him to her aunt. "Alv—" she caught herself, "Al, this is my aunt, Betty Jones. Auntie Betty, this is Al Williams."

He shook her hand and said, "Please to meet you." Darlene pointed to her cousins. Darryl was the only one he wasn't familiar with. He had seen Robert hanging on corners and he knew Crystal, but Darryl didn't associate with the same crowds his sister and brother did. Al sat in a chair next to the sofa. Darlene sat on the end of the sofa close to his chair. Crystal started with the questions.

"So, Al. How did you end up with Darlene?" Darlene wanted to just get up and leave. She looked at Al as if to say ignore her cousin, but he chose to answer her question.

"Let's just say I found her to be irresistible," he said and reached over and held her hand.

Then Betty asked a few questions of her own. "Al, do you go to school with Darlene?"

"No, I don't."

"Then what do you do?"

"I'm a salesman at my brother-in-law's car dealership. Speaking of which," he looked at his watch, "I have to stop by there and help him with something. Darlene we need to get a move on."

"Okay," she said and they got up to leave.

"It was nice meeting you," he said to her aunt.

"It was nice meeting you, too, Al."

They left and headed to the car. Darryl was already outside waiting. The three of them got in and headed to the store.

Al drove them to a furniture warehouse. They walked to the section with bedroom furniture and looked around. Darryl wanted to walk around and look at other things so he left.

Al and Darlene looked mostly at the oak bedroom sets. She came across a white canopy bedroom set. She moved closer to get a better look.

"No way, Darlene."

"What?" she asked innocently. She knew the bedroom was strictly feminine. She just thought it was pretty. It wasn't like she planned on getting it.

"I'm not going to sleep in a bed like that. Find something brown or black. You can pick whatever you want then." They walked along the warehouse some more. Al's cell phone rang. "You go on ahead and I'll catch up with you," he said and answered his phone. She walked farther along and a salesman approached her.

"Good afternoon. Can I help you with anything today?" he asked cheerfully.

"Yes. I'm looking to buy bedroom furniture." She looked over in Al's direction then said, "Preferably something brown or black."

"We have a lot to choose from in oak and lacquer. They're towards the back of the warehouse. Any particular size?"

"Queen. I'd like to look at mattresses, too."

They walked to the back of the store where there was a vast assortment of furniture. Darlene saw a black lacquer set that was unlike anything she'd ever seen. The headboard was huge. It spanned about seven feet wide and four feet high. It was mostly black with gold sparkles inside the color with an oval-shaped mirror positioned in the center. There was a double-dresser with a mirror, an armoire, a six-drawer chest, and two nightstands that completed the set. It was shown with full-size bedding since most sets were displayed for that particular size. The salesman assured her it would accommodate king or queen size bedding.

The salesman was standing close to Darlene explaining about ways to avoid scratching the furniture when Al was approaching. He walked up startling them both. "Found what you wanted?" He sounded irritated to Darlene, but the salesman didn't take notice.

"I was just looking at this set right here. How do you like it?"

He looked over at it without really noticing it and said, "It's all right."

Darlene wanted to look around a little longer before she made a decision. The salesman gave her his card and left them.

"What's wrong with you?" Darlene asked.

"Nothing's wrong with me. I just didn't know how close you have to be under someone to sell them furniture."

"Were you jealous, Alvin?" He looked as if he didn't know what she was talking about. "You don't have any reason to be jealous. He was telling me how to avoid scratching the furniture and how to maintain the glossy finish. I'm marrying you so stop being jealous. Now do you like this set or do you want to look at others?"

"No. This one here is fine," he said, pointing to the furniture.

"Let's find the salesman and see how much it cost," she said, standing on tiptoe to see if she could spot him.

"It doesn't matter. If you want it, we'll get it. Here." He handed her a Gold Master Card.

"What's this?" she said, looking down at the card.

"A credit card," he said.

"I know that. I mean what's it for?"

"To buy the furniture. I don't have that kind of cash on me. The card is yours temporarily. I authorized you to use it. You can buy the bedroom set and everything else you have to buy with it."

"Why are you doing this?" she asked. She couldn't get over how much he seemed to trust her. She wouldn't have had a problem if they were a couple in love, but they weren't.

"Dee," he said her name like he was losing patience with her. "We're getting married aren't we?" She nodded her agreement. "You might as well start getting used to buying things without me. Anyway, I have to leave once we finish up here. I'll drop you off and you can get whatever else you need."

"Okay."

The salesman found them before they located him. They decided on the black lacquer set. Darlene wanted new mattresses and the salesman showed them the best they had. Darryl joined them near the mattresses.

When the salesman calculated the bill, it came to almost three thousand dollars. Darlene turned and looked up at Al with nervous eyes. He looked down at her and smiled. He realized she felt uncomfortable about him spending so much money on her. He remembered taking one woman shopping for clothes and she hadn't cared how much he had spent. Albeit it was nowhere near the amount he was spending on Darlene.

"Give him the credit card, Darlene," he said so only she could hear him. He then slipped his arm around her waist and kissed her near her ear. The delivery date wasn't for another week because they didn't have the queen sized bed frame in stock. They offered to deliver the other pieces of the set and provide them with temporary bedding, but Darlene chose to wait for the entire set. The salesman handed Darlene the receipt. They left and headed back to her aunt's house. Darlene was wondering what he would do with his other bedroom set.

"What are you going to do with the furniture you have, Alvin?"

"I don't know. Get ride of it somewhere."

"Would you mind if I ask my aunt if she wants to buy it?"

"Yeah, I mind. If she wants it, give it to her."

They were soon parking in front of her aunt's house. Darlene stayed in the car while Darryl got out. Al reached into his pocket and handed Darlene a key, which she looked at strangely. "That's a key to my apartment," he explained. "In case you plan on buying anything else, you can leave it over there. You do remember how to get there don't you?"

"Not really," she confessed.

"Okay. Let's go now and you can drop me off where I have to go." He started the car up again and pulled off before she could answer.

It didn't take long to get to his apartment. They went inside for a few minutes and went into the bedroom. Darlene looked around and noticed he had a nice oak bedroom set. When Al came up behind her, she turned to him and he started kissing her. She didn't resist when he subtly eased her back on the bed. He pulled her shirt from her shorts and exposed her bra-covered breasts. He started rubbing and squeezing them. He pulled at the buttons on her shorts, unfastening them. Darlene knew what he wanted. And she suddenly wanted the same thing. After all they were engaged and he had just bought her a three thousand-dollar bedroom set.

"Alvin, aren't you supposed to be somewhere?" she asked, reminding him.

"Yeah. But we have time for this," he said, referring to sex. "Just a quickie. C'mon, Dee." He had been celibate for weeks. And the way she had him turned on the previous night he couldn't wait to have sex with her. He was already hard. He felt like he could bust the zipper on his jeans.

"Use a condom, Alvin," she said and he quickly took one out of his wallet. He opened his pants and let them drop around his ankles. He pushed his briefs down to join them. Once he readied himself with protection, he pulled down her shorts and panties. He entered her quickly and started moving. It was a little painful to Darlene because he didn't give her time to adjust to him. She hadn't been intimate with a man in months. And she realized Al was more concerned with his own pleasure. She was turned off so she just laid there until she heard him grunt his satisfaction then laid on the bed next to her. She eased from under him and asked, "Where's the bathroom?" He told her and she left.

Al laid on his bed and wondered what had happened. He was used to responsive women, but Darlene hadn't seemed to be enjoying the sex as much as he was. And he definitely enjoyed it. Darlene came back to the bedroom fully dressed. While he was in the process of fastening his pants, he looked at her and asked, "You all right?" For some reason he thought something was bothering her.

"Yes."

"Let's go then." They walked back to the car. When they got in, Al opened his glove compartment and handed her his beeper. "Keep this on you. I'll let you know when to pick me up. And while you're out, use my car. I don't want it parked by your aunt's house too long."

"Sure."

They drove in silence. Once they got to their destination, Al got out and Darlene moved over to the driver's seat. He reached in his wallet and pulled out two fifties and held them out to her.

"What's that for?" she asked, looking at the money.

Al usually gave the women he would have sex with a little cash, but never that much. Not that he thought of them as prostitutes or anything. They were always willing so he would give them twenty or forty dollars here and there.

"Just something for you. I can't wait to test out that new bed we're getting."

"Oh, so now I see," she said, nodding her head. Now she was beginning to get the picture. "Payment for services rendered. Keep your money for your whores. I'm not your whore." She put the car in gear and pulled off leaving him standing with the money in his hands. She couldn't believe he had tried to give her money as some kind of payment for having sex with him. It wasn't that good anyway, she thought, because she sure didn't get anything out of it. She was mad as hell by the time she got home. She decided to show him a thing or two. Since he wanted to treat her like a whore she would show him.

As soon as she got home, she took a bath and changed clothes. She was going shopping and Crystal jumped at the chance to join her. Crystal walked outside assuming they were going in Darlene's car. Then she saw her cousin heading toward a white Mercedes.

"Girl, this Al's car?"

"Yeah. He had to be somewhere and I dropped him off. He'll beep me when he wants me to pick him up." They got in the car and left heading for the nearest shopping mall.

Darlene went to the mall and got carried away. She bought comforter sets and all the accessories to go with them. She bought three different queen-size sets. She bought the sheets, decorative pillows, and draperies to match the sets. She also bought shower curtains, towels, and rugs for the bathroom floor. She also bought every popular kitchen appliance. She hoped she could see Al's face when he got the bill.

They couldn't carry everything she bought so someone at the store helped carry the rest of it to the door and waited while she and her cousin went to get her car. As she and Crystal were nearing the car in the parking lot, they noticed two girls hanging around the car. At first Darlene didn't think anything of it, but when she saw one of them looking inside the car she got a little suspicious. When her and Crystal were closer, she asked, "May I help you with something?" catching the girls off guard.

"No. We're just waiting for the man who this car is for."

"I'm sorry, but the car is mine," Darlene calmly lied and the two girls looked at one another.

"I know for a fact that this car belongs to a man named Al. That's his license number," she said, pointing to the plate.

Darlene was starting to find the whole thing funny. Al had girls hanging around his car, knowing his license plate number. "Okay," Darlene said. "I see we have a problem here. As it happens, my husband's name is Al. Why don't you describe your Al to me?" Crystal looked at her cousin in amazement. She knew they were talking about the same Al. One of the girls started describing Al and Darlene looked at her cousin and smiled. "Sounds like my husband to me. Well, if you two will excuse me," Darlene said, taking her keys out of her purse. "I would like to get in my car. Would you like me to give Al a message?"

"No," one of them answered and then they walked off.

"I can't believe you did that," Crystal said and they got in the car.

"Did what?"

"You knew those girls were talking about Al. I *know* it'll be all over streets that he's married now."

"That's the point." They drove to the store to pick up their purchases.

Once everything was loaded in the car, they decided to stop and have lunch. While they were sitting down eating, they talked about the wedding.

Chapter six

Darlene was watching TV when Al beeped her. She immediately called him and he answered the phone on the first ring. "Al here."

"Are you ready for me to pick you up?"

"Yeah. The same place you dropped me off earlier will be fine. Dee, about the money—"

"I'm on my way, Alvin," she said not letting him finish. Then she hung up. She wasn't in no mood to hear any trumped up apologies from him. She left and got in the car. It didn't take her long to get there, about fifteen minutes. She saw him and slowed down and stopped. She didn't get out. She just moved over to the passenger side. He got in and turned off the car. She just looked out the side window.

He turned to face her and said, "I didn't mean anything by giving you the money, Dee."

"Sure, Alvin."

He reached for her shoulder and turned her to face him. "I'm serious. I didn't think you would take it like that. You still marrying me right?"

"I said I would. I just wish you would stop treating me like those other women you used to mess with." He leaned over and kissed her softly on the lips then he started the car. "By the way, I saw a couple of friends of yours."

"Friends of mine?" he asked, frowning.

"Yeah. Two young-looking girls were hanging around your car. They knew it was yours because they knew your license plate number."

"Uh, Darlene, some people, women in particular, know my car. That don't mean nothing."

"I didn't say it did. I was just telling you."

"Oh," he said. He looked over at her sitting in the car. She was wearing a short skirt and a T-shirt that stopped at her waist. He removed his right hand from the steering wheel and placed it possessively on her left thigh and began rubbing. He eased his hand higher. It moved all the way in between her legs. Darlene was getting irritated and she brushed his hand away and that angered him.

"Whatcha did that for?" he demanded.

"I told you, Alvin, I'm not your whore or bitch."

"Damn, Darlene. I just wanted to touch you. You sittin' over there looking all sexy and making me get all hard."

"So you're trying to say you want sex?" she asked, getting pissed off.

"What the hell you mean by do I want sex?" he asked. It was true he wanted to have sex with her, but she made it sound so cheap.

"That's what it would be wouldn't it?"

Al was finding it hard to concentrate on driving and argue with Darlene at the same time. He didn't answer her question right away. He found somewhere he could pull over to talk. It was a side street behind an abandon warehouse. He turned off the car's engine and faced her.

"What are you talking about?"

"Just what I said. What would you call what happened earlier?"

"Sex. I don't believe in that making love crap."

"Well, I do. And I hope you got something out of just having sex earlier because I didn't." She didn't mean to say that to him. It just came out. She soon saw anger building in his facial features. He turned in his seat and looked out the front windshield. "I'm sorry, Alvin. I shouldn't have said that."

"You damn right. You tryin' to say I can't satisfy you? We'll just see about that," he said and reached over and started pulling on her clothes. Darlene tried to stop him, but she couldn't. Once he had her breasts exposed, he squeezed them roughly and hungrily sucked and bit on them. Immediately he felt Darlene's body tremble and he thought she was enjoying it. Instead she was crying and wondering how could she have agreed to marry him. She didn't know this man in the car with her.

Al looked up and saw her crying. He immediately stopped what he had been doing and sat back in his seat and took a deep breath. He swore under his breath and hit the steering wheel hard, with both palms of his hands. "I didn't mean to do that." He took another deep breath and released it. Darlene just sat in silence. Her silence wasn't doing anything to his punctured ego. "How do you think I'm supposed to feel when you tell me I can't satisfy you?"

"I didn't say you couldn't satisfy me. I said I didn't enjoy it. All you did was got your satisfaction. You didn't think about me at all."

"Whatchu talkin' about?"

"All you did was climb on me and started humping. You didn't kiss me. Not once. And it was painful."

Al never thought about any of that. He was used to being with women who were always ready and willing, the promiscuous types. He didn't have to do any foreplay. But he was beginning to realize just how totally different Darlene was. Wasn't that the reason why he wanted her as his wife?

"Listen, I'm sorry. It won't happen again. C'mere," Al said and beckoned her to sit on his lap. He adjusted his seat to accommodate them. "Dee," he turned her face to look at him and he kissed her softly. "I won't ever do that to you again." Then he put his hand on the back of her head and pulled her to him to receive a deeper kiss. She kissed him back with a great need. She reached her hand down and started feeling his manhood. She wanted to give him an example of how he could make her feel good. Al's muscles tightened when she started feeling him.

"Alvin?" she said still kissing him.

"Hmm?"

"Do you have any condoms?" she asked, kissing his neck.

"What?"

"Condoms."

"I think so. Why?"

"Take one out," she ordered, pulling free from him. "I'll show you how good making love can be."

Al hurriedly pulled the condom from his wallet. Darlene took the plastic packet away from him and said, “Magnum large?” after reading the packet.

“You wouldn’t want it to break would you?”

Darlene looked down at his engorged sex and said, “I guess not.”

“Then I have to wear the size that fits.”

Al removed the opened pack from her hand and proceeded to put on the condom. Darlene took off her shirt, bra, and panties, leaving on her skirt. She raised it around her waist and sat on his lap, facing him in a straddling position. She started kissing him aggressively. She unbuttoned his shirt and started kissing his chest. Then she guided his head to her breasts. He started sucking her chocolate colored nipples.

“Lay the seat back.” He did as she instructed. She kissed from his chest to his stomach. Al moaned and groaned in pleasure. She raised herself up to allow him entry into her. “Now just lay back and relax.” Darlene did all the work. Al just held on to her at her waist. “Don’t cum until I say so, okay?”

“What?” Al asked. He was almost ready for his release.

“Trust me. If it gets to where you can’t wait tell me.”

She rocked and drove him to the edge. Al had never had a woman to take charge during sex. He had to admit he was enjoying it. Soon he muttered a curse through clenched teeth and she knew he was beginning to lose control. “Hold on, Alvin,” she said, quickening her movements. Soon they both exploded together. She laid down on top of him and he circled her in his arms.

They both laid still until their breathing returned to normal.

"Damn, that was good. Oh, I love you." Darlene moved to get up off of him in order to start putting her clothes back on. "Hold up. I want some more of that."

"Do you have another condom?"

"No. But we don't need none. C'mon, Dee," he said pleadingly

"No, Alvin. Not until I see your test results," she said adamantly.

Al swore under his breath while he was raising his seat upright. "Well, I wanna know whether or not you have something, too. And I want you to move in with me," he stated then he started dressing himself.

"I only have two weeks before I leave. And I'd like to stay at my aunt's house."

"Can't you just spend a few nights with me?" he asked hopeful.

"Sure. Starting Saturday night."

"Why so long away?"

"Because that's when the new bed will be delivered."

He thought it would be best to let the conversation drop for now.

Monday at work, Marie noticed the ring on Darlene's finger. She didn't mention it at first. She wanted to see if Darlene would. It was getting close to lunch and Darlene still hadn't said anything. She invited her to lunch. Once they were seated at the table, Marie couldn't wait any longer. She had to say something about the ring. "Nice ring," she said.

"It is, isn't it," Darlene said, looking down at her left hand. "But I guess you knew, huh?"

"Knew what?" Marie asked.

"You didn't know?"

"Know what?"

"Alvin gave me the ring. We're getting married the week before Christmas." Darlene was taking in the shocked expression on Marie's face. "I take it he didn't tell you. He gave it to me Friday night. He wanted to give it to me the day we were supposed to have lunch together, but something happened."

"I can't believe this. You and my brother are getting married. I guess when he decides to do something he does it. He's always been like that though," Marie stated.

"I'm beginning to realize that. I was hoping you would be my matron of honor."

"Girl, yes indeed. I'm just glad he's marrying someone like you. At least you have a brain. I couldn't stand those sluts he used to have around him. But enough about that. I hope you're going to finish school."

"No question about it."

"What are your colors? Where are you going to have the reception?" Darlene started laughing because Marie sounded just like Crystal.

"Slow down, Marie. I haven't had a chance to decide anything yet. I was hoping you can help me out a lot since I'll be at school."

"No problem. But you should still have the final say so."

"I know. I'll have to come back on some weekends."

"Do you have a color scheme in mind?" Marie asked.

"Yeah. I was thinking about velvet hunter green and black. It won't be a big wedding. I'll only have you as my matron of honor, my cousin as my maid of honor, and a couple of my friends from school as bridesmaids."

"Okay. We can go and look at some dresses this weekend. I can probably get a hold of some tickets for this bridal show this weekend, too. When do you have to be back at school?"

"The first week in August."

"Good. After the show this weekend, we'll see where to go from there." Their food arrived and they discussed other matters concerning the wedding. They finished eating their lunch and headed back to work.

The week passed fast. Darlene had arranged for someone to bring Al's old furniture to her aunt's house. They moved her aunt's old bedroom furniture into Crystal's room. They gave away Crystal's old furniture.

Darlene was at Al's apartment waiting for the deliverymen to show up when the telephone rang. She wasn't sure she should answer it so she let the answering machine pick up the call. When she heard Al's voice, she grabbed the receiver.

"Don't hang up, Alvin," she said over the recording. He waited until the out going message stopped.

"Turn the machine off, Dee," he ordered. When she did, he asked, "Why didn't you answer the phone?"

"I didn't know if you would have wanted me to."

"Dee, I want you to consider my apartment your apartment. Have the delivery people come yet?"

"No, not yet. I have the room empty and waiting."

"Sorry I couldn't be there to help," he apologized.

"Don't worry about it."

"I love you, you know that?"

"Is there any direction in particular you want the bed to face?" she asked purposely ignoring his question. He had been telling her he loved her all the time. She just didn't believe him. She still felt he had a reason for wanting to marry her in particular. And she wanted to find out that reason.

"How ever way you want it is fine with me. Just as long as you are in it tonight. And I have something for you."

"What?" she asked curiously.

"You'll have to wait until tonight."

"Why tonight? I won't see you until then?"

"I have something to take care of. I should be home by about eight o'clock."

"Fine. I think I hear a truck. Call me here or beep me. Bye, Alvin." She hung up and opened the door just as the deliverymen were approaching. She supervised them while they brought in the furniture.

When Al hung up the phone, he was feeling happy. He just realized that he was really beginning to love Darlene. He didn't really know why she had agreed to marry him. She never asked him for money. She didn't expect much from him. He hadn't called her in days. And when he did, she acted like it didn't bother her. He knew that in the business he was involved with, having a wife and family made him look good in the eyes of the law. Not that he was having problems with the law. But it was always better to be safe than sorry. And the wife he was choosing was going to be a college graduate. And on top of that, she was majoring in accounting. The same as his sister. Al knew that Marie had help Jeff out a lot with financial matters. Him too for that matter. He couldn't have made a better choice, Al thought to himself. He was aware that his sister knew a good deal about what he and Jeff were in to. But Darlene had told him to keep it away from her. He agreed at the time, but now . . ..

Al was pulled away from his thoughts when Jeff came into the room.

"How's it going, man?" Jeff asked.

"Everything's cool," Al replied.

"I hear you gettin' married," Jeff stated.

"Yeah. I wanted to do it now, but she wants a wedding so we'll do it a week before Christmas."

"Say, man, have you told her anything?" Jeff didn't have to go into specifics.

"Nah. She just knows what she's heard. As far as she knows, I supply certain people and they go deal on the street. Just small time stuff."

"That's all she needs to know for now. When you get married, we'll see if we can trust her before you tell her anything else. Got it?"

"No problem. So what's the deal for tonight?" Al asked then they went on to discuss what they had planned for that night.

Darlene had put the new sheets and comforter on the bed and hung the drapes. The whole room looked different. She had her results from her Pap smear and

HIV test from her last check up three months ago. She had gone back to her aunt's house and gotten a few of her clothes and brought them over. She wanted to cook, but Al didn't have much food in his refrigerator. She went to the store and bought a few groceries. She baked steaks and potatoes. She sat and waited for Al to come home. It was going on ten o'clock. She decided to go to bed at half past ten. At around eleven thirty, she heard the front door open. She was mad and decided to pretend to be asleep.

Al walked into the kitchen and saw the food on the stove. He knew he was later than he said he was going to be. A lot later. But things got out of hand and they ran into a little bit of trouble. When he walked into the bedroom, he turned on the light and was amazed by what he saw. The room didn't look familiar to him anymore. And there was Darlene, lying in the bed sleeping. His bed. He went and sat beside her and rubbed her hip and she slapped his hand away.

"Dee, what's wrong?"

"You tell me. You had fun tonight? I guess you stopped in on one of your whores. Did you need release tonight?"

Al looked at Darlene shocked because he didn't expect that kind of reaction from her.

"No, Dee. I wasn't with another woman. I'm sorry I'm late. Things got out of hand tonight. I need to go to the bathroom." He got up off of the bed with a groan. Darlene laid there for a while before deciding to follow him in the bathroom.

When she walked into the bathroom, she stopped in her tracks. Al was standing in front of the mirror with his shirt off and a cut on his shoulder. Maybe it was at that moment that she really started to care for him.

"Alvin!" she screamed, startling him. He turned to see her standing in the doorway staring at his shoulder. "What happened to you? How did you get cut?"

"It's nothin'. It'll heal by itself. It's not deep." She walked up to him and started examining the wound. He had peroxide, gauze bandages, and tape sitting on the bathroom counter. She began to clean the cut. He just stood there while she bandaged him up. When she was finished, he pulled her in his arms and said, "Thank you."

"Are you hungry?" He nodded and they went to the kitchen to eat. Soon after they sat down to eat, he left the table to go and get something for her. When he came back, he handed her a package. She looked at it then she looked at him.

"It's and engagement present," he explained. Darlene opened the package and saw his medical results, which proved he was HIV negative and that he didn't have any other sexually transmitted disease. There was a cell phone and a jeweler's box. She opened the box and saw a wide gold herringbone chain. She looked at him again.

"What's all this for?"

"You asked for the medical paper. And I would like to be able to reach you at all times. That's what the phone is for. And I just wanted to get you the jewelry."

"Oh, Alvin," she said and got up and carefully hugged him and kissed him. "Thank you. But I can't keep the phone."

"Why?"

"What if you decide to call while I'm in class?"

"Okay. Then I'll get you your own beeper, too. I don't know who may still have the number to mine."

"I can't have a beeper either. They're too loud."

"All you have to do is put it on hum."

"Hum?" she said. He got his beeper and adjusted the button and handed it to her. Then he dialed the number. She felt the vibration and said, "Oh. I didn't know about that."

"So now you do. By the way, the room looks nice."

"I'm glad you like it. Too bad we can't break it in tonight."

"Why not?"

"Remember your shoulder?"

"That doesn't affect the bottom part of my body. And I'm in the mood about now. How about you?"

"That depends," she said.

"On what?" Al asked.

"Are you going to make me feel as good as I made you feel the last time?"

"Definitely."

They left the kitchen and went into the bedroom. And true to his word Al made her feel good. And from that night on, they made love without using condoms. Darlene was taking birth control pills so there wasn't a risk of pregnancy.

While they lay in bed together in the dark Al started talking.

"Dee, you know I love you right?"

"That's what you tell me," she said not really agreeing with him.

"I do. I need to know how you feel about me."

"I care for you or I wouldn't be with you." At least he knew she cared for him. It wasn't love, but it was something.

"I need you to do something for me."

She was silent for a moment.

"Dee?"

"Huh?"

"I said I need you to do something for me."

"What?" she asked, holding her breath.

Al reached over to the nightstand and turned on the lamp. He looked at her and said, "I need you to say I was here with you tonight from as early as eight o'clock if anyone ask."

"Why?"

"You don't want to know that. I just need you to do that for me. Can you?"

Darlene raised up in bed and looked in his face then she kissed him. When she ended the kiss, she looked at him and said, "Of course I can, Alvin."

Chapter seven

When Darlene and Marie went to the bridal show, they sampled wedding cakes, received brochures from various florists, photographers, and hotels for possible places to hold the reception. They had a lot of information to choose from. They had already gone shopping for a bridal gown. Darlene wasn't satisfied with what she had seen so far. She had seen beautiful dresses for her bridesmaids though. She will have to talk to her friends at school before she decided anything definite. Darlene wanted Marie to pick whatever style of dress she wanted as long as it was velvet hunter green with a little black in it. Crystal was getting her dress made since she would have recently had her baby.

It was now nearing the time for Darlene to go back to school. She had saved the bulk of her money from working during the summer because Al didn't want her to spend any of her money. He paid the credit card bill plus he gave her money to buy groceries for the apartment and for her to buy lunch at work.

A couple of days before Darlene was due to leave, Al brought up the subject of money with her again over dinner one night.

"Darlene?" She looked at him. "How are you paying for college?" She was hoping her finances would never have to be discussed.

"I've been going on scholarship," she said, hoping it would be enough. It wasn't.

"But how do you afford food and your books? And your car note?"

"I don't have a car note. My car is paid for."

"It is?"

"Yes. I used some of the money I had left over from my parents' insurance after I buried them to buy my car. And what was left along with the part-time job I get during tax season, I can pay for my books and eat."

"How much do your books usually cost?"

She thought for a minute. "Between two hundred and fifty to three hundred dollars a semester. That's if I get them new from the bookstore. Sometimes I can buy used books from someone else. But if they change the books every semester, I have no choice but to buy them new."

"I'll give you enough to buy them new," he said.

"I can buy my own books, Alvin."

"Let me take care of you. Save your money. I can still put you in an apartment right off campus," he suggested.

"No. I like it on campus. My dorm isn't far from the library. And when I need to study late, I don't have far to go."

"All right. But are there any hotels close by?"

"I think so. Why?"

"Because when I come to see you, I want some privacy. And I'll be taking you back to school."

"And how are you going to get back?"

"I'll rent a car. I want to see your school."

"Okay."

Darlene stopped by her aunt's house the morning before she left. It was nine o'clock. She was hoping she could say goodbye to them all. Robert was outside somewhere and Crystal was still sleeping. Darryl walked her out. She would miss him the most.

"Look like this is it. My last year."

"Yeah. Mine, too. Darlene . . ." he began and stopped.

"What?" she asked, looking up to him and encouraging him to finish.

"Is Al treating you okay?"

"Yes. Don't worry about me. I can take care of Alvin. Tell you what. One weekend I'll send for you to come to one of the football games at school," she said and his face brightened.

"You will?"

"Yes. I'll send you the schedule and you find out if it's okay with Auntie Betty and I'll send you a bus ticket."

"All right."

"Here," she said, handing him a piece of paper. "That's my beeper and cell phone numbers. You are the only one, besides Alvin, who has them. You call me if you need me."

"Okay."

"I'll talk to you later. I'll send the schedule as soon as I get it," Darlene said then she got into Al's car and left. He had been asleep at home when she had left earlier that morning. They had packed her car up the night before.

When Darlene got back to the apartment, it was almost ten o'clock and Al was still asleep. She went into the bedroom and woke him. "Alvin, it's time to get up," she called to him, but he didn't move. She shook him a little and he jumped up. His sudden movement scared her. "Alvin?" she said cautiously.

"I'm okay," he said, rubbing his eyes with his hands then he yawned. "What time is it?"

"Ten o'clock. You don't have to bring me to school you know."

"I know. I want to. Let me get dressed and I'll be ready in a few minutes." He got out of bed naked. He always slept nude. Darlene didn't have any complaints at all. She went to sleep wearing a nightgown, but woke up naked most of the times herself.

They hit the road a half an hour later. Darlene was a bit surprised at Al's enthusiasm. He asked a lot of questions about her school. He had only finished high school, but he was smart.

Darlene directed him where to go. When they pulled up near her dorm building, she got out and went in while Al waited in the car. Al sat for about five minutes and became restless. He got out of the car and leaned against it. A couple of guys walked past and looked in his direction. Just then, Darlene came out of the door and started walking toward him. She was grabbed from behind by one of the guys and picked up off her feet. Al's first reaction was to think that it was somebody trying to get at him. He quickly banished that thought because no one he was associated with knew about Darlene except Jeff. Then he saw Darlene smiling. He walked over to her and the guys.

"Everything all set?" he asked, looking at her then giving the two guys a menacing look.

"Yeah," she answered as the two guys walked off saying they would see her later.

"Who were they?"

"Just friends," she answered. She didn't see any need to tell him she used to have a relationship with the one that had picked her up. They were just friends now.

"Just friends, huh? Do all your friends greet you like that?"

"No, Alvin. Let's get my things to my room. I want you to meet Chris," she said and they headed back to the car.

They carried her things to her room. On the last trip to her room, her roommate came in. Chris was a little chubby in the midsection. She's shorter than Darlene and very light skinned. She was shy and didn't have many friends when her and Darlene first met. She had been Darlene's roommate since their freshman year. They got along great. Every time Darlene would go somewhere, she would usually coax Chris into going also. And since Chris had lost some weight she has become very open and outgoing.

Darlene pushed the door opened with her free hand. She pointed to where she wanted Al to put her suitcases down. She then reached for his hand and introduced the two.

"Chris, this is Al . . . my fiancé. Al, this is my roommate Chris."

"Hold up a minute," Chris said before Al could say anything. "Your *what?*"

"Her fiancé," Al said. "We're getting married a week before Christmas."

"When did this happen?" she asked, looking at Darlene. She had always been aware of the guys Darlene went out with. On occasions, she had to cover for her. But she never recalled Darlene mentioning anyone named Al. "How come I've never heard of an Al?" she asked. Her shyness now a thing of the past.

"That's because she hadn't either," Al said. "We met this summer. It was love at first sight. Ain't that right, Dee?" he said, hugging her to him, daring her to say otherwise.

"What can I say? You swept me off my feet," she said, looking up at him sharply.

"Well, I've seen it all. Leave at the end of the school year breaking hearts and come back engaged."

Al looked down at Darlene and asked, "Breaking hearts?"

"Oops," Chris said. "I think I'll leave you two alone. See you later, Darlene. Nice meeting you, Al." She left the room.

"What hearts have you been breaking?" he asked.

"I don't know what Chris is talking about." She really didn't want to discuss the previous guy she was involved with. "She exaggerates sometimes. It's just that the last guy I was involved with didn't want to accept the break-up," she said by way of an explanation.

"He still goes here?" he asked, referring to the school.

"As far as I know."

"I hope you make sure that he knows it's over between you two and that you're married now."

"Engaged. And if I see him, I'll let him know. And I'll wear my ring all the time, Alvin." She stood on her tiptoe and kissed him.

He pulled back and said, "If he bothers you, let me know, okay?" She nodded. He raised her chin up so she could look in his face. "I'm serious."

"I will, Alvin. Are you ready to go and get your rental car?" she asked to lighten the mood.

"Yeah, but I'm not ready to leave yet. Why don't we try one of those hotels we passed on our way here? I need some lovin'."

"You're crazy," she said, hitting him in his chest playfully. "You're lucky I need some lovin', too." They left her things on her side of the room and headed for the hotel.

After they made love Darlene got up and showered. Al walked into the bathroom just as she stepped out.

"When are you coming home?" he asked.

"Well, I usually stay on campus until Thanksgiving—"

"I know you're coming home before then," he said, cutting her off voicing his objection. "I can't go that long without making love to you."

"That's nice to know. So if I have to be away for a long time I guess you would start having sex with everything in sight."

"Damn, Darlene. I didn't mean that the way it sounded. I just meant I would want to see you before Thanksgiving. Can't you come home any sooner than that?"

"I was going to suggest the very thing, but I was cut off," she said, walking out of the bathroom and to the bedroom. "And it won't be every weekend. I enjoy the football games here. And I promised Darryl I would send for him to come to a game."

Al walked toward her and removed the towel she was using to cover herself. The draft made her nipples harden. He bent down and captured one with his mouth, nibbling on it with his teeth. Darlene's body reacted to him and she arched toward him. She reached down and stroked the part of him that was currently lifting and hardening. It became hard and throbbing in her hands. He led her back to the bed and joined their bodies again.

They lay in bed afterwards, rubbing each other's sweat-soaked skin. Al was wondering how he would get through the week.

"Do you want me to come and get you Friday?"

"Alvin, I just got here. I'll call you and let you know when I'm coming home. I want to see what my schedule will be like. You can always call me. You can wait for me can't you?" She wanted him to. She was beginning to have very strong feelings for him. But she wouldn't let him know just yet.

"Yeah, I can wait for you. And if I can't, I'll be on my way here for you."

"I'll be here waiting. But I think we should go. I have to unpack and you have to go and rent a car." They got up and dressed and went to check out. Al picked up one of the brochures on his way out.

Two days later, Al called Darlene. She had just walked in her room.

"Hello?" she answered.

"Where have you been?"

"Who is this?"

"This, Al. Who did you think it was?"

"Hey, Alvin," she said happily.

"Where have you been? I've been trying to call you for hours."

"I'm sorry. I forgot my phone and beeper in my room. I was down in Gail's room. Her, Chris, and I were discussing the wedding. What's wrong?"

"I've been sitting in this damn hotel room for two hours. I missed you."

"What hotel?"

"The one we were at before," he said as if she should have known.

"You're here?" she asked excitedly. "Why didn't you tell me you were coming?"

"I wanted to surprise you."

"I'll be over soon. I'm on my way." She hung up and left her room. She got over to the hotel in fifteen minutes. It dawned on her that she didn't know what room he was in. She asked the receptionist and was given the room number and a key.

Al was lying in bed with nothing on but a towel wrapped around the lower portion of his body. After he had gotten off the phone with Darlene, he left a key at the receptionist desk for her then he went back to the room and took a shower.

She walked in and saw him stretched out on the bed in nothing but a towel. It seemed like it had been two months, instead of two days, since she'd seen him. She started taking off her clothes, leaving a trail on the floor and joined him on the bed.

Two hours later Darlene had to leave and get back to her dorm room. Al handed her an envelope containing five hundred dollars. Darlene was really getting tired of him choosing to give her money right after they would make love.

"Why do you do that?"

"Do what?"

"Give me money after we make love. You make it seem like it's a payment."

"Dammit, Dee. It's—okay," he said, calming down. "I'm sorry it seemed like that to you. It's for your books. And if I had to pay for how good you make me feel, I'd have to start robbing banks." He smiled and so did she. She accepted the money and bent down to kiss him goodbye before she left.

As the weeks passed, Darlene was either spending time with Al at their usual hotel or at his apartment. They got to know quite a lot about each other. She found out that his father had abandoned him, his sister, and their mother when he was young and that his mother had died three years ago. Then they talked about school and the things they both liked and disliked.

On her visits home, she and Marie got together and talked about the wedding. She had finally decided on a wedding gown. She made sure her cousins were fitted for their tuxedos. Al was paying for everything, but she drew the line at her gown. She wanted to pay for that herself.

Darryl wanted to come to just about every home game at the college. Darlene would send him a bus ticket and pick him up at the bus station the morning of the game. She would get an extra game ticket just in case Al had time to come. He never did though. She usually went to the games with her friends. A lot of them thought Darryl was cute. He enjoyed the games. He especially enjoyed the band and the dancing girls. He would get caught up in all the excitement.

"Darlene, this is the kind of college I wouldn't mind going to."

"Then do that," she stated.

"I can't."

"Why?"

"My grades aren't as good as yours were when you were in high school."

"Are you flunking out?"

"No. But my Mama can't afford to send me to college."

"Try to bring your grades up. We'll apply for grants and other financial aid for you. Also, apply to the colleges you want to go to. It doesn't have to be this one. And once you're accepted, we'll take it from there. Talk to your counselor at school."

"I'll do that when I go back to school," he said.

Later that night, they had a victory party in the gymnasium. Darlene usually didn't go when they were so close around mid-term exams, but Darryl was excited about it. Plus he was mistaken for one of the students because of his height.

Darlene watched him enjoy himself until her beeper hummed. She recognized Al's number. He was calling her from his cell phone. She called and found out he was on his way there and that he wasn't too far away. She told him to come to the gym because she was there with Darryl. She found Darryl and told him she was going to wait outside for Al.

While she was waiting, her most recent ex-boyfriend approached her. He was the one who hadn't wanted to break up with her. She had seen him at the football game and the dance, but she had ignored him.

"Hey, Darlene," he greeted.

"Hi, Shawn."

"Is that the guy you left me for in there?"

He thought she was involved with Darryl. She thought about letting him believe it, but didn't. "No. He's my cousin. And I didn't leave you for anyone, Shawn," she said to set the record straight. "Things just wasn't working out."

He stood closer to her and said, "You know I still love you."

She couldn't be bothered with Shawn. He was nice and all, but he was boring in the bed plus he wanted to hang under her too much. And she didn't want to be with him anymore.

"Listen, Shawn . . ." She let what she was about to say trail off because she noticed Al's car pull up in the parking lot. She was watching Al as he got out of the car. Shawn on the other hand was watching her. He grabbed her and turned her to face him. She tried to push him away, but he was so much bigger and a lot stronger. He started kissing her and holding her body close to his.

Al saw what was happening. He knew this was different from the playful act that had happened before. He reached back into the car and removed his gun from under his seat. He hurriedly walked to them holding the gun at his side. When he was close to them, he yanked Shawn by his collar, pulling him away from Darlene. It happened so fast that Darlene hadn't seen Al coming. He threw Shawn against the wall with one hand and with his other hand he pointed his nine-millimeter handgun in the middle of Shawn's forehead.

Darlene put her hands to her mouth in horror and begged Al not to do anything. "Oh God, Alvin don't," she pleaded.

Al turned his attention toward a scared Shawn. "What's your damn problem? Don't nobody put their hands on my wife like that."

"I-I-I d-d-didn't kn-kn-know she was m-m-married," Shawn stammered.

"Alvin, please. Just leave him alone," Darlene said, wrapping her arms around him.

Al slowly lowered the gun. "I'd better not catch your ass touching my wife again. In fact, you better not look at her. Now get the hell away from here," Al said to Shawn and watched as he backed away and soon started running. Al put his gun in the back waistband of his pants then he looked down at Darlene. "You all right, Dee? Did he hurt you?"

"Oh, Alvin. Why did you do that?"

"What was I supposed to do?" he asked, feeling hurt because Darlene sounded disapproving of his actions. "I see him all over you and you were struggling. He's lucky I didn't shoot his ass then ask questions. Who was he anyway?"

"The guy I was going with last semester."

"Didn't I tell you to let me know if he bothered you?" he asked, getting angry himself.

"He hasn't been bothering me. I don't know why he did what he did tonight."

"He better not do it again."

"You have to leave, Alvin. He might tell the campus security guards that you had a gun."

"All right."

"Can you give Darryl a ride back home. I don't think I could drive him to the bus station in the morning," she said. She usually arranged for him to sleep in one of her friend's room overnight.

"Yeah. Let's go and get him," he said, walking off still hugging her close to him.

"No. You go and wait in the car. I'll get him."

Al walked to his car while Darlene left to find Darryl. He was dancing with some girl when she interrupted them. She tapped him on the shoulder. He turned to see who it was and saw his cousin. She tiptoed and told him in his ear, above the music, that it was time to go. He ended the dance. As they were walking out he saw that she was nervous.

"What's wrong, Darlene?"

"Nothing. Alvin will give you a ride home tonight. I don't feel well."

Al got out of his car when he saw them coming. Darryl was quick to think Al must have done her something.

"Did Al do something to you?"

"No, Darryl. Just go on home. I'll talk to you later." Darryl walked to the car and looked at Al suspiciously. Al walked up to Darlene and put his arms around her.

"I'm sorry. I just lost it for a minute. I love you, Dee. And I won't stand by and let some man put his hands on you like that. I'll call you tomorrow, okay?" He felt her head nodding against his chest. He walked her to her dorm and kissed her goodbye.

On the drive home, Al noticed Darryl wasn't too comfortable riding with him. For some reason, he thought the boy hated his guts.

"Look Darryl, Darlene wanted me to give you a ride home. It wasn't my idea," he said. Darryl didn't respond. They drove in silence for a while before Darryl said anything.

"What did you do to her?"

"What?"

"What did you do to my cousin? She was happy before you got there. Now all of a sudden she don't feel good."

"Darlene didn't tell you anything?" Al asked, not wanting to go into exactly what happened with her cousin.

"No."

"Well, I'll tell you this much. When I got there, some guy was grabbing on her and I made him stop." That was all he needed to know, Al thought.

"Did he look like he could be a football player or something?"

Now that Al thought about it, the guy was big. "Could be."

"Was he real black?"

"Yeah. Why?"

"He sounds like the same guy that's been close around us all day. He was even checking me out when I was with Darlene at the game. I told her he was looking at us all funny, but she told me to ignore him."

"That was him. He won't be bothering her again. Would you tell me if he does when you're with her at the games?"

"No problem. What did you do to him?"

"I just told him, in no uncertain terms, to leave her alone." They rode the rest of the way home talking about the football game and halftime show.

Darlene was a nervous wreck in her room. She couldn't stop shaking. She had never seen a real gun that close before. And to know Al was capable of using it really scared her. It was as if he had transformed before her eyes. He wasn't the same person she was falling in love with. And she realized she was definitely falling in love with him. But she was going to have to do something about Al's temper where she's concerned.

Chapter eight

When Darlene went home for the Thanksgiving holiday, Crystal hadn't long had her baby. A little girl she named Desiree. Darlene's wedding was only a couple of weeks away. Both of her friends from college had given her their money to pay for their dresses. She left her wedding gown at Marie's house because she didn't want Al to see it.

Marie was giving her a surprise bridal shower before she went back to school. She invited Darlene's two bridesmaids also. She had called the dorm room and found out they were going home for the holiday, but would be back the Saturday after Thanksgiving. She had sent them round trip bus tickets and met them at the bus station. She had also told Crystal about the shower. A few of the people who liked Darlene from her job at the bank were also invited. There were only about a dozen women there. Darlene thought her and Marie were going to go over menu selections for the reception at the hotel she had decided on.

When she arrived, she didn't take notice of the cars. Marie answered the door calmly. Once she walked into the living room, everyone yelled Surprise! Darlene was more surprised to see her friends from school. They were all talking when the doorbell rang. Marie went to answer it. It was a guy delivering four large pizzas. He walked in and placed the pizzas on the coffee table in the living room. She paid him for the pizzas and pulled out a twenty dollar bill and asked, "Pizza man, what can I get for this twenty-dollar tip?"

"What do you want?" he asked in return.

Darlene was shocked because Marie was married and flirting with the pizza man.

"So far I can't see it yet," Marie replied. The pizza man pulled off his T-shirt revealing his muscular chest and all the ladies starting shouting for him to take off the rest. Darlene couldn't believe what was going on. The other ladies took out money and waved it at him. He started stripping right there in the living room. Marie put on some music. Chris and Gail started dancing with him. All of a sudden it dawned on Darlene that he was a stripper and she let everybody else know. "He's a stripper!" she yelled informing them as if they didn't know. They all laughed.

Marie sat next to her and said, "We knew he was a stripper. You're the only one who didn't."

"For a minute there, I was beginning to think he was giving a whole new meaning to home delivery." Darlene sat back and enjoyed the show. Some of the ladies were getting a bit carried away. Darlene was feeling sorry for the poor man. They were feeling all over him, but he seemed to enjoy it.

Darlene was given all kinds of lingerie as gifts. Some of the items were very sexy and some were skimpy. She wondered how she would fit in those. Her friends left to go back to the school that night. She dropped Crystal off at home then headed back to the apartment.

Al was lying in bed watching TV when she got home. He knew his sister had planned a party for her. He had paid to have Darlene's friends there.

"How was the party?" he asked when she walked into the bedroom.

"You knew about it?"

"Sure."

"It was great. They bought me a lot of nice gifts. I don't think I'll be able to look at a pizza man the same way again though," she said, taking a seat next to him on the bed.

"Why's that?"

"The one that delivered the pizzas stripped. The women there went crazy. They were all over the poor man. Even my friends from school were there."

"Were you all over him, too?" he asked, pretending to be interested in what was on TV.

"No, Alvin. Why would I want to be all over him when I can be all over you?" she said and laid on top of him.

"Just checking." Al put his arms around her waist. "These two weeks are gonna be hell on me," he said, holding her tight against the length of his body.

"The time will pass fast. You'll see."

"I hope so," he agreed not really believing it himself.

"Have you and the other guys been fitted for the tuxedos yet?"

"Uh, we'll get it done this week. I promise," he assured her. She had been telling him to get that done for weeks. She had taken Robert and Darryl herself.

"Yeah, yeah. You told me you were going to do that two weeks ago."

"I'm serious this time."

"Okay. I won't be back until the Wednesday before the wedding."

"Why so long?"

"It's just a week and a half. I have final exams to study for and you distract me too much."

"But I thought you liked my distractions," he said, pretending to be hurt.

"I do, but it's barely two weeks. I'm going take a bath. I'll be back in a few minutes."

Darlene left and went to the bathroom to take a bath. While she was in there she thought about how close the wedding actually was. She wasn't having seconds thoughts. It was just that she was starting to love Al. She never told him. He always told her and he never asked her in return. She guessed he just sort of grew on her. She think it was his sense of humor that she found irresistible. Plus he had a sexy body and was awesome when it came to making love. Plus he sort of swept her off of her feet. She hadn't had anyone to really take care of her since her parents were killed. It was one of the reasons why she excelled in school. She knew she would only have herself to depend on. But now she had Al.

A week later, on a Friday afternoon, Al beeped her. She was in between classes and returned his call.

"Dee?" he answered on the first ring.

"Hey, Alvin."

"Sweetheart, listen to me. I need you to go and check us into that hotel we usually go to. Use a credit card. Reserve the room until you leave to come home. Go there and use the towels and mess up the bed so it will look like we're staying there. Got that?"

"But why, Alvin?"

"Just do this for me. Please, baby. Go as soon as you can. Call me on my cell phone and let me know when you've reserved the room. I'll talk to you later. I love you." He hung up.

Darlene stood there holding the phone. She had one more class that day. When she found out it was canceled, she left campus and checked them into the hotel. The receptionist at the front desk was familiar with her and Al since they have been there quite often. Darlene went to the room and called Al back. "Hello?" he answered not expecting her to call back so soon.

"I've reserved the room. Anything else?"

"Stay in the room tonight. I'll be there sometime tonight or early tomorrow morning. Make sure you order something to eat. And when they bring it, have the shower running so they'll think I'm already there." Darlene was quiet on the other end of the phone. "Dee? You still there?"

"Yes, Alvin. What's going—"

"I'll talk to you later. I love you. I gotta go. Bye, baby." He hung up again.

Darlene knew what she was about to do was serious. She had a choice to make. She could choose not to do what he asked or choose to do it with no questions asked. Her mind was made up. She loved him and she would do it. She went back to her dorm room and packed a few clothes to spend the weekend at the hotel. She tried to do a little studying, but she was too worried about Al. She had ordered room service and did as he had instructed. She even left her suitcase in plain sight for anyone to see. She stayed up until about eleven o'clock that night and Al still hadn't shown up.

After Al had gotten off the phone with Darlene, he nodded toward Jeff. Jeff had told him to make sure he had an alibi in case things got out of hand like they had before. They were supposed to meet with some men from Florida. They wanted to start buying from them. Al and Jeff usually got a hold of large amounts of items and sold them in bulk. Sometimes it was blank credit cards, different types of electronics, or drugs. That night it was drugs. These men were rivals with Jeff's usual buyer. The deal with them had gone sour and there had been bloodshed. Jeff and Al met the men up front while they had others positioned in case something went wrong.

They met at an abandoned shipping yard in a nearby city. One of the other men tested the merchandise with Al while Jeff watched the other guys carefully.

"It's pure," he verified. Another man opened the briefcase and showed them the money. As soon as they exchanged briefcases, they heard sirens. It was a set-up.

"*Sonofa—*" Jeff said and pulled out an oozie and shot one of the guys. The other one shot at Jeff and the bullet grazed his arm. Al shot him dead. He grabbed both briefcases and he and Jeff made a break for it.

They were familiar with the area so the police didn't see them leave. Al didn't speed. He drove at a normal speed. He saw that Jeff was bleeding. He dropped him off at his house and headed straight for the hotel where Darlene was waiting. He went straight to the room. She had told him the room number after she'd called him when she reserved the room. The front desk attendant got someone from housekeeping to let him in the room after he lied about leaving his key inside while he went to get something out of his car and not wanting to wake his wife. Once inside the room, Al sat his bag on the floor next to the dresser. He placed the briefcases on the dresser. One was full of cash. He took off his clothes and climbed into bed with her.

Darlene turned over in bed at about six o'clock the next morning and turned right into Al's chest. She grabbed him so hard from being so glad to see him it scared him. Al jumped up and pushed her off him. When he realized it was her and how frightened she looked, he pulled her back to him. "I'm sorry, baby. You just scared me," he said apologizing.

"When did you get in? I waited up until eleven o'clock."

"It was sometime after one. But I was here since early yesterday evening. What time did you order room service?"

"About seven o'clock last night."

"Then I was here since then. All night? You got that?"

"Yes," she said quietly, laying back down with her back to him.

He positioned his body behind hers and said, "Baby, I need you to agree. If anyone ever ask, we were together last night. All night. Can you do that for me?"

"Alvin, I'll say whatever it is you want me to say anytime you need me to say it. Just don't hurt me or play me for a fool," she warned.

"Baby, you know I wouldn't do that. I love you," he said and kissed her on her bare shoulder.

"Yeah, well I hope not. Because I love you, too." It was the first time she had ever said it to him. After what she had agreed to do for him, she figured she might as well tell him.

"You do?" Al pulled her closer to him. "Baby, I'm so glad. I didn't mind getting married if you didn't love me back. I figured you would in time. But I'm so glad you love me."

"Just don't hurt me."

"I won't," he said and they laid there, not saying anything for a while longer before they went back to sleep.

Darlene woke up before Al. She called room service and ordered some breakfast. She saw two briefcases on the dresser and wondered what was in them. She looked back at Al and saw that he was still asleep. She stood in front of the briefcases, debating with herself whether or not she should open them. Her curiosity won out.

The first one she opened was filled with money, all one hundred-dollar bills. She stood there staring at the money. She couldn't begin to guess how much was in there. She quietly closed the briefcase. When she opened the second case, her whole body tensed with fear. It had cocaine in it. A very large quantity of it.

Al was awake by now. He had heard the click of the second briefcase. He got out of bed and stood directly behind Darlene. He slowly reached around her and closed the briefcase. Darlene started visibly trembling with fear. Al didn't quite know what to do at first. He led her to the bed and sat her down on his lap. They both sat silently for a few minutes. He waited until she stopped trembling before he said anything.

"Dee? Are you okay, baby?" he asked, genuinely worried about her.

"Why did you bring that here?" she said, pointing to the briefcase with drugs in it. "I told you to keep it away from me." She removed herself from his lap and walked into the bathroom. She soon heard Al come in.

"Don't you think I've been trying to do just that?"

"Why do you have to mess with that stuff anyway?" she asked. She had always wanted to know. She tried to ignore it. But now . . ..

"Look, Dee, something happened last night and we ended up with both cases. I didn't plan on having either one of the cases with me when I got here, but Jeff got shot—"

"Shot?" She quickly forgot about the question she had asked. Forgot that he hadn't answered her. "Oh God. Is he . . .?"

"He's okay. The bullet only grazed his arm. And after I took him home I came straight to you," he said, hoping she would understand. He walked to her and put his arms around her.

"Alvin, what if it had been you? And the bullet didn't just graze your arm, but killed you?"

"Nothing's gonna happen to me, Dee," he said, trying to assure her. But he knew the possibilities were out there. There was a knock on the door and Al's arms tightened around Darlene.

"It's room service. I ordered it while you were still sleeping," she said and he loosened his hold on her. "Go and put those cases away." He left the bathroom and went to lock the cases and put them in the closet.

Darlene opened the door and the young man walked in and put the trays on the table. He nodded to Al, who was sitting on the edge of the bed, in his pajama bottoms. They ate in virtual silence. Darlene barely touched her food, but Al devoured his meal.

When Darlene finished all she was going to eat, she went and got her books. She spread them out on the vacant bed and began to put them in a particular order to study. Al remained at the table and watched her. He thought about how Jeff being shot had affected her so much. What if it *had* been him? What if he *was* to get killed? He had never given those types of questions much thought. But now he was about to have a wife. A wife he loved and who loved him in return. He would have to talk to Jeff and see how he deals with being married.

Later that morning Al went to check on Jeff. He got to his sister's house about an hour and a half later. Jeff had gone in to work that morning as usual but was only going to stay there half a day. He was due to be home in thirty minutes. Al sat and talked to his sister.

"Is Jeff okay?" he asked concerned for his brother-in-law.

"He's fine. It wasn't as bad as I thought. It was just a scratch."

Al was noticing how calm his sister was handling the whole situation. Whereas Darlene was stunned to see a small knife wound on his shoulder. "Marie, tell me something. How do you deal with it?"

"I take it Darlene isn't handling things too well?"

"It's just . . . I've never had no one but you who really worried about me. When I told her about Jeff being shot . . . Marie you could see how scared she was."

"I can imagine."

"No," he said, shaking his head. "True, she was concerned about Jeff, but she was more worried about what if it had happened to me. And that what if I would have been killed." Just then the door opened and Jeff walked in. He took a seat on the sofa.

Marie excused herself to give them some privacy. Jeff asked Al, "Everything went all right last night?"

"Yeah. You heard anything yet?"

"Nah. Where are the cases?"

"They're at the hotel." He paused a moment then said, "Darlene saw what was in them."

"How did that happen?"

"It was an accident. It's all right though."

"It better be," Jeff said, getting off the sofa. "Want a beer?" he asked, walking toward the kitchen.

"Yeah," Al said, getting off of the sofa also. "Can I ask you something, man?" he asked, following him.

"Sure. What's on your mind?" Jeff got the beers and they sat at the kitchen table.

"Does Marie worry a lot about you?"

"Yeah. Why? Was Darlene worried last night?"

"More like terrified," he said and took a swallow of beer. "She told me last night, well this morning, that she loves me."

"I see your point. Do you feel the same way about her?"

"Yes indeed. I've been feeling that way about her."

"Listen, man, Marie used to be the same way. In time Darlene will adjust. But you know I love your sister a helluva lot. If something ever happened to me, she would be living very well off. I have money put away plus I have various insurance policies with her as my sole beneficiary. And if this fertility stuff works out, her and our child or children will be set for life financially. This house is in Marie's name. So are most of the accounts. We have money spread out. Marie makes sure everything is in order. Why don't you let her talk to Darlene." Al nodded. "And if you're so worried about Darlene, get some life insurance when you two are married. That should make her relax. I doubt if anything will happen between now and then. Let me get you the names and numbers of the companies we deal with," Jeff said and left the table.

Al sat and thought for a while. He knew it would make him feel a lot better to know that if something were to happen to him, he would still be taking care of Darlene. Jeff handed him several business cards. Al put them in his pocket. They then proceeded to discuss the contents of the briefcases.

Darlene's birthday was the next day and Al wanted to get her something special. On the way back to the hotel, he stopped at a shopping mall. He went into a jewelry store and bought her a pair of diamond-studded earrings. On his way to his car, he passed a lingerie shop. He had never considered buying a woman anything from a store like that, but he saw a satin sleepshirt that he thought would look sexy on Darlene. He bought that, too.

Darlene had been studying for her last two final exams. She had a hard time concentrating at first because she was still worried about Al. Then she took a hot bath and was able to relax and study. It was almost five o'clock in the evening when she decided to stop. She was putting her books away when the door opened and Al walked in. She stopped what she was doing and ran to him and hugged him.

"What's this for?" he asked surprised and pleased by her greeting.

"I'm just glad you're back. That's all," she said in his chest and he kissed the top of her head.

"Come and see what I bought you for your birthday," he said, trying to get her to stop worrying. He took her by her hand and led her to the bed.

"My birthday isn't until tomorrow."

"I know that. I just wanted to give you one of your presents now."

"One of my presents?" she said, looking at him suspiciously. "What all did you get?"

"I only bought you two things so relax." He gave her the bag with the lingerie in it and she held it up to her body after pulling it out of the bag. Al wanted to see her try it on. "Why don't you try it on to see if it fits," he suggested.

"It'll fit. You just want me to take off my clothes," she said and he smiled his agreement.

"Let's go out tonight and have dinner to celebrate your birthday. I have to leave tomorrow evening and I know you still have some studying to do."

"Okay. Do I still have to keep the room reserved?"

"Yeah. I'll be back Tuesday night so we can drive back together."

They went to a nearby restaurant. They sat and talked about their wedding of a week away over their meal. Al assured her that he and the other men in the wedding had gotten fitted for their tuxedos. He wanted to know where she wanted to go for their honeymoon, but she wanted him to surprise her. They finished their meal and went back to their room.

After bathing, Darlene slipped into the sleepshirt Al had bought for her. She walked to the bed where he was waiting for her. He had taken off his clothes and was lying on the bed in his briefs. He stood up when she entered. He walked to her and lifted his hands to caress her satin clad body. She indicated that the bathroom was all his and sauntered over to the bed to wait for him.

Al took the quickest shower he ever had. Before Darlene could get comfortable in bed, he was walking out the bathroom with a towel loosely wrapped around his waist. He stood next to the bed and removed his towel, letting it fall to the floor. He pulled the covers back and lowered himself on top of her.

The next morning Al woke up before Darlene and ordered room service. Darlene woke up when she heard the door close. She saw the food on the table and a small, gray, velvet box. She got up and went to the bathroom startling Al. "Good morning," he said, standing in the bathroom doorway.

"Good morning. Have you been up long?" she asked, getting ready to brush her teeth.

"An hour or so. Did you sleep good?"

"You know I did." After the night they had just had together, she couldn't help but sleep like a baby. She started brushing her teeth and Al went and sat at the table and waited for her. She came out a few minutes later and sat down at the table and prepared to eat.

Al picked up the box and handed it to her. "Happy Birthday, baby?" She took the box and opened it. Her mouth fell open while she stared at the earrings. "You like 'em?" She nodded. "Let me see how they look on you." She started taking off the large gold hoop earrings she had on while he took the other ones out of the box. She put them on and Al liked the way they sparkled on her ears. "Will you wear them for the wedding?"

"Yes. Thank you, honey." She got up and hugged him. "I hope you won't be borrowing them," she said teasingly to him.

"They're all yours. They're too big for me anyway."

When breakfast was finished, they spent the rest of their time together in bed. When it was time to leave, Al followed her back to campus before he left to go back home.

Chapter nine

On the morning of the wedding, Darlene was a nervous wreck. She was worried about every little thing. Her, Crystal, and her friends from school were staying at Marie's house for the weekend. The wedding wasn't until six o'clock that Saturday evening. Marie had made hair appointments for the five of them with her usual hairstylist. Darlene had looked at hairstyles while the others were getting their hair done. She couldn't decide so Marie took over. She explained how the veil would be positioned on Darlene's head and the stylist took it from there. Everyone was satisfied with the finished results. Even Darlene.

The men were assembled at Al's apartment. They had given him a bachelor party the night before and the men who were in the wedding party stayed the night. Darryl and Robert weren't allowed to attend the party. One of the men had gotten two strippers. They were just a couple of women who obviously needed money desperately.

There was an ample supply of alcohol and drugs at the party. Most of the men were high as the sky. One of the strippers focused her attention on the groom-to-be. She danced and shook half-naked all in front of Al. He had a little too much of the provisions and had started fondling the stripper's breasts a few times. Jeff brought him back to his senses quickly and he let the other men enjoy the strippers. They offered them some of their drugs and alcohol.

One of the men had some triple X-rated videotapes. They sat and watched the tapes until about three o'clock the next morning. Some of the men had slipped into the other bedroom with the strippers during the viewing of the videos. At around 5 a.m. the strippers and the men who weren't in the wedding left.

The men that were in the wedding were so drunk that they slept until the next evening. The phone ringing awakened Jeff. It was Marie.

"Hello?" Jeff answered still half asleep.

"Jeff?" Marie said unsure.

"Yeah."

"Were you still asleep?"

"Yeah. What time is it?"

"It's three o'clock."

"What?" He sat upright in bed swinging his feet to the floor.

"Yeah. I was calling to remind you that the limousine will be there at five o'clock. Why are you still asleep?"

"We had a lot to drink last night. I'll get everybody up. See you later, sweetheart." He hung up the telephone then woke up Al. Al had a hangover. All of them did. They all started getting ready slowly, but surely.

Darlene called her aunt's house to make sure Darryl and Robert had everything they needed. Everything was fine at her aunt's house. She let Darryl use her car that day so he could drive the rest of the family to the church and reception.

Marie had picked up the bridal bouquet and bridesmaids bouquets from the florist. A white limousine will bring the bridesmaids to the church and reception while a white Rolls Royce brings Darlene. The Rolls was Al's idea. Jeff's niece and nephew were the flower girl and ring bearer. His sister would bring them to the church. Once they were all dressed, they waited for the cars to come.

They arrived at the church at about six o'clock. Darlene stayed in the car until Darryl came to get her. He was speechless when he saw her. She nervously took his hand when he extended it to help her out of the car. They walked into the church together.

When Darlene heard the introduction to the bridal march start up, she stopped. Darryl looked down at her and asked, "You all right, Darlene?" She felt lightheaded. She didn't know if she would be able to make it down the aisle. Too much had happened too fast. She felt like a deer caught in a car's headlights. She couldn't move. All the guests were looking at her. The bridal march played again. Her instincts told her to turn around and run. But she couldn't just back out now, she thought. She nodded and they proceeded to walk down the aisle.

Most of the groomsmen were still hung over. Jeff was about the only one who had a clear head. Al was still a little high. When everyone stood up signaling the bride was about walk down the aisle, he took his place at the altar. He sobered up immediately when he saw that Darlene wasn't moving. But that soon changed. Darlene looked beautiful, he thought. He watched her as she walked down the aisle wearing a dress made of white satin with an open neckline and a bodice covered and designed with lace and pearls. The sleeves were puffed at the shoulder and fit her arms snug. There were also pearl designs down each sleeve. The bottom of her gown was plain satin and trailed six feet in the back. She wore a veil made of the same lace and pearls that were in her dress. It covered her face and stopped just at her breasts and trailed to the floor in back. Al was mesmerized. He had never seen Darlene look more beautiful than she was at that moment. He had figured the wedding wouldn't be a big deal. He had just wanted to get married. A Justice of the Peace would have sufficed. But at the moment he saw her in a wedding gown, he wouldn't trade it for anything in the world.

When they were standing at the altar together, hand in hand, Al felt her trembling. He was ignoring most of what the minister was saying because he was focusing his attention on Darlene. As she repeated her vows to him in a shaky voice after the minister, he looked into her eyes and a tear rolled down her face. When they were pronounced husband and wife, Al lifted her veil and saw her tear streaked face and kissed her.

There were a lot of people at the reception. Darlene hadn't invited that many people. She invited a few people her aunt wanted to attend and some people from the bank she and Marie worked at. The rest were people who work with Al at the dealership and other associates.

Al didn't let go of Darlene's hand the entire time. He would introduce her to people or they would dance. It was the first time they had ever danced together. It was kind of awkward because she had to maneuver her gown. She wanted to dance with Darryl and he reluctantly let her go. She found Darryl and went on the dance floor with him.

"You look like you're having a good time," she said to him.

"I am."

"I'm glad. How are your grades so far?"

"I think I might get a couple of A's this quarter," he said, feeling proud of himself.

"That's good."

"After Christmas break, they're going to have a College Day at the school. A lot of people from different colleges will be coming in to talk to the juniors and seniors."

"That's good. We'll see about applying for grants after you've applied to a school and get accepted." He looked doubtful. "You *will* get accepted, Darryl."

Al came over and tapped Darryl on his shoulder and said, "Mind if I cut in?"

"Not at all," he said, releasing his cousin.

Al gathered her in his arms and they danced until the song ended. He whispered in her ear, "Let's leave."

"What?" Darlene asked, pulling back to look him in the face.

"Let's go. We have a suite right here in the hotel. Nobody will miss us. C'mon, baby," he said, pleading with her.

"We can't leave right now. Wait a little longer."

"How much longer?" he asked, looking at his watch.

"About another half hour."

"Another half—okay," he agreed. "I'll be looking for you in exactly thirty minutes." They danced until Jeff cut in. He handed her a twenty-dollar bill to dance. That started a trend. The other groomsmen did the same. Some of them handed her five or ten dollar bills. The fast songs weren't a problem for Al. It was the slow songs. Each man would dance with her for about two minutes before the next one would cut in. Al was finding it funny until the other male guests joined in. He didn't like the way some of them were holding his wife. He walked on the dance floor and announced that no one else was going to dance with his wife. He was serious, but the guests received it as fun. He pulled Darlene with him intending to leave the reception.

She stopped him and said, "Alvin, we can't leave until I throw my bouquet and you throw the garter."

"Fine," he said then he went to the DJ and borrowed the microphone and announced the bouquet was about to be thrown. The single women gathered and Darlene threw the bouquet. She didn't see who caught it because Al was telling everyone to clear the floor so the single men could catch the garter. Once the men were assembled, he put his hands under Darlene's gown to retrieve the garter. He started rubbing up and down her leg and he heard a few lewd shouts from the men. He quickly removed the garter when he saw how uncomfortable Darlene was becoming. He threw it as quickly as she had thrown the bouquet. Neither saw who caught it because Al left with her in tow heading for their suite. Marie saw their quick departure and took it upon herself to make sure the gifts would be taken care of along with everything else.

When they arrived at their suite, Darlene was out of breath. Al had rushed her to the elevator then rushed her to the room. He held the train of her dress so it wouldn't slow her down. Once inside the room, Al was trying to figure out how to get her out of her dress. Darlene wasn't as anxious as he was. She wanted to savor the moment a little while longer. But when Al started acting as if he was all thumbs, she gave in realizing he was nervous. She couldn't imagine why. It wasn't like it was their first time making love. Maybe he didn't want to ruin her dress, she thought. That's it. She instructed him where to unfasten her gown and he eagerly went to it. He was in for a shock once he shed her wedding gown off her.

Darlene had anticipated this moment. She wore one of the sexy lingerie outfits she received at her bridal shower. It was a white satin and lace teddy. Al was enthralled. He had seen her naked on countless occasions, but she looked the epitome of a bride on her wedding night. All he could do was stare. When Darlene walked toward him, he staggered back a step. All of a sudden he felt like a young teenager about to have sex for the first time. He had backed up against the bed and Darlene stood in front him. He looked down at her. That was all he seemed able to do. Speech was something he couldn't quite use at the moment. Darlene pushed his tuxedo jacket off of his shoulders and it fell quickly and quietly on the bed. She unfastened his pants and pulled out his shirt. She unbuttoned it and discarded it along with the tie. While he stood before her bare from the waist up, she took advantage of his hypnotic state. She caressed his chest and planted kisses all over it. She knew he was getting aroused. She unzipped his pants and pushed them, along with his briefs, to the floor. Once she eased him down on the bed, she removed his shoes, socks, and his clothes from around his ankle.

Kneeling on the floor between his legs she began to kiss him. He took her in his arms and kissed her as if he hadn't kissed her in years. She ended the kiss and gently pushed at his shoulders, indicating that she wanted him to lay back on the bed. She then held his throbbing erection in her hands. Al clenched and unclenched his hands on the bed spread. She kissed him from his neck to his stomach all the while holding him firmly, but gently in her hands. She stroked him before she took him fully into her mouth. It happened so fast that Al was bewildered. He wasn't expecting it. He had wanted to experience oral sex with her, but since she had refused that first time he never mentioned it again. So now he was trying to figure out what could have changed her mind when the feelings she started evoking in him took over. She was making him feel like no other woman had. Maybe it was because he loved her or because they were married. Whatever it was, it was giving him a mind-blowing, heart-stopping experience. He captured her head with his hands and he was in ecstasy. He was feeling . . . he was feeling . . . feeling too good. He pulled at her head, removing himself from her mouth and soon experienced his release. He hugged her against the length of his body. He had almost lost control and he would have hated to do to her what he has done to other women by not pulling out. For a moment he was afraid of what she would say to him. He held her so tight against his body that she could hardly breathe. He loosened his hold so she could breathe easier then smothered her face with kisses. A few moments later he turned over and positioned her under him. He kissed her slowly. And as much as he liked what she was wearing it became a hindrance. He hurriedly took it off her. He kissed and sucked her breasts. Then he moved lower. He hoped he could give her the same pleasure she had given him. He had received oral sex many times, but he had never reciprocated. He had never really been interested in it in the past. But for some inexplicable reason he had to do it with her. He spread her legs and slowly started kissing her inner thigh and she trembled and moaned. So far so good, he thought. He kissed her intimately and he achieved his goal. Darlene wiggled and screamed in pleasure. He couldn't believe he had made her feel that good without being inside her. He then moved up and positioned himself between her legs and entered. They made love all night long. When they fell asleep, either he would wake her up during the night or she would wake him up and they would make love again.

About five o'clock the next morning after a session of lovemaking, Al wanted to give her the wedding present he had for her. He got up and found his tuxedo jacket. He handed her a white envelope with a red ribbon tied around it. She took it and opened it. It was an insurance policy for a half a million dollars and she was the sole beneficiary. She looked up at him with questioning eyes.

"In case anything ever happens to me I want you to be taken care of. It's paid up for a year," he said by way of an explanation. Tears started rolling down Darlene's face. Al jumped to the conclusion that he had done something wrong so he pulled her into his arms to soothe her.

Darlene didn't know what to say. It was extremely thoughtful of him to think about her. All she could do was hug him tight. She was too overwhelmed with conflicting emotions. One being that how much he loved her to be considerate enough to provide her with such a substantial amount. The other being the possibility that she would probably have to use it too soon.

Al rocked her in his arms until she went back to sleep. He dressed back in his tuxedo shirt and pants and went to retrieve their suitcases from his car. They had packed for their honeymoon and Al had someone drive his car to the reception at the hotel and park it. They were only going to take a four-day honeymoon because Darlene wanted to spend Christmas with her aunt and cousins and Al had agreed.

When he got back to the room, he called room service and ordered their complementary breakfast. He hurriedly took a shower. Darlene was waking up when he came out of the bathroom. He let her know that breakfast was on the way up. She quickly got out of bed and went to take a bath. She heard the door open and close while she was in the tub and knew that breakfast had been delivered.

Although she had told Al to surprise her for their honeymoon, she had become inquisitive. All he had told her was to pack for moderately cool weather.

"Are you going to tell me where we're going?"

"I thought you wanted to be surprised."

"I changed my mind. Where are we going, Alvin?"

"Cancun, Mexico."

"*Mexico?*" she asked in disbelief.

"Yeah. Why? You don't want to go there?"

"I've always wanted to go to Mexico." She got up and kissed him all over his face saying thank you in between kisses. They finished their breakfast and headed for the airport.

They spent four days and three nights there. During the days they went on guided tours to see the sights. The nights were mainly spent in bed. Darlene was curious to try all the native cuisine and she coaxed Al into tasting a few also. Darlene brought souvenirs back for her aunt, cousins, and new in-laws.

When they got back to the apartment, it was almost three o'clock in the afternoon. Al placed all the packages Darlene had in the spare bedroom. He noticed that their wedding presents had been brought home. He quickly shut the door because he didn't want Darlene seeing them just yet. He wanted her seeing him so he pulled her into their bedroom. They were both eager to be together again.

While they were lying in bed together, Darlene thought about the upcoming holiday season.

"Alvin?"

"Hmm?"

"Do you have a Christmas tree?"

"Nope."

"You don't?" He shook his head. "Then what do you do for Christmas?"

"Nothing much. Watch a little TV sometimes and get something to eat. Sometimes I stop by Marie's house." He never was in to celebrating Christmas that much since his mother died.

"Would you mind if we did a little decorating? Not much. Just get a little tree and some lights. That's all."

"Fine with me."

"And can we eat by my aunt's house?" she asked hopefully.

"Sure."

"Good. Then let's get up and go shopping," she prompted, getting out of bed herself.

"Shopping?"

"How else do you expect to get a Christmas tree?" She stood with her hands on her hips, looking at him as if he was a dense child.

He got out of bed and went into the bathroom to shower. Darlene went into the kitchen to see if she could find something to eat. But it looked as if Al hadn't been grocery shopping in weeks. She had only gotten home a few days before their wedding. She was so nervous that she never took time to eat that much. When she did eat, it was either at her aunt's house or while she was out. She stood in front of an almost empty refrigerator. A six-pack of beer, a two-liter bottle of soda, a pitcher of water, and a carton with three eggs were inside. The freezer was empty. Al came up behind her and stared also. Then he said, "We'll eat while we're out. And tomorrow you can go to the grocery store."

"Okay. Let me get a bath and I'll be ready in a few minutes."

They went to the store, but there wasn't much left to choose from. She found a nice three-foot artificial tree she liked and Al put it in the basket. She went to get a sales paper. When she was on her way back, she heard someone call her name. She stopped and turned around and saw Vincent. He was walking toward her.

"Hey, Vincent. How you doing?" she greeted him.

"Oh, I'm hanging in there. So I hear you and Al are actually married now," he said, looking over her body with appreciative eyes.

She thought he was a nice and very handsome man. And if she and Al hadn't been sort of together back then, she would have gotten to know him better the night she met him at that club.

"Yeah."

"Would you mind if I congratulated the bride?"

"No," she replied. He bent down and kissed her cheek a little too close to her mouth for a friendly kiss, she thought.

Al had been watching her when she left and he saw when she stopped. He started looking at tree lights for a minute or two and when he looked back the man she was talking with was pulling his face away from hers. He began to wonder what had just transpired between the two.

When Darlene came back and started looking at lights and bulbs, Al asked, "Who was that?"

"Who was who?" she asked in return even though she knew who he was referring to. She started placing lights and bulbs in the basket.

"The guy you were talking to."

"Oh. That's just someone I met a while ago. He heard I got married and congratulated me."

"Uh-huh," he said, looking around to see if he saw the guy. "You about ready to go?"

"Yeah. I think this is enough for a first Christmas." They left and stopped at a restaurant and ate.

Later that evening they sat at home and decorated the tree. Darlene called her aunt to let her know they were back at home and to find out what time was Christmas dinner then she wanted to speak to Darryl.

"Hey, Darlene. When y'all got back?"

"This afternoon. How's everything?"

"Good. But I, um, um," he said, stalling.

"Spit it out, Darryl," she ordered.

"It's nothing really. I didn't think you would mind. I just been driving your car sometimes," he confessed.

She had given him permission to drive her car to the church and reception and told him to watch it while she was on her honeymoon. She didn't really say he couldn't drive it. She knew it would be too much of a temptation for him.

"Did you wreck it?"

"No!" he yelled through the receiver.

"Then what's the problem?"

"You don't mind that I've been driving it?"

"As long as you were careful. We'll be there day after tomorrow for dinner. I want my car back with gas in it, Darryl."

"No problem."

"Okay, bye."

She and Al were just about finished decorating the tree when the telephone rang. It was Marie. She was calling to remind Darlene to bring her gown to the cleaners to get it heirloom and for Al to return his tuxedo. Darlene promised she would do it the next day.

She stood and looked at the finished tree. It still looked like it was missing something. She sat it on one of the end tables near the fireplace.

"Alvin, don't you think it looks naked without presents under it?"

"I guess. Why don't you put some under it."

"Oh, that'll help. We'll put what you buy for me and what I buy for you under the tree. That'll put between two to four gifts under it."

"Put the wedding presents under it."

"I forgot about them. We left the reception and—"

"They're in the other bedroom," he said, cutting her off. She looked at him uncertain and he pointed to the door indicating for her to check. She went to see for herself and screamed her joy at seeing the gifts. See called for him to help her bring them into the living room and to put them under the tree and on the floor near it. She had found a good deal of cards among the presents. She made Al sit down while she read them. Al was familiar with almost every card sender. The cash in the cards totaled almost one thousand dollars. Al wanted her to keep it and use it however way she wanted to. She put a rubber band around the cards and placed them under the tree also.

Chapter ten

Darlene decided to do a little last minute Christmas shopping. Although they had all the wedding presents under their tree to open, she still wanted to get Al something. She went shopping at a nearby mall. She bought him a three-fourth-length leather coat. She also picked up a few things for her aunt, cousins, and in-laws. She stopped and got everything gift-wrapped. She was getting hungry so she stopped at the food court in the mall.

While she was eating at one of the tables, she overheard two women at another table talking. One was telling the other that her usual man was no longer available because he had suddenly gotten married. It didn't matter to the other woman because she was still going to have him. And if push came to shove, she would settle for his friend.

Darlene was finished with her meal and decided to leave the two women to their man troubles. But she couldn't resist a quick look in their direction. They were both nice-looking women, she thought. She couldn't see why either of them would have a hard time keeping a man. But everyone had his or her faults, she thought.

Darlene and Al arrived at her aunt's house in the afternoon. The weather was lovely. The sky was blue without a cloud in sight. The temperature was cold, but not freezing. Al got out the car wearing his new leather coat and retrieved the presents from the trunk of the car. They walked in the house and the aroma of the food was tantalizing. Al hadn't smelled holiday cooking since his mother died. His sister always bought food already prepared. She would heat it up, but it didn't have the same aroma as home-cooked food. They put the presents on the floor near the tree. Al sat in the living room with Robert and Darryl while Darlene went into the kitchen to see if her aunt needed any help.

Once the food was finished, her aunt announced that they could eat. Al and the boys opted to eat in the living room so they could finish watching the football game. Darlene fixed Al a little of everything and brought him a plate of food and a soda. She sat in the kitchen and ate with her aunt and cousin. The baby was in Betty's bedroom sleeping.

When Crystal had moved out, they moved one of the twin beds and a dresser out of the room Darryl and Robert shared into her old room. That way both boys had their own room.

Crystal was living in a government Section-8 apartment. She was lucky and got it fast. It was mainly because she was trying to better herself by attending school. She had moved in the month before Thanksgiving.

Darlene talked about her honeymoon. After they had eaten, her aunt went to lay down with the baby because she was tired. She had been up late the previous night and early that morning cooking. That gave Darlene and Crystal time to talk.

"You know I have been asked a hundred questions about you," Crystal informed her.

"About me?" Darlene asked surprised.

"Everybody knows Al married my cousin. And with Robert broadcasting it, a lot of women wanted to find out about you."

"What have they been asking?" Darlene asked and Crystal started listing the questions.

"Things like," she started counting her fingers, "Where have you been? How did Al hook up with you? Why did you two get married so fast? Were you pregnant? That's what a lot of them thought. They assumed he only married you because you must have been pregnant." Darlene laughed a little. "*Are* you pregnant?" Crystal asked. She was curious herself.

"Crystal, if Alvin and I had gotten married because I was pregnant, wouldn't I be about five months now?"

"Yeah you're right. I was just checking. Knowing you, you probably didn't give him none until you were married anyway."

"Girl, I sampled what I was getting first," Darlene replied to her cousin's remark.

"Girl, stop," she said and playfully pushed Darlene on her arm. "Is he as good in bed as he looks?"

"Better. And not only in a bed either," she answered.

"You are too kinky for me. So where are you two headed when you leave here?"

"By his sister's house."

"That's still the baddest house I ever saw. You and Al gettin' a house like that?"

"No indeed. We don't need a house that big. A pool either. But enough about me, what's up with you?" Darlene asked, changing the subject.

"Girl, I met this new guy. He works at a cleaners his family owns near my apartment."

"What about Desiree's daddy?"

"When I told him I was pregnant, he said my baby wasn't his. I even told him when it happened and he still denied it."

"Has he ever seen her?" He would have to change his mind then, Darlene thought, because the baby didn't look anything like Crystal.

"Yeah. He still said the same thing. I hear his new girlfriend is pregnant and he's living with her."

"I'm sorry, Crystal." Darlene could tell her cousin was a little hurt by the rejection.

"That's all right. But wouldn't it be something if *her* baby turns out to be for somebody else?"

"It would serve him right," Darlene said and Crystal laughed. "In fact, we ought to call one of those talk shows and make him take a paternity test."

"I don't want to waste my time on him," Crystal said.

"I don't blame you."

Darlene got up and emptied the remains of her food in the trash and put her plate in the sink. She went into the living room to retrieve Al's plate. He had eaten just about everything. She decided she would ask her aunt for the recipes so she could cook meals as good. She cut two pieces of sweet potato pie for her and Al then she and Crystal joined the others in the living room.

They left that evening and headed to Marie's house. When they got there, they talked about what all happened after they left the reception. Marie had saved the top of their wedding cake for them. She told them they were to eat it on their first wedding anniversary. Jeff extended an invitation to a New Year's Eve party at a club he and Marie were invited to. Al and Darlene accepted since they didn't have any other plans.

An associate of Jeff's owned the club. It was a very classy place. There was a sign that let patrons know that entrance was allowed to patrons 25 years and older and ID required. Darlene had recently just turned twenty-one. She knew Al and Jeff must have seen the sign, too. If they did, they didn't seem to let it bother them. She held Al's hand a little nervously and he gave her a reassuring squeeze.

At the door, there was an older guy in his late forties checking for identification on the people who looked too young. When the couple was turned away, Darlene really got nervous.

When they reached the entrance, the guy greeted Jeff and Al happily. He smiled and greeted Marie. Then he looked at Darlene and said, "Now who is this pretty young thang?"

Al had been holding her hand, but now he slipped his arm around her waist and pulled her closer to him and proudly said, "This is my wife."

"Your wife? C'mon. You," he pointed to Al, "married? I can't believe it. The playboy has settled down with *one*," he held up his hand, pointing his index finger up, "woman?"

"That's right," Al said, caressing Darlene's waist. The man moved aside and let them in.

Once they were inside, someone else greeted Jeff and Marie then they were shown to a secluded table where they all sat down then ordered drinks. Jeff and Marie sat at the table while Al and Darlene went on the dance floor. They practically dance all night. They were getting a few curious stares, but Darlene didn't give it much thought. She was enjoying herself too much to care.

When they got back to the table, Al and Jeff excused themselves. Marie and Darlene were talking when three women approached their table.

"Nice to see you again, Marie," one of them said.

"Is it?" Marie said doubtful. It was clear there was no love lost between the two women.

"So, this is Al's wife," she said, ignoring Marie's sarcasm. "I just came over to say hi."

"Hi and goodbye."

This was the first time Darlene had seen Marie display antipathy toward anyone.

"I'm going to congratulate Al personally when he comes back. He just loves the things a mature woman can give him." It was obvious to Darlene that the woman was closer to Al's age than she was. Maybe older. But she ignored the little comment. Then she remembered seeing the woman before. It was at the mall. "I guess I should congratulate you on your pregnancy."

Before Darlene or Marie could respond, Al and Jeff walked up. At that point Darlene had had about all she could take from this woman. She stood up and greeted Al with a very sensual kiss. Everyone at the table was so shocked that all they could do for the moment was stare. When she brought the kiss to an end, she said, "Al, this woman has something to say to you." She could tell he was feeling a bit awkward so she turned to the woman and said, "I believe you have something to tell my husband." The woman seemed to be at a temporary loss for words. Darlene turned back to Al and said, "She came over to our table to congratulate us on our marriage and the expectancy of our baby." Al looked down at Darlene and a smile curled his lips. "Don't get excited. I'm not pregnant. But some people seem to think that's why you married me." She looked back at the woman. "So you see, we didn't get married because of a baby. And it's obvious I can give him more than some older woman can. If I couldn't, he would have married some older woman instead. Now wouldn't he? Youth does have its advantages." Darlene looked back at her husband and said, "Let's go dance, honey." She grabbed his hand and led him to the dance floor.

Throughout the entire episode, Jeff and Marie watched in astonishment. The other women were silent. And when Darlene walked away with Al, Marie just all of a sudden started laughing. She looked at the other woman and said, "I guess you can kiss that meal ticket goodbye." The woman turned on her heels and walked away with the other two following close behind.

On the dance floor, Al was amazed at his wife. Usually when there was a confrontation between his women, they would go at each other's throat. And the one who was just at their table would come out on top. She was a few years older than Al and had been his main woman for a couple of years off and on. But she didn't stand a chance against Darlene. Maybe it was because Darlene knew where she stood with him, he thought. He wanted to explain things to her about the other woman.

"Dee?" she looked up at him. "About that woman—"

"I don't care, Alvin. It's in the past. Let it stay there." Then she snuggled up to him.

"I love you," he said. "Let's go, home." She looked up at him and agreed. They decided to go home and bring in the New Year together in bed.

It wasn't long before Darlene was back at school. She would go home every weekend to be with her husband. But Al didn't like coming home to an empty apartment now that he was married. They had a few mild arguments on the matter, but they were always settled in bed later.

About two months later, Darlene didn't come home for the weekend. It was the weekend right before midterms. Al made it through the weekend, but that was as far as it went. He couldn't wait until she came home the following weekend. He drove to their favorite hotel late that following Tuesday evening and called her dorm room. Her roommate answered and told him that she was at the library studying. He decided to go over to the campus and surprise her.

When he got to the library, he started walking around looking for her, but he didn't see her. Then he noticed a group sitting at a table in the back corner of the library. He was about to turn and leave, but then he saw Darlene stand and stretch. One of at least five guys that Al could see gathered around the table pulled her back into her seat. They were laughing with each other. Al noticed it was the same guy who had picked her up when he first brought her to school. He walked over toward them. It wasn't until then that he noticed another girl at the table. They were so engrossed in their studying that no one noticed him until he was standing right next to Darlene. She looked up at him surprised, which was the opposite of the expression on his face.

"What are you doing here?" she asked.

"Can I talk to you for a minute?" All eyes focused on the two of them.

"Sure." She looked at the people in her study group and said, "I'll be back." They were about to call it a night so she gathered her books and notebook and put them in her book bag and walked off with Al. He took her book bag from her and carried it and headed toward his car. "Are you going to answer my question?" He was silent. "Alvin, what are you doing here?"

He stopped and turned to look at her. "Do I need a reason to come and see you?" he asked in a brusque tone.

"No. I was just wondering," she said and continued to walk along side him. When they got to the car, she said, "We don't have to drive the short distance to the dorm. We can walk."

"We're not going to your dorm. We're going to the hotel."

"Alvin, we can't make love tonight," she informed him.

"What?" he said, stopping in front of his car.

"Just what I said. We're not making love tonight."

"And why the hell not?"

"Because I'm tired and I still have to study for a test tomorrow. I told you I would be home at the weekend."

"Well, I can't wait to the weekend. If you stayed in an apartment like I wanted you to we wouldn't have this problem. I could come by at any time and be with you."

"Well, since I don't, there's no need to discuss it," she said, getting angry herself.

"You messin' around with that guy in there?"

"What guy?"

"The same one who picked you up the first time I brought you here. Now I see him pulling all on you. What's up with that, Darlene?"

"There's nothing to it. We're friends. We all get together and study for our tests. That's all. Look, Alvin, I don't feel well and I'm starting to get a headache and I really have to study. Call me before you leave in the morning."

"You've got to be kidding. You think I drove all this way and I'm not going to be with my wife? Oh no, Dee. We're making love tonight." He opened the door to let her get inside the car.

Darlene couldn't believe his audacity. She had just given him reasons as to why she didn't want to make love, but he totally ignored them. She decided to give him a more definite reason. She took his hand and placed it between her legs. Al was caught off guard and let her take control of his hand. "Do you feel that, Alvin? It's a maxi pad. I'm having my period this week. *That's* why we can't make love. Next time call before you drive *all this way*," she said before she snatched her book bag from him.

Al stood there shocked. Since they have been together, he had never been with her during her period. It always occurred the times when she was at school. And this was a totally new experience for him.

"I'll call you if I come home this weekend," she said and started walking off.

Al grabbed her by her arm when she was about three feet away from him and turned her to face him. "What do you mean by *if* you come home?"

"My period might just last until then. And what sense does it make for me to come home and we can't make love?" She knew her period wouldn't last until the weekend. She was just mad at him. "So I guess we'll just have to wait and see won't we?"

Al grabbed her by her upper arms and pulled her to him and said, "No we won't. You *will* be home this weekend whether you're having your period or not." When she didn't seem to be listening to him he shook her a little. "You heard me?"

Darlene didn't like his behavior one bit. "Take your hands off of me," she ordered. His fingers momentarily tightened on her arms then he released her. He didn't plan on getting into another argument with her. He just missed her every time she left to go back to school. He knew he only had two more months to put up with it, but that didn't make it any easier. Plus it didn't seem to bother her as much as it did him.

"Look, Dee, I'm sorry. I'll call—"

"No. Don't call. I'll just see you at home." She turned at walked toward her dorm without looking back. Al just stood there and let her leave. Once he saw her enter the dorm, he got in his car and left. He headed back to the hotel and went to sleep.

The next morning he called her before he left.

"Hello?" she answered.

"Good morning, baby," Al greeted. She didn't say anything. "Dee?"

"What do you want?" She was being cold to him. It was just the mood she was in. She had midterms to worry about and she had cramps. And the way he had acted the previous night didn't help matters.

"I just called to say I was leaving and that I'll see you when you get home."

"Fine."

"Dee—" He stopped himself. He wanted to tell her how lonely he felt when she wasn't with him, but he didn't. "Never mind. I love you."

"Yeah."

"You're not gonna say it back?"

"I love you, too."

"Damn, I had to ask you to tell me?"

"No you didn't. You should already know. I have to get up and study."

"I thought you did that last night."

"I think I remember telling you I was getting a headache last night so I didn't get a chance to study."

"Oh."

"Yeah, oh. I have to go. Bye," she said and hung up. She wasn't in any mood to be bothered. She got up and went to take a shower. Her test was in a few hours so she still had time to do a little more studying.

For some reason Al thought Darlene was changing. She didn't seem like the same person she used to be. She seemed so serious now. Maybe it was because she was in her last semester of college. Or maybe it was them being married that was making their time apart unbearable for him. Maybe it was both. He decided to give her as much time as she needed.

The next day, Darlene found out she didn't do as well as she thought she did on her exam. She scored an A, but it was in the lower ninety percentile. She almost always scored in the upper nineties or received a perfect score of a hundred percent. Of course she blamed it all on Al. When he called her later that night, she told Chris to say she wasn't in. Chris shrugged her shoulders indifferently and did as told. It was the same for the next few days. He called her room, her cell phone, and beeped her, but she wouldn't return his calls.

One night, Marie called her. She was genuinely happy to talk to her sister-in-law.

"Hey, Marie," she greeted.

"How's school coming along?"

"All right. I just finished up mid-terms."

"I know you're glad they're over."

"Yes indeed. And guess what?" she asked excitedly.

"What?"

"I have a job interview with your bank."

"That's good. I'll put in a good word for you since you're my sister-in-law."

"They don't know I'm married. I still use my maiden name."

"I'll still tell them how good you worked when you were here anyway."

"Thanks. So, how've you been?"

"All right considering."

"Considering what? Has something happened?" Darlene began to worry because she had been avoiding talking to Al and something could have happened to him.

"Nothing has happened. I've just been a little sick lately."

"You could be catching a cold or the flu that's been going around."

"No, it's not a cold. I think I'm pregnant."

"What?"

"I think I'm finally pregnant. You know Jeff and I have been trying."

"I know. Is Jeff excited?"

"I haven't told him yet. I wanted to be sure before I get his hopes up high. I have a doctor's appointment tomorrow. I'll be sure then. Are you coming home this weekend?"

"Yeah. I might wait until Saturday morning to leave though," she said. She usually left on Friday afternoons after her last class.

"Good. If my test is positive, we'll have dinner together that night and celebrate. If it's negative, I can cry on your shoulders."

"I'll look forward to that dinner. Good luck tomorrow. Even though you won't need it."

"Okay. I'll see you Saturday." Marie hung up. She turned to her brother and said, "She'll be home Saturday morning. I still don't see why I had to call her and find out. Why couldn't you do that?"

"I couldn't never seem to catch her in her room. And she wouldn't return my calls."

"Has something happened between you two?" she asked with sisterly concern.

"I just got mad about something I shouldn't have that's all. Thanks. I owe you."

"Well you could make it up by treating us to the dinner I promised Darlene. After all, I am pregnant and I told Darlene we would have dinner to celebrate."

"No problem," Al said and left for home. He had been feeling extremely lonely since he had left Darlene at school. It was one thing not seeing and being with her. But to not be able to talk to her was agony for him. He went to the grocery store that night and made sure there was food in the refrigerator and freezer. He was up early that Saturday morning. He was eager to have his wife home. He didn't have much cleaning to do since he was basically a neat person. His eagerness started to dwindle away when noon came and went. He started worrying. He called his sister wondering if she had heard from Darlene.

"Hello?"

"Hey, Marie. Have you heard from Darlene?"

"Yeah, about an hour ago. Why?"

"Where was she calling from?"

"I thought she was home with you. She wanted to know how my tests came out. Is everything okay with you two?"

"I don't know. I'll see you tonight." Al hung up. He wondered why had his wife called his sister and not him. He wasn't worried anymore. He was angry. Where had she called from? Why she didn't call him? He was just about to pick up the phone and call her aunt's house when he heard a key opening the front door.

Darlene walked in carrying her suitcase. Al was so mad he didn't give her a chance to put her suitcase down before he started yelling.

"Where have you been?" he demanded in a raised voice. "I thought you said you were going to leave this morning to come home. It's after three o'clock." Darlene looked at him, turned, and walked toward the bedroom to put her suitcase down. He followed close on her heels. When she sat on the bed, he yanked her up off the bed by pulling her by her upper arms, bringing them face to face. "I asked where have you been."

"Alvin, please let me go," she said as if she was worn out.

He shoved her back on the bed and stood there staring at her. She didn't respond to him at all. "I don't know why I wasted my time worrying about you," he said and was about to turn to leave the room. She responded then.

"So, I'm a waste of your time am I?" she asked, getting off of the bed. "Okay. Fine." She walked out the room, grabbed her keys, and walked out the door. Al followed her.

When she was getting in her car, he noticed it was wrecked on the passenger side front fender.

"What happened to your car?" he asked.

"While you were having your time wasted, I was in an accident," she said and started the car.

"Where are you going?" he asked with belated concern.

"Why should you care? I'm just a waste of your time." She put the car in reverse and slowly backed up from the parking space. Al walked along side the car.

"You know you're not a waste of my time."

"That's not what you said." She stopped and sat still in the car then asked, "What time are we supposed to have dinner with Marie and Jeff?" she asked, looking straight ahead.

"Seven o'clock."

She put the gear in drive and drove off. She didn't have anything else to say to him. She drove to her aunt's house. Darryl was outside when she pulled up.

"What happened to your car?" he asked, looking at the dent.

"I was on my way home from school and stopped to get some gas. And when I was pulling in, some lady was backing out and backed right into my car."

"You weren't hurt were you?"

At least her cousin was concerned for her. It was more than she could say about her husband.

"No. I just had to wait to get a police report for the insurance company. I have to get an estimate to give her insurance company."

"I know this shop that does good body work. We can go there now if you want."

"Maybe in a lil' while. I want to see Auntie Betty first." She went inside and talked with her aunt for a while. Betty was playing with her granddaughter. Darlene saw that Crystal's daughter must still look like the father because she couldn't find any resemblance to Crystal in her. She stayed by her aunt's house for a couple of hours. Darryl didn't know how long the shop stayed open so they left.

They drove to a shop that must have been good at what it did because they had a lot of business. They got out of the car at the same time. Darryl went to find someone to help them. Darlene was leaning against her car when she heard a familiar voice call her name. She turned around and saw Vincent.

"Hi," she said when he got closer.

"What brings you here?"

"A fender bender," she said and walked around to the passenger side of the car and showed him. Darryl was coming out with an older man. Vincent waved him off saying he would handle it. "Is this where you work?"

"Yep."

"So how much will it cost to fix it?"

"About five to six hundred maybe. You have insurance I hope."

"Of course, but my insurance won't be paying. I have to give it to the other person's insurance company."

"You wasn't hurt or anything, huh?" he asked.

She wondered why she couldn't have heard that question from her husband. Or why she couldn't have gotten any of the concern she had gotten from her cousin and was getting from Vincent from her husband.

"No, I wasn't hurt," she answered.

"Good. I can write up the figure and give you my card."

"Thanks. How long will it take to fix?"

"About a week," he estimated.

"That long?" she asked.

"It could take longer, but since I know you I can squeeze you in."

"I'll talk with the insurance company and see about renting a car and get back with you," she told Vincent.

"Okay," he said and he watched her as she walked away. She and Darryl got back in her car and left. She dropped him off and headed home. It was almost six o'clock. She noticed Al's car in the parking lot when she arrived. When she went inside, Al was sitting on the sofa watching TV. She didn't say anything to him nor did he to her. She noticed the refrigerator and freezer were full of food. After she had a drink of water, she went to take a bath. She heard the doorbell sound while she was in the tub.

Chapter eleven

Al answered the door and was greeted by two police detectives, one white and one black.

"Mr. Alvin Williams?"

"Yeah. Can I help you?" Al answered.

"I'm Detective Jackson," he showed his identification, "and this is Detective Waters," he pointed to the white cop. "May we come in and ask you a few questions?"

"Sure." Al opened the door wider and let them in and gestured for them to have a seat in the living room.

"We're investigating a murder and have reason to believe you may know something about it."

"Me? I don't know nothing about a murder," Al said.

"This happened last December. The sixth to be exact. Can you tell me where you were between the hours of nine and eleven that night?"

"The sixth of December?" he said as if he had to think about it. Then he said, "Yes, I can. I can tell you exactly where I was."

"And where was that?" he asked with pen in hand ready to take notes.

"I was out of town with my wife."

"Oh. We didn't know you were married. Have you been married long?"

"Nope. Only few months. We're still newlyweds."

"Is your wife home by any chance, Mr. Williams?" the detective asked.

"Yeah."

"We'd like to ask her a few questions."

"She's taking a bath. Excuse me while I go and get her."

Al left the two detectives sitting in the living room. He went to the bathroom and knocked on the door before entering. Darlene was still in the tub. She looked up and saw him standing inside the doorway. She stood up and stepped out of the tub. Al watched every move she made. He watched as the bubbles from her bath slid down her smooth, curvaceous, brown body. It has been two weeks since he'd made love to his wife. And if it weren't for the two cops in the other room he'd take her right then and there in the bathroom.

Darlene ignored him standing there gawking at her. She reached for a towel and began drying herself. When she was slipping into her robe, she looked at him. "Was there something you wanted, Alvin?" Her question brought his mind away from the lusty thoughts he was having.

"Yeah. There are two cops in the living room who want to ask you a few questions."

"About what?" she asked.

"Something that happened last year," he said vaguely.

"Last year when?"

"In December." There was a moment of silence. "Dee, I'm sorry for—"

"Now I get an apology, Alvin?" she said, cutting him off. "I don't need it now. Tell them I'll be out in a few minutes." He turned and left. He walked back to the living room and let the cops know that his wife would be out soon.

Darlene stood in front of the bathroom mirror and looked at her reflection. She had an idea of what the cops probably wanted to ask her. It amazed her how Al had been so mad at her earlier and didn't say anything to her when she came back home, but the minute he needs her, he was ready to apologize. It didn't matter to him that by her being in the car accident was terribly upsetting for her because it reminded her of her parents' accident. But the first reaction she got from her husband was anger. She didn't realize she had been standing there so long until she heard Al call her. She walked into her bedroom and quickly slipped into a pair of shorts and a shirt. She then walked to the living room.

The two cops stood when she approached. They introduced themselves and shook her hand. Darlene sat down next to Al. Detective Jackson began speaking.

"Mrs. Williams, I only have a few questions for you." She nodded and listened. "Mr. Williams tells us he was with you on the night of December sixth of last year. Is that correct, Mrs. Williams?"

"December sixth?" She thought for a moment before answering. "Yes, he was."

"You don't seem to be too sure, Mrs. Williams," the white cop said, speaking up.

Al was a little nervous not that it showed. Deep down he knew Darlene wouldn't say or do anything that would hurt him. But since the past week and what had happened earlier that day he honestly didn't know.

"I was trying to remember the day. It was a Friday and Alvin had come to the hotel we usually share together."

"A hotel?" the black cop asked.

"Yes. I'm a college student and I live on campus. We frequently went to the same hotel near the college. I checked us in and he joined me later that evening sometime between six and seven o'clock. We spent the whole weekend there because that following Sunday was my birthday. That's why I remember the date so well."

"I see. Can you tell me the name of this hotel?" Darlene told him the name. She would have shown him the receipt, but it was back at her dorm room.

"Oh," she said, causing both cops to look at her. "When I registered us, it was in my maiden name because we weren't married yet. I can send you the receipt if you want it," she offered.

"That won't be necessary, Mrs. Williams." They thanked them for their time and left.

Once they were gone, Darlene went back into the bedroom to get dressed for dinner. It all seemed to make sense to her now. She now had her answer as to why Al wanted to marry her in particular. She was someone who was honest and trustworthy. She guessed that he thought she would be his automatic alibi all the time.

Darlene was in the bedroom taking off her shirt when Al came in. He went to her and placed his hand on her exposed breasts. She had only put a shirt on, not bothering with a bra. She brushed his hand away and went about getting dressed.

"Darlene, I said I was sorry. I didn't know you were in an accident."

"I know that. And it seemed to me like you weren't too worried either. Let's just drop it. I don't care to discuss it. It's over and done with," she said and stood by the closet, contemplating what to wear. Al sat on the edge of the bed. "Where are we going tonight?" she asked. He told her the name of the restaurant. She didn't say a word to him while they dressed.

When they were on their way out, Al stopped her before opening the door.

"I love you, Dee. I'm sorry about the police being—"

"There's no need for you to be sorry. I said what you wanted me to say right? I guess I finally have an answer to my question," she said.

"What question?"

"I always wanted to know why you wanted to marry me. I guess a wife makes a good alibi. Doesn't she?"

"Why are you acting like this?"

"Acting like what? Like I just lied to the police? Or like I don't really know where my husband was that night or what he was doing? I'm not stupid. I can put two and two together. And you wouldn't have to worry about having an alibi or worry about the police if you leave that stuff alone." She opened the door and walked to his car. Al locked the door and followed.

They drove in silence. Al was hurt by what all she had said. It was true that he wanted to marry someone who would make himself look good. He married her because he loved her. But she made it all sound so calculating and deceitful. He tried to make things better and started up a conversation.

"How did you do on your tests?" he asked.

"On one I got a hundred percent and the other one I didn't."

"Why?"

"I had a headache the night before and didn't finish studying."

Al knew what headache she was talking about. He felt partially to blame. "Did you make a real low grade because of me?"

"It wasn't because of *you.* I just let my mind get sidetracked. I still made an A so your conscience can be relieved."

Why did it seem like she was deliberately trying to make him angry? He gave up and they rode the rest of the way not talking.

When they arrived at the restaurant, Marie and Jeff were already seated. They sat down and joined them. Practically throughout the entire meal, Darlene only talked to Marie or Jeff about their good news. She rarely said a word to her husband. And when she did, it was short and quick. Her tone of voice would go from excited, as it was when she talked to Marie, to impassive when she would talk to Al.

When the meal was finished, the two ladies excused themselves and went to the ladies' room. While they were washing their hands, Marie asked, "What's up with you and Al?"

"Nothing."

"Then why are you giving him the silent treatment?" She had picked up on it early during dinner.

"According to your brother, I'm a waste of his time," Darlene stated flatly.

"What?"

"I had an accident on the way home this morning. It wasn't nothing serious, just a dent in my car. I called you from the gas station where it happened. And when I got home, I didn't get no 'Hey how you doing?' no 'I miss you' no 'What took you so long?' I got a 'Where have you been?' And it wasn't meant to be caring. Then he went on to say he was wasting his time worrying about me."

"Aw, Darlene. I'm sure he didn't mean it. He was going crazy when you wouldn't talk to him last week."

"Well, he shouldn't have said it. And to top everything else off, the police showed up right before we came here."

"Did everything go all right?"

"Of course. I made my husband happy. I said what was expected of a wife. I think we should get back," Darlene suggested and they left.

Al and Jeff had been talking while their wives were in the restroom. Al told him about the police and what had happened. Jeff had noticed that something was going on between the two. He thought it was the deal with the police.

"Is that what's bothering Darlene?" he asked Al.

"Nah. That's about something else."

The ladies were soon on their way to the table. They sat and had dessert. It was starting to get late and Darlene was tired. She had been up all that day and she had some things she wanted to get done before she went back to school. They said goodbye to Marie and Jeff in the parking lot.

When they got home, Darlene went straight to the bedroom to change and go to bed. Al went into the kitchen instead. When he entered the bedroom, Darlene was already in bed. He undressed and climbed in with her. Moments later she turned over and faced him. He was still awake watching her. She closed the small distance in the bed that was separating them. Their bodies were now touching. Darlene started rubbing her hand along his body. She was still mad with him, but that didn't mean she didn't want to make love with him. He was her husband after all. For better or for worse.

Al was already aroused. That happened the moment he got in bed with her. He leaned closer to kiss her. They made love slow that night. When they were finished, Darlene was about to get up, but he stopped her. He held her close and said, "Oh, Dee," he took a deep breath, "I was so worried about you this morning."

"You didn't seem to be."

"I know. And I'm sorry. I was at Marie's house when she called you. Since you wouldn't talk to me I figured you'd talk to her. She told me you were going to come home this morning. And when you hadn't shown up by noon, I started worrying. I called Marie and she told me you had called her. Why didn't you call me?"

"I was just anxious to find out if she was pregnant."

"Marie thought you were calling from here. That's when I got mad. I was wondering why you didn't come straight home. I guess I missed you so much that I just didn't think. You forgive me?"

"Yes, Alvin."

"And I married you because I love you, Dee. Please believe that," he said.

Darlene got out of the bed and went to the bathroom. She didn't want to discuss the reasons why they got married. They were married so she would have to accept it. She entered into it with her eyes wide open.

The next morning over breakfast she told him about the accident and her job interview with the bank. He suggested a place where she could take her car.

"I've found a place," she informed him.

"You have? When?"

"Yesterday. Darryl brought me to a paint and body shop. I got an estimate to give to the insurance company. I'm calling them later to see about a rental car."

"What do you need a rental car for?"

"I need one to get back to school and get around."

"I can bring you to school and rent you a car. How long will it take to get your car fixed?"

"Vincent told me about a week?"

"Vincent?"

"Yeah. He's the guy I talked to. I might wait until the week after next when it's spring break."

"You'll be home for spring break won't you?"

"Of course, Alvin. The only times I don't come home is when I have major exams. And I don't have any more of them until May."

"Yeah and that will be the end of you being away from me. I can't wait."

After they finished their breakfast, Darlene called the insurance company and was told that the lady didn't have rental coverage. She gave them the estimate and the name of the shop she got it from. That made up her mind. She would wait until she was home for spring break and have her car fixed.

The weeks flew by and Darlene was back home before too long. She got in on a Friday evening. Al thought he would surprise her and fix dinner. It wasn't anything major. He fixed spaghetti with meat sauce. The meat sauce wasn't seasoned at all. He must have just poured it out of the jar and heated it up, Darlene thought. But she was pleased with the effort he made.

She decided to bring her car to the shop the next day. Al had to work so she dropped him off then picked up Darryl. She drove the Mercedes and he followed in her car.

Vincent was busy working on another car when they drove up. He stopped what he was doing to help her.

"You finally bringing your car in to get fixed, huh?" he said, walking toward her.

"Yeah. I had to use it at school. The other lady's insurance wouldn't pay for a rental car and I wasn't about to. So while I'm out of school for a week, I'll get it fixed. You're sure it'll only be a week?"

"Yep," he assured her.

"Good because I'll need it to go back to school next Sunday."

"You have my word. I'll work on it myself."

"Okay. Here are my keys."

"Give me your number so I can call you and let you know when it's finished." He handed her a card and she wrote her name and phone number on the back. She thanked him and her and Darryl got in Al's car and left.

On the way to her aunt's house, Darryl told her all about College Day at his school. He had applied to several schools and his counselor had given him financial aid packets. When they were parking, Darlene's cell phone rang. While she was talking, the mailman delivered the mail. Darryl went to get it out of the mailbox. There were five letters for him from prospective colleges and universities. He went straight to Darlene. She was finishing her conversation with Al when he handed the letters to her. She looked down at them and recognized that they were acceptance or denial letters. She could tell Darryl was nervous. Once they were inside she asked, "Do you want to open them?"

He shook his head. She was about to open the first one, but he stopped her. He looked around to see if anyone was coming. "Let's open them in my room." He didn't want anyone else to know. He hadn't told his mother he was applying for college. And his sister and brother would have only made fun of him. Darlene was the only person he could talk to about it.

Darlene sat on the bed while he leaned against the door. She offered him the letters again, but he still refused. Before she opened them she said, "Don't get upset if you don't get accepted, okay?" He nodded. "I didn't get accepted to some of the schools I applied to." That seemed to calm him a little. She noticed three of the letters were from universities in their state, but in different cities. One of the letters was from the school she was attending, another from a rival college, and the last one was from a local school. The other two colleges were out of state. She decided to open the ones from the out-of-state schools first. She opened the first letter and it was a denial. Darlene was reminded of how it was for her when she applied. But the second letter was an acceptance and she handed it to him. He was elated. He couldn't believe a college had accepted him. She opened the three remaining letters. The one from the school she was attending was a denial. So was the local college. But his mood wasn't dampened. The last letter was another acceptance. He had two college acceptance letters. Two more than he had ever expected or ever dreamed. He jumped and hollered. Darlene was truly happy for her cousin. Darryl was so excited he didn't consider the tuition and room and board costs. He just ran out of his room excited.

"Mama! Mama!" he yelled when he saw his mother in the kitchen. "I'm goin' to college. Look," he said, waving the acceptance letters in front her face.

Betty took the letters from him and read them. She was so proud of her son. The schools that sent acceptance letters would send a packet with the school's fees, starting dates, and other information at a later date. They sat and talked about college, possible majors, and everything else Darryl could think of to ask Darlene. He had always been able to draw practically anything he looked at. It was usually pencil sketches though. Darlene suggested he consider majoring in art. He gave it some thought and agreed. His art classes at school were the only classes he always received an A in. Darlene ended up spending the entire day there. Darryl was leaning toward the school in the same state. They decided to fill out his financial aid forms. She left when it was time for her to pick Al up from work. She was a little early so she sat in the car and waited.

Al was out giving someone a test drive. He was getting really tired of trying to convince the man to buy the car. The man had been in three times that week. He finally decided to get the car and Al was relieved. He was happy to receive the commission, but happier to not have to go on another test drive with that customer.

When they pulled up in the lot, he saw his wife sitting in his car waiting. He showed his customer to a seat then went to talk to his wife. She was reading a magazine when he approached the car.

"Hey, baby," Al said in greeting.

"Hi. You're about ready to go?"

"No, not yet. I just have to finish this last sell. I may be another half-hour or so. Sorry," he apologized.

"That's okay. I'll go and pick up a pizza for dinner tonight. Is that's all right with you?"

"Fine." He leaned in the car and gave her a kiss.

When they got home, they sat at the kitchen table and ate their dinner. They talked about her day from dropping off her car to Darryl's college acceptances.

Darlene's interview was Tuesday morning. She dropped Al off at work and headed to the bank. She talked to the person who hired her as an intern. They talked then she was introduced to a few other people. She was hired to start work after she graduated with a starting salary of thirty-five thousand dollars a year. She informed them of her current marital status and they made a note to change her name on all the necessary paper work. She called Al as soon as the interview was over and he offered to take her out to dinner that night to celebrate.

For the rest of the week, Darlene brought Al to work and picked him up. Darryl called her on Thursday evening telling her that the information from the colleges had come in the mail. She called Al at work and told him about Darryl's good news and told him to call her at her aunt's house when he was ready, but he would get a ride with Jeff and he would see her at home.

When she got to her aunt's house, they had the information on the kitchen table waiting for her input. The out-of-state university was a bigger school so the tuition was more. They wanted a total of eight thousand dollars a year for tuition and room and board. The in-state university only wanted six thousand dollars for the same thing. The college fees seemed to diminish Darryl's aspirations for going to college. Darlene looked at the financial help he had qualified for. He was able to get a grant for three thousand dollars and a student loan for one thousand dollars. She explained that only the one thousand dollars would have to be paid back with interest after Darryl graduates or drops out. She also explained that the amounts were for the entire year and would be divided up for the two semesters. Darlene did the calculations and showed them the figures. That brought the total cost of going to the closer university to one thousand dollars a semester. Darlene was able to pay it with no problem. But she wanted to talk it over with her husband then her aunt. She wanted Darryl to seriously think about what he will be doing if he goes to college and he promised to think about it long and hard.

Al was already home by the time Darlene got there. He had started frying chicken and French fries for dinner. She gave him a kiss and went to take a shower. While she was still in the bathroom, the telephone rang. Al answered. "Hello?"

"May I speak to Darlene?"

"Who's calling?" Al asked, wondering who was the man on the other end of the phone and why he wanted Darlene. Had she been talking to other men while he was at work? He quickly scratched that thought because he trusted his wife.

"Vincent."

"Darlene can't come to the phone. You wanna leave a message?"

Darlene had finished her shower and had just walked in the living room and saw Al on the phone. She looked at him wondering who was on the phone, but he didn't make any gesture to give it to her so she went into the kitchen.

"Tell her she can pick up her car tomorrow after two o'clock."

"Okay. I'll tell her," Al said and hung up. He turned to see her removing the chicken from the deep fryer. How could he have thought of such a thing as his wife cheating on him? She never gave him any reason to think such thoughts.

"Who was on the phone?" she asked, bringing him back to the here and now.

"Some guy from the shop where your car is. You can pick it up after two o'clock tomorrow."

"That's good." She started fixing them both a plate of food.

"So, how did it go with your cousin?" he asked.

"I want to talk to you about that," she said, setting his plate in front of him and then taking a seat herself. "The two colleges sent a packet which contained the tuition fees. The out-of-state college wanted too much so he decided to go to the one closer to home."

"And?" Al asked, knowing she was leading up to something.

"The grant and loan helped out a lot but he still has to pay a thousand dollars a semester since he will live on campus," she said and looked down at her food.

"I see. So, how is he going to pay it?"

"I was hoping you wouldn't mind if I paid it. I have money saved up and with my new job I can afford it. I'll tell my aunt that the money I give her every month I can use to help Darryl go to school. It means so much to him, Alvin. You should have seen his face when he received those acceptance letters."

Al wasn't worried about her cousin's face. He was watching her face while she was obviously sharing in her cousin's joy. He had come to realize how fond of her cousin she was.

"You really care about your cousin don't you?"

"Yeah. Darryl and I have always been close. I'd do anything for him."

"What about the other two? I noticed you're not as close to them."

"Crystal and I were close before I went away to school. I think she kind of felt I was better than she was. And Robert was always trouble as far as I'm concerned. But he's still my cousin."

"I've noticed. But he's a cool kid."

"So, is it okay?" she asked hopefully.

"That you help your cousin go to school? Sure. You didn't have to ask me."

"Why not? You're my husband. You don't let me pay for anything as it is. That's why I'm able to do this for Darryl."

"You're my wife and I'm supposed to take care of you. You don't need to spend your money on bills," he said and continued eating.

Darlene got up and went stood behind his chair. She slid her hands over his shoulders and down the front of his chest. Al stopped eating. She then went down to the zipper on his pants. Immediately he got aroused. He reached for her and she moved away. He got up and she started backing away playfully. He smiled and she ran to the bedroom. They played together until their playing took on a sexual nature.

That next evening Darlene went to her aunt's house. She explained it to her aunt and Darryl the same way she did with Al. Darryl was all for the idea. Her aunt had a few reservations.

"Are you sure you can afford this, Darlene?" she asked, referring to her son's education. "And your husband won't mind?"

"Of course I can afford it. It's really because of Alvin that I can do this for Darryl. He pays all our bills. And he told me that if I wanted to do this I could. I'd be the one responsible for Darryl's bills at school. Auntie Betty, it will be a load off of you. Now you only have to support Robert." Her aunt nodded. "So, is it okay if I take financial responsibility for Darryl?"

"If you're sure you can handle it."

Darryl hugged his mother tight then grabbed his cousin and lifted her off her feet, spinning her around. After he calmed down he walked her out to the car. When they were standing beside it, she asked, "Can you do me a favor?"

"Anything."

"Call the apartment tonight and thank Alvin. I know you don't care too much for him—"

"It's not that, Darlene. As long as he treats you right and keeps you happy, I have nothing against him. I'll call him tonight." Darlene said goodbye and got in the car and drove off.

Al was ready when she arrived. They went to the body shop to pick up her car. Al sat in his car while Darlene went in to find Vincent. She was standing where Al could see her when Vincent approached her from behind. He extended his hands and touched her on her waist. It scared her at first, but when she saw it was only him she smiled.

Al recognized him from when he and Darlene were Christmas shopping. And when the other man touched her on her waist he remembered him from the club before him and Darlene were married. This was the third time this man was in her face, Al recalled. He decided to wait until they get home to ask Darlene about him. But that idea changed quickly.

When Darlene was backing out the parking space, Vincent was walking along side her car. Al could tell they were talking. And he wanted to know about what. She stopped the car and Vincent leaned over to be on eye level with her. Al got out of his car and walked toward them to find out what was going on. Vincent saw Al coming toward them and stood up. He waved goodbye to Darlene and walked back in the garage. Al looked from his wife to the man walking away and back to his wife. He placed his right hand on the roof of the car and looked down at her and asked, “What was that all about?”

“What?”

“Don’t play like you don’t know what I’m talking about. That’s the same man who was so-called congratulating you last Christmas. So what was he all in your face telling you now?”

Darlene realized that Al was getting jealous again. Some women may like it when their man or husband is jealous, but she didn’t. And she didn’t want to get into an argument right there in front of the body shop.

“Wait until we get home, Alvin. I’ll tell you about it then.” He stared at her for a few seconds then walked off in the direction of his car. She watched as he climbed in, slammed the door, started the car, and sped off. She knew she would have to do something about his insecurities. And fast.

Al was already home by the time she got home. As soon as she walked in the door, he came toward her and pulled her roughly into his arms and kissed her. Her first reaction was to pull away, but then she realized it wouldn't do anything to help with the matter of banishing his insecurities. Instead she made the kiss more intense. She moved her hands and caressed his back. She knew from experimenting with him that that particular touch aroused him quickly. And he got fully aroused and led her to their bedroom.

After an energetic bout of lovemaking, they both lay on the bed exhausted. When she regained a normal breathing pattern she brought up what had happened earlier.

"Do you want to talk about why you were so jealous earlier?"

"I wasn't jealous," he stated.

"What would you call it? You probably started jumping to all kinds of conclusions in your head." Al was silent because he had been wondering if she was seeing the other man behind his back. "He's just someone I know. I didn't bring my car to that shop knowing he worked there. Darryl brought me there. And he was telling me about getting my car painted."

"Why is he so worried about your car?"

"He's not worried. He noticed a few scratches on the hood that's all. And I told him I wasn't worried about the scratches. And that's when you came up." She laid on top of him and cradled his face with her hands. "Alvin, I love you okay. Only you. You don't have to worry about no one else," she assured him and gave him the softest and gentlest kiss Al had ever received. She just laid on him for a while and he wrapped his arms around her. They laid like that until both their stomachs growled from hunger. They both laughed and got up to eat dinner.

They sat in the living room and ate while they watched TV. The phone rang and Al answered. It was Darryl calling to thank Al like Darlene had asked him to. She could tell that Al appreciated her cousin's thanks. Marie called as soon as he had replaced the receiver. Darlene had intended on calling her to let her know about the job, but with all that was going on with her cousin she had totally forgotten.

"Hey, Marie."

"Don't hey me. What happened with the interview?"

"I got the job. I start after graduation. I'll be working in an entry-level tax accounting position."

"That's good. It won't take you long to get moved up. You two busy tomorrow afternoon?"

Darlene asked Al and he shook his head. "No, why?"

"Why don't you two come over. We're having a few people over and I need to talk to you about something."

"About what?" she asked interested.

"I'll tell you when you get here. See you tomorrow."

Darlene hung up then sat back down by Al and told him of their plans for the next day.

Chapter twelve

They arrived at Marie's house around noon that Saturday. The other guests weren't due to come until an hour later. Darlene wanted to get there before the other guests so she could help Marie. Jeff was going to grill chicken breasts and steaks. Marie was seasoning the meats and fixing salads. She was making pasta, potato, and fruit salads because she had cravings for all three.

Darlene joined her in the kitchen. They talked about this and that. But when they were finished, Marie wanted to talk to her in the den. Both their husbands were in the backyard getting the grill prepared. The two ladies had a seat on the sofa and Marie started the conversation.

"So how are things with you and Al?"

"They're all right. I'm just going to have to do something about his jealousy."

"I never knew he was the jealous type. But then again, I've learned a lot about my little brother. Anyway, there is something in particular I want to talk to you about."

"Okay."

"Has Al ever discussed with you his other job so-to-speak."

"Not really. I told him to keep it away from me. But some things he couldn't keep away."

"I know. Jeff told me about that. I don't know if or when Al may ask you for help, but I'll tell you what it's all about." Darlene sat more attentive and listened carefully to what Marie was about to tell her. "Some of the people Jeff and Al are associated with have a great deal of money. Of course a good portion of it is not legally earned. I do their income taxes and advise them on how to allocate their money. Those who have children get tax breaks from college funds and savings bonds and other tax shelters along the way. It is all legal on paper. It depends on the person I advise that I get paid anywhere from five hundred to two thousand dollars."

Darlene stared at Marie. Was she hearing what she thought she was hearing? Was Marie doing people's income taxes who would ordinarily end up getting audited? Or worse get sent to jail? And she was getting paid good money for it. But she said everything was legal on paper.

"Don't look so shocked," Marie said. "The extra money comes in handy."

"But aren't you scared?"

"I was at first. But I've been doing it for four years now. I do them from my office here at home. I never bring any of it to work with me. Everything stays locked in my file cabinet. And if I think there will be a problem with a client, I don't do it. That's where I draw the line."

"I guess that's why you can afford this lovely house."

"Yeah. And we have a vacation house in the Bahamas."

"You do?"

"Yeah. We go every summer."

"I wish I had known. I would have told Alvin that's where I wanted to go for a honeymoon," she said and smiled.

"He asked, but someone was using it at the time," Marie told her.

"But can both your incomes afford the houses. I mean—"

"I see what you're getting at," Marie said not letting her finish what she was saying. "We rent out the house in the Bahamas when we don't use it. We let friends or associates have use of it. So the income earned from the house there would have a bearing on our income."

"I see. Did Jeff just tell you you had to do this for the people he's associated with?"

"He brought the subject up a few times. I started off just advising them by suggesting things they should do with the money they earned from legal paying jobs to make them more money. Some consider me their financial advisor. I only point them in the right direction. That's when the doing of their income taxes came into play."

"How many clients do you have?"

"Sometimes it's as many as fifteen a month, but that's usually during tax season. But on an average I have about five a month."

"That's a lot on top of your job," she said, but she also thought about how much money Marie was making a month on top of what she was already making at the bank.

"Not really. I work at my own pace and my own hours. To tell you the truth, I'm going to start cutting down with the baby coming. There are a few people that will be here today that I want you to meet. I want you to have a look at their taxes. They file the basic 1040 and 1040EZ. If you meet them and don't want to deal with them, I'll do their taxes. And we'll see about others for you to handle. Fair enough?"

"But what if Alvin doesn't want me to?"

"We'll see. And speaking of Al, I guess you can do his taxes from now on. He always waits until the last minute to bring his things to me. Maybe you can get them done on time for a change." Marie stood up ready to leave. She looked down at Darlene still sitting. "It's not as bad as it sounds," she said, trying to put Darlene's anxieties to rest.

Al poked his head inside the doorway. He had been looking for them. "There you are. I've been looking for you two. Some of your guests are arriving, Marie," he said, entering the room. "I just wanna sit with my wife for a few minutes." Marie took that as her cue and left them alone. Al sat on the sofa next to his wife. "Are you okay?" he asked, taking in her worried expression.

"I'm fine. Let's go outside." She stood up to leave and Al followed.

They went out to the patio. It was a casual get together. Darlene wore a pair of stonewashed jeans and a short-sleeved, pink, polo shirt. She wasn't in much of a mood to socialize just yet so she sat in one of the patio chairs. The sun was shining and the weather was mild.

Three other couples were there. Al and Jeff were talking to a couple of the men. One was middle-aged around forty-five to fifty. The other appeared to be closer to Jeff's age, late thirties. They walked over to where she was sitting. Al stood next to her and placed a possessive hand around her shoulder and introduced her to the two men. They were both polite and offered her their congratulations on their marriage and were sorry they weren't able to make it.

Marie came out of the house with two women who were the wives of the men and the other couple. The other couple seemed a lot younger. The guy was closer to Al's age. He wasn't as tall as Al though. He was maybe five feet, nine or ten inches tall. He had curly, sandy-brown hair and he was very light skinned, a high-yellow brother. He was also on the slim side. The girl with him looked like she had just gotten out of high school.

The rest of the evening was pleasant. The men gathered on one side of the yard while the women on the other. The women talked about Marie's pregnancy. Marie has known the two women who were the wives of the men Jeff and Al had been talking to for years. The young girl was new. Al and Jeff knew her boyfriend. The other two ladies were telling Marie what to expect during her pregnancy and the best baby products to use. The conversation stayed on that topic for a while.

Darlene went back into the house to get something to snack on until the meat was finished. She didn't hear anyone come in behind her. It was the young guy, Vaughn.

"So you're Al's new wife. I always said he had good taste in women," he said, letting his eyes blatantly roam over Darlene's body. "Are you as friendly as the other women he used to have?"

Darlene just stared at him. This was too much, she thought. He had a woman. Darlene assumed the girl was at least eighteen. But he was coming on to her big-time. Where was her jealous husband when she needed him? She wouldn't get scared at all if Al were to put a gun to this creep's head. If she had a gun she would do it herself. Marie walked in and Darlene finished putting some potato salad on a small paper plate.

"Hey you two. I'm glad I got you two alone." Marie didn't take notice of the tension that was emanating between the two of them. "Vaughn, I was wondering if you wouldn't mind my sister-in-law doing your income taxes this year," she said to the man Darlene wanted to put a bullet in.

"No, not at all. Whenever she's ready to do it it's okay with me," he said with a sexual connotation that Darlene picked up on.

"Good." Marie didn't wait to see if Darlene would object or not. She started gathering plates and napkins to bring outside and left.

"So you're the smart lady Marie was telling me about. Smart as well as fine. I think we can have dinner one night next week and discuss taxes."

"I don't think so."

"Then another night. I can be available for you anytime."

"There's no need. I won't be doing your taxes," she informed him and started to walk off, but he grabbed her arm roughly detaining her.

"Look, I know your type. You'll hop into bed with anybody who can throw money your way. And I can throw more your way than Al. I don't see where you're no different from the other women me and Al passed each other. You know I can give you everything Al can. Maybe even more. So what's it gonna be?" he said arrogantly. It was true that he and Al had always tried to take each other's women friends. It had been fun to them. But that was before Al was married.

Was he implying that he and Al shared women? Darlene thought. She had to be jumping to the wrong conclusions. She thought for a minute or two. Was he telling the truth about Al? Did Al do that with his other women? Well, she was pretty sure he wouldn't do it with her. And she really didn't want her husband to kill this bum and have it on her conscience. So she looked up into his face and smiled and he released the pressure on her arm.

"I'll tell you this," she said. And before he knew what hit him, he had a plate of potato salad in his face. "Go screw yourself you conceited bastard," she said and walked out to the patio just as calmly as she had walked into the kitchen.

Jeff passed her on his way to the kitchen. Once he got inside, he saw Vaughn wiping the salad off his face with a paper towel.

"What happened to you?"

"That bitch just hit me in the face with some salad," he said.

"Who?"

"Al's wife," he stated.

Jeff was finding this hard to believe. From what he knew of Darlene, she was a nice person. "Darlene?"

"Yeah. That bitch must be crazy or something," he said and threw the dirty paper towels in the trash.

"What happened?"

"I don't know. One minute she was smiling in my face then the next thing I know she hits me. You better tell Al to do something about her."

"I'll talk with him." The other guy left Jeff and went back outside.

Darlene had been talking to Marie and one of the couples she wanted her to do the taxes for. These people were nice and Darlene agreed to work with them. She looked around and saw Vaughn watching her.

Jeff came back out and was manning the grill ready to remove the food. He noticed how often Vaughn watched Darlene. He also saw how she rolled her eyes at him. Something more than what Vaughn had said had happened in the kitchen, Jeff thought. He called his wife to stand next to him at the grill. He told her what Vaughn said had happened in the kitchen and what he saw happening outside. Marie started watching them, too. She also noticed how Vaughn always seem to be watching Darlene. She decided to find out exactly what was going on. She wanted Darlene to help her bring out dessert. Once they were inside, Marie made sure they were alone.

"What's going on?"

"What are you talking about?"

"What exactly happened between you and Vaughn?"

Darlene was wondering how she knew anything had happened. "What makes you think something happened?"

"Vaughn told Jeff you hit him in the face with a plate of potato salad."

"Did he tell Jeff why?"

"No. But Vaughn's been watching you the entire afternoon. So what happened?" They sat at the table and she went on to tell Marie exactly what had happen from before she walked in on them until the potato salad incident. "I don't believe he said that to you," she said shocked.

"Believe it."

"And here I thought he and Al were good friends."

"Well, I guess they are to be sharing the same women."

"But that was before Al was married. He couldn't possibly think Al would do that with you. Wait until I tell Jeff this."

"No. Promise me you won't tell Jeff," she almost begged.

"Why?"

"Because Jeff will tell Alvin. And the last guy to put his hands on me against my will Alvin put a gun to his head."

"When did this happen?" Marie asked shocked.

"It was before we were married. And I'd hate to think about what Alvin would do now."

"Me, too," Marie agreed. They gathered the dessert dishes and went back outside. Darlene went to where Al was sitting. Marie went to her husband and told him she would tell him all about what she found out later.

Vaughn and his friend came and sat with Al and Darlene. They talked about nothing in particular. Vaughn kept telling his friend all about Al. It was as if he was trying to sell her on Al. And while Al smiled and talked with the young girl, Vaughn looked at Darlene with sexually appraising eyes. He had been doing it since their encounter in the kitchen and it was really starting to bother her. She excused herself and went to the bathroom. But when she came out, she noticed she wasn't the only one who had left the table. Vaughn was standing right outside the door. She tried to walk around him, but he blocked her by stepping in front of her.

"Do you mind?" she asked.

"Yeah, I mind a lot."

Darlene just wanted to get away from him. She noticed he kept looking at her breasts. At the moment they were rising and falling very noticeable with her breathing.

"What's your hurry?"

"I'd like to get back to my husband."

"He's otherwise occupied at the present time. My friend seems to be holding his attention. And I think it's only fair if you hold mine."

"I have better things to do with my time," she said and attempted to walk away again. This time he grabbed both her arms and pulled her to him. That action caused her body to rub up against his.

"What's with you?" he asked. She could feel his hot breath on her cheek since she had turned her face away from him when he grabbed her. "You think you too much since you go to college? If Al's good enough for you I'm better."

Darlene thought that if a class on conceit or arrogance were ever offered anywhere he would be the perfect teacher. She noticed his hold on her upper arms relaxed. He removed one hand and touched her breasts.

"Take your damn hands off me," she ordered.

"Why? Doesn't it turn you on? You have nice size titties," he said. "I'd enjoy sucking your titties. Especially right here," he said and pinched the nipple of one of her breasts. She slapped his hand away and snatched her other arm out of his grip. But before she could get away, he backhand slapped her across her face. She instantly covered the stinging area of her face with her hand. Then she just raised her knee and hit him in the groin. The hit was unexpected and hard as hell. It caused him to groan and slump against the wall.

They had both been unaware of someone else in the house. Marie had come in looking for Darlene when she didn't notice Vaughn in the backyard anymore. As she was walking through the house approaching the bathroom, she heard Darlene telling someone to take his or her hands off of her, but she didn't know who. Then she heard the sound of someone getting slapped then a groan. She hurried her steps and almost collided with Darlene, who had tears falling from her eyes. Marie tried to slow her down to calm her. Then she saw Vaughn walking slowly from the direction of the bathroom. She knew he must have done something to Darlene. She watched as he walked past them. She took Darlene to her bedroom. She noticed Darlene was holding one side of her face. She got a small towel and put some cold water on it and handed it to Darlene.

"What did that bastard try to do?" At this point she knew something serious had happened.

"He touched my breasts then he slapped me," she explained.

"Of all the—I'm going tell Al about this," she said, getting off the bed.

Darlene grabbed her hand to stop her. "No, Marie. Just get him to leave. What Alvin doesn't know won't hurt him. I'll stay in here a little longer if you don't mind. I'll come out in a little while."

Marie left her in the bedroom. She was torn between going outside and telling Jeff to tell Vaughn to leave or telling Al and let him beat the hell out of him. She decided she had to tell her brother. But she would tell him an edited version.

When Marie went outside, she saw Vaughn sitting near Al and smiling in his face. He was one two-faced individual, she thought. She calmly walked to her husband and pulled him to the side and filled him in on part of what had happened. He was shocked. It was getting late and the other guests were about to leave. Jeff pulled Al aside and told him about the come on. They went to the den to have a few heated words with Vaughn in private. Al was mad as hell. Sure he had played the game with Vaughn in the past, but that was with friends. He didn't think Vaughn would try it with his wife.

When Vaughn entered the den with Jeff, Al shouted, "Have you lost your damn mind?"

"What are you talking about?" Vaughn asked innocently.

"How in the hell could you think I would include my wife in the dumb ass game we played?"

"A bitch is a bitch as far as I'm concerned. Married or not."

Before Vaughn or Jeff could do anything, Al had cocked his arm and let his fist collide with Vaughn's mouth and Vaughn staggered back from the blow.

"Don't you *ever* call my wife a bitch," he said, pointing his finger at him. "I ever catch you anywhere near her again I'll kill you," he threatened and Vaughn walked out with his hand covering his bleeding mouth. When he was about to leave the house, he grabbed his friend, almost dragging her and left.

Marie had heard what all had been said. She walked into the den where they were talking and she looked at Jeff. Al saw how they both looked at each other. Then he realized he hadn't seen his wife in about half an hour.

"Where's Darlene?"

"She's in my bedroom laying down?" Marie answered. She and Jeff adjoined to the living room. Al turned and headed toward the bedroom. He found Darlene laying on the bed on her side with her knees drawn up almost to her chest and her hands tucked under her chin. He went in and sat next to her. She was sleeping. He had never seen her sleep in such a child-like position. He kissed her on the cheek and she flinched a little. He thought she was just stirring in her sleep so he headed back to the living room.

Darlene had pretended to be asleep when she heard Al come into the room. She just didn't want to discuss what had happened.

Jeff and Marie had been sitting on the sofa waiting for Al to come tearing out of the bedroom. She had filled Jeff in on what else had happened. Jeff was appalled at the behavior Vaughn exhibited in his home. And after the altercation in the den earlier, he was glad he didn't know everything. Al walked from the bedroom normally. They both watched him carefully.

"Did you talk to Darlene?" Marie asked.

"No. She was sleep," he said, taking a seat on the love seat.

Marie thought that was odd because she had just talked to her right before Al went in the bedroom and Darlene had been awake.

Al looked at Jeff and Marie a little harder. He realized they were acting kind of strange. He knew something was wrong and asked, "Something else happened didn't it?"

"Al, I don't want you to overreact." She waited until he appeared to be calm. "Well, you know Vaughn came on to Darlene." She waited for his reaction, but he just looked at her and waited for more. "Twice."

"What?!"

"Darlene told me not to tell you," she said and his mouth dropped open in disbelief. "She told me about the last man who touched her and what you did. She didn't want any trouble."

"I wouldn't have—" He stopped suddenly as if to think about something. Then he said, "What do you mean touched her? You said he made a play for her."

"He slapped her, Al."

Al jumped up so fast it startled her. "He . . . did . . . *what?!*" Al screamed, clenching and unclenching his fists.

Darlene had been hearing their voices. She couldn't quite make out what was being said though.

By now she was aware that Marie or Jeff must have told Al what had happened.

"He touched her breasts and when she made him stop he slapped her," Marie explained.

Al started breathing really hard and then he started swearing out loud. Darlene had gotten off the bed and was heading to the living room. Suddenly Al stopped swearing. It was an abrupt end. Then he just stared at the wall. "I'll kill him." He said it with so much conviction Darlene froze in her tracks.

"That's just why Darlene didn't want you to know. She knew how you would react."

"Well, you shouldn't have told me."

"Al, just let it go, man," Jeff said. "You've made your point to him."

"Have I? 'Just let it go.' Tell me, Jeff, would you let it go if it had been Marie?"

Jeff wasn't going to sit there and lie and say he would. He would have been out the door already.

"No, I wouldn't."

"Well I'm not about to let it go either. I wish I had known this before. Someone would have taken him out in a body bag," Al said.

When Darlene came into the room, all heads turned in her direction. Marie got up and approached her. She carefully inspected Darlene's face where it was slapped. It wasn't bruised, but it was a little sensitive. Both Al and Jeff noticed it also. Al walked immediately to Darlene. He tilted her face and looked at her cheek. He touched it and she flinched a little. He pulled away from her and stormed out the door. Jeff hopped off the sofa and ran after him. Marie and Darlene stood in the doorway. Jeff had to physically restrain Al from getting in the car. Darlene ran to where Jeff had him pent against the car. She squeezed in between them and wrapped her arms around Al, begging him not to leave her and to just forget about Vaughn. It took all of his will power not to push her away from him and to go and find Vaughn. But when she started crying, he relaxed a little and held her. They just stood there for a while. Soon Al put Darlene inside the car. Once he got inside, he just sat for a moment looking straight ahead. Then he started the car and left. They drove home in silence. Al was too furious to say anything and Darlene was too scared.

When they got home, Darlene took a long relaxing bath. She wanted Al to sit with her. She wasn't upset anymore. She just didn't want him sneaking out while she was bathing. So he sat and watched her. He didn't say a word though. They didn't make love that night. Al had too much pent up anger in him. He just held her in his arms all night and thought about all the ways he would get back at Vaughn.

Darlene went back to school the next morning. She made Al promise not to do anything while she was gone. It wasn't what he wanted to promise her, but he reluctantly gave her his word. If something were to happen to Vaughn he wouldn't literally do it. It was probably that night that they both realized how much they both loved each other. Al for letting what happened that night pass because it was what she wanted and Darlene for not wanting to see him get in any trouble that could easily result in someone killing or being killed.

The weeks seem to fly by and it was getting close to final exams. This time Al was more understanding since she would be home all the time in a matter of weeks. He called her every night though. And if she wasn't in her room he called her on her cell phone or beeped her. And she would return his calls as soon as she could.

Chapter thirteen

A couple of days before graduation, the senior class organized a picnic at one of the nearby local parks. Most of the jocks and fraternity boys did all the cooking. The other students helped set up the foods, plates, napkins, spoons, forks, and cups on nearby tables. Everyone was participating in one game or another. Darlene, Chris, and Gail were playing volleyball with a group of friends. There were eight players to a team, three girls and five boys. Their team was winning.

When Darlene jumped to return a serve, she came down a little off balance and fell down twisting her ankle. One of the guys on her team picked her up. It was the same guy who picked her up before, her old boyfriend, Jesse. He was in one of the fraternities. That was how they had met. It was at one of their step shows. He was also an accounting major.

"Darlene, you've put on some weight since the last time I carried you," he said.

"Oh, thanks. And here I am trying to watch my weight," she said, pretending to be hurt.

"Feels good though," he said, tightening his hold a little. He walked over to a bench and sat her down and examined her ankle.

Darlene never could tell whether or not he was serious because he joked a lot. She was hoping he didn't want to start anything up again. Their relationship happened when they were between relationships with other people. She couldn't remember if she had told him she was married or not.

The picnic was on a Friday and Darlene had invited Al to come. He had been able to get off work early that day. Jeff even gave him that Saturday off too so he could move Darlene's stuff out of her dorm room. He found the picnic site without any problems. The directions Darlene gave him were exact and easy to follow. He parked and was walking toward the joyous crowd when he spotted Darlene playing volleyball. He hadn't made love with her in a couple of weeks. And watching her jump up and down was torture on his libido. She had on cut-off blue jean shorts and a red T-shirt that stopped just below her breasts. And when she stretched, her stomach was visible. Al was thinking about what all he wanted to do to that exposed area when Darlene fell. He saw some guy pick her up and carry her. Of course he recognized him. To Al it was the guy who couldn't seem to keep his hands off his wife. Picking her up or pulling her down. And she always seemed to be enjoying it. He watched them head toward a bench then he heard someone call his name. It was Chris inviting him to play.

Darlene heard Al's name being called while she was on the bench getting her leg rubbed when it didn't need to be. She slapped at Jesse's hand and looked over at Al and waved him over. He was wearing beige jean shorts, an olive colored T-shirt, white tube socks, and white leather sneakers. She figured she'd better tell Jesse of her current marital status.

"Who's that?" Jesse asked, looking in Al's direction. "He looks familiar."

"You saw him a couple of times at school. He brought me at the beginning of school last year and you saw him in the library once."

"Oh, yeah. The mean guy."

"He's not mean."

"Well, he looked it then, especially in the library. And he looks it now." Al was coming near them with an expression on his face that said he was anything, but friendly. "You go with him now?"

"He's my husband."

At that, Jesse quickly removed his hands from her leg and asked, "When did you get married?"

"Over the Christmas break?" she told him.

"And you didn't invite me? I'm crushed. And here I thought I was going to have another chance with you," he said, trying to sound let down.

"Yeah, right. You have enough women as it is."

"True, but you were my favorite," he said, smiling.

Al was a few feet away by now. Darlene's ankle felt better so she stood up and greeted him with open arms and a kiss. She made the introductions. "Al, this is Jesse. Jesse, my husband, Al." They didn't shake hands. They just nodded their hellos. "Jesse and I have been friends since our freshman year." Al still didn't say anything.

"So I hear you and Darlene are married. Looks like my loss is your gain. It happens like that sometimes. See you two later." He left them to go back and play volleyball.

Al looked at Darlene and said, "His loss?"

"He was just playing," she said.

"He didn't look like he was playing when he was rubbing your legs."

"He wasn't rubbing my legs. I twisted my ankle and he was checking it. Him and I used to go out when we were freshmen, but it only lasted a month or so. We are better at being just friends. So there's nothing for you to worry about."

"Whatever you say, Darlene. How long do you have to stay out here?"

"I don't *have* to stay out here, Alvin. I *want* to be out here. Why?"

"I just thought we could go to the hotel."

"You are so hot. As soon as you get here you're ready to get me in bed," she said, teasing him.

"That's what's husbands are for. So when do you plan on leaving?"

"Probably in a couple of hours. I gave Chris and Gail a ride here. I wouldn't want to cut their fun short."

"Okay," he said and they went and got something to eat.

After that, Darlene played a little softball. Al sat on the sidelines and watched. He never knew she was so athletically inclined. She was playing catcher. Al noticed that the guy he had pulled his gun on was out there, too. He was acting as umpire. Al would look at him from time to time since he was standing so close to Darlene.

When Darlene stepped up to the plate to bat, Jesse sat beside Al. Jesse did a lot of yelling for the team Darlene played on. A pitch was thrown and the ump yelled strike. Jesse jumped up and shouted his disapproval of the call. When the umpire looked over in the direction the shout came from, he almost panicked. He recognized Al instantaneously. Al saw the recognition on his face. Another pitch was thrown. It was a strike, but the ump called it a ball. Jesse was about to yell again, but caught himself just in time. The next two pitches were also called balls. The other team was yelling all kinds of insults at him. On the next pitch, Darlene didn't swing and it was called a ball and she walked to first base.

"I wonder what's with Shawn," Jesse said, talking to Al. "He's usually fair when he calls games."

"He is?"

"Yeah. I know he had a thing for Darlene, but that's been over for a while. I hope he's not thinking that he can get her back now."

"I don't think he thinks that," Al said, sounding very sure.

"I guess he knows you two are married, huh?"

"Yeah."

"I never liked him all that much anyway. I never knew what Darlene saw in him." The next player hit the ball out to right field. Darlene made it to third base and the hitter to second base.

"I don't care for him that much myself either," Al said. They watched the rest of the game. The next person at bat hit a home run. That won the game for them. After Darlene made it to home plate, she went to where Al was and sat beside him.

"You about ready to go?" Al asked.

"Let me see if Chris and Gail are ready to leave."

"I'll give them a ride back if they're not ready to leave yet," Jesse offered. Darlene went to check and they decided to get a ride with Jesse later. She and Al left and headed to the hotel.

As soon as they got inside, Darlene started taking off her clothes. Al just watched her. She looked at him and said, "What are you waiting for?" He quickly started taking off his clothes too. They joined their bodies the minute they were on the bed. They were so hot and horny for each other they didn't waste time pulling the cover back.

Darlene went back to her dorm room to change so they could go out to eat. She had packed most of her things already. She just grabbed a pair of shorts, a shirt, socks, and underwear to put on the next day. They left her car parked in the parking lot near the dorm and rode in Al's car.

The next morning they started loading up both cars with her things. She had a small microwave oven, a refrigerator, all of her books, clothing, and other college paraphernalia. Al put all the clothing in his car. They loaded all the other stuff in her car. It was pretty full by the time they were ready to leave. The trunk and back seat were full. Al only had the trunk of his car full. He was wondering where they were going to put all of her things in their apartment. It wouldn't have been much of a problem, but he had made a few changes at the apartment for Darlene's graduation present.

They left the campus for home with Al leading the way. When they arrived at home, he wanted her to leave the things inside the cars and come inside for a minute. Once they were inside, he covered her eyes and led her to the spare bedroom. He had gotten rid of the old furniture that was in there and turned it into an office for her. His sister had helped him out a lot. Al had gotten her a top of the line computer, a copier, printer, and scanner trio, and a fax machine. It was set up on an oak computer work center.

On the other side of the room she noticed floor-to-ceiling bookshelves made of the same oak as the computer center. The room was also furnished with a jade and beige multicolored futon sofa and chair, and oak cocktail and end tables. There were forest green lamps with beige shades on each end table. Darlene was so shocked she was speechless.

"Do you like it?" Al asked and for an answer she threw herself in his arms.

They unpacked all her things. He had moved some of his clothes to the closet in the newly converted office. So did she. They only kept the clothes they would be wearing to work in the closet in their bedroom. After everything was settled, Al had to leave. He kissed her goodbye and hurried out the door.

Darlene went to her aunt's house. Her aunt was glad to see her. She even had some good news to tell her. Crystal had gotten a job due to the computer courses she had taken and Darlene was genuinely happy for her cousin. Darryl had started working part-time as a bag boy at one of the large supermarkets in order to earn money for college. He worked after school during the week and during the day on the weekends and holidays. He would start working mornings the two months in the summer. But all the joy seemed to disappear from her aunt's face when she asked about Robert. He always seemed to be in some kind of trouble or another. This time he had been caught trying to steal beer from the corner grocery store. The owner didn't call the police because he knew her aunt. He just didn't want Robert in his store anymore. And if he did catch him trying to steal again, he would call the police the next time. Darlene decided to change the subject and talk about Darryl again.

"How has Darryl been doing in school? I haven't heard much from him?"

"He wanted to wait until school was out, but I can tell you some of it."

"What?"

"Well, on his last report card he made the honor roll," she said, feeling very proud of her son.

"He did?"

"Sure did. He wanted to see if he could make it again before he told you though. You know," Betty said and pondered a little before going on. "You and Darryl are more like brother and sister. You two have so much in common. Crystal and Robert are two peas in a pod. But Crystal seems to be gettin' her act together. But I don't know about Robert." She shook her head as if to be giving up on the situation.

"He'll probably get his act together, too, Auntie Betty," she said, hoping to convince her aunt.

"I don't know, Darlene. I've tried and I've tried with that boy. But it's no use."

"Do you want me to talk to him? Maybe he'll listen to me."

"You can try." Her aunt stood up and went into the kitchen. She got herself a soda and offered one to

Darlene. They talked about her graduation ceremony that was the next day.

"What time does Darryl get off work?"

"In about an hour," her aunt said.

Darlene decided to pick him up instead of letting him ride the bus home. She was a little early when she got to the store so she did a little shopping to pass the time. She got in the line where he was bagging. She kept a magazine in front of her face so he couldn't see her. When she handed the cashier the magazine she was reading, that's when her cousin recognized her.

"Hey!" he greeted excitedly. "What are you doing here?"

"Buying fruit and waiting to bring you home. I'll be waiting in the car when you get off."

He looked at his watch. He only had ten more minutes before he clocked out. "I should be out in about fifteen minutes."

They talked on the drive home. Darlene expressed how glad she was to be finished with school and eager to start her new job. And Darryl was just as excited about going to college. He had two hundred dollars saved up from working and it made Darlene feel good to know that he was willing to help himself financially instead of leaving it all up to her. She didn't mind helping him, but it felt good to know he was willing to help himself. She would let him use his money for other expenses he may incur. They also talked about the possibility of him finding a job. She thought it would be best if he concentrated on his first year without worrying about a job. And if he found out he could handle his studies and a job, then he should give it a try. He fully agreed. He mentioned he had the next day off and was planning on riding the bus to her school to see her graduate. It wouldn't be necessary because she would leave her car for him to bring the rest of the family.

The next morning, she and Al drove to their hotel near the college. She had questioned him on his whereabouts the previous day, but he had only told her he was getting her a graduation present.

Al and Darlene walked around until her family showed up. A few minutes later, Jeff and Marie came and soon the graduates, families and friends, faculty and staff, and distinguished guests started to gather in the designated area. When the ceremony was about to start, Al and the rest of the family took their seats and she lined up with the rest of the graduates. While they were marching in, family and friends were snapping pictures of the graduates.

The ceremony was a bit long and boring. Some of the seniors started talking amongst themselves. And just by coincidence, Jesse was sitting behind Darlene. Every time a speaker approached the podium, he would say something funny and she would laugh. She got a few stares from her fellow graduates because Jesse would lean close to her from behind and tell her. That way no one else had heard. And of course while she received the stares, he sat back in his chair innocently.

They were finally ready to hand out degrees. The degrees for a Bachelor of Arts in Accounting were first. They announced for family and friends to hold their applause until all the graduates received their degrees. Those directions were followed for about the first five recipients. Family members were too proud and excited to not show their appreciation.

When Darlene was fifth in line to receive her degree, she looked into the audience and spotted her family. She saw her aunt looking very happy. Darryl looked at her with admiration. Crystal even looked excited with a bouncing baby on her lap. Robert looked as if he'd rather be somewhere else. Jeff and Marie looked happy for her, too. But none of their happiness could compare with what she saw on her husband's face. His whole face seemed to be lit up. She was so enthrall with watching him that she didn't hear her name being called. All of a sudden she saw her family jumping out of their seats applauding. But Al's whole facial expression changed. Sure he clapped, but that glow was gone. Jesse gave her a subtle push. They called her name again. Darlene Carson graduating Cum Laude. She walked across the stage and received her degree. She couldn't see her family from where she was seated. She would just have to wait until the ceremony was over, which was about another hour.

When everything was over, the seniors threw their caps in the air. Just about everyone wanted to get pictures with one another. A few of Darlene's friends wanted to take pictures with her, but she wanted to find her family first. They found her instead. She ran to Al and threw herself in his arms and he lifted her off the ground, hugging her. He seemed to be in a much better mood, she thought. Darryl wanted to see her degree. He opened it and showed it to his mother. Al glanced at it and his happiness seemed to dampen just as it had before.

"What was that they said after your name when they called it?" Betty asked.

Marie was so proud that she explained. "That means that my sister-in-law here is a whole lot smarter than I thought she was."

"How?" This time Al was interested.

"She ranked in the top ten percent of the smartest graduating seniors."

Everyone was extremely proud now. They all walked to the parking lot. There was a black, four-door BMW with a red bow on top in the parking lot receiving a lot of attention. Al turned Darlene in his arms, kissed her, and said, "I'm so proud of you and I love you. Congratulations." Then he dangled a set of car keys in front of her face.

This was not happening, Darlene thought. She shook her head in disbelief. She looked to Jeff and Marie for verification and they both nodded. She looked back at the car. She still hadn't moved from the spot she was standing in. Al took her by the hand and led her trance-like body to the car.

The car was beautiful with gray leather upholstery and a sunroof. Al put the keys in her hand, but she was too excited and nervous to get it inside the door lock. He took the key and unlocked the door with the remote. She turned to him and gave him the biggest hug she could. Then she started crying she was so happy. Al thought it was the car.

"What's the matter, baby? You don't like the car?"

"I love the car. And I love you," she said in his chest. A few of her friends passed by and commented on the car. Jesse came by after he'd heard the car had been for her. Al was more cordial to him this time.

Chris and Gail came by also. They weren't accounting majors, but they were just as lucky as she was in the job department. They both got great job offers in their hometowns.

When they left, Jeff suggested treating everyone to dinner. Darlene realized they were going to have an extra car. She found out that Jeff and Marie had driven her car there and they would drive Al's car home.

When they were inside the car, Darlene decided to ask Al what had bothered him earlier. It had nagged at her throughout the rest of the ceremony. "Alvin?" she said while he was backing out the parking lot.

"Hmm?"

"Was something bothering you when I was getting my degree?"

"Why do you ask?"

"Because I was watching you and your expression changed. It did it again when Darryl was looking at my degree."

"I was expecting to hear them call you Darlene Williams, not Darlene Carson." He knew it was silly for him to be upset. But he had been expecting to hear her be called by her married name. His name. And it hurt him a little that she didn't use his name.

"I'm sorry, honey," she said, looking at him from her seat. "I didn't change my name on any of my school records because I didn't want to lose my dorm room. And I didn't want to risk anything going wrong in my last year. They probably would have forgotten to change my name on certain forms and messed my grades around and I wouldn't have graduated. Those were the only reasons I didn't change it," she said and he seemed to be satisfied.

They drove to a seafood restaurant. The staff had to pull two tables together to accommodate them. Crystal's daughter was sitting up so the waitress brought a high chair to their table. Everybody sat at the table and talked until their meals came. Marie wanted Crystal to sit next to her with the baby because she was feeling a bit maternal.

When the food arrived, everyone started eating. Every now and then Desiree would grab at something on the table. If Crystal wasn't taking it away from her, Marie was.

"That's what you have to look forward to Jeff," Darlene said to him.

He looked at his wife and said, "It'll be worth it." Then he said, "How about you and Al? Our baby will need some cousins."

Al smiled, but Darlene was quiet.

"Jeff, they just got married and she's starting a new job. They'll have plenty of time to have a baby," Marie said, seeing how uncomfortable Darlene looked.

She and Al had never discussed having children. Sure she wanted one or two, but not this soon. She wanted a career first and she wasn't ready to put it on hold.

When they finished eating, they all hit the road for home. On the drive home, Darlene wanted to know what made Al buy her a car for a graduation present when he'd already gotten her a computer.

"Alvin you didn't have to get me a car. The computer was enough."

"I wanted to get it. You're not some college student anymore. You'll be working in a bank. I can't have you driving that old car of yours. I want my wife to drive in style."

"'That old car'?"

"You know what I mean."

"But what are we going to do with three cars?" she asked.

"Why not sell your old car," she shoved him, "I mean the other car."

"Can I—never mind. How much are my car notes going to be?"

"There are no car notes," he stated.

"What do you mean 'no car notes'? Then how did you get the car?"

"It's bought and paid for," he replied.

Darlene had never asked Al about how he paid all their expenses. He had told her to keep her money and he would take care all the bills. And she let him. But this was a little too much.

"Alvin, how could this car be bought and paid for? It's brand new. It must have cost more than forty thousand dollars. What did you do?" she asked accusingly.

"Damn, Dee. I didn't do nothing." He was beginning to get a little mad because of her accusation. So he decided an explanation would appease her. "When I left you yesterday, I went with Jeff to an auction. He usually buys used cars for the dealership. And when this one came up I wanted to get it for you. But if someone would have out bid me for it, Jeff was going to buy it. Then I would have bought it from him. But I was able to get it and it's not brand new. It's slightly used. It's a year old, but everything is just like new. So now you see I didn't steal it if that's what you were thinking."

"I'm sorry," she said and looked down at her lap. "How did you buy it?" The not knowing was awful. She doesn't know how she would feel about her graduation present if it was bought with drug money.

"I put it on a credit card."

"Oh," she said and felt much better. "Thank you for the best present I could have ever wanted."

"You're welcome. So what is it you want to do?"

"What are you talking about?"

"You were about to ask can you do something earlier."

"Oh. It was nothing."

"Sure, Dee. If you don't tell me now, you'll tell me eventually." She didn't respond to him. She busied herself with all the knobs and buttons in her car. It had a radio, cassette player, and six-disc CD player. Everything was in perfect working order. The air conditioner had the front area cold and it was only blowing on low. Al showed her how to adjust the temperature to keep it at a comfortable level.

Darlene started getting horny. She reached over and started rubbing Al's thigh and he looked over at her. She moved her hand up and started rubbing his crotch.

"You better stop that, Dee," he said.

"Why?" she asked and continued to rub him. "I want to feel you," she said and started unfastening his clothes. Once she freed his sex, she started stroking him until he got hard. Darlene had heard some of her friends talk about having oral sex in a moving car and she wanted to try it with her husband.

When Al was hard enough, she bent down and placed her mouth over him. She wasn't worried about anyone seeing them because it was a bright and sunny day and the windows on the car were tinted. And the brighter the day, the darker the tint. She kissed his abdomen teasingly. She licked up and down the length of him. Al was holding on to the steering wheel so tight that it looked like the blood in his hands had seeped out. And when she took him into her mouth, he accelerated too hard and started speeding. He was losing it. He wanted to tell her to move, but he couldn't talk. Oral sex with her always affected him that way. Especially when she did it when he wasn't expecting it. He reached down and pushed her head away and soon he heard a police siren. So did Darlene.

Al looked at the odometer and saw he was doing only sixty miles per hour in a fifty-five mile per hour zone. Darlene tried to fix his clothes while he pulled over to the shoulder of the road. Al finished fixing his clothes before the cop approached.

A black highway patrolman approached the driver side of the car and Al rolled down the window. He hoped he wouldn't have to get out of the car. If he did it would be embarrassing.

"Do you know you were speeding? You were doing seventy in a fifty-five mile per hour zone," he told Al. Al didn't know how fast he had been driving. He would just accept the ticket without attempting to get out of it like he usually did. "Can I see your license, sir?" Al reached in his pocket for his wallet then gave his license to the police.

The police looked over at Darlene then glanced at the back seat. He saw her graduation gown and asked, "Are you two coming from the nearby college?"

"Yeah. My wife," he pointed his thumb toward Darlene, "just graduated."

The highway patrolman let him go with a warning. He didn't give him a ticket since his daughter was attending the same school. Al and Darlene thanked him. Al looked over at Darlene and she looked embarrassed.

"I'm sorry. I didn't think we would get stopped by the police," she said.

"That's okay. I knew I was speeding. You just took me by surprise that's all. Let's finish when we get home," he said and she sat back and enjoyed the ride home.

Chapter fourteen

When they arrived home, Darlene wanted to make love to her husband and thank him properly for her gifts. And thank him she did. They both were too tired to move. As they lay together sexually sated, Al brought up Jeff's remark at the restaurant earlier.

"So when do you want to give my niece or nephew some cousins?"

Not *a* cousin, but cousins, Darlene thought. "I don't know, Alvin. Let's just wait and see. We're still newlyweds. Let's see how things work out with us living together full time. Plus I'll have to adjust to my work schedule. And I'm going to have to go shopping for work clothes."

"Use the credit cards, but not the platinum Master Card. Better yet, I'll give you cash."

Darlene started rattling on and on about what all she had to do. It seemed like she was finding all kinds of excuses not to have his baby, Al thought.

Darlene wouldn't start work for another week so she did some shopping the following week. She bought a few dresses. Slim skirts were bought in just about ever color they had. She bought blouses to go with them and a few suits. She was on her way out the mall when she passed by a dress shop. There was a dress that caught her eye. She went in and took a closer look. The dress was sleeveless and low cut in the back and made of green stretch lace. Al's birthday was coming up soon so she stopped and got something for him also.

That weekend, she wore her new dress when she took Al out for his birthday. She had looked around the mall some more in order to find a shirt for Al that would match her dress. She didn't find an exact shade of green, but it was close.

Al worked late that Friday. He didn't get home until almost eight o'clock that night. Darlene wasn't upset. She just figured they would get started celebrating a little later than she had planned. Al really didn't want to go out dancing or anything. He just wanted to stay home. But when he saw Darlene slip into her dress he changed his mind. The dress accentuated every curve of her body. They left the house at about nine-thirty that night.

Darlene drove them to a restaurant. It wasn't that crowded because of the lateness of the night. They both ordered steak dinners. Once when Darlene got up to go to the restroom, Al noticed a few men looking at her. It didn't bother him because he knew she was fine. And what made it so good was that she belonged to him. But when they got to the club it was another story. They went to a club Al used to frequent. It was the same club he'd seen her in before they were married. He saw a lot of people he knew. Darlene even noticed a few people she knew. She was surprised to find her cousin there. They joined her cousin at the table where she and a guy were sitting. Crystal introduced them to her new friend, Carl. He was the same guy she had been telling Darlene about. Al ordered drinks for all of them.

When a fast song played, Darlene was ready to dance. She and Al went on the dance floor. Al had always liked the way she danced. But now it was totally different. With that dress on, her moves looked very suggestive and seductive. Al would lose his rhythm because he kept his eyes on her body. And he wasn't the only one. A lot of other men were doing the same. Darlene didn't seem to notice that her dancing was stimulating so many men. It was the same way she always danced. Just not in such a figure-hugging dress. She just wanted to look special for her husband on his birthday.

On a slow song, she and Al danced together. Her moves weren't suggestive then. Al just couldn't seem to keep his hands still. He caressed her exposed back and slid his hands down to her hips. She had to stop him from going any further. Al wanted to sit the next song out. So did Crystal's friend Carl. The two ladies went on the dance floor. Carl and Al talked for a while about sports.

When the ladies came back to the table, it was only to get their purses to go to the restroom. When they got there, Darlene wanted to know more about Carl.

"Are things with you and Carl serious?" Darlene asked, starting to touch up her lipstick.

"I don't know. We see each other all the time. And he's crazy about Desiree," she said a little unsure of his feelings for her.

"How do you feel about him?"

"I like him a lot. He's the nicest guy I've ever met. I think I'm falling in love with him."

"Good for you," Darlene said and they left the restroom.

On the way back to their table, Darlene saw Vaughn. And he was with the woman she had encountered New Year's Eve. They were made for each other, Darlene thought. She tried to ignore him, but he wasn't about to be ignored.

"Well, well, well. What have we here? I see you look as if you want someone tonight."

He had to be the most disgustingly, aggravating person Darlene had ever met. He was abominable. "Not you," Darlene said and saw a flicker of anger flash across his face. She knew now that it infuriated him to get insulted or rejected.

"Baby, don't waste your time with her," the woman beside him said.

"I guess since you couldn't get Al, you settled for second best I see," Darlene told the woman referring to Vaughn.

"You bitch," the woman said and pushed Darlene.

Darlene stumbled back a few steps to a table close by and a few people started gathering around. She picked up a glass containing the remains of someone's drink and tossed the contents in the woman's face in retaliation. The woman gasped then slapped Darlene across her face. But before she anticipated the next move, Darlene grabbed a beer bottle off the table and cracked it across her head. The woman staggered back and fell to the floor. Vaughn grabbed a handful of Darlene's hair and held it tight in his fist. But that was about as far as he got before Al's hands were around his neck choking him.

Al and Carl had been watching for their ladies to return from the restroom. Al saw when Vaughn came in. He had been considering leaving as soon as Darlene returned to the table. But when he saw Vaughn approach Darlene, he knew something was about to happen. He got up and headed toward them.

"I told you what would happen if you came near my wife," he said, reminding Vaughn and tightened the pressure around his neck. Vaughn's entire face was turning red. His eyes were bulging and he was gasping for air. Once Darlene was able to remove her hair from his hand, she tried to get Al to stop before he choked Vaughn to death. Everyone was standing around watching, but no one tried to stop Al from choking him. It appeared as though Vaughn wasn't well liked. And a lot of people there would have gladly cheered Al on in killing him. Darlene tried in vain to pull Al off him. Carl began helping her, but Al had a death grip on Vaughn's neck.

The security guards came through breaking up the crowd. With the help of them, she and Carl were able to get Al to release Vaughn, who slumped to the floor and started coughing and gasping for air. Darlene was so scared about what Al could have done with his bare hands she was shaking. Crystal led her back to their table and tried to calm her down.

The manager threw Vaughn and his friend out of his establishment. The spectators were quick to point out who started the altercation and how. And since Al wasn't at fault, he didn't have to leave. He and Carl went back to the table. Darlene wasn't in a partying mood any longer so they left.

When they got home, Al went straight to the kitchen and got a beer to drink. He sat on the sofa in the living room and drank it. Darlene had gone to the bedroom to change. She took a quick shower and put on a nightgown. By now, Al was on his second beer. He looked up when she came into the room. The gown she had on was transparent. He could see her breasts and her bikini panties. He wanted her and he wanted her desperately. He pulled her down on the sofa with him and raised her gown over her head and took it off. He started taking off his clothing. He then laid her back on the sofa and proceeded to make love to her with an urgent need. Nothing was said. No words of love or words of pleasure. When he experienced his release, he grunted then collapsed on top of her. After a minute or two, he got up and pulled her with him and led her to their bedroom where he proceeded to make love to her again. Afterwards, he held her for a while.

"I'm sorry your birthday was ruined," she said because she felt she was partly to blame. "We should have went somewhere else or stayed home like you wanted to."

"That's all right. It wasn't your fault. It was Vaughn's fault. When I saw him grab you . . ." He tightened his hold on her. He couldn't put into words the rage he had felt. "I won't let him get away with that. I let him slide the last time. Not this time."

Darlene was getting scared. "I'm all right, Alvin. I don't want you to do anything that will get you in trouble. Or worse killed."

He released his hold on her and sat on the edge of the bed and said, "Well, damn, Dee. What am I supposed to do? Let him get away with man-handling you like that and do nothing?"

"But you did do something," she said, trying to change his mind. "Everyone there saw you choke him."

"I can't let it go, Dee. Don't ask me to. You did that before and look what happened."

Darlene saw how tense he was. She crawled over toward him and kneeled behind him. She began rubbing his tense muscles and he began to relax. She planted kisses across his shoulder blades. He turned around and grabbed her. It was so sudden he scared her. He laid her down on the bed and looked at her for a very long moment before asking, "Do you know how much I love you?"

"How much?" she asked, looking at his intense expression.

"Enough to kill," he said and then he started kissing her desperately. He ended the kiss and looked at her long and hard and said, "You're mine. I won't let no one hurt you or have you." Then he united their bodies with one hard thrust. It was a desperate union. That night of lovemaking was unlike any other time they had been together. He couldn't get enough of her. The next morning was the same. He woke her up to make love. She had to put a stop to it after the first morning session because he had gotten a little carried away the night before. She was sore everywhere. Her breasts, inner thighs, legs, and especially her most intimate area. They spent the rest of the day at home.

Monday was her first day at work and things went smoothly. She had her own private cubical to work from. Her work area consisted of a desk with several drawers and a computer on it, a file cabinet, a telephone, and an adding machine. Only two chairs were provided. She had been shown around the floor she would be working on. She was also shown the workroom, which was where all copy machines, printers, and the fax machine were located. Then she was shown the Finance Department, which was where she was to turn in her work. She was glad everything was all on the same floor.

Marie stopped by later that morning to see how she was settling into her new job. She talked with a few of the supervisors she knew and they had nothing but positive things to say about Darlene. She went over to Darlene's work area and said, "Hey, girl. How you doing?"

Darlene looked up surprised to see Marie. "Fine. This is sure a lot more work than I was doing last summer," Darlene informed her.

"I know. But you're getting paid a lot more," she said, sitting in the only available chair. "It'll slack up soon. Don't worry," Marie said, trying to comfort her. "Do you have any plans for lunch?"

"Nope."

"How about if we go together? My treat since it's your first day."

"I'll be ready at a quarter 'til noon."

"I'll meet you here," Marie said, rising from the chair to leave. "I'm surprised Al didn't want to take you out for lunch."

"Oh, Lord," she placed the palm of her hand on her forehead, "I forgot to call him. I told him I would call him this morning to let him know how things were going. But I got so busy," she said, waving a hand at the paperwork occupying her desk.

"Well, call me upstairs if he has plans for you. Bye." Marie walked off leaving her to make her phone call.

"Crawford Mercedes BMW may I help you?" the receptionist said, answering the phone.

"May I speak with Al Williams please?" she asked.

"One moment please."

Al was on the line a minute or two later. "Al Williams."

"Hi, honey. I'm sorry I didn't call you sooner. I had a lot to do this morning."

"That's okay. Do you wanna have lunch?"

"If you do. Marie already offered—"

"That's fine. Go with her. I'll take you out tomorrow. Can you give me a number where I can reach you?"

"Yeah. It's the number at my desk," she said then gave him the number. He had a customer and had to go. She then called Marie and told her their lunch was still on.

Later that day, Al called her at work to tell her he loved her and that he wanted to take her out for dinner since it was her first day and he didn't take her out to lunch. They went to a nice restaurant and she told him about her job and the people there. She invited him to go with her to Darryl's graduation which was the coming Sunday.

"Is that what you wanted to ask me about before?" Al asked.

"Before?" She was wondering what he was talking about.

"Yeah. After your graduation, you were about to ask me something and you stopped." She thought back to that and remembered what she wanted to ask.

"No. It was something else. I was wondering would it be all right for me to let Darryl use my Jetta while he's at school since I have another car. And having a car when you live on campus makes a big difference. I've seen a lot of people stranded in their rooms."

"Sure. It's your car. Do what you want. You didn't have to ask me."

"Why do you say things like that?"

"Like what?"

"Every time I want to get an okay on major decisions, you say I don't need to ask you. Would you want me to do things without your knowledge?"

"It wouldn't bother me," he said.

Those four words made Darlene feel as if he didn't take their marriage seriously. She didn't bring it up anymore. She was beginning to think that the only sharing that went on was when they were in the bedroom. There was no decision making on money matters. He handled everything. And even though she was working he still gave her money.

Darlene got her old car washed and waxed the day before the graduation so Darryl could use it to bring the rest of the family to the graduation ceremony. She had called her insurance company and got him listed as the primary driver.

Darlene was getting dressed when Al walked into the bedroom. He had left earlier that evening saying he had something to do and she hadn't questioned him. He came and stood behind her and started kissing her on her neck, but she pushed him off of her because she wasn't in the mood for making love. The past week had been tiresome. She was overloaded at work and he was coming home late every night. He tried to kiss her again and this time she pushed harder and said, "I'm trying to get dressed. The graduation starts at eight o'clock and it's almost seven now."

"C'mon, Dee. We have time for a quickie," he said, fondling her breasts.

"You should have come home earlier if you wanted a 'quickie'."

"What's that supposed to mean?"

"Just what I said. You knew I wanted to go to Darryl's graduation tonight."

"All you talk about is Darryl. Darryl this and Darryl that. If he wasn't your cousin, I'd think you were sleeping with him." Darlene looked at Al as if she wanted to slap him silly. How could he think something like that about her? She never gave him a reason to think she would want another man. Unlike him who had been coming home late every night that week.

"You've been coming home late every night. Maybe I should be wondering whether or not you're out sleeping with somebody," she said in retaliation and walked out of the room to go to the bathroom. No sooner had she walked inside that Al grabbed her and spun her around to face him.

"What the hell are you talking about?"

"Just what I said. You come home late and don't say anything. You just climb in bed ready to make love. I guess it's been busy at the dealership. Everybody must have been buying cars this week," she said sarcastically.

"I can't make love to you when I come home? Is that what you're tryin' to say?"

"Did it ever occur to you that I be tired and that's why I'm in bed asleep? No. You just—"

"Forget you, Darlene," he said and walked out of the bathroom, slamming the door.

Darlene was so mad that angry tears flooded her eyes. But she held on to her temper and finished getting dressed. They didn't leave the house until five minutes to eight. She knew they were going to be late when she saw how Al was dragging around the house. It was as if he wanted them to be late or didn't want to go at all.

"You don't have to go if you don't want to, you know," she told him.

"Didn't I say I was going? We wouldn't want to miss seeing your precious cousin graduate," he said and finished dressing. She knew Al could be jealous when it came to other men. But of Darryl?

By the time they made it inside, all the graduates were seated. Her aunt had held two seats for them because she knew Darlene wouldn't miss Darryl's graduation.

The program wasn't as long and boring as her graduation had been. When they started handing out diplomas, Darlene wanted to get closer to the stage to take pictures since she'd missed taking them when Darryl marched in. When she got up to leave, Al wanted to know where she was going. She told him and he volunteered to take the pictures while she sat with her family.

When Darryl's name was called out, they all clapped and screamed. He looked in their direction and saw Darlene and waved his diploma at her. While Al was walking back to his seat, he saw how proud Darlene was. It was all over her face. He sat down in his seat and wondered why she couldn't look at him that way.

After the ceremony, all the graduated seniors went to find their family and friends. Darryl found his family before they found him. "Darlene and Al!" he yelled, walking through the crowd toward them. "I didn't think you two would get here in time."

"We wouldn't have missed it," Darlene said then looked at Al for confirmation.

"Yeah. Congratulations, man," Al said, extending his hand to shake Darryl's.

"Let's go out to eat," Darlene suggested.

When Al and Darlene got in his car he said, "I didn't want to go out tonight. I wanted to be at home with you."

"Well, I wanted to take Darryl out and since I didn't need your permission I made reservations. You are free to just drop me off at the restaurant. I'll get home safely."

He mumbled something under his breath and put the car in gear and left. There was a long line of cars waiting to exit the parking lot. Al didn't say a word to her and she didn't care. Not anymore.

Al was quiet throughout the entire meal. When the others were discussing something, she leaned closer to him and asked, "What's wrong with you?"

"I just don't want to be here."

"Then leave," she told him. She had gotten tired of his attitude. From the time he had come home he had been complaining about one thing or another.

"Are there any parties tonight?" Darlene asked, talking to her cousin.

"A few," Darryl replied.

"You're not planning on going?"

"I was, but they are all kind of far away."

"So what's stopping you from going?"

"You'll let me borrow your car to go?"

"My car is at home."

"Not your new car. The Jetta."

"Ohhh, the Jetta. That's yours to drive," she said and a silence fell over the table.

"M-mine?"

"Yes. You'll have to put gas in though. It's your graduation present for Al and me. A college student needs a car." He got up and hugged her tight and pumped Al's hand a few times in thanks.

As soon as they were finished their meals, Al announced that he and Darlene were calling it a night and placed a twenty-dollar tip on the table. She cut her eyes at him then agreed. On their way out to pay the check, Darlene was about to pay with cash and Al took out a credit card and paid the bill. She was wondering why he would pay when he knew she wanted to. The whole night started off strange, she thought.

When they got home, he got a beer and sat in the living room on the sofa. She didn't want to talk to him anyway. She changed and got in bed. About an hour or so later, Al climbed in the bed next to her. She felt him rubbing on her body. She figured if she pretended to be asleep he would just leave her alone. Finally after minutes of trying to get a response out of her, he gave up and went to sleep.

Darlene got up for work Monday morning and gave him the silent treatment. He called her at work wanting to take her to lunch, but she told him she had brought her lunch and didn't want to leave. He called later that day, but she told him she was busy and hung up.

When she got home, she smelled food cooking. Al had made a point to get home early. He knew she was mad with him, but they had always made up the same night. And after the way she had treated him when he called her at work, he felt he had to make amends.

He had been setting the table when she walked in the door. He stopped what he was doing and went and hugged her. "I'm sorry, baby. Whatever it was I did, I'm so sorry."

"Okay."

"I just love you so much," he said and tightened his hold on her. "More than I thought was possible." He kissed her on her temple. "Go change and comc eat."

A week later, Darlene was watching the news and heard a report about a decomposed body being found in the trunk of an abandoned car. The body had been bound and gagged and had multiple bullet wounds. It was apparent that the body was closed inside the trunk then shot. The identity of the victim wasn't given. But based on an autopsy, the murder occurred a week ago due to the decomposition of the body. She thought it was awful, but there was always some kind of killing almost everyday on the news.

She stopped by her aunt's house a few days later after work. She was surprised to find Crystal there. She was there with Desiree and Carl. She waved at them and picked up her little cousin. The baby giggled the whole time Darlene played with her. Then the baby reached for Carl and she threw her little arms around his neck once in his arms. They looked so good together, Darlene thought. He would blow in her tummy and she would fall out laughing. Crystal wanted to talk to Darlene so they went into the kitchen. Darlene noticed she was nervous.

"Is everything okay?" Darlene asked, leaning against the counter.

Crystal had taken a seat at the table. "Carl wants to get married," she said.

"Is that why you look so nervous? I hope you told him yes," Darlene said being glad for her cousin.

"I haven't given him an answer yet. But that's not what I wanted to talk to you about," she said, looking to make sure no one was about to come into the kitchen with them. "Vaughn's body was found."

"Is that who they were talking about on the news the other day?" Darlene asked, getting a piece of the cheesecake her aunt made.

"Yeah. And Darlene?" she said, getting her attention.

"Hmm?"

"Darlene," she said and Darlene turned around and looked at her.

"A lot of people are saying Al did it." Darlene vaguely remembered how she got from the counter to sitting in a chair at the table. "You know because of the fight at the club that night. I just thought you should know."

"He didn't do it," she said, shaking her head as if it could numb the feeling she had in the pit of her stomach.

"I didn't say he did," Crystal quickly said. "I'm just telling you what I heard."

"I have to go," Darlene said. She waved goodbye to her aunt and Carl. She got in her car and left.

After about forty-five minutes of driving, she was at Marie's door. Marie was expecting her. Darlene had called her en route. She didn't go into details as to why she was coming there so late. She was a nervous wreck by the time she'd gotten there. Marie saw how wound up she was and gave her a glass of orange juice to calm her. She called Jeff at the dealership and told him to bring Al home with him because Darlene was there and she looked too upset to drive back home. She sat down beside Darlene on the sofa.

"Do you want to talk about it now?"

Darlene looked at her and nodded. She took a shaky breath and said, "Vaughn is dead."

At first Marie didn't have a reaction. She was expecting to hear something about her or Al, not Vaughn.

"Vaughn?"

"Yeah. I heard it was his body that was found decomposed," she said, wiping at the tears that were falling.

"And that's why you're upset?" Marie thought Darlene would be the last person to shed a tear over Vaughn.

"No. People are saying Al did it," she said and stood up to pace the floor.

"Al had let what had happened go. He couldn't have done it."

"Something else happened," Darlene said and stopped pacing. She had Marie's full attention at this point. She went on to tell her about what happened on Al's birthday at the club. Marie didn't know what to say. "That's why I'm so upset. A lot of people saw the fight. I'm so scared, Marie."

The door opened and Al and Jeff came inside. Al rushed over to Darlene and looked at her. He saw fear in her eyes. The first thing he thought was that somebody had done something to her.

"What's wrong? What happened to you? Are you all right?" All she did was start crying. He encircled her in his arms. Then he looked at his sister. "What happened to her?!" he screamed at his sister, letting all his concern show in his voice.

Jeff went and stood beside his wife and hugged her to him. He didn't want her getting upset about anything since she's pregnant. "She heard Vaughn was killed and she said people are saying you did it because of some fight you had with him," Marie told him.

Al looked down at Darlene in his arms. She was trembling. He tilted her face up and looked at her. Her eyes were red from all the crying she had done. "I didn't kill him, baby. Please believe me. I didn't kill him." She buried her face in his chest and desperately wanted to believe him.

When they got home, Al took Darlene into the bedroom. He sat her on the bed and undressed her. She sat on the bed and just stared at nothing. Once she was free of her clothing, she curled her body up and laid down wearing her bra and panties. Al went to hang up her clothes and when he came back he saw her lying in the same fetal position he'd seen her in before. He didn't like what had made her lay like that the last time. He went and sat on the edge of the bed next to her.

"Dee? You okay, baby?" She looked up at him. "You want something?" She nodded. "What? Anything and I'll get it."

"Hold me," she whispered. He leaned closer to her in order to hear her. "Just hold me tonight." Al hurriedly took off his clothes, climbed in bed with his briefs on, and held her. She soon drifted off to sleep. Afterwards he slipped his arm from around her so he could get up. He was hungry and he wanted to get something to eat. He was in the kitchen fixing a sandwich when he heard Darlene scream. He dropped what he was doing and ran to check on her. When he got in the bedroom, he saw her thrashing about in the bed. She was swinging her arms violently. He couldn't quite tell if she was awake or still asleep. He moved closer to her and reached for her upper arm and she swung her other arm around and punched him in his jaw. He tried shaking her, but he had to duck her punches at the same time. She wasn't doing anything, but fighting him. He released her and turned on the light. He grabbed both her wrists and penned her to the bed with his body to still her. Then he clasped both her wrists with one hand and patted her cheek in an attempt to wake her up. She stopped struggling and opened her eyes. Then the tears started flooding out. Al immediately got off of her and pulled her into his arms.

"Shhh. It's okay. I'm right here," he said, trying to soothe her. After the sniffing and shuddered breaths stopped, Al wanted to know what happened. Because one minute she was sleeping peacefully and the next she was going wild. "What happened?"

"I dreamed Vaughn was chasing me. He was all zombie looking and he grabbed my arms. I was trying to fight my way free, but when I hit him worms and stuff started oozing out of him. I was calling for you to help me, but I didn't know where you were," she said then buried her face in his chest.

"Vaughn can't ever hurt you again. Nobody will ever hurt you," he assured her.

Chapter fifteen

The next morning Al wasn't sure she should go to work, but she assured him she was fine. He called his sister and told her to keep an eye on her for him.

Darlene was busy as usual working when Marie came to her area at about three o'clock that afternoon. She had received a call from Jeff saying Al had been taken in for questioning concerning Vaughn's murder. Marie had talked to both their supervisors and they were given permission to take the rest of the day off. Darlene smiled when she saw Marie.

"Hey, girl. What brings you here?" Darlene asked. Then she stopped what she was doing because usually Marie would sit down. This time she only stood in the doorway.

"Darlene, we have to leave. Al was arrested. We can take the rest of the day off." Darlene didn't hesitate a minute. She quickly grabbed her purse and they left in Marie's car.

They went to where they brought recently arrested prisoners. They gave Al's name and were told that he hadn't been formally arrested, but he was being held for questioning. They were directed to where he could be found.

Al was sitting in a room while a couple of cops, the same two cops who had questioned him before, were questioning him about the fight he and Vaughn had. Apparently the woman Vaughn was with that night named him as a possible suspect. He explained to them what had happened and where he was at the time of Vaughn's actual death, which had been determined by an autopsy. It was the same night as Darryl's graduation. He told them his wife and her family were with him and that they went out to dinner afterwards. He even had a credit card receipt to prove it. They decided to check out his alibi and released him.

When he walked out the room, he saw his sister and his wife waiting for him. Darlene threw her arms around him. She was so relieved that her husband wasn't going to be in jail. Marie drove them back to the bank's parking lot so Darlene could get her car. Then Darlene and Al went to the dealership so he could pick up his car. They went home afterwards.

Darlene was so upset she could hardly keep her mind on the road, but she made it home safe and sound. When they got home, she fixed a nice hot bath for Al. She ordered Chinese food to be delivered while Al went to take his bath. When he was finished his bath, he wasn't in a mood to eat. He just wanted to lay down and relax and try and put the day's experience behind him. He heard when the food was delivered. Darlene poked her head inside the bedroom and offered to fix him a plate, but he didn't want to eat. He wanted her to lay down with him. She had taken off her work clothes and slipped into some shorts and a T-shirt. She climbed in bed next to him. All they did was snuggle with each other.

"Al?" Darlene called to him after about ten minutes.

"Hum?"

"Why did they arrest you?"

"They didn't arrest me. They just questioned me," he explained.

"But why you?" She was sure Vaughn had many enemies who could have killed him.

"That broad who was with Vaughn that night at the club told the police that I may have done it. But since the time of death was estimated as being the night of your cousin's graduation, they let me go. I told them I was with you and your family and that we had dinner later that night and they could check and see. So that was it."

"I wish we would have stayed home for your birthday. Then none of this would have happened."

"Well, it has. C'mon," he patted her rear end, "let's go and eat. I'm hungry."

There were no further problems from the police. They checked out Al's alibis and everything was in order. They ended up saying Vaughn's death was a drug-related-incident.

The summer was ending and it was getting time for Darryl to leave for college. Darlene really wanted him to succeed, but she knew the temptations college life had to offer. She had already talked with him about what to expect as far as campus life, classes, and parties. He had his priorities straight. But she wanted to talk to Darryl about practicing safe sex so he wouldn't get any diseases or get some girl pregnant and have to drop out of school. She didn't think he would want to hear it from her so she asked Al to do it. At first he laughed. Then he saw how serious she was and became serious, too.

The day before Darryl was due to leave, she told him to stop by her apartment. He came by as soon as he finished his last day of work. Al was home alone. Darlene had gone to the store in order to give them some privacy.

"Ready for school?" Al asked once they were seated.

"Yeah."

"Good. I'll get straight to the point. Darlene really cares about you. She doesn't want you goin' to college and messin' up. She wants you to graduate. Now she wanted me to talk to you about sex."

"I know about sex."

"I would hope so. But seriously use condoms. It doesn't matter how pretty and fine those girls might be don't be careless and stupid." Al had been careless a few times in the past. He was lucky he didn't end up getting any of the women he had had sex with pregnant or contracted any sexually transmitted diseases. Or worse AIDS. "Because if you end up getting some girl pregnant and have to drop out of school, it'll break Darlene's heart and I'm not about to see her hurt. So you better take care of things on your end," he said and Darryl nodded. "She'll be giving you a check for your first semester's tuition and room and board when we stop by your house tomorrow. But take this for your books," Al said and reached into his pocket and handed him three one hundred dollar bills.

"I have money saved up from my job. I can buy my books."

"Do you know how much college books cost?" Darryl shook his head. "Well, I bought them for Darlene and they cost five hundred dollars. So you use your money for other things. Like buying condoms for one thing." Darryl laughed. "Gas for another. And you will need to get other stuff for school. Use your money for that. Don't tell Darlene about the money. And don't let her down, Darryl."

"I won't. She means too much to me and she's done too much for me. Tell her I appreciate her concern and I'll be careful." Darryl was touched by Al's offer of the money. He had been harboring doubts about Al's feelings toward his cousin, but not anymore. He figured if she could make a conscious choice and look past what he did on the streets so could he. He shook hands with Al, thanking him for all he has done for his cousin and what he was doing for him. "Check you later, Al. Tell Darlene I'll see her tomorrow." Then he left. Darlene came home about fifteen minutes after he'd gone.

"Is Darryl gone already?" she asked Al.

"Yeah. We talked and he left."

"Aw, Alvin. Did you threaten him?"

"No, Dee. We had a nice chat about sex. And speaking of sex," he said, getting off the sofa and looking at her very peculiar.

"Oh no you don't, Alvin. You're going to tell me what you said to Darryl," she said, backing away from him.

"How about if I show you," he said, unbuttoning his shorts. "Got any condoms handy? You know it's good to practice what you preach. So let's have some safe sex." By now he was naked. He had slipped out of his shorts and briefs and pulled his T-shirt over his head. Darlene ran to the bedroom. She kicked off her sneakers and jumped in bed. Al was only seconds behind her. The playing stopped and they made love. It was without condoms, but it was safe because they only made love with each other.

The next morning they went to her aunt's house. Crystal was there with Carl and Desiree. Al and Carl helped Darryl get his things packed and loaded in the Jetta. Darlene had given him the miniature microwave and refrigerator she had used in college. His mother was crying because she was so proud of her son. Robert didn't know what was the big deal since he was only going to school.

On one of the trips to the car, Darlene went with Darryl. "Here's your tuition check. It's already made out to the school. And take this," she said, handing him three hundred dollars.

"What's this for?"

"Your books. I know you have your own money, but you'll need it later."

"I won't need it for my books."

"Of course you will. You'll have to buy all new books for all of your classes. Plus a lot of other stuff too so take the money," she insisted.

"I don't know who's worse. You or Al. He already gave me three hundred dollars for books. So you can keep your money."

Darlene felt touched by her husband's generosity. "Call me. Anytime. And call collect."

"I will. I might not call too often because I'll be busy studying."

"You do that. We'll see you whenever you decide to come home. And don't feel as if you have to come home every weekend."

"Don't worry." He looked up and down the block he lived on. "I'm glad to get away from around here. I'll call you when I get settled in my room."

"Okay. Me and Alvin have to go. But I'll be waiting for your call." She hugged him tight. Al came outside while they were hugging. He knew she was crazy about her cousin. And very protective.

"You all set?" he asked Darryl, causing them to end their goodbye-hug.

"Yeah. I'll talk to you later, Darlene. Bye and thanks, Al. For everything."

"No problem. Just remember what I said," he warned Darryl.

"I will." And with that he went back inside.

Al looked at Darlene and asked, "Are you ready to go?"

"How come you didn't tell me you gave Darryl money for his books?"

"Because you wasn't supposed to know."

"I tried to give him money for his books, too. I was about to stick it in his pocket and make him take it until he told me you had already given him money."

"Why didn't he just take the money you wanted to give him too? I would have."

"Darryl's not like that. He knows I'm doing a lot for him as it is. He wanted to get a job to help pay some of his expenses, but I told him to concentrate on studying now."

"Good. C'mon let's go home."

Chapter sixteen

Weeks passed and things went on pretty okay after that. Darlene didn't have any more dreams about Vaughn, Darryl was doing well in school and she was adjusting well at her job. She made friends with everyone in her section. Male as well as female. Almost all the women were married. Only a few were single. There were only a few married men. There were two single men in particular that were big flirts. One white and one black. They flirted with everyone. Darlene told them she was married, but they didn't seem to care. She used to get offended by some of the things they would say. One of the ladies told her they weren't serious, but only playing. Darlene didn't seem to think they were playing until the other lady showed her how phony the black guy's flirts were.

He came by one afternoon and asked her out and she told him she was leaving her husband and would be willing to go out with him anytime and anywhere. He came up with so many excuses that both Darlene and the lady started laughing. So from that point on, she didn't let the so-called flirts bother her.

Marie called and invited her to lunch one afternoon. They went to a nice restaurant that Marie had found. She was in her eight month of pregnancy and her workload had lightened. But she still had her other clients on the side. And that was what their lunch meeting was about.

Marie had invited a few other people. All three were middle-aged men. One black and the other two were white. She had been advising them on ways to spread out large sums of money. But the further along she got in her pregnancy the less work she wanted to do. She introduced Darlene to the men. They talked and she had a lot of suggestions for them, but they couldn't go into them there.

Marie took out a few of her business cards and wrote Darlene's phone number on the back and gave it to the men for them to call her when they would have a chance. They finished their lunch then went back to work.

Darlene was home before Al so she started cooking dinner. She saw that the laundry was starting to pile up so she went to the apartment's Laundromat and washed their clothes. All the clothing they wore to work went to the cleaners. So all she washed were underwear, socks, towels, and the clothes they wore at home. Once she had the clothes in the washer, she went back to the apartment and finished up dinner.

Al was late getting home that night. She had finished cooking dinner and was on her way back from getting the clothes out of the dryer when she saw him opening up the door. She called to him and he held the door open for her.

"Why are you so late today?" she asked casually once they were inside.

"I had something to do."

She had always respected his privacy in his other work, but she didn't like the way he answered her sometimes. She knew she had told him to keep it away from her, but he could be nice about it, she thought.

"You can't tell me?"

"Why? When I give you money, do you ask where it come from?" he yelled.

"Have I ever asked you to give me money?" she screamed at him and dropped the basket on the floor. "No, I haven't. You can keep your damn money. All I asked was why you are so late coming home. And you start in on me about money." Darlene wasn't in such a good mood herself because she was starting her period. "Keep your money. Your food is on the stove," she said and went into the bedroom. She was changing into some jeans and a T-shirt when Al walked into the bedroom a few minutes after her. She had to leave. She didn't like to argue when she was starting her period. It was bad enough that she was cranky at that time of the month. She didn't want to risk saying something she might regret later.

"Where the hell do you think you're going?" he asked, looking at her getting dressed.

"I don't know just yet, but I won't be spending your money if that's what you're worried about," she said, stepping into her sneakers.

"I'm not worried about you spending money, Darlene," he said.

"You could've fooled me," she said then looked at her watch. She saw it was almost eight o'clock. "I'll be back later," she said and walked out of the bedroom then out of the front door. Al was too shocked to stop her. He just started undressing. He fixed a plate of food and started eating.

Darlene went by her aunt's house. With Darryl gone, it was pretty quiet there. She sat and talked with her aunt a while. She found out her aunt was having all kinds of problems with Robert. He was hanging on the street corners more than he used to. And he was wearing all kinds of new clothes, expensive sneakers, and jewelry that his mother hadn't bought for him. Darlene's first guess was that he was starting to sell drugs. She wanted to talk to him, but her aunt didn't know his whereabouts. Darlene decided to drive around and see if she could find him and bring him home.

She started by asking a few of the boys hanging around the house. They told her a few places she could try. She found him hanging on a street corner a few blocks away with a bunch of other boys. She parked her car and got out. She didn't have any time to be patient with him.

"Robert get in the car and let's go," she ordered.

He turned and looked at her and so did the other boys. "Where we goin'?" he asked.

"Home. And if you got any of that mess with you, you better get rid of it now."

"Whatchu talkin' 'bout?" he asked, pretending not to know what she was referring to.

"Don't play stupid with me, Robert. If I have to go through your pockets, I will," she threatened. He saw how mad she looked so he took what he had out of his pockets and handed it to one of his buddies, who took it gladly.

They were just about to get in her car when two police cars pulled up and ordered everybody to get up against the police cars. All of the boys there did as told. It must have been a routine thing for them, she thought. They stopped her and Robert from getting in the car. The police searched one of the boys and found some crack on him so they started searching everybody else. A few other boys had marijuana on them. Robert would have been one of them, but he had just given it to one of the other boys. One of the policemen approached her.

"I know you don't plan on searching me," Darlene said. She didn't have anything to hide, but she recalled reading something about a woman cop was supposed to search women.

"Is that your car?" he asked, pointing to the BMW.

"Yes," she answered. One of the other cops ran a check on it and came up with the identity of the previous owner who was a big-time, murdering, drug dealer. It appeared that was the reason why they stopped. She explained to them that her husband had recently bought the car at an auction and that all the papers were in the glove compartment. She showed them her license and registration and they checked it out.

They kept everyone there for about twenty minutes. Another car pulled up and a woman cop was in it. She got out and searched Darlene. A couple of the cops were making remarks about how they wished they could be doing the searching. Darlene had never been so humiliated in all of her life. Soon she was free to go.

Robert sat silently while she drove and cursed under her breath. He went straight inside. She told her aunt what had happened and what could have happened. Robert went to his room. It was after ten o'clock and Darlene wanted to get home.

When she opened the front door, she noticed the house was dark and quiet. She had planned on getting something to eat while she was out, but she forgot with all that had happened. She fixed something to eat and sat in the kitchen and ate. Then she went to take a bath afterwards.

Al had been watching TV. He turned it off when he heard her key in the door. He was now lying in bed, waiting for Darlene to come in. She was taking mighty long, he thought. Then he heard the water in the bathroom. He got out of bed and went to the bathroom.

Darlene was lying in the tub filled with bubble bath. She opened her eyes when she heard the bathroom door open. Al came in and leaned on the bathroom counter and asked, "What took you so long coming home?"

"I don't want to talk about it," she said because she was still too upset to calmly discuss what happened.

"What do you mean by 'you don't want to talk about it'? I wanna talk about it."

He sounded mad, Darlene thought. She didn't know why he was so mad. He was the one who came home yelling at her. He was the one at home while the police was searching her. So if he wanted to know, who was she not to share her unforgettable experience.

"Okay, fine. First of all, I went to my aunt's house and she told me Robert is selling drugs. So I decided to go and find him and bring him home. Secondly, the police stopped on the corner where I found Robert and they searched everybody. Including me once a lady cop came. And you know what, Alvin? They stopped because of my car."

"What?"

"My car. I guess you don't know who the cars used to belong to at those auctions. Apparently my car was for some big-time dealer. I'm getting it painted and a personalized license plate," she said and looked at him. "I'll pay for it myself so don't worry. I'll ask Marie to stop and pick me up on the way to work or I'll get there some other way. I do not want to drive that car."

"You can use my car. I'll use one from work."

"You're sure it won't be a problem? I wouldn't want you to spend any kind of money on me," she said, trying to start an argument.

"Do what you want." He left and went and got in bed and went to sleep. Darlene came in a few minutes later. She got in bed and went to sleep, too.

Darlene woke up in a much better mood. She even snuggled up to Al in bed. She decided against the paint job, but she wanted to get a different license plate. She told him what she decided and he said he would take carc of it. He would drive her car until the new license plate was in place. She suggested getting her name or birthday on it, but Al said he had an even better idea for hcr.

The following week was Marie's last week at work. Darlene gave her a baby shower on her last workday. They had it at the office during lunchtime.

They used one of the conference rooms that wasn't being used that day.

Darlene had ordered a cake and they had meat, vegetable, and fruit trays. Sodas were also available. Everybody bought nice gifts. Marie opened them all. She was so happy she cried when she saw the pretty baby things. All the women who had children said hormones at the same time.

When the party was over, Darlene put all the presents in Marie's car. She put the cake in the break room with a note for others to help themselves. She took some of the fruits and vegetables down to where Marie was working. She knew Marie got hungry about every half an hour. She wrapped the rest of the food up to take home. She worked late that night. By the time she got home, she saw her car already parked so she knew Al was home. She looked at the license plate. It read I-M-4-A-L. She was wondering how could that be a personalized plate.

Al had pulled a few strings and got the license plate a lot faster than usual because he worked at a car dealership. He had started dinner since he'd gotten home early. She put her briefcase down and carried the food she had brought home to the kitchen. She kissed him and asked, "What kind of license plate did you put on my car?"

"Something personal," he replied.

"I didn't see anything personal about it."

"C'mon. Let me show you," he said and grabbed her by her hand. They walked back out to the parking lot. "Now tell me what you see when you look at it?" he asked, standing behind her.

"I see I-M-four-A-L," she said still not comprehending anything personal.

"Dee, baby, it says I'm for Al." She looked at it again and repeated what he said silently and she saw it finally.

"Ohhh, now I see. But the car is for me," she told him.

"I know, but the owner is for me," he said and he kissed her behind her ear. They went back inside. She put the food from the party in the refrigerator and ate what Al had cooked.

The telephone started ringing and Darlene answered. It was one of the men she had met through Marie. He wanted to know when would be a good time for him and her to discuss business. She was nervous about the meeting. She put him on hold before answering. She wanted to make sure Al would be home. She quickly told him about the call and he told her any day would be fine. She told the man to come over the next Monday evening, but he preferred to come over Saturday evening instead. After she hung up, she couldn't remember if Mr. Davis was one of the white men or the black man. She would have to get a planner to keep her clients and appointments straight.

Al was waiting for her when she came to bed. It had been a couple of weeks since they had made love nice and slow. When she's on her period, he doesn't touch her. And the week after that, she had been so busy at work and planning Marie's baby shower they only made quick love. But he wanted to take his time.

Darlene was in the bathroom. She had just taken a bath. She was in the mood for some good lovemaking herself. She didn't want to just put on any nightgown.

She put on a sheer nightshirt without any panties. It was completely see through with the exception of satin pockets that covered her breasts.

When she walked in the bedroom, Al was sitting up in bed with the covers over him from the waist down. The lamp on the nightstand was on so he was able to see her entire body. When he saw her, he removed the covers and she saw he was already naked and hard. He swung his legs down and sat on the edge of the bed. Darlene walked over and stood right in front of him. He hugged her to him, burying his face in her breasts. He pulled back and started unbuttoning her shirt. He didn't take it off. He just let it hang open. He captured her taut nipple with his mouth. The heat from his mouth made her tremble. Al didn't want to neglect her other breast so he gently started massaging it. He grasped the other nipple with his thumb and forefinger. Then he slid his hands down in between her legs. She was wet. Just the way he wanted her and the way he liked her. She pushed him back to lie on the bed. She laid on top of him and started kissing him. She straddled him, letting him slide into her wetness. It wasn't long before he exploded within her. He turned and laid her beneath him and began moving slowly within her. She placed her hands on his butt urging him deeper. Al began to thrust within her harder and harder and deeper and deeper. She moaned his name and they went over the edge together. They were both so exhausted that all they could do was sleep afterwards.

Darlene was the first one to get up the next morning and she initiated the lovemaking. Al dozed off to sleep again and she got up and fixed breakfast. She carried his food to the bedroom on a tray. He was still asleep so she woke him up.

"What's all this for?" he asked sleepily.

"Do I need a reason to fix my husband breakfast in bed?" He looked at her. "I'm thanking you for my new license plate," she said and handed him the tray.

"I thought you did that last night," he said and smiled.

"You don't have to do anything special for me to make love to you. That's a perk to being married. We can make love whenever, wherever, and however we want," she said and leaned over and kissed him. "I'm going to get my food. I'll be right back," she said then left.

Al noticed she was wearing shorts and a shirt. He sure would have liked to see her wear what she had on the previous night. He sat his tray aside and found her nightshirt on the floor on her side of the bed. At some point time during the night it was tossed to the floor. He picked it up and laid it on the bed right on her pillow where he was sure she would see it.

Darlene walked back in the bedroom with her tray and saw Al sitting up in bed innocently eating while her nightshirt laid on her pillow next to him.

"What's that for?" she asked as she neared the bed.

"I thought you might want to dress the same way we were last night. I am," he said. She put her tray down and changed right in front of him. He stopped eating and got up to put his tray of food on the dresser. Darlene was just about to slip into her shirt when Al came up behind her. He cupped her breasts with both his hands and she let her head fall back on his chest. She could feel his erection against her bottom. He lifted her right leg and positioned it on the bed. Then he penetrated her softness from behind. Darlene was enjoying this new position. She reached back and caressed his face. Al moved her closer to the bed and laid her face down on the bed without breaking their connection. He started humping faster and faster until they both climaxed. They were both extremely hungry after that quick experimental lovemaking.

Darlene went about doing the laundry and cleaning the apartment. She and Al had stayed in bed until almost noon. Her meeting was at five o'clock that evening. She had one of her work suits hanging on the back of their bedroom door. She was planning on handling this meeting very professionally.

Al came home and saw what she was planning to wear and disapproved. "What's that for?" he asked, pointing to her clothes.

"I'm wearing that for my meeting. Why?"

"Why do you have to wear that suit? The skirt is too short," he said, complaining.

"No it's not. You never said anything about it before when I wear it to work."

"That's because you wasn't going to be in a private room with a man."

Darlene didn't say anything. She just removed the suit and took out a pair of slacks and a blouse. She went to take a quick shower. She was dressed and ready by the time her appointment showed up.

When she opened the door, she was relieved to find the black man standing outside her door. She introduced him to Al. Al had seen him at his sister's house a time or two, but they didn't know each other.

He seemed to be in a hurry so they were going to get to work.

Al sat in the living room trying to watch television. An hour passed and Darlene was still in her office with the man. Al was getting restless. He opened the door and the man quickly covered the papers he was showing Darlene. Al offered them something to drink, but they didn't want anything so he closed the door.

Finally, after two hours of being in the room together their meeting was concluded. She had helped him allocate tens of thousands of dollars. He was so pleased with all the advice she gave him he paid her five hundred dollars. He offered to take her and Al to dinner that night and introduce her to some possible clients. He said he would call Marie personally and thank her for recommending Darlene to him. She agreed to the dinner since she and Al were already going to go out to dinner. He told her what restaurant and the time.

When he walked out the room, Al was approaching the door. The man expressed how he was looking forward to seeing them later that night as she walked him to the front door. When she closed the door, Al was standing right behind her.

"What did he mean by that?"

"He invited us to dinner tonight. I accepted because we were going out anyway and this way it's a free meal."

"It won't put a dent in our finances for me to take us out to dinner, you know," he said, feeling pissed at the man for still wanting to spend time with his wife.

"I know, Alvin. He can't be all that bad. Marie knows the man." Al just walked off. "We have to be at the restaurant at eight o'clock," she said to his retreating back.

Darlene decided to ask for Al's opinion on what to wear because she didn't want to put on anything he thought would be too revealing or clinging. She knew how he could get when he was jealous or angry and she didn't want to give him any reasons to be either.

Al was familiar with the restaurant they were going to. It was a very expensive restaurant. When they walked in, Mr. Davis greeted them. He had been waiting for them. They followed him to a table where there were two other couples and his wife. One couple was young, closer to Al's age and the other was middle-aged like Mr. Davis and his wife. He introduced Darlene and Al to all of them.

A waiter came by to take their orders. They all were ordering appetizers so she and Al did the same. She and Al ordered shrimp cocktails. The others ordered soups that were offered. Darlene ordered steak and lobster and Al ordered steak and fried shrimp.

They all talked over dinner. Mr. Davis was praising Darlene to the other guests. Al excused himself from the table. Soon after he left, the men subtly suggested that their wives go to the restroom. Darlene thought she'd missed something when the other ladies stood up. She was about to get up, too, but Mr. Davis gestured for her to stay. He started telling her about the other men in general. They wanted to meet with her and discuss financial matters. She didn't have her planner with her, but it didn't seem to deter them. They pulled out their business cards and handed them to her. The older man wanted her to call him and set up an appointment. He circled his cell phone number on it for her to reach him at that number.

Al had gone to the bar to get a drink. He looked back at the table and saw Darlene and only the men at the table. He didn't like the way one of them had been looking at her during the meal so he decided to leave the table before he told the guy something. He went back to the table when he saw the women returning. He was ready to leave, but dessert was about to be served. It was strawberry cheesecake, one of Darlene's favorite desserts.

The other women were talking amongst themselves and so were Mr. Davis and the older man. The younger man watched Darlene. Every time she would place the fork with a piece of cheesecake on it in her mouth he would focus on her mouth. And when she closed her lips around the fork he would lick his lips. She didn't notice his actions, but Al did. And he didn't like them one bit. Al leaned over and whispered in her ear that he wanted to leave. She saw he hadn't eaten his dessert. She wanted it, but he offered to stop on the way home and buy her a whole cheesecake. He wasn't about to let the pervert across the table from them get off on watching his wife eat. They stood to leave. Darlene thanked Mr. Davis for dinner then said goodbye to everyone and shook his or her hands. Al followed suit. The man who had been admiring her eating ability was the last one whose hand she shook. He held her hand a little longer than necessary, Al thought. He was about to snatch her hand away, but the other man released it when he saw Al's outstretched arm. Al shook his hand more firmly than necessary. He looked up at Al and received a subtle but intimidating look before Al released his hand.

On the ride home, Al told Darlene he didn't want her meeting with the man. She asked why, but he didn't elaborate.

Chapter seventeen

Darlene and Marie went shopping one Saturday afternoon. It was early October so the weather wasn't too cold, but a little cool. Marie wasn't due to have her baby for another week. Darlene went and picked her up because Marie couldn't drive comfortably anymore. Plus Jeff didn't want her driving anywhere. But she wanted to get some last minute things for the baby's room and he was at work. Darlene couldn't possibly wonder what she wanted to get. The room was equipped with everything there was for a baby. But Marie dragged her to a store to get curtains with a certain pattern.

They got back to the house and Darlene hung the curtains for her. Marie came into the baby's room having contractions. Darlene didn't know what to do. She had never been around anyone who had a baby. She was away at school when her cousin gave birth. But she calmed herself enough to help Marie into the car and get them safely to the hospital.

Marie was examined and was definitely in labor. Darlene called Jeff and told him what happened. He and Al were at the hospital thirty minutes later. Al had to drive because Jeff was too nervous. Al and Darlene stayed in the waiting room while Jeff was in the labor room with Marie. After about twenty minutes, Jeff and one of the nurses came out. The nurse wanted Darlene to come back in and give Jeff a break. Marie hadn't been handling the pains too well and she blamed Jeff. She had been much more relaxed when Darlene had been in with her.

Jeff and Al sat in the waiting room patiently. Hours passed, but neither of them wanted to leave. Darlene would come out and the three of them would alternate in sitting with Marie. Jeff and Al's sitting time always seemed shorter than Darlene's time. Marie was mad at men in general. She was even mad at her doctor. He would come and examine her periodically. She wanted to hurry and have the baby, but he would only look at the machines then leave.

Marie was in labor for fourteen hours and she wasn't progressing as she should. They recommended doing a Cesarean Section operation if she didn't progress any further in the next few hours. They explained everything to her and Jeff. But after two more hours she was ready to have the baby naturally.

They took Jeff to get him prepared for the delivery room. Al and Darlene sat and waited. Al started thinking about him and Darlene having children soon and told her, "I can't wait until we have a baby."

From what Darlene had seen so far, she could wait. And wait patiently. When she held Marie's hand, she felt the pains of the contractions through her hand.

"We'll have a baby one day," she said vaguely. She did want to have a baby. Just not any time soon.

Al and Jeff had been buying sandwiches, snacks, and sodas from the cafeteria then from the vending machines all night long since the cafeteria was closed. Seven-thirty Sunday morning Jeff came in feeling very proud and announced that he had a daughter. He belated said that Marie was fine. Al and Darlene wanted to see the baby, but it would be a few minutes because they had to get her fully checked. Then Jeff went on to try and tell Al the feelings he felt when he saw his baby come into the world and when they showed him his daughter.

Darlene walked off to find the nursery. When she found it, she saw a few babies in there asleep. They all looked so small and cute. Then she saw a nurse rolling a baby up to the front. Darlene read the card and it said Baby Crawford.

Al and Jeff came up while she was looking at the baby. She pointed the baby out to them. Jeff couldn't help but to be proud. She was the baby he and Marie had been trying to have for years. They all went home to change since Marie was going to be in the recovery room for a while. Al left his car for Jeff to use and he rode home with Darlene.

They were all back at the hospital within a couple of hours. Marie had been moved to her own room. Jeff was already there when Al and Darlene walked in.

Darlene thought Marie looked worn out. A few minutes later the baby was brought in. Jeff picked her up immediately and handed her to Marie. She was a beautiful baby. Al went and stood by his sister and held his niece's little hand. He seemed to be in complete awe of her. Marie held the baby out to him and he reached down carefully and removed the sleeping baby from his sister's arms. He walked over and stood closer to Darlene. He looked from his niece to her. She saw it in his face how bad he wanted them to have a baby. And in all probability soon. She wasn't the only one to notice either. Marie looked at Jeff. He was looking at how Al was holding the baby. It was the same way he held her in the delivery room.

Darlene looked away from Al and noticed Jeff and Marie looking at her. She calmly lied about wanting to use the bathroom. There was one in the room, but she left the room before Marie could tell her.

Darlene felt as though she was suffocating in the room. She was genuinely happy for Marie and Jeff. Their baby was the prettiest baby she had ever seen. But that didn't mean she wanted to go out and have a baby. She returned back to the room knowing she couldn't stay away for too long. When she got back, she learned that Marie and Jeff had named the baby Jasmine. The baby had awakened and Jeff was changing her diaper. He seemed so at ease handling the baby. Al grabbed a hold of Darlene's hand and held it. She seemed uncomfortable for some reason, he thought. He decided they should leave, but would stop by later and visit Marie and the baby.

As the weeks passed, Al would often bring up the subject of the two of them having a baby. It would usually occur when they went to see Marie and her baby. Darlene would always point out that she wanted them to be married a year first before they tried to have a baby. Al decided to bide his time since they only had a little over a month before their first anniversary.

Darlene received a call from Darryl while she and Al were having dinner one night. Her whole face seemed to light up at hearing his voice. He told her about his mid-term grades and naturally she was proud of him. He seemed to be doing well in all of his classes. He would be home for the Thanksgiving break and he was looking forward to it. Then she received a call from Crystal with some good news. She and Carl were going to get married the following year in June and she wanted her to be matron of honor. Darlene automatically said yes, of course. But that kind of put a damper on things after she thought about it. She had told Al that they would start a family after their first anniversary. And knowing him he would want to start that night. And if she got pregnant, she wouldn't be able to stand up for her cousin. Which did she want more? To be in her cousin's wedding or have a baby?

For Thanksgiving, Darlene tried her best at cooking some of the foods her aunt had cooked the previous year. Her aunt didn't really want to do too much since it was just her and Robert. She had become so worried about him that she seemed worn down and about to just give up on him. It was only going to be the three of them. Darryl had gotten home a couple of nights ago. He spent time hanging with old friends. He was going to have dinner with Al and Darlene. She would send her aunt and Robert something to eat home with Darryl. Crystal was spending the day with Carl and his family. And Marie and Jeff were going to visit his parents with the baby.

The three of them were sitting at the table when the telephone rang. It was Eugene Miller, the man from the restaurant who had been admiring her eating skills. He wanted to know if he could meet with her the next day. She had the next day off from work, but Al didn't. She was about to ask his permission, but decided against it. He suggested taking her to lunch as opposed to coming to her apartment. She agreed and quickly wrote down the time and place. She returned to the table and finished talking about college with Darryl. Al felt left out so he left the table and went into the living room.

The next day Darlene was at the restaurant a little before noon. She couldn't remember which man was which. She was going to have to work on associating names with faces. She didn't dress as if she dressed for going to work. She wore black slacks and a red sweater. She was hoping it wasn't the man her husband didn't want her seeing. But as soon as she walked in and saw him, she knew he was the one Al didn't want her seeing.

As she neared him, she realized he wasn't that much taller than she was. A little on the husky side though. But he seemed to be nice. He wore gold-rimmed designer glasses. She didn't know why Al didn't want her to see him. He definitely didn't have a reason to be jealous, she thought.

Darlene followed him to a table. She was ready to get down to business as soon as they were seated, but he wanted her to have something to eat first. She couldn't seem to make up her mind so he suggested the club sandwich. It came with French fries and a couple of spear-shaped dill pickles on the side. Darlene wanted to get an idea of what he wanted to talk about. And from the way he was dressed, he was probably on a lunch break from work. She figured they only had an hour at most.

"What is it you wanted to see me about, Mr. Miller?" she asked, hoping she wasn't being rude or anything.

"Eugene, please," he said, insisting she call him by his first name. "I was so impressed with what I heard about you that I wanted to see what you could do for me with a little problem I'm having," he said. He didn't get to elaborate any further because their food arrived. He suggested they eat first then discuss it further after their meal.

He watched as she took one of the French fries, dipped it into some ketchup, and bit into it. He thought she had sexy lips. Darlene was oblivious to him watching her. She picked up a quarter of her sandwich and bit into it, savoring the taste of it with a moan. It had been a long time since she had eaten a club sandwich. And it tasted so good to her that she didn't bother hiding the fact.

"Do you like your sandwich?" he asked in a strained voice before taking a drink of water.

"Yeah. It's really good," she said after swallowing.

"The pickles are very good, too," he said. As far as he knew, they were no different than any other pickles. He just wanted to see her eat one. And he did.

Darlene picked up the spear and placed it in her mouth and bit into it. The juices started running down the side of her mouth and she sucked on the pickle before removing it from her mouth. She quickly grabbed her napkin and wiped her mouth. Eugene stared at her. The way she had just eaten the pickle seemed so erotic to him. He had gotten hard by just watching her. And he liked the fact that she was unaware of it. It made it all the more exciting and stimulating to him.

Once they finished their lunch, he started giving her a vague idea about his problem. While their table was being cleared, the waitress suggested dessert, but Darlene declined. That was until Eugene mentioned cheesecake. She couldn't resist then. And he enjoyed the cheesecake a lot more than she did. He had never been so turned on so quickly before. She was so innocent that she didn't have the faintest clue that she had him sexual aroused.

Darlene had to do some checking on his problem, but would get back with him. She wanted to make an appointment for him to come by her apartment in a week, but Eugene wasn't about to see her in her apartment with her husband looming around. He was determined to only see her in a restaurant, somewhere he could watch and enjoy her eat. He suggested meeting her at another restaurant the following Monday evening.

"I won't have much information by then, but I may have something by Wednesday," she suggested.

"I can't make it then," he lied. "Just show me what you'll have then. And before I forget, here," he said and pushed an envelope toward her.

She picked it up and opened it. There were two one hundred-dollar bills inside. She looked at him. It had barely been an hour and he was giving her so much money. "But—"

"I think we should call it a day," he said, cutting her off. "I'll see you Monday, Darlene. Is it okay if I call you Darlene or would you prefer Mrs. Williams?"

"Darlene's fine. But Eugene, about this," she patted the envelope that was still on the table, "I didn't do anything." Eugene knew she had done a whole lot, but he wasn't about to tell her. He looked at his watch feigning to be in a hurry to leave.

"See you Monday," he said and stood up kind of awkwardly holding his briefcase in front of him.

"Sure."

When Darlene left, she stopped at a bank to open an account. The bank had a branch close to the bank where she worked. Her regular checking account was at the bank where she worked. She wrote a check from her other account for the five hundred dollars she had gotten from Mr. Davis. She used that along with the two hundred she'd just gotten and opened a new checking account. She was going to deposit all the money she earned from her advice work into the account.

She did a little shopping when she left the bank. She decided to take advantage of her day off. She bought a planner, a file cabinet, folders, legal pads, and two fire-proof security boxes, one for her own personal papers and one for other important papers.

She went to see Marie who was still home on maternity leave. The baby was asleep and Marie was starved for adult conversation so she sat and talked with her for a couple of hours. Marie loved being with her baby all day, but she needed to talk normal for a change. Then Marie told her something that shocked her.

"I'm so glad you and Al are watching Jasmine tonight while me and Jeff go out to dinner. It's been so long since we've been out," Marie said and went on and on.

Darlene didn't know anything about her and Al watching Jasmine that night. He hadn't mentioned it to her. And she didn't have the heart to tell Marie, who seemed so excited about going out with her husband.

On the way home, Darlene kept telling herself that she wouldn't get angry with Al. She would just make him do everything and maybe he wouldn't want to rush into having a baby. When Al came home, she didn't mention anything about knowing they were baby-sitting and he didn't mention it to her either. She was almost tempted to tell him she wanted to go out just to see what his reaction would be.

Marie and Jeff came through the door with so many baby things that Darlene was wondering how long they were going to be gone. Marie looked at Darlene's confused expression and assured her they would be back that night.

Al sat on the sofa with the baby in his arms and patted a spot next to him indicating for Darlene to sit beside him. When she did, he draped one arm around her. They sat on the sofa as if they were a nice, little, happy family. And Darlene just knew Al would bring up the subject of children again. She decided to take a bath and give him some time alone with the baby. She purposely made it a long bath. She must have stayed in the bathroom for at least an hour. She had heard the baby crying, but the crying had soon stopped. She put on a nightshirt and went back in the living room and found Al feeding the baby. She felt hungry herself. She hadn't eaten since lunch earlier. She fixed a sandwich and went back to sit with Al. He was just laying the baby in the portable crib Jeff had brought over. She watched how carefully he was handling the baby. After he laid the baby down, he came and sat down beside her and started kissing her on her neck. He couldn't be in the mood, she thought. He was baby-sitting.

"Stop it, Alvin," she told him.

"Why?"

"Because you're supposed to be watching the baby that's why."

"She's sleep. C'mon, Dee," he said, running his hand across her breasts.

"And what if she wakes up?"

"Then I'll stop. We can hear her from the bedroom. C'mon," he said and took the sandwich from her hands and sat it down. Darlene got up and followed him to their bedroom. Al took off her nightshirt and laid her down on the bed. He started sucking her breasts and she shivered. He quickly took off his shirt and shoes and joined her on the bed. Darlene was ready for him. Al was about to take off his pants when he heard the baby crying. He hopped off the bed and went back into the living room, leaving Darlene laying on the bed, feeling neglected. Their lovemaking had never been interrupted. If the phone rang while they were making love, they ignored it. If there was a knock at the door, it was also ignored. She was used to them starting and finishing. She figured nothing was going to happen so she got out of the bed and picked up her nightshirt.

Al walked back in and saw her about to redress. "Why are you putting your clothes back on?"

"Isn't the baby awake?"

"No. Her pacifier came out of her mouth. She was still sleep. C'mon, baby," he said, taking the shirt from her hands. "We have a little time before Jeff and Marie get back."

"Why don't we wait until they pick up the baby, Alvin."

"I want some now though, Dee," he said and laid her back on the bed. This time he didn't waste any time with foreplay. He joined them quick. Darlene enjoyed it as much as he did. The problem was that she didn't want to stop, but Al promised her it would be a whole lot better later that night. And it was. He was ready to get in bed as soon as Marie and Jeff picked up the baby.

On Monday morning, Darlene let Al know that she would be late coming home, but he didn't question her why. She told him she was meeting a new client and he still didn't seem to be interested. She didn't bother telling him anymore.

She got to the restaurant expecting to only find Eugene. Instead she found a couple of other men. Both were white men. They looked as though they were in their mid to late twenties, but she wasn't sure. They wore suits and were average looking men. She went to the table and they stood when she neared. Eugene pulled out her chair so she could sit. Then he made the introductions.

"Darlene Williams, this is Doug O'Conner and Tom McMillian." She shook hands with them using their sir names, but they quickly wanted her to call them by their first names. She noticed the two men weren't wearing a wedding band like Eugene.

Eugene suggested they order appetizers before they ate. He informed Darlene that the shrimp cocktails there were very delicious. He remembered she had ordered it the first time they'd met. While she was eating the shrimp cocktail, she happened to notice the other two men staring at her. She thought she must have gotten some sauce on her face so she took her napkin and wiped around her mouth. She picked up the last shrimp, dipped it into the sauce and bit into it. She loved shrimp and she relished every bite. One of the men, Doug, accidentally hit his glass, spilling some of the water. He was able to stop the flow of the water with his napkin before it made too much of a mess on the table.

A waiter came by to clear their table and give them menus. Darlene didn't know what to order. Eugene did a lot of suggesting. She had trusted his choice the last time so she let him order for her while she went to the ladies' room. After she left, Eugene had a chat with his associates.

"What did I tell you?"

"You were right, Eugene. She's beautiful," Doug said. "Is she married?"

"Yes. And her husband is very observant. She would rather do business in her home, but I prefer watching her eat."

"Me, too," Doug said.

"Well, try not to be too obvious. She doesn't know that I watch her." Doug nodded in agreement.

"I didn't see anything all that special," Tom said.

"Just wait. If dinner doesn't do it for you, dessert definitely will. She loves cheesecake. And with the variety of desserts they have here she may like something else just as much."

Darlene returned back to the table and they discussed a little business. She had brought the information she had for Eugene. The other two men didn't really have anything to discuss yet.

When the waiter brought their dinner, Darlene was pleased to see that Eugene had ordered pasta and shrimp in a garlic butter sauce for her. The men ordered steaks. All the men ordered an alcoholic drink. She ordered a virgin strawberry daiquiri. They all ate and kept the conversation light. Darlene would twirl the pasta around the fork and pick up a shrimp and open her mouth to accommodate the amount of food on the fork. There were also garlic bread sticks on the table. When she placed one in her mouth and took a bite, she heard Tom groan. She looked over at him and he pretended to be full on the food. Doug had little beads of sweat on his forehead and the restaurant was comfortable.

"Would you like any dessert?" Eugene asked.

"I'm too full," she said.

He waved the waiter over and he brought the dessert cart to their table. Darlene soon found out she wasn't as full as she thought. The cart had all kinds of artificial pies and cakes on it. She ordered a piece of strawberry shortcake.

The cake looked too good to eat, Darlene thought. The whipped cream was neatly swirled atop and the strawberry glaze dripped off the sides of the cake. She took her fork and picked up a piece. She closed her eyes after her mouth closed over the piece of cake on the fork. It tasted heavenly, she thought, as she licked her lips removing any whipped cream that might have been there. "You should all try a piece," she said and they all shook their heads, not trusting their voices.

When she was finished, Tom cleared his throat and made an appointment with her. So did Doug. She took out her appointment book and scheduled them for the following Wednesday and Thursday at 6 p.m. They chose different restaurants so she wrote down the name and address. They gave her their business cards. She wrote her home and office number down for them. Eugene kept his appointments on Friday during lunch. He paid her another two hundred dollars.

"Gentlemen, I really should be going," she said, standing and they stood up also. She waved goodbye and left.

When she was gone, the three men talked amongst themselves. Tom started the conversation.

"She doesn't have any idea at all how she looks when she eats?"

"None what so ever," Eugene told him.

"I thought you were joking at first, Eugene. And her husband doesn't mind her seeing us?" Doug asked.

"I don't think so," he answered.

"But is she trustworthy?" Tom asked.

"I met her through Charles Davis and he had nothing but good things to say about her. The woman is very smart. And she was very helpful for me. It's your choice though gentlemen."

Darlene met with the two men on their scheduled nights. She enjoyed talking with them and made a few suggestions to the problems they had. And they thanked her the same way Eugene had. They made appointments the next week so she could get back with them on the information she would have for them. It was at the same restaurants. It would have been easier for them to come to her office, but they preferred discussing business in public places. She met with Eugene at the same restaurant and they discussed their business. And he made another appointment.

Later that Friday afternoon at work, Darlene was told that a new computer system was going to be installed and she would have to go to the main branch, which was in a neighboring state, to stay a week for the training. The bank would pay all expenses. She and four other employees were going. There were twenty people who worked in the section she worked in and they would go in intervals.

When she told Al the news, he didn't take it that well. Going on the business trip meant she would be leaving the week before their anniversary. He again brought up the subject of children and she promised they would talk about it when she got back from her trip. She had to call and cancel her appointments with Doug, Tom, and Eugene. They always looked forward to seeing her and were a little disappointed when she canceled. She rescheduled them for the following week.

After working hard all that week, Darlene was glad to be going home. They all flew out late that Friday evening. Al met her at the airport. Among the five of them, there were four women. And the man with her was the black man who always flirted. He and Darlene were laughing about something as they were coming through the gate from the plane.

Al had been sitting and waiting patiently for Darlene. He had missed her a lot. It was different when she was still in school. Now he had gotten used to making love to her just about every night and waking up to her every morning.

He stood up anxiously waiting for Darlene when it was announced, over the airport intercom, that her flight had arrived. He watched as the people came through the door. Then he saw his wife, smiling and laughing. She looked up and saw him and waved. The man with her looked, too. She introduced Al to her co-worker when they were closer. Al barely nodded to the man. She waved goodbye to him as he walked away. Darlene hugged Al tight after her co-worker was gone. She didn't get the welcome she had been expecting. They had been having some pretty heated phone conversations while she was gone. Al would tell her what he planned on doing to her when she got back. And she was looking forward to it. She pulled back and looked up at him and saw that he was looking past her at her co-worker. She knew then what was wrong with him. She took him by the hand and led him away to claim her luggage.

Al was quiet on the drive home. He hardly said anything. He answered the questions she asked, but he didn't initiate any conversation. The only time he did have anything to say was when he talked about his niece. Then his whole face seemed to light up.

All Darlene wanted to do when she got home was take a hot bath. But as soon as they were inside, Al wanted to make love.

"Alvin, I'm tired and I want to take a bath."

That's when he exploded. "You messin' around with that man you work with?"

She just looked at him. The question had come out of the blue and she was too stunned to answer.

"That's probably why you don't want to get off them birth control pills. You might get pregnant for somebody other than me. You been working late a lot and you're always tired. So what going on, Darlene?"

"I'm not having an affair with anybody, Alvin," she said.

"So why don't you want to have a baby?"

"It's not that I don't want to have a baby. It's—"

"What Darlene? You too busy working and having men laughing all in your face?" he said, cutting her off.

Darlene walked away from him. She went to her dresser and removed the packs of birth control pills she had. Then she got the packet out of her purse. She quietly and calmly handed them to Al. Then she left the bedroom and went into the bathroom. She was in the bathtub soaking when Al walked in. He was still holding the pills. She closed her eyes and hoped he would go away because his accusations had hurt her really bad.

"Dee?" he called softly, but she pretended not to hear him. "Baby?" he said again, walking further into the bathroom.

She turned her head toward him and said, "What?"

"Why did you give me your pills?"

"You said you wanted to have a baby. I can't get pregnant if I'm still on the pill can I. So do whatever you want to do with them," she said and started bathing.

It wasn't how Al wanted them to decide on having a baby, but it was a start. He left her alone. He went and threw all the packets of pills in the trashcan. Then he decided to carry the bag outside and put it in the trash dumpster because he didn't want her changing her mind and taking them out the trashcan.

When she walked into the bedroom, Al pulled the comforter and sheet back invitingly. She climbed in bed and Al immediately made love to her. It wasn't like the other times. Correction. It was just like their first time. And Al didn't even seem to notice that she wasn't responsive. After he rolled off of her, she turned her back to him. He didn't say anything to her and she didn't say anything to him. She was so exhausted that she was asleep in minutes.

Al laid awake a little longer. He wasn't expecting her to hand over all of her birth control pills to him. He knew she wasn't cheating on him. He had just been lonely and didn't like the fact that she had been smiling with some other man. He had planned exactly how he was going to make love to her that night, but it just didn't happen. He had gotten her an anniversary present. But now he wanted to get her something extra for what she was doing by agreeing to have a baby.

Chapter eighteen

For their anniversary, Al took Darlene to a music concert featuring her favorite singer. He had gotten the tickets weeks in advance. He took her to a nice and cozy restaurant for dinner. After dinner they went to the concert. Darlene was excited throughout the entire concert. She wore the same dress she had worn for his birthday. He had bought her a gold choke chain. And it looked great on her with that particular dress. Darlene kept her arm linked with his when they were walking and he kept his arm around her when they were sitting. He looked over at her and watched her sing along with the singer. She looked so beautiful to him. She had always been pretty to him, but she was absolutely beautiful to him now. And she was all his. And he would do anything to make sure she stayed all his.

It wasn't long before Darryl was home from college. He had passed all of his classes and he was excited to be home. At least for a while that is. Him and his brother stayed at each other's throat. Darryl didn't like the trouble his brother was putting their mother through. Even though he hated leaving his mother, he was glad to go back to school. He had talked to Darlene about the way he felt and she assured him she would look after her aunt. And she did. She saw the road Robert was heading down and she made sure her aunt had his insurance policy paid up. Darlene made sure she knew where any important papers were in case of an emergency.

As the weeks passed, Al started to complain about Darlene coming home late. To make him happy she started seeing Doug and Tom during lunch. She really didn't know why they kept making appointments with her. Sometimes they wouldn't even discuss business. They mainly asked about her likes and dislikes, her job, and her childhood.

With the beginning of a new year at hand, Darlene knew it was tax time. She made sure her and Al's taxes were filed as soon as they both received their W2s. A lot of Al's associates wanted her to do their taxes. She had to do them from her home office so she was busy for the next few months. In case anyone wanted to file electronically, she could do it from her computer. But if they didn't, she would let them drop off all the necessary information and call them if she had any questions or when she finished.

Al didn't mind that people came by because he knew most of them. Some of the people he knew had told friends and they had started calling for Darlene. She was charging a flat fee for doing the taxes for standard deductions. Itemized and large income earners paid a bit more. But when a white man knocked on the door, Al thought the man must have had the wrong door. Darlene had told Al she was expecting someone to stop by, but he thought it would be someone he knew.

Darlene was on her way to answer the door, but Al had already opened it. She walked up and greeted Doug with a smile. She had gotten to know a lot about him. He was a nice guy. Al looked at the other man then to his wife and walked away from the door. Darlene noticed Doug was holding a bag. She showed him to her office. She hadn't sat down good before Al knocked on the door and opened it. She excused herself for a few minutes. Al took a good look at Doug before she closed the door and asked, "Who's he?"

Darlene pulled him by the arm and led him to kitchen. "He's a client I work with sometimes," she told him.

"How come I ain't never seen him?"

"Because we usually work during lunch or after work."

"After work where?" Al asked not liking what he was hearing. "You been goin' to his house?"

"No, Alvin. We work at restaurants. Somewhere nice and public. So relax. This shouldn't take too long," she said and tiptoed and kissed him. Then she went back into the office where she found a strawberry cheesecake sitting on the coffee table. She looked at Doug who was smiling shyly.

"I know how much you like cheesecake so I . . ." he said and shrugged his shoulders.

"Thank you, Doug. Would you like a piece while we work on your taxes?"

"Are you going to have a piece, too?" he asked hopefully.

"Yes."

"Then I'll have a small piece."

Darlene took the cheesecake and left the room and went to the kitchen. Al saw her from the living room and followed her. He saw her get two small plates, a knife, and two forks. She cut two pieces, one larger than the other one.

"Where did that come from?" Al asked, referring to the cheesecake.

"Doug bought it for me," she told him.

"Why is he buying you a cheesecake?" Al asked suspiciously.

"Don't tell me you're jealous of Doug, Alvin." She wanted to laugh, but she didn't think he would find it funny.

"I just don't trust white people," Al stated flatly.

"I didn't know you were prejudice. Anyway, he found out that I like cheesecake from our meetings."

"You've been meetin' with him a lot?"

"Yes and I have to get back. We'll talk later." She gave him a kissed on his jaw and headed back to her office.

Doug was waiting patiently for her. He was sitting in one of the folding chairs she had Al bring in when she started having a lot of people come over. She handed him the plate with a small piece of cake and a fork and a napkin. She noticed he had turned and was facing her.

He remembered what Eugene had said about her husband and said, "Your husband doesn't seem to like that I'm here."

"It's not that. He just wasn't expecting me to work tonight," she said not wanting to hurt his feelings. He didn't ask anything else and she continued to eat her cake.

"This is the best cheesecake I've ever had," she said.

"I'll get you one anytime you want one. Just tell me," he said quickly.

"I may have to cut down on these desserts. They're too fattening."

"I don't think you have to worry about that," he said, looking at her body and admiring it. "But I can get the low fat kind if you'd like."

She didn't know where his strange behavior was coming from all of a sudden. She thought a change of subject was quite necessary so she suggested they do his taxes.

The next day Tom came by and Al reacted the same way. He had bought her bread sticks. So while she did his taxes, she ate one and Tom loved it.

Saturday evening was when Eugene came by. Al was at work. He brought her a strawberry shortcake. They had been working for an hour when she decided to take a break and get a piece of cake. So did he. They went into the kitchen to eat.

Al came in a few minutes later. And what he saw in the kitchen wasn't what he was expecting. It didn't take Al long to recognize Eugene. And even if he hadn't recognized him instantly, the way the other man was watching Darlene eat would have refreshed his memory.

Darlene looked up when she heard the door open. She smiled when she saw Al, but it died when she saw how he looked. He was angry. He had told her not to see Eugene and she was sitting in the apartment with him. He looked at her and turned and went into the bedroom. Darlene excused herself from the table and went to talk to Al. He was lying across the bed watching TV when she walked in.

"What's wrong, Alvin?" she asked concerned. Maybe he had a bad day at work, she thought. He just looked at her and turned his head. She started wondering if it was something she had done, but she couldn't think of anything. "What are you mad about?"

"I thought I told you not to see him," he said, still looking at the TV.

"I know what you said, Alvin, but you can't possibly be jealous of Eugene," she said, hoping he wasn't.

"Eugene? So you're on a first name basis with him. And I'm not jealous. I just don't like the way he looks at you."

"He has never flirted with me, if that's what you're worried about."

"He's done more than flirt."

"What are you talking about?"

"I mean he gets off by watching you eat." Darlene laughed. She didn't mean to, but she couldn't help it. "You think I'm joking?" She didn't say anything. "Is this the first time you've seen him since that night?"

"No."

"What other times then?"

"We usually work during lunch."

"How often?"

"About once a week," she said. Then she started wondering why Eugene always shied away from coming to her home to work.

"He's a pervert, Darlene. Every time you ate a piece of that damn cheesecake that night he was watching you and licking his lips."

"No he wasn't. You're making this up," she said, refusing to believe him.

"Did you meet those white guys through him?"

"Yes."

"So all three of them have probably been jerking off after meeting with you," he said angrily. "Tell him you ain't seeing him no more."

Darlene didn't like Al's attitude. She didn't tell him who to see and not see. Plus she enjoyed the extra money she was making. And the three men were nice and pleasant company. She turned and left the room.

Eugene had suspected something was wrong when she returned so he decided to end their meeting. He wanted to know if he could see her the coming Friday at their usual time and place. She hesitated a moment before she agreed. On the way out, he told her he would see her Friday just as Al was coming out of the bedroom.

He waited until she closed the front door before he grabbed her upper arm, jerking her away from the door. "He's not seeing you at all." Then his anger turned insulting. "That's unless you like him gettin' a hard on for you."

"Let go of me," Darlene said and snatched her arm loose. Then she said something she knew she shouldn't have, but she couldn't help it. "If he is getting a hard on at least it's for *me*."

"What the hell is that supposed to mean?"

"You only seem to want to make love just to make a baby. Forget about pleasing me. It's just wham, bam, thank you ma'am."

"Fuck you, Darlene," Al said and turned away.

"You already have." And before she knew what happened, he grabbed her and pulled her into the bedroom.

"So you think I've been fucking you, Darlene. Okay, let's fuck then." He threw her on the bed and she quickly hopped off. But Al was quicker and he grabbed her and threw her back on it.

"Get out," she screamed at him.

"No. I'm not goin' nowhere," he said, shaking his head. "And I'm gettin' a hard on for you, Darlene. Just like your pervert friends."

"Then go find somebody else and leave me the hell alone."

"Oh no, Darlene. You're my wife 'til death do us part. And if I want you, you're mine to have."

"Like hell I am," she said and tried to run out of the bedroom, but he stopped her. Darlene just started swinging her arms wildly, hitting him. He picked her up off the floor hugging her to him in an effort to restrain her. Then she started kicking him. One kick landed hard on his shin and at the same time she hit him in the jaw. He dropped her suddenly as a reaction from the hard hits. And when Darlene fell, her head hit the dresser. Al tried to catch her, but he couldn't. She was on the floor unconscious and Al panicked.

There was a hospital not too far from where they lived so he picked her up and carried her to the car. He was hoping he was doing the right thing. He just didn't want to go out his mind waiting for an ambulance.

Al was at the emergency room entrance in five minutes. He picked her up and carried her inside where someone immediately wheeled a gurney toward him. The staff took over from there. He had to give them information and tell them what happened.

Al had to wait while they examined Darlene. It was only then that he realized he only had on pants, an undershirt, and socks. He didn't think about anything other than getting Darlene to the hospital.

Darlene had regained consciousness in the examination room. She was disoriented at first. Then she heard someone telling her where she was. She remembered her and Al arguing then him picking her up. But then all she remembered was falling. And now she had a headache from hell. It felt like her head was growing and growing and any minute it would explode.

They wanted to keep her overnight for observations since she had a head injury. She would be able to see her husband in a few minutes. The way her head was pounding she didn't want to see anyone. The nurse had given her something to relieve the pain, but it hadn't taken affect yet.

Al walked into the room very cautiously. Darlene was lying on the bed. She looked like she was sleeping. He didn't want to wake her up so he sat in the chair next to her bed. It squeaked a little and she turned toward him. He looked different to her for some reason. Then it dawned on her what it was. He looked scared. She had never known him to be scared of anything.

Al was looking at her wondering what she was thinking. He moved the chair closer to the side of her bed.

"Dee, baby, are you okay?"

"My head hurts," she said in a sleepy voice.

"I'm sorry. It was an accident. I tried to catch you," he said.

She started remembering the whole episode. All the mean and nasty things he had said to her. "Leave me alone," she said and turned her head and closed her eyes.

That was a slap in the face to Al. In that instant, he thought she was going to leave him. He felt paralyzed to the spot he was in.

Darlene knew he hadn't left. But she refused to look at him. At that moment, she didn't care what he was thinking or feeling. And to show him exactly that she turned her back to him. And a minute or two later she felt him lean over and kiss the side of her face then he was gone.

Al didn't quite know how he got home, but he did. All the way home he kept thinking about what he would do if Darlene left him. He didn't like those thoughts so he decided he wouldn't let her leave him. He would make this up to her. He knew he didn't mean the things he had said, but she didn't. His pride was hurt and he had lashed out at her. Visiting hours was over so he didn't go back to the hospital that night. But he was there the first thing the next morning. He bought her some flowers and hoped she liked them.

Darlene hadn't long finished eating breakfast when a doctor came in and checked on her. She looked fine and everything seemed okay. She could leave that day, but she should stay in bed for the rest of the day.

Al walked in with a basket of flowers while the doctor was still there. The doctor repeated what he'd just told her for Al's benefit. He also had a prescription for pain medication when she checked out. Al sat the flowers on a table next to her bed and sat down on the bed this time.

"How do you feel?"

"All right."

"You need anything? You want me to do anything?"

"No."

"Are you ready to go home?"

She didn't answer. She just looked at the wall not saying anything. She had thought about everything that was said and had happened the day before. And to be honest, she was scared to go back home.

"Dee?"

"Why did you do what you did?"

It was time to be honest, Al thought. To hell with his pride. If he wanted to keep his wife, he'd better tell her exactly how he felt.

"I wasn't going to do anything, Dee. It just made me mad to know what those perverts were doing. And if one of them was to touch you . . ."

"They haven't, Alvin. I think they just enjoy my company. And I get paid good money for helping them."

"Forget the money."

"Will you forget the money and stop doing what you're doing?" she asked.

Al got off of the bed and walked to the window. His back was facing her. “I can’t, Darlene,” he said with no explanation at all.

“Not even for me, Alvin?” she asked, hoping he would say ‘I’ll do anything for you’ then agree to stop dealing with drugs.

“It’s not that easy, Dee. I just can’t right now.”

“Then when? In a few weeks? A few months?” she asked very hopeful.

“I don’t know,” he said, raising his voice as if her questions were aggravating him.

“Do you love me, Alvin?” she asked.

Al turned around and faced her and said, “You know I do.”

“Then why?” she asked. For an answer he turned his back on her again. She didn’t ask again. Her eyes burned with tears and one tear rolled down her face.

Al turned around before she could wipe it away. “Baby, I’m sorry,” he said and moved closer to her.

“You don’t have to be sorry. Could you get my clothes out of that closet for me,” she said changing the subject. She now knew where she stood with him—second.

Al went to the nurse’s station to get the necessary paperwork they had for her. Then he went back to the room to make sure Darlene was ready. On the drive home, she sat in the car and didn’t say anything. When they got home, she went straight to the bedroom to lay down. It was in her fetal position. And when Al saw her lying like that, he knew she was hurt. He just didn’t know what to do about it since he was the one to cause it this time. He walked over and climbed in bed and arched himself behind her. She was about to move away from him, but he begged her not to and she didn't.

Later that day Darlene woke up hungry. She was about to get up, but she felt Al behind her. It was still daylight outside. She moved his hand intending to get up and it woke him up.

"What's wrong?" he asked, tightening his hold on her.

"Nothing. I have to go to the bathroom," she said and got up.

Al was following her when the telephone rang. He answered the living room extension while Darlene was in the bathroom.

"Hello?"

"Hi, Al."

"Hey, Marie."

"You and Darlene busy tonight?"

"Why?"

"Me and Jeff were invited to some function and I was wondering if you two wanted to watch the baby tonight."

"Not tonight. We had an accident here last night and Darlene had to go to the hospital—"

"The hospital? Is she all right? What happened?" she asked not letting him finish.

"She's fine. She hit her head and was knocked out. She just came home, but she has to stay in bed today."

"Tell her I'll see her at work—"

"She's not going to work tomorrow. And tell Jeff I won't be in either."

"Okay. I'll call tomorrow. Bye, Al."

Darlene had come out of the bathroom while he was on the phone and went back in the bedroom. Her head was still hurting.

Al checked the bathroom and didn't see her so he went back to the bedroom. She had turned on the TV and started watching it.

"Where are my pain pills?" she asked and he got her one and some water.

"Are you hungry?"

"Yes. I'd like a burger and fries."

Al kissed her and left.

On his way to get her something to eat, he saw a billboard advertising new homes for sale. He drove to the area and looked at the houses. They were all nice looking. He wrote down the name of the Real Estate Company. He knew Darlene would love having a house. He didn't know how many rooms they had, but they weren't all that expensive. At least the starting price on the billboard wasn't. He'd bring up the subject of house hunting with Darlene when he got home.

Darlene had decided to take a shower after Al left. She was tired and hungry and her medicine hadn't started working. She wished the pills worked instantaneous. She was lying in bed under the covers when she heard the key in the door. Al walked in with her food on a tray. She would have preferred a piece of either her strawberry cheesecake or strawberry shortcake to go along with it but she didn't say anything. He had gotten something for himself also. He sat in bed next to her.

"Dee?"

"Hmm?" she answered after biting into her sandwich.

"I saw some newly built houses and I thought maybe we could take tomorrow off from work to go and look at them."

"Why?"

"Because I think we should get a house."

"There is nothing's wrong with living here."

Al put his tray down on the floor beside the bed. He took hers also. Darlene was wondering what he was doing. He laid his head on her lap and held her tight. He started saying how sorry he was for saying the things he had said and for how he had acted. Then he did something that shocked her. He raised up and looked at her and almost begged her not to leave him.

"What makes you think I'm leaving you?"

"I don't know. You were so mad the other night that I thought . . ."

"If I were to leave because I get mad and we argue, I would have left you a long time ago, Alvin."

Somehow that made him feel better. She wasn't leaving him. He was so relieved.

"So do you want to start looking for a house tomorrow?"

"Yes."

"Good. I'll call your job and tell them you won't be at work. Doctor's orders."

"But that was only for today."

"So. They don't know that." He handed her the tray and he picked up his. Soon after eating, Darlene went to sleep. Her medication finally kicked in.

Monday morning, Darlene woke up feeling a lot better. Al was already dressed and she thought he had changed his mind about the house.

"Where are you going?"

"I have something to do before we go look at houses. We will go and talk to the Realtor at one o'clock." Al made a call to the Real Estate office that handled the houses. He wanted to know in advance what would be the minimum down payment for any of the houses. The lady was nice and polite and told him the different price ranges of the houses and the monetary down payment that coincided with each.

"You've already made an appointment?" she asked in disbelief.

"Yeah."

"But where are you going now?"

"We need a down payment if you see a house you want, so I'm going make sure I can get it today if necessary."

"But—"

He cut her off by kissing her. "I've already called your job. I should be back," he looked at his watch and saw it was nine o'clock, "at about ten o'clock. We'll get something to eat while we're out." He kissed her again then he left.

The houses were all beautiful. They were being built in a new area that was between the city and the suburbs. It was quieter than the city, but not as isolated as the suburbs. Darlene liked the location. All of the houses had fireplaces. The exterior of the houses was made of brick and wood. Some with more of one than the other. Darlene wrote down the house numbers of all the houses she wanted to see on the inside.

It was almost noon by the time they were finished looking. They went to a seafood restaurant and ate lunch. Darlene was so excited she couldn't stop talking about the house. She thought about the money she had in her mutual fund.

"Alvin?"

"Hmm?"

"I can help with the down payment. I have money—"

"*I'm* buying the house for *you*. Let me, baby. Let it be my early Valentine's Day present to you."

"I love you."

"I know, Dee. Believe me, I know." And he did. He knew that if the roles were reversed he would have left her. But not matter what he accused her of or how mad and jealous he got she stayed with him.

They were at the Realtor's office promptly at one o'clock. A few of the houses on Darlene's list were scratched off because they were sold. Since the houses were almost finished they sold quickly. She wrote a few descriptions next to the house numbers she liked. There were three houses she really liked. The agent showed them the floor plans. Two of them were basically the same and were priced the same. The other one was quite different. It was one of the two-story houses she had seen. The other two had been marked off her list. With keys in hand, the agent took them to see the houses.

They saw the one she really liked first and she was hooked. It had three bedrooms, all upstairs, a living room, dining room, kitchen, den, two and a half baths, a utility room, a two-car garage, and a nice backyard. All Al had to do was see how she fell in love with the house instantly and knew it was the house he was going to get for her. He didn't care that it cost more than the other two. It wasn't by much. It was only a few thousand dollars more, but that was no big deal to him.

Back at the office, the real estate agent had to do a credit check. When she told them how much the down payment was Al didn't bat an eye. He just agreed to have it for her if everything checked out. And of course everything did.

Chapter nineteen

Darlene put most of the furniture she had in storage in the other two bedrooms. Her office would now be set up in the den. The only major purchase made was buying a dining room set. She had a washer and dryer and refrigerator in storage. The dinette set Al had went in the kitchen. Marie went shopping with her for an entire dining room set. In fact, Marie helped her decorate the house. Darlene always did like Marie's house so she asked her for help. And usually on Saturdays or Sundays, they would go shopping. They would bring the baby with them on Saturdays, but Jeff would keep her on Sundays.

Darlene wanted to buy as much as she could herself so she used her checking account with the money from her extra work. She had more than five thousand dollars in that account. She bought curtains for the other bedrooms and carpeting for the master bedroom's bathroom floor. Mirrors and tables were bought for the living room and foyer. And all that plus a few other items about cut that account balance in half. She was working so hard at fixing up the house that it started taking a toll on her. She was exhausted. Her workload at the bank had picked up and every night she would do a little something at home.

Al came home from work one Saturday and found her on a stepstool hanging curtains in one of the bedrooms. She turned when she heard him come in, but she turned too fast and felt a little dizzy and she slipped. Al caught her this time. He thought it was probably some delayed reaction from when she hit her head. She tried telling him that was nearly two months ago, but he didn't want to hear it. He helped her downstairs and put her in the car and drove her to the hospital.

When they got to the hospital, Darlene was seen quickly. She told the doctor what happened. He started asking her other questions. And one question he asked left her stumped. With the moving into their new house and the decorating, she hadn't notice that her period hadn't come. As far as she could remember, February was the last time she recalled having her period. But it was now April.

The doctor got a urine sample and ran a few tests and sure enough Darlene was pregnant. At first she was in shock when the doctor told her, but then she thought about how happy Al would be.

Al had been sitting in the waiting room for about an hour wondering what could be wrong with his wife. If it had anything to do with her hitting her head he would never forgive himself. Then he started feeling bad about not helping her more at home. But he didn't know anything about decorating a house. He looked up and saw her approaching. He walked toward her and hugged her saying how sorry he was. And that she wouldn't be there again if it weren't for him. She didn't mean to make him feel bad. She was only joking when she said, "You're right this time, Alvin. It is your fault."

That was like a slap in the face to Al. He removed his arms from around her waist and walked away from her, out of the hospital, leaving her there. Darlene didn't know what was wrong with him. She followed him out to the parking lot and to the car. He got in and waited until she got in then started the car without saying a word. She wondered what could be wrong with him. He was getting what he has wanted for months. Maybe he had changed his mind about a baby, she thought.

"Alvin, what's wrong?"

"I told you how sorry I was for what happened and you just go ahead and blame me anyway," he said angrily.

Now she was getting the picture. He was hurt by what she said. "Oh, Alvin," she said, placing her hand on his arm. "I didn't mean it the way it sounded. I meant that it was your fault this time because I'm pregnant."

Why didn't she wait until they were at home to tell him the news? They were at a traffic light and the light was red. It turned green while she was telling him and he hit the brakes. The car behind them ran into the back of them. Al turned horror-stricken eyes toward Darlene, but she quickly assured him that she was fine. They got out to see how much damage was done.

The driver of the other car was an elderly lady. At first Al was mad, but Darlene pointed out that he was really at fault so he calmed down. There was no damage to the lady's car, but one of the taillights on Al's car was broken.

The lady was getting her insurance company's name and number to give to him. She had honestly thought she had caused the accident. She had been looking down at something on the passenger seat. When she glanced up, the light had changed and she just accelerated. If she had been paying more attention, she would have seen Al stop.

Since nothing was wrong with her car and it was only a light broken on his car, he wasn't worried about it. The lady didn't seem to believe him and she was insistent on giving him her insurance information. He then lied to convince the lady by implying that his brother would fix the damage to his car for free. The lady thanked him and Darlene. This time Darlene did the driving. He just sat in the car in a daze.

"Alvin?" Darlene called to him. "Are you okay?"

"Yeah." He didn't say anymore until they were home which was about fifteen minutes later. They were living a little further away from the hospital now.

When they got home, Al went to the kitchen and got a beer. For some reason Darlene thought he would be jumping for joy. After all, he was the one who wanted a baby. She didn't know what else to say. He had been asking her whether or not she was pregnant just about every week. That was why she was able to remember her period the first two months of the year. Then he stopped asking. She didn't think anything of it. That was probably why she had forgotten that it hadn't come. She decided to go back upstairs and finish in the bedroom she'd started with.

Al sat and wondered about how long had she been pregnant. He wondered why she didn't tell him or would he have only found out when she started showing. He remembered how happy his sister had been when she found out she was pregnant. But Darlene didn't look happy at all. He knew she didn't even want to have a baby so soon. He realized this was the third time he has gotten her to do something she didn't really want to do. First, it was their engagement. Next, it was the wedding. He knew she would have rather waited until she had graduated, but he didn't want to wait. And now it was this baby. She had wanted to put it off. But she gave in after his unforgivable accusations. She just gave him all of her pills and said nothing.

After the first two months, he thought she was using some other kind of birth control since she hadn't gotten pregnant. There had been so many men calling to talk with her and coming to see her that he got suspicious. Deep down he knew it was only business, but he was jealous. He knew a lot of women liked making their men or husbands jealous. But not once since he and Darlene have been together had she done that. And she never seemed to be jealous at all. Well, there was that one time before they were married. But it was nothing compared to the many times he had behaved like a jealous fool. And now she was pregnant. At least he wouldn't worry about being jealous any more. Other than his sister, all the women Al usually saw pregnant didn't look pretty anymore. And with that thought in mind, he went to look for his wife.

Darlene had slid the curtains on the rod and was about to hang them up. She had just stepped on the bottom step of the stepstool when Al came in.

"Don't get up there, Darlene," he said. "I'll hang it up. You almost fell the last time you were up there," he said, coming forward and taking the curtains away from her. He climbed up and hung the curtains. After that he stepped down and pulled her to him and asked, "Why didn't you tell me you were pregnant?"

"Because I didn't know myself. And when I told you, you seemed like you weren't all that happy," she said in his chest.

He pulled back so he could look down at her. "You thought I wasn't happy?" She nodded. "I'm more than happy. When are you due?"

"I don't know yet. I have to call and make an appointment with an obstetrician."

"Can I come?" he asked.

"Why?"

"Because I want to," he said without any further explanation.

"Sure. I think I'll stop for now and get something to eat."

"Let's go out and celebrate," Al suggested. They hadn't been out in a while. She was usually too tired and didn't feel like going anywhere. Darlene really didn't feel like cooking anything so she agreed.

It was only six o'clock in the evening when they left. They went to a nice restaurant and had a delicious meal. Al wanted to go to his sister's house and tell them the good news.

Jeff answered the door. He hardly ever worked late anymore if he could help it. To him his wife and daughter were the two most important people in his life. He had even cut back on a lot of the business he did with Al.

"Hey you two. We just called your house. We wanted you to come over," Jeff said as they walked inside the house.

"We wanted to talk to you and Marie, too," Al said.

Marie was in the living room with the baby. There were toys and stuffed animals inside the playpen with her. If anyone indulged a baby, it was those two. The baby screamed in delight when she saw Al and Darlene, especially toward Darlene. As much delight as a six-month-old baby could show that is. When Darlene and Marie were shopping and decorating, she always played with and held the baby. And now she went over and picked her up out of the playpen and was rewarded with smiles and giggles. She raised her up in the air. She knew that was something Jasmine liked. Al went over and took the baby saying she was too heavy for her to be lifting over her head. Darlene was about to protest, but Jeff wanted them to have a seat.

When they were seated with Jasmine sitting on Darlene's lap, Jeff announced that he and Marie wanted them to be their daughter's godparents. Darlene was speechless. Al wasn't though. He quickly told them yes and asked them to be godparents to their baby. Marie and Jeff were happy for them. Marie wanted Darlene to let her know when she found out when the baby is due. Darlene tried her best to keep her attention on the baby on her lap. Maybe she would have wanted someone else to be godparents to her child. She didn't have anything against Marie and Jeff being her child's godparents. It was just the way Al handled the situation. He didn't bother discussing it with her. Then why should he. He always seemed to get what he wanted anyway, she thought. And it was starting to wear a little thin.

Al went with Darlene to her doctor's appointment and they found out her baby was due the first week in December. He wanted to go and buy baby furniture that day, but she told him it was too early for that. Now she would have to eventually put the furniture from one of the bedrooms back into storage since one of the rooms was going to be for the baby.

She went to visit her cousin to see how the wedding plans were coming along and to tell her about her news. Crystal was happy for Darlene. She told her that she could get her last fitting for her dress about two weeks before the wedding. Darlene had been fitted for her dress months ago, but she had probably gained weight due to her pregnancy. She didn't notice any weight gain, but the seamstress would have to make sure the dress fit. They talked about everything that had happened in the past year and a half. The only sore spot of their conversation was Robert. He had gotten worse. Between work and the wedding, Crystal hadn't been by her mother's house that often. And with Darryl back at school, Darlene hadn't been around as much as she used to. Her aunt had all but given up on Robert. She didn't know if he was still going to school or not. Some nights he would come home and some nights he wouldn't. Darlene thought about getting Al to talk to her cousin, but that would be hypocritical. That would be the pot calling the kettle black, she thought so she decided to visit her aunt more often.

When she would see Robert hanging on street corners, she would make him leave.

Darlene had been suffering from morning sickness for the past month and her cousin's wedding was only a few days away. Darryl came home from college with a 3.0 grade point average. He decided to major in art and was considering pledging one of the fraternities.

The wedding was nice, but the reception was better. This was the first time Darlene and Al had been out dancing in months. The reception was held in a nice and spacious hall. Darlene was having a good time. Her pregnancy wasn't showing yet. And the dress her cousin had picked out for her to wear was strapless and figure hugging. The wedding colors were peach and cream. The other four bridesmaids' dresses were all peach, made with satin and lace material. The lace overlapped the satin. Darlene's dress was cream with peach lace. All the dresses were made differently. Crystal picked the dresses according to her friends' personalities. And the one she picked for Darlene was perfect for her, sweet and sexy. Al thought so. And so did half the men in attendance.

During a toast made by the best man, everyone in the bridal party had champagne. Then everyone in the bridal party danced with their partners after the bride and groom danced. Some of the people were married, but it didn't seem to bother anyone. The best man was single and handsome. He was Carl's best friend. He had been subtly flirting with Darlene at the rehearsal and the rehearsal dinner that was at Carl's parents' house, which Al didn't attend.

During the dance, he was caressing Darlene's bare shoulder a bit more than necessary. They were all still holding their glasses. She was wondering how he was maneuvering the glass and caressing her back without spilling champagne all over her. She looked around and saw Al looking directly at her. The song was almost over so she stopped the dance and went to her husband. She knew he didn't like the dancing. She felt how tense his body was when she hugged him. It took him a while to notice the glass in her hand.

"What's that?" he asked, looking at the contents.

"Champagne. We had a toast—"

"You shouldn't be drinking while you're pregnant," he said flatly. He also thought she shouldn't have worn that sexy dress since she was pregnant. And to drive the point home he attempted to pull up the bodice.

She slapped his hand away and asked, "What are you doing?"

"All your titties are showing. And that guy you was dancin' with was gettin' an eye full."

"It's not my fault my breasts are getting bigger." And they were. She had cleavage for days showing. "If it'll make you feel any better, I'll put your coat on." Al had worn black slacks, a black collarless shirt with a beige sports coat. She didn't have to ask twice. He quickly shrugged out of it and helped her put it on.

The hall was very well air-conditioned. She was a little cool, but she really didn't need his coat. She kept it on throughout the rest of the reception. Crystal and Darryl questioned her and she told them she was getting chills being almost naked up top.

Al and Darlene danced together the rest of the night. Al didn't really drink much that night. The times he left to get a drink for himself or Darlene he would return to find some man talking to his wife. So he decided not to leave her side.

For the Fourth of July, Jeff and Marie had a barbecue at their house. Marie was nice enough to extend an invitation to Crystal and her husband. She insisted they bring their daughter so her daughter would have someone to play with. A few friends and associates of Al and Jeff's were at this party. No one from the bank or dealership was there.

Darlene was four months pregnant and starting to show. She bought a maternity swimsuit that didn't look maternal at all. It wasn't that different from a regular swimsuit. It was loose around the stomach, but it didn't look too baggy. Granted no one seven to nine months pregnant would be able to wear it. Darlene knew she would only wear it a few times and she wouldn't be that far along in her pregnancy. She hadn't liked the other suits she'd seen. And the one she liked, which was solid black on the bottom and black with small white polka dots on the top with spaghetti straps was kind of cute. Plus, she didn't look pregnant in it.

Al liked the way the pregnancy was having its affect on Darlene's body. He never had any complaints in the past, but the way her body was changing he liked it all the more. Her breasts had grown and her hips that were almost non-existent were beginning to noticeably show. He saw how other men were looking at her, but he remained calm. At least for a while. He noticed that often she would engage in a conversation with some of the men and a card would exchange hands.

Darlene went inside because she had to use the bathroom. Al was waiting for her when she came out.

"Hey," she said happily.

"What did that guy want?"

"What guy?" she asked because she had talked to a number of men that day.

"The one that's in your face every time I looked around. That tall one."

"It was business," she said and was about to walk off.

"Yeah, I bet. You've been doing nothing but business almost everyday. Especially with your pervert friends. And let's not forget the ones whose names I haven't heard of before."

Darlene had only taken a few steps away before she turned around and stood there and looked at him. How would he know how often she saw people? And who she saw? She had never thought that she had to hide her appointment book from him.

"How do you know who I see and when I see them?"

"Because I looked in your book," he said not caring if she thought him to be nosy or not. "If you're not having lunch with somebody, you're having dinner, or closed up in the den. Maybe I should schedule an appointment with you."

Darlene was raging mad. First, because he had the nerve to look through her book. Then, because he seemed to be mad because she was working a lot. Most of the people she was seeing were people he knew. And those were the flirty ones. Not her "pervert friends" as he put it. But she didn't tell him that. And finally, she would check with him before she made appointments after work with anyone to make sure he didn't have anything planned for them. She never planned more than a week in advance.

"I can't believe you looked through my book," she said in disbelief.

"Why? You had something in it you didn't want me to see?"

She wondered why he was trying to start an argument. But if it was an argument he wanted, she wasn't in the mood for one.

"I want to go home. I'll be waiting in the car," she said and pushed past him. And that's exactly where she was. Sitting in the car. Al went back to the backyard and told his sister Darlene wasn't feeling well so they were heading home. It wasn't exactly a lie. Her moods weren't all that good the farther along she was getting in her pregnancy.

Darlene didn't say anything to him in the car. Al drove home in deep thought wondering why couldn't his wife get fat and out of shape when she was pregnant, why did she have to look prettier, and why did she have to be so smart in money matters. She had their money invested, in tax-free accounts, and other shelters. At least with the money she was aware of. Al had assets she didn't know anything about.

When they got home, Darlene had cooled off and was in the mood for love. Al never could figure out how she could be mad with him, but when she wanted to make love none of that mattered. And he was ready. Or so he thought. Darlene was acting as if they were in a marathon for sex. She didn't want to stop. Al tried prolonging it with foreplay, but she wanted him inside her. After two back to back sessions, he was tired on his back, but that didn't stop her. She just straddled him. After an hour, Al was too tired to get it up. Darlene was frustrated because she wanted more. And that only started an argument. With the end result of Al getting up and leaving the house. It happened about twice a month or so for the next two months.

Al would usually drive around or stop and get a drink. He didn't know what had gotten in to Darlene. Their sex life had always been good. He thought it was perfect. They both satisfied each other. But now . . .. Now she was like a nymphomaniac, he thought. During the times in between her sexual overload, their sex life was the same as it had always been. They were both satisfied. But on the times when she wasn't satisfied he just knew she thought about leaving him or at least getting satisfaction somewhere else. But so far she hadn't left him or given any inclination of doing so.

Tragedy struck Darlene's family in her ninth month of pregnancy. It was the Sunday before Thanksgiving. Darryl was due to come home from college the following Tuesday night. Darlene hadn't long gotten to her aunt's house. They were discussing recipes. She was going to have Thanksgiving dinner at her house again. But this time she had invited Crystal and Carl, Marie and Jeff, and of course Darryl, Robert, and her aunt. She had been talking to her aunt when Robert came inside. Her aunt's whole demeanor seemed to change. She had been full of smiles, but not anymore. She pleaded with him to stay inside that night and talk a while, but he walked out the house as if he didn't hear her. And that was impossible because he passed right by her when she said it.

Twenty minutes later Darlene decided it was getting late and got up to leave. But before they reached the door, they heard gunshots. Darlene was scared. She had gotten so used to not hearing gunshots where she lived that it was quite frightening for her to hear the shots sounding so close. But her aunt didn't seem to be concerned. She just calmly sat back down on the sofa and started singing gospel hymns.

Darlene wanted to know what had happened outside, but she was worried about her aunt. She sat back down beside her aunt, but all her aunt said was that her baby was gone. Darlene went to the door to see if she could at least see Robert. All she saw was a crowd on the corner from her aunt's house.

One of the neighbors came walking toward the house. Darlene felt tears burning her eyes and blurring her vision. And then she knew that her aunt was telling the truth. She tried her best to hold herself together. At least until she could get a hold of her husband or Crystal. A neighbor came and sat with her aunt while she used the phone. She called 911 and told them what happened. She called her house and told Al what had happened and he left immediately. Then she called Crystal. She was so glad that Carl answered the phone. They were on their way, too.

Darlene and Crystal sat and cried. Al and Carl went down to the corner to see if they could find out what happened. All they were told was that some guys drove by and got out the car and started shooting and then left. Robert was dead on the scene with multiple gunshot wounds.

Darlene handled all the necessary funeral arrangements. She had suggested they wait until after the Thanksgiving holiday to have a burial, but her aunt didn't want to prolong it. Darlene wanted to go up to the school and get Darryl, but Al and Carl volunteered.

The wake service was that following Tuesday night. Darlene stayed with her aunt and Darryl that night. She was off work all that week. They went to the funeral parlor that night. There were a lot of people in attendance, especially a lot of high school kids. Darlene sure hoped they would learn something from Robert's death.

Darlene saw Marie and Jeff. They questioned her about Al's whereabouts. She was wondering the same thing herself. She had told him where the service was going to be held and at what time. But he hadn't shown up yet. Darryl escorted his mother to the front pew while Carl escorted Darlene and Crystal. Darlene had never felt so alone in her life. Here she was nine months pregnant and grieving and her husband was no where in sight. A lot of the people were sympathetic toward her because of her condition. They, along with her family, thought the trauma would be too hard on her. She didn't worry about anything because she knew she would have her husband beside her. So she thought.

During the service, Crystal couldn't take it anymore. She broke down. Carl had to almost carry her out. That left Darlene alone. At least until Vincent came and sat beside her. She was so happy to see a friendly face that she just used him for comfort. He had heard about the killing and found out that it was her cousin. He thought he should pay his respects. He placed his arm around her shoulder and she leaned on him. Suddenly she didn't feel so alone anymore.

Al had been doing business that night. He thought he would have been finished in time to meet Darlene at the services, but he wasn't. It was late when he arrived at the funeral parlor. The family was viewing the deceased. As he stood in the back, he felt as cold as the body in the casket when he saw his wife being led to the casket by another man. A man he recognized. A man who was holding her tight against him as if to absorb all of her hurt and pain. That was his job, he thought. He was her husband. He should be there for his wife. Then why wasn't he? Al didn't like the answer that came to mind to that question so he just turned around and left.

At the end of the service, people gathered and had coffee and cake. Darlene was exhausted. She didn't want Darryl leaving her aunt to bring her home so she asked Vincent would he give her a ride home. She waited inside until he went to get his truck and bring it to the front of the building. While he did that, she let her family know she was leaving and that she would see them the next morning.

Al's car was in the driveway when Vincent pulled up. He didn't mention it and she thought that was very considerate of him. She hadn't seen him in a while. In fact, not since he had fixed her car. And that was more than a year ago. But he acted like they had been in contact with each other often.

“Are you going to be up to going to the cemetery tomorrow?”

“Yeah. And thank you, Vincent. I’m sorry about messing up your clothes,” she said. She had done a lot of crying. In fact, there had been a lot of crying going on. It was mostly from the young people.

“Don’t worry about it,” he said and looked toward the house. “Are you going to be all right tonight?” he asked a little concerned.

His concern touched her and she appreciated it. But she figured he was concerned because she was pregnant that’s all.

“I’ll be fine. Good night, Vincent. And thanks again,” she said and began to remove her seat belt.

“Wait. I’ll come around and help you out,” he said and was out and around before she could protest.

Al had heard someone drive up. The house was practically dark with the exception of the foyer and porch light. He stood by the bedroom window and looked out and noticed that they didn’t instantaneously get out the truck as soon as it stopped. Then he watched as the same man from the wake service help his wife out of the truck and walk her to the door. He couldn’t see them once they were at the door. But he noticed it was taking the other man a long time before he walked away from the door. Al was imagining them standing on the doorstep kissing. Never mind the fact that his wife was pregnant. He still found her to be attractive so why wouldn’t other men? Finally, he heard the front door open and close and then saw the other man walk back to his truck and drove off.

Darlene slowly made her way upstairs. She wasn’t up to arguing with Al or hearing any explanations or excuses from him. She just wanted to go to sleep. She went into the other bedroom and took off her dress. She hung it up neatly in the closet because she was going to wear it the next day because that was the only black maternity dress she had. She took off her shoes and pantyhose and laid on the bed in her slip, bra, and panties.

After Darlene didn't come into the bedroom, Al searched the house. He found her in the other bedroom. He stood and watched her sleep for a few minutes then he went to bed.

Darlene woke up early the next morning and started getting ready to leave. She didn't bother checking to see if Al was going with her or not. She just put her clothes on and left. At her aunt's house, everyone was so wrapped up in their own sorrow that they didn't ask her about Al. And she was glad.

They were all outside, with the exception of Betty, waiting for the limousine when Al pulled up. He looked mad. And for the first time Darlene really didn't care. She barely spared a glance in his direction. He stood by her and put his arm around her, but she subtly pushed away and went into the house. Soon the limo arrived and they all got inside, including Al.

The service was short and they were soon on their way back home. Al tried to console Darlene, but he was a day too late. When she really needed to be consoled, he wasn't there. And now she didn't want him to touch her.

Friends brought over pots and pans of food. They offered their condolences and stayed and talked. Darlene avoided Al as much as possible. He wasn't stupid. He knew she was avoiding him. He had to leave so he cornered her in the kitchen. She didn't say anything. She barely stopped from flinching when he kissed her lips before he left.

Darlene stayed with her aunt until everyone had gone with the exception of the family. Crystal convinced her to go on home because she looked tired on her feet. She didn't argue the point. Her aunt told her not to bother with cooking for Thanksgiving because she could take some of the food they had there. People had brought small turkeys with stuffing, pies, hams, and a lot of other foods. Carl and Darryl loaded some of the food in her car and she left.

It didn't bother Darlene in the least that when she drove up to her house she didn't see Al's car. She knew then that things had changed drastically in their marriage. She opened the front door and started unloading her car. She sat most of the foods on the stove and the counter. Any foods that were in non-disposable pans, she transferred to her own pans or dishes then she washed them in the dishwasher so she could return them to her aunt's neighbors and friends. She finally fixed something to eat. She didn't get around to eating nothing much that day now that she thought about it. And at her aunt's house she was waiting on others in order to keep herself busy and away from Al. But it was catching up with her.

Chapter twenty

Darlene had just finished eating when she heard the front door open and close. It was eight o'clock at night. She had been home alone since six o'clock that evening. She got up and went upstairs to her bedroom to take a shower. She was glad that there was a stairway that led from the kitchen to upstairs. She had just slipped into her nightgown when the bathroom door opened. She looked at Al only to acknowledge he was there. Then she walked past him to get to the bedroom. She turned on the TV and got in bed. Al stood there dumb-founded because she was practically ignoring him. Forget practically. She was definitely ignoring him. So he went and took a shower.

Darlene didn't bother pretending to be asleep when he came out. She just continued to watch television. Al got in bed and laid close to her and she moved away from him. He moved even closer. This time she got out of the bed.

"Where are you going?" he asked. She didn't answer. She just looked at him. Then she turned her head. He got out of bed only wearing his briefs. "I asked you a question?"

"I'm going where I can watch TV in peace." And with that she walked out the door and headed downstairs to the living room. Al slipped on a pair of pants and followed her.

Darlene was sitting on the sofa with the remote control in her hand. She started flipping through the cable channels, but she couldn't find anything on TV she really wanted to see. Then Al came downstairs. He sat next to her and tried to talk to her, but she kept her eyes focused on the TV. He tried to take the remote control from her, but she wouldn't let him. He stood in front of the TV, but it didn't stop her from flipping through the channels.

"Give me the remote control," he said, but she ignored him. Then he demanded it in a harsher voice. He got it then. She threw it at him. "What the hell is wrong with you?" he yelled after he ducked out of the way of the flying remote.

"You wanted it, didn't you," she said sarcastically.

"What's with you? You been acting funny since last night."

"Nothing's wrong, Alvin. What makes you think something could be wrong?"

"You tell me."

"There is nothing to tell."

"I think there's a lot to tell. Like for one, why was that guy, Vincent I think that's his name, bringing you home?"

He was back to his same old jealous self, she thought. She didn't care anymore. "He brought me home because I didn't have anyone else to bring me home. God only knew where my husband was."

"Oh, I was there, but you didn't look as if you needed me there."

Darlene knew she hadn't seen him there. "What are you talking about?"

"You were all hugged up with Vincent. What was I supposed to do?"

"You were *supposed* to be there with me. You were *supposed* to come to me when you got there. I needed someone to lean on. I needed *you* to lean on. So tell me Alvin, where were you?"

"I had business to take care of."

"And this business was so important that you couldn't be with me when I needed you the most?" She didn't give him a chance to answer. "And what was so important today, huh, Alvin? More business? Well, Alvin, you can finish taking care of your business because I don't want you taking care of me anymore. So have a nice life with your *business*." She got up to leave and that's when Al knew she was going to leave him. He didn't mean to grab a hold of her so tight, but he felt like his whole life was slipping away from him. And the more she struggled trying to get him to release her, the tighter he held her. He started shaking her to stop her from struggling. That's when she started cursing him and calling him every degrading name she could think of. His ego couldn't take it anymore. And then she told him flat out that she was leaving him. His hands just let go of her as if she had burned him. She fell back on the sofa and landed on the recliner end and it reclined. The footrest came up and hit Al on the shins and he stumbled back and fell to the floor.

When he sat up, he saw Darlene's body drawn up in pain. He quickly got to his feet. He went to touch her, but she slapped his hands away and clutched her stomach.

"Dee, what's wrong? Is it the baby?"

"I think so," she said through clenched teeth.

"But you ain't due. How can you be having it now?"

"Do I look like a damn doctor to you? If you can't bring me to the hospital, give me the phone and I'll call an ambulance," she said in torturous agony.

"Hold on, baby. I'll bring you to the hospital." Al rushed and slipped on his shirt and shoes. He grabbed Darlene's coat and helped her put it on. He went out and started the car. Then he went back to get her. He was almost ready to pull off when Darlene told him he'd left the front door to the house wide open. He ran and closed the door. Now they were finally on their way to the hospital.

The trauma and stress she'd been under the last few days, plus the sudden fall on the sofa had caused her to go into premature labor. She was only two weeks early so the baby wasn't in any real danger. Al went into the labor room where Darlene was. She waited until they were alone then she told him to get out. He stared at her then wondered if he had misunderstood her. But the look in her eyes before she turned her back to him was unmistakable. He left, but he stayed in the waiting room.

After hours and hours had passed, a nurse came and told him they were about to bring Darlene to the delivery room and asked if he wanted to be there. He didn't care how mad she was with him. He was going to be there for the birth of his first child.

Darlene wasn't even aware of Al being in the delivery room with her. She was in that much pain. She was only aware of him when she was about to give her last push. At least she hoped it was the last push. The doctor told her the baby's head was out. One more push and she was rewarded with a six-pound, two-ounce son at 3:50 a.m. that Thanksgiving morning. And Darlene was thankful. Thankful to be out of all the pain more than she was about her son for a minute.

After Al cut the umbilical cord, he left the room. He sat in the waiting room totally shocked. He was happy to have a son, but he hadn't planned on actually seeing him being born. While he was in the delivery room, he happened to look up in the mirror that reflected the birth. He wanted to see if he would feel the way Jeff had when he had seen his daughter being born. But when Al saw the baby's body come out his wife, he felt like his whole sex life with his wife was over. He knew he was very well endowed in his manhood. But to see a six-pound baby come through what he had been receiving so much pleasure in made him feel inadequate. He didn't think he would be able to see his wife in the same way again. Then he shook his head of those thoughts. It was almost four o'clock in the morning. He didn't want to call anyone that early in the morning. Besides, he wanted to wait until he saw his wife again. He really didn't know how she was going the act toward him.

A couple of hours or so later, a nurse came and told him what room Darlene was in. Al went to her room feeling nervous. All he could think about was that she said she was going to leave him. He hoped she only said it because she was mad. Maybe with the baby coming early she would change her mind. At least he hoped she would.

Darlene was tired. She felt like she couldn't move a muscle. All she wanted to do was sleep. But before she was about to close her eyes, the door to her room opened. She saw Al walk in slowly. He came and stood next to her bed and leaned over and kissed her forehead.

"How do you feel?" he asked.

"Tired and sleepy," she said softly.

At least she wasn't yelling at him. He was glad for that. "Well, I'm gonna let you get some rest. I'll see you later this morning, okay," he said, pushing her hair away from her face.

"Okay. And bring my bag I had packed," she said then drifted off to sleep.

Al got home and was bored out of his mind. He didn't have anything to do. He fixed some breakfast and sat down and ate. That only took about half an hour. He decided to call his sister and tell her the news. She was happy and she told him that she was afraid Darlene would have the baby early. Then she asked him where was he during the services. Al cut the conversation short by giving his sister the name of the hospital and Darlene's room number and got off the phone. He thought about calling her aunt, but decided to go there instead.

Darryl answered the door. He greeted Al sleepily. He asked about Darlene and Al told him that's why he was there. Although it was still early, her aunt was already awake. She greeted Al happily. She didn't seem like she had just buried her son the previous day. Maybe it hadn't really sunk in yet, Al thought. He took a seat on the sofa. Darryl chose to stand. Al cleared his throat before he began speaking.

"Uh, I didn't mean to come over this early, but I was already up. I just came by to tell you that Darlene had a little boy."

Her aunt's face lit up. She had been more worried about Darlene's condition than she was about her son's funeral. She knew it was only going to be a matter of time before something had happened to him. She had tried and tried until she couldn't do anymore. But it would have been doubly worse if Darlene would have suffered, too.

"I'm glad. Is she and the baby all right? I mean with her having him early."

"Yeah. I didn't want to call as soon as she had him. That was about four o'clock this morning. I'm about to head back to the hospital now," he said and stood up. He gave them her room number and told them what hospital she was at. They told him they would go to the hospital later that day to see her.

Darlene was in her hospital room sitting up in bed watching TV. She had eaten breakfast and wasn't able to go back to sleep. She got out of bed and slowly walked to the bathroom inside of her room. It was only about ten feet away from her bed, but it seemed like a mile away. She had to rest once she made it inside. She heard someone walk into the room then there was silence.

Al had picked up some flowers from the hospital's gift shop on his way up to her room. He walked into her room with her bag in one hand and the flowers in the other and all he saw was an empty bed. His first thought was that she had taken the baby and left. He went back out to the nurses' station and found out where was the nursery. He went there and he was somewhat relieved when he saw his son inside a bassinet sleeping. Then he thought that she had left him *and* the baby. No. She wouldn't leave her baby. Or would she? He remembered that she wasn't too keen on the idea of them having a baby anyway. He decided to go back to her room. This time she was in the bed when he walked in. He walked straight to her. He put the bag and flowers down and hugged her to him. He kissed the side of her face near her ear. Then he whispered, "I thought you left me," in her ear. Darlene tried to pull back, but he wouldn't let her. He didn't want her to see the tears in his eyes. He quickly blinked them back. He started rocking her a little saying, "Please don't leave me, Dee. Baby, please don't leave me." Darlene didn't have to see his face to know he was crying. She could tell by the tremble in his voice and by the way he was holding her. It was as if he thought she would run if he loosened his hold on her.

She had only been letting him hold her. She was too stunned by what he was saying to reciprocate his hug. But now she put her arms around him in reassurance. "I'm not going anywhere, Alvin," she said and turned a little and placed a kiss on the side of his neck. "No where at all." After Al composed himself, he risked looking at her. "Why would you think I would leave you?" she asked.

"You said it last night."

She *had* been planning on leaving him. That night anyway. She just needed to get away from him. But she didn't tell him that. "I was just mad. I'm sorry, Alvin," she said.

Al couldn't believe she was saying she was sorry. After the way he had acted by not being with her when she needed him and then causing her to go into labor early, he wouldn't blame her for wanting to leave him.

The telephone in her room rang and Darlene answered. It was a nurse in the nursery asking did she want to see the baby. She had only seen her baby briefly after the delivery. And if she were honest with herself, she probably wouldn't be able to tell him from any other newborn black baby.

Soon they heard crying coming from outside the door. Then the nurse came through the door and Darlene sat up in bed. It was her son doing all the crying. The nurse picked him up and handed him to Darlene and he immediately stopped crying.

"There are bottles and diapers in the drawer under the bassinet. And it is about time for his bottle," the nurse said then left the room.

While Darlene looked down at him she realized she hadn't given him a name. She burped him after she fed him an ounce of the formula. A few minutes later there was a stench in the air. The baby had a bowel movement. Since Al had been practicing with his niece, he got all the necessary things out the drawer to change the baby. He laid the baby back in the bassinet.

He didn't put a new diaper on the baby immediately because he saw something that surprised him.

"Look, Darlene," he said, moving the bassinet closer to the bed where she was.

"What?" she asked, looking at her son with his little legs drawn up almost to his stomach.

"Look how long his thang is," he said, referring to his son's penis. "He's gonna be puttin' it on them girls when he get older."

"Like father, like son." And right after she said that the baby urinated and Al jumped back. "You better wipe him off again and put a diaper on him," she told him. Al quickly did so without any delays.

About an hour or so later, Jeff and Marie came in with their daughter. Jasmine wanted to go to Darlene, but Marie wouldn't let her. She looked at the sleeping baby and saw how cute he was and said, "Darlene, he looks just like you. I guess boys look like their mothers and girls look like their fathers because Jasmine is the splitting image of Jeff." The baby squirmed a little then she asked, "What's his name?"

"I haven't decided on one yet since the baby came kind of unexpectedly," she said and noticed how Al looked over at her.

He didn't see what was the problem. The baby should be named after him. He told her she could pick any name she wanted if they had a girl. He just assumed she would name a boy after him. But he didn't say anything. He would wait until they were alone. And that was thirty minutes later.

"What's wrong with naming him Al Junior?" Al asked as soon as Marie and Jeff left the room.

"Nothing. I just had other names picked out."

"Like what?"

"I like the names Armaud, Jamal, Dante', and Darell."

Right after she finished saying the names Darryl and his mother walked in. Al got up and gave her aunt the seat he was sitting in. They talked for a while. The baby woke up again and Darlene reached into the bassinet for him. She held him close to her. Darryl went over and stood next to her. And it hit Al like a bolt of lightning. Their baby didn't just look like Darlene. He looked a little like Darryl. Al left the room saying he wanted to get something to eat. Darlene's lunch tray was soon brought in. She ate her food with the help of Darryl. Her aunt held the baby while Darlene finished eating. He started to cry so Darlene held him and fed him. They left soon afterwards.

She had gotten him to go back to sleep by the time Al came back and he was in one of his moods, she noticed.

"Now what's wrong?" Darlene asked.

"Why don't you just name him Darryl. He looks like he could be the baby's daddy anyway," he said and slumped down in the chair.

That was the last straw for Darlene. She thought she could forget about all the other hurtful things he'd said to her in the past. But the implication he was making now was going too far.

"Get out of my room. I don't want you here. I am sick and tired of all your accusations. If you think he," she pointed at the sleeping baby, "is Darryl's baby, then you can keep on believing it. I don't care what you think or believe anymore. Now just leave me the hell alone."

It was Al's pride that stopped him from begging her for her forgiveness. He just got up and left. He didn't go to see her the next day. He figured he would give her a day to cool off. A big mistake on his part.

Saturday afternoon he decided to go and see her. He was shocked to find out that she had checked out of the hospital. He was told that she had checked out that morning. He quickly went back home thinking that was where he would find her, but all he found was an empty house.

Darlene couldn't check out on her own so she had called Darryl to come and pick her up from the hospital. He didn't ask her any questions. But when they were in the car and she told him to bring her to a hotel that was near where she lived he started getting worried.

"Why do you want to go to a hotel and why Al didn't pick you up?"

"Because Alvin is an asshole." That was all she said and Darryl just drove her where she wanted to go.

Once she checked into her room, he started questioning her again.

"What happened with Al, Darlene?"

"I was telling him the names I had picked out for the baby and he got this crazy idea in his head that I should name the baby after you since you look like you could be the baby's daddy." Darryl was looking at her with an expression of humor and disbelief. "And here's the funny part. Once before he was jealous of you."

"But why? I think of you more as sister than a cousin."

"I know that. I'm just sick of Alvin's jealousy. And yesterday was the last straw. I just don't feel like going home to him."

"Okay. You need anything?"

"Yes." She made a list of everything she would need. She didn't have much cash. She was paying for her room with a credit card she had packed in her hospital bag just in case. She gave her cousin the credit card and pin number and told him to get three hundred dollars out of one of the ATM machines and buy all the things she had on her list.

"How long do you plan on staying here?" he asked, looking at the list of items.

"I don't know. I just want to make sure I have enough things to last me for a while. And Darryl, don't tell Alvin where I am."

"I won't," he said, knowing he wouldn't.

"I mean it, Darryl. He'll ask you and you are not too high on his list of favorite people now."

"Well, after I get you these things, I'll make sure Crystal keeps an eye on our mama and I'll go on back to school," he said and left. He was back in about an hour. He sat the bags with all the things she wanted on the other bed. She really did appreciated what he'd done for her. And she knew that she would have done the same thing for him. Darryl went and got her something to eat before he left.

Al was about to go stir crazy sitting at home. He didn't know where his wife and son were. He called his sister hoping she had heard from her. Nothing. He even called her aunt. Nothing again. So Al didn't know what to do. He decided to pass by her aunt's house and see if her cousin had any idea where she might have gone. After all, they were close.

Darryl was putting his bag in the car when Al pulled up. He tried his best to look calm. Al walked up to him and asked, "You heard from Darlene?"

"No. I was going to stop by and see her on my way back to school," he said, lying easily. Well, he wasn't exactly lying. He didn't say where he was going to see her.

"She's not at the hospital."

"Then I'll stop by your house."

Al hated having to tell her cousin that he didn't know where his wife was, but he had to. "She's not there either. I thought she might have called you. I don't know where she is." Al looked lost. He looked like he had lost his best friend. Darryl was almost tempted to tell him exactly where she was, but his loyalty lay with his cousin. "If she calls you, tell her I'm worried about her and I'll be at home. Tell her to call me."

"Okay, Al." After Al left, Darryl went back inside and called Darlene. He told her about Al's visit and the things he said. He thought she should at least call him.

Later that night, she decided to call Al at home. He picked up the phone on the first ring.

"Hello?"

"Hello, Alvin. I called to let you know that me and Jamal are fine."

"Jamal?"

"That's what I named your son. Jamal Alvin Williams." She started not to give him a middle name at all. But she decided at the last minute to give him his father's name as a middle name.

"Where are you, Dee?"

"Somewhere I can do a lot of thinking. And I can't do that at home with you."

"I won't give you a divorce," he said, trying to hold on to her with a threat.

"Did I ask you for one?"

"No. But what else am I supposed to think? You leave without telling me anything—"

"Maybe if you would have come to see me yesterday none of this would have happened." She had been really hurt when he didn't come by or call. She had been up with the baby all night and she was tired that morning. Plus she had to take the baby to get circumcised. And she had been looking forward to seeing Al, but he never showed up. She had refused to call and ask him to come and see her after the things he had said to her. She felt she shouldn't have to call her husband and ask him to come and visit her in the hospital after she had just given birth. Given birth to a baby she wasn't ready to have. "But no, you had to accuse me of not only having sex with my cousin, but having his baby. I have been taking all your accusations and lack of trust for the past two years. And after all I've been through this past week, I just couldn't take it anymore. I would have thought that after all that has happened between us in the past you would know how much I loved you, but I guess you didn't."

It took a minute for Al to register her saying loved instead of love. Past tense not present tense. He didn't know what he would do if she stopped loving him.

"You tryin' to say you don't love me no mo'?"

"No, Alvin. It's just that I'm tired. I'll be home Monday."

"Why Monday? Why I can't come and get you now. Please, Darlene, come home to me."

The desperation in his voice was getting to her. She stilled loved him. After all the things he had done and said, she still loved him. "Not tonight. I'll call you tomorrow. Bye, Alvin," she said and hung up before he could protest any further.

Al sat on the sofa partially relieved. He now knew she hadn't left him. At least not for good anyway. That was some consolation. But what lay ahead was a whole other story. He was going to have to try his best to make her happy again. He didn't know how, but he was going to try.

It was Sunday evening and Darlene still hadn't called him. He was frantic. What if she changed her mind? What if everything she said was a lie? How was he going to live without her? There was a knock on the door. He rushed to it thinking it was probably Darlene, but was disappointed when it was Marie and Jeff. He greeted them as they came inside. Marie noticed that her brother didn't look at all like a proud father.

"Where's Darlene and the baby?" she asked after looking around the empty room.

"I don't know," he said and went sat on the sofa.

"You don't know?" Both Marie and Jeff echoed.

Al filled them in on what had happened with the exception of accusing Darlene of having a baby by her cousin.

"How could you be so stupid, Al?" Marie asked. "I don't blame her. It was bad enough you weren't at the wake service for her cousin. I for one thought she would go into labor there. Then you turn around and do something like that. What's the matter with you?" She was incensed with her brother. Darlene was the best thing to happen to her brother and all she saw was him messing it up.

"Calm down, sweetheart," Jeff said to his wife.

"Calm down nothing. If you would have pulled something like that you'd be living somewhere else by now." The telephone rang. Al was about to get up and answer the phone, but Marie reached it first. "Hello?"

"Marie, is that you?"

"Yes. Are you okay?" she asked and Al got up to go to the phone.

"Yes, I'm fine. I was calling to tell Alvin I'm on my way home," she said. She had decided to call a taxi to bring her home because she didn't want him to know where she'd been just in case she needed refuge again.

"I'll come and get you if you want," Marie offered.

"No. I've already called a taxi. I'll see you when I get there. Bye."

Al watched as his sister replaced the receiver on the phone without giving him a chance to talk. "Why did you hang up?"

"Because she didn't want to talk to you. She's on her way," she said and went and stood at the window next to the door, watching and waiting for the taxi to pull up.

"How is she getting home?"

"She called a taxi. Did you think she had somebody else to bring her home?" she asked not bothering to hide the sarcasm.

"No I didn't think that. It's just that I wanted to go and get her."

As the minutes ticked by, they all waited. "Well, you can go and get her out the taxi. It just drove up," Marie said.

Darlene had gotten so much stuff she had barely used any of it. Most of it would have been used if she had stayed a few more days like she planned. But she didn't think she should have to be alone anymore. She was able to get everything in the diaper bag and the duffel bag she bought. Some things went into the bag she had with her at the hospital. The duffel bag was stuffed with unopened diapers, baby wipes, cans of ready-made formula, and baby clothing. She kept a few diapers and bottles in the diaper bag.

She noticed Al, Marie, and Jeff were all standing outside waiting. Al was at the door to help her out. The driver retrieved her bags from the trunk. She only carried her sleeping baby in her arms. She didn't resist any help Al offered. She just wanted to get inside and lay in her bed. Marie helped her to the house while Al carried the bags. Marie remembered how she had felt after coming home from the hospital. She didn't want to get out of bed. And here was Darlene on her own for a couple of days as soon as she gets out of the hospital. She took the baby and held him with one arm and helped Darlene with her other arm. When they were inside, all Darlene wanted was a shower and a bed. Marie helped her up the stairs. The baby was sleep so she went and laid him in his bed. Good thing it was already assembled, she thought. She plugged in the baby's monitor and carried the parent one downstairs with her.

Darlene stood in the shower for ten minutes before she started washing herself. The water shooting from the showerhead felt very therapeutic to her aching body. She slowly washed herself. Her breasts still felt heavy. She didn't want to breast-feed so she was taking pills to dry up the milk. But she knew it wasn't going to shrink her breasts to their pre-pregnancy size. They were noticeable bigger. She was so preoccupied with the size of her breasts that she didn't hear the bathroom door open.

When Al walked into the bedroom, he heard the shower still going. He went to see if she was all right. He had only walked in seconds before the shower curtain was pulled back.

It had been weeks since he had seen his wife's nude body. Their lovemaking had lessened and when they did make love it was short and sweet. He hadn't touched nor seen her breasts in months because she had complained that they hurt too much when he touched them. Al knew they had gotten bigger, but he had no idea how good they would look in the flesh.

Darlene saw him staring at her breasts and she immediately started feeling self-conscious. She felt a cool draft and that made her nipples harden. She grabbed a towel and started drying herself off being careful to keep her body covered most of the time.

Al picked up her panties and nightgown she had hanging on the rack on the back of the door. He walked over and helped her with the gown. He wanted to help with the panties, but she was able to manage herself.

A few minutes later, Marie and Jeff came in the bedroom. Jeff was holding Jasmine and Marie was holding Jamal. She had heard him crying on the monitor and came upstairs to change him. They were getting ready to leave so she was bringing the baby to Al and Darlene.

"Look who's awake," Marie said as they entered the bedroom. Darlene looked over and smiled. "I've changed him, but I think he wants to eat," she said, handing him to Darlene. "Where are his bottles?"

"There are some in the diaper bag I had with me. And can you put the other ones in the refrigerator for me?" Marie nodded as she left. Darlene started focusing all of her attention on the baby. She was smiling at him and talking baby talk.

Al just looked at them. He was happy. Marie came back with the bottle. They were leaving and Al went to see them out. While he was leaving, the telephone started ringing. Darlene answered it. "Hello?"

"I was wondering where you were. I called the hotel and they told me you checked out." Immediately she knew it was Darryl.

"I decided to come home earlier than expected," she said in a hushed voice.

"Is everything all right now?" he asked worried about both of them really.

"So far. I'll have to talk to you later. Bye." She hung up because she didn't want Al to come in and find her talking to Darryl.

Al came back in the bedroom a few minutes later. She wanted to talk before things go from bad to worse. She waited until Al sat on the bed next to her.

"Alvin, we need to talk," she said.

Al started feeling like his life was going to fall apart. He refused to believe she would come back to him just to leave again.

"About what?" he asked stupidly.

"About what you said at the hospital."

"Dee, I'm sorry—" he said before she raised up a hand to silence him.

"All I want is for you to answer this one question for me right now," she said, looking at him. He nodded. "Have I ever, I mean since I agreed to marry you, given you any reason to think that I have had sex with or been remotely interested in any other man?"

"No, but—"

"But what, Alvin?"

"You seem so close to Darryl," he said solemnly.

"We seem as close as you and Marie are. He's always been more like a brother to me than a cousin. And I'll never have any reason to want another man as long as I have you." Al leaned over and kissed her and he wanted her. He started caressing her breasts then down to her thighs. "Alvin, we can't do anything," she told him and he blew out a frustrated breath.

"Then when can we?" he asked, still holding on to her.

"Not for four to six weeks at least."

Al released her and fell back on the bed looking up at the ceiling. He wondered how was he going to do without making love for that long. When he thought about how long it had actually been he got even more frustrated. It had already been about a month since they had last made love. Now it was going to be another one. But what could he do about it? Nothing.

Chapter twenty one

Everything checked out fine when Darlene went in for her postpartum check-up weeks later. She was fine and the baby was doing fine also. Al accompanied her on both appointments. She was still on maternity leave from work. She had canceled all of her appointments with her other clients and reschedule them for after the New Year. She talked with Marie often. Marie had her daughter in the daycare center located inside the banking facility. She had already inquired for a vacancy for Darlene. Darlene was thankful. She was starting to get bored at home and anxious to get back to work. She kept in close contact with her aunt and Crystal. She found out her cousin was expecting another baby. Although Carl was just like a father to Desiree, it was good they were having a baby of their own.

Christmas had passed and the New Year was upon them. Darryl stopped by often to see her and the baby. He would see Al sometimes. He usually visited Darlene during the day. He had become an excellent student. He always maintained nothing less than a 3.0

grade point average. She was glad she had been able to help him go to college and get him away from the streets. She doesn't know what she would do if what happened to Robert were to happen to him.

Marie called and invited Darlene and Al to a New Year's Eve Party, which was a couple of days away. Darlene really didn't want to leave her baby alone just yet. But she reluctantly gave in. She called her aunt and asked if she wouldn't mind baby-sitting for her. Her aunt was pleased to watch the baby.

Darlene planned to tell Al about the party when he came home later, which was what he had been doing quite often. And when he did, he smelled of alcohol. She usually didn't bother saying anything to him, but that night she wanted to talk to him.

Al had a hard day at work. His mind had been occupied all that day. He didn't go straight home. He took care of a little business then stopped and had a few drinks. He had been stopping to drink in order to be able to go straight to sleep when he got home. All he could think about when he got home was making love to his wife. The doctor had said it was okay for them to resume with their normal sex life, but Darlene didn't seem interested. Most of the time she was already asleep. He thought they would have made love for their anniversary, but they didn't. He had plans to take her out to dinner and dancing, but she was tired after dinner and they went home.

Darlene heard the front door open. She had gotten too impatient waiting in bed so she went downstairs to greet him. Al had just closed and locked the door by the time she made it down. He turned and saw her.

"What are you doing up so late?" he asked, taking off his coat.

"Waiting for you."

"For what? Is something wrong?"

"Yeah. I think I'm suffering from a lack of loving. Can you help me out?" she asked teasingly. Those were the words he had been waiting for. He had waited so long.

"Oh, I think I can help you out," he said.

"I'll be upstairs waiting," she said and headed for the stairs and Al was right behind her.

Darlene had on a robe so Al didn't see what she had on. She had put on the nightshirt he had bought her for her birthday before they were married. She took off the robe then laid on the bed while he took a shower.

Al was trying to calm himself down while he was in the bathroom. He hadn't made love to her in months. He has wanted her so bad, especially in the mornings when he would wake up rock hard from having a horny dream about her. And now it was happening.

He walked out and saw her lying on the bed with the covers pulled back. He started getting harder. He removed the towel he had wrapped around him. He really didn't want to waste time with foreplay. He wanted to be inside of her warmth, but he took the time to kiss her.

Al laid in bed beside her and pulled her to him. Then he noticed he wasn't the only one who didn't really want to waste time with foreplay. Darlene was stroking his nature and pleading with him to put it in. She rolled on her back and spread her legs apart. Then everything went down hill. Al looked down and the flashback of the delivery hit him. All he could see was how wide she had stretched and his erection immediately began to disappear. He moved and laid back down on his side of the bed. He felt angry, frustrated, and humiliated.

Darlene was wondering what had just happened. One minute Al was ready to make love to her then the next minute he wasn't. She turned to look at him lying next to her.

"Alvin, what's wrong?"

"Nothing. I'm just tired," he said.

Tired? How could he be hard and ready one minute and tired the next minute?

"But what happened? I thought you wanted to make love tonight."

"I did, but I changed my mind. I'm just tired," he said and turned his back to her.

Darlene felt as if all the air was sucked out of her body. In an instant, her eyes flooded with tears. She reached over and tried to turn him to her, but he pulled away from her. That only made the tears fall. She started crying and got up and ran to the bathroom. Al cursed under his breath and got up and ran after her.

Darlene stood in front of the sink with a wet towel wiping her face. She stood there looking at her reflection, wondering what was so different about her. Wondering what was it about her that had turned off her husband so suddenly? What had she done wrong? She turned when she heard the door open.

Al had put on his underwear before he went in after her. He stood in the doorway and saw his wife looking like she had just lost her best friend. All he did was go to her and pulled her in his arms. He wanted to make everything better. When Darlene thought it was her fault, Al felt like the wind had been knocked out of him. His pride wouldn't let him tell her the truth, but he couldn't let her believe it was something she did so he blamed it on the drinks he had earlier that night. And that he wanted their first time together again to be without any alcoholic influences. He didn't know if she believed him or not. She just went back to the bedroom and got in bed. She didn't tell him about the party until the next morning. He didn't seem to want to go at first, but she told him that she was looking forward to getting out of the house.

Darlene was glad she was able to still fit into her clothes. She was getting dressed when Al called her and told her he would meet her at the club. She was a little disappointed, but she didn't say anything.

Marie and Jeff were already there when she arrived. The party was from ten o'clock that night until two o'clock the next morning. She had taken the baby to her aunt's house earlier with enough things so he could spend the night. That way she would have had a little time with her husband before they left. But that didn't happen.

She went over to the table where Marie and Jeff were sitting. A few other couples were there also. Jeff introduced her to everyone. Once she was seated, she told Marie and Jeff that Al was going to be late. Jeff frowned a little because he didn't know of anything that would be detaining Al. He didn't mention it though.

While the couples danced together, Darlene sat at the table alone. Jeff danced with Darlene a few times and so did some of the other men on fast songs. Usually on the slow songs, Darlene would either go to the restroom or to the bar. While at the bar that time, she decided to call it a night soon and go home. It was almost half past eleven and her husband wasn't there yet. She felt lonely sitting at the table with nothing but couples. Then she felt someone tap her on her shoulder. She looked around and saw Vincent. Why did he always seem to be there when she was feeling alone?

"Hey, Vincent," she said.

"Hey. I'm surprised to see you here," he said, looking at her closely. Darlene was wearing a strapless, black velvet dress. The dress fitted her like a glove.

"I'm here with some friends," she said and picked up the drink she had ordered and took a sip.

"You're not with your husband?" he asked surprised. Then he saw a sad look cross her face before she was able to dismiss it.

"He'll be here later," she said not believing it herself. "I'll see you around. Bye, Vincent." He watched as she left.

It was only minutes before midnight and everyone was on the dance floor waiting to dance in the New Year. Everyone except Darlene. She sat at the table all alone.

Vincent had been watching her the rest of the night. He saw her dance a few times with the other men at the table. But for this particular dance, she was alone. He took a chance and approached her. She looked up and saw him. He held out his hand to dance and she didn't hesitate. He led her to the other side of the dance floor, away from the people she was there with.

When he pulled her close to him, she smelled the scent of his cologne. At that moment, she thought it was the best smelling cologne there was. She was enjoying smelling him and dancing with him. It had been months since she had been held and caressed by her husband. Her husband, she thought and loosened her hold on Vincent. She shouldn't be dancing with him. And she shouldn't be enjoying it as much as she was. She was about to pull free when the count down started.

Vincent felt her trying to pull free, but he wouldn't let her go. He leaned down and kissed her when everyone else started kissing in the New Year. Darlene knew it was wrong, but she couldn't help it. She kissed him back. The kiss was short and sweet, but she felt guilty because she enjoyed it.

"I have to leave, Vincent," she said, removing her arms.

"Why?"

"I just have to."

"I'm not worried about Al," he said, looking down at her. "I'm worried about you."

Oh God, Al, she thought. What would he do if he had seen her kissing Vincent? She knew how he could get when he was jealous. And that was when she hadn't done anything. And she didn't want anything to happen to Vincent. He was a nice man and she would blame herself if something happened to him.

"I'm all right. I'm just going to go home. Bye," she said and walked away from him. She sat at the table and waited for Marie and Jeff to return. She feigned a headache as an excuse to go home. She drove home trying to figure out what had happened to her. She shouldn't have responded to Vincent the way she did. She decided it was just that she had been without intimacy for too long. That's what it was. Wasn't it?

Al had been doing business that night. He wanted to be with his wife, but he couldn't get finished quick enough. He didn't arrive at the party until around half past midnight. He got a drink and looked around for his wife. He located his sister at a table on the far side of the club. He sat down at the table and asked, "Where's Darlene?"

"She went home because she *said* she had a headache," Marie said, but she didn't believe it. Then she asked, "Where have you been?"

"I had something to do." That was all the explanation he gave.

"I don't blame Darlene for making up an excuse for leaving. She must have felt out of place all by herself."

"I told her I would meet her here. She should have waited."

"That was hours ago."

"So."

"That's all you have to say is 'so'?" Marie said.

"Yep. So while I'm here, I might as well enjoy myself," he said and got up and left the table.

Vincent had been watching Al. He saw when Al left the table. He also saw how he was flirting with other women. Vincent couldn't believe it when he saw Al leave with a woman. And he wasn't the only one to see it. Marie had been watching her brother also.

Vincent followed Al's car and saw him drive to a motel. Him and the woman got out and went into one of the rooms. Vincent decided to go and tell Darlene himself.

Al had been feeling like less than a man since that night when he and Darlene had tried to make love and he couldn't perform. He wanted to know if it was him or just a reaction to her. He picked up a woman he knew at the party and decided to test his theory. He brought her to a motel to see if he would be able to perform.

When they got there, he found out the woman had her own supply of drugs. They both got high. He was able to get it up this time and keep it up. Then when she spread her legs for him he penetrated her. He wanted to pull out, but he didn't. In his mind he was seeing Darlene in bed with him. And after penetration he began thrusting.

"Dee, baby, you feel so good."

"I'm not Dee," the woman said.

The knowledge of what he had done hit him with full force. He looked down at the woman in bed with him. He was just about to experience his release and he realized he didn't have on a condom. He got off the woman just in time.

"What's wrong, Al?"

He started swearing. He couldn't believe what he had done. He picked up his pants and took out his wallet. He took out three twenties and threw them at the woman and said, "Get out." She only stared at him. "Get the hell out of here!"

Darlene was wondering who was ringing her doorbell so late. She looked out the peephole and saw Vincent and her heart rate accelerated. She opened the door and said, "What are you doing here?"

"I have to talk to you," he said. "And I know your husband ain't home."

"But he could come home any minute," she said, feeling scared.

"No he won't, Darlene," Vincent said matter-of-fact.

"How do you know that?"

"Because I saw him go into a motel room not long ago with another woman." He didn't mean to say it so bluntly. But he didn't like seeing her hurt.

"No," she said, shaking her head in denial. "Not my husband."

He walked inside the house and closed the door behind him. "I saw him, Darlene. He came to the club after you left. And he left soon afterwards with a woman." He reached his hand out and cupped her face. "And there could be only one thing they did once they were inside." He saw the tears rolling down her face. "Don't cry over him, Darlene. Just leave him," he said and wiped away her tears. He wanted to tell her to come to him, but he didn't.

Darlene felt numb. She didn't want to believe her husband was cheating on her. But why would Vincent come to her house and tell her that? He couldn't be lying could he? She knew he was attracted to her. She's known it from their first night at that club. But would he stoop to lying on Al to try and get her? Something in her wouldn't allow her to think that about Vincent.

"Thanks for telling me, Vincent," she said, wiping her tears away. "I'll be all right though. I just have a few things I need to do before he comes back tonight."

"*If* he comes back," Vincent said and she turned hurtful eyes toward him. He forgot about what he'd said earlier and pulled her in his arms. She didn't resist. "I'll take care of you, Darlene. Leave him and come to me. I may not be able to give you the material things he's able to, but I'll never be unfaithful to you."

"It's not that easy. I have a son to think about." Was she crazy? She couldn't possibly be considering Vincent's offer.

"I would want you and your son," he said seriously.

"I need to be alone."

"Okay," he said and sighed, releasing his hold on her. "Take my card and call me if you ever need me." She took the card. And when he left she just stood in the middle of the foyer and cried.

It was almost three o'clock in the morning when Al finally came home. Darlene had been sitting on the sofa waiting. And when she heard his key in the front door she stood up.

Al was feeling like dirt. He didn't know how he was going to react when he saw his wife. He had showered in the motel before he left. He had been driving around trying to figure out what he was going to tell his wife. It had been times when he would go from one woman to another woman and it wouldn't bother him. But now he was nervous. He was hoping she would be asleep. That way he would have more time to compose himself. He had no such luck.

Al looked right at Darlene when he walked into the living room and he turned his head immediately. For some reason he couldn't look at her for too long. He went into the kitchen pretending to look for something to eat. It took all of Darlene's willpower to make herself go behind him.

"Where were you tonight?"

"Huh?" he asked, pretending like he didn't hear her.

"Why didn't you come to the party?"

"I did. Marie said you left," he said, taking some cold chicken out the refrigerator.

"So why didn't you come home then?"

"I did."

Darlene looked at the clock. It was three o'clock in the morning. She had left the party a little after midnight. The party was over at two o'clock. If he had gotten there right when the party was over he should have been home at least half an hour ago.

"The party was over an hour ago, Alvin," she told him.

"So, what are you tryin' say?"

"I'm not trying to say anything. I just want to know where you were," she said.

"Do I ask you where you be all the time?" he asked defensively.

"No. But I don't be sleeping around," she accused. She knew she had hit the nail on the head because guilt was written all over Al's face. "I wouldn't believe it. But I guess now I don't have a choice but to believe it. I hope you had fun," she said and walked away.

Al cursed under his breath. He had hoped he could have hidden what had happen from her, but somehow she knew.

She only made it as far as the living room before he came up behind her and turned her around to face him and asked, "What are you talkin' about?"

"I'm talking about you leaving the party with some whore and going to a motel with her. That's what I'm talking about," she said and snatched her arms from his hold.

Al stood there too stunned to move. How could she have known? He may have given away that he had done something, but she knew details.

"You had someone following me?" he asked, thinking it was the only way she could have known.

She turned and looked at him and said, "It never crossed my mind to have you followed. I always thought you loved me and that I could trust you to be faithful. I guess I was wrong on both counts." She walked over and sat on the sofa. Al went over and sat next to her and she moved away from him.

"Darlene, I do love you," he said. She just looked at him. "It's just that I thought I wasn't going to be able to make love to you no mo'." The hell with pride, he thought. He was going to tell her everything. "After I saw the baby come out of you, I felt like I wasn't going to be able to satisfy you."

"Is that the best you can come up with?" she said very unsympathetic. And why should she be sympathetic? He was the unfaithful one. Not her. Although she could have been many times, she didn't because she was in love with her husband and very happy with him. "Let me get this straight. Since you thought you couldn't satisfy me sexually, you go out and have sex with somebody else?" He didn't say anything. "I must have stupid stamped on my forehead or something. Just answer one question for me. Did you use a condom?" Al covered his face with his hands. He removed them then turned and looked at her, not saying a word. That was answer enough for her. She stood up and told him, "Get out of my house. Go find your whore and be happy."

"Dee, baby, I'm sorry. It won't happen again."

"I know it won't happen again because I don't want you. You can go on a fucking spree for all I care."

"Baby, please," he said and went and held her. She stood unresponsive in his arms. She didn't have the slightest impulse to put her arms around him.

"I told you a long time ago not to play me for a fool or hurt me. And you managed to do both at the same time. So I hope you, your business, and your whore will be happy together." She walked out of his arms and headed up the stairs.

She locked the bedroom door once she was inside. She had put up a brave front fueled by her anger while she was downstairs. But she was hurting deeply. She sat on the edge of the bed and cried. After all the things she had forgiven him for, this was how he treats her. She heard him knocking on the door, but she ignored him. He broke the lock and came in the room. She jumped off the bed and screamed, "Get out of my house!"

He stopped where he was and said, "I said I was sorry, Darlene."

"That's where you're right. You *are* sorry. You are one sorry excuse for a man. You didn't even have the sense to use a condom. I guess you would have come home and fucked me, too. That's if you would have been able to get it up."

That was a cutting blow to his ego. He walked over to her and slapped her hard across her face and she fell back on the bed. He squeezed his eyes shut and clenched his fist. He didn't mean to hit her. He just lost control for a moment. And when he opened his eyes, he saw blood near her mouth. "Oh God, Dee, I'm sorry," he said and attempted to go to her.

Darlene thought he was coming to hit her again so she picked up the TV remote and threw it at him since it was to closest thing she could grab. Then she scrambled off the bed and grabbed the clock, the lamp, and anything else she could get her hands on and started throwing.

"You lying, cheating, abusive *bastard!* I *hate* you! Get out of my house before I call the police." She couldn't do it then because she had thrown the handset to the cordless phone at him.

Al knew he wasn't going to get anywhere with her that night. "I'll leave, but I'll be back later."

"Don't waste your time coming back."

"I *will* be back," he said and walked out of the room then out of the house.

Darlene wasn't able to go back to sleep. She sat down in the kitchen and decided what she was going to do. She didn't have any doubts in her mind that her marriage was over. She was glad that Al had insisted on paying all the bills. She could use the money she's been saving to pay the mortgage and other bills. And the money she made from her clients would help out a lot. She made a list of things she wanted to do that day. And number one on her list was to buy new locks for the house.

Chapter twenty two

Darlene called her aunt at about nine o'clock the next morning to let her know she was on her way to pick up the baby. She was just about to leave when the telephone rang.

"Hello?"

"Hey, Darlene. How are you feeling this morning?" It was Marie calling.

"Fine. I was on my way out though," she said. She really wasn't in a mood to talk to anyone. Especially anyone related to Al.

"Al came by looking for you last night."

"So I've heard. But he obviously made other plans."

"What happened?" Marie asked concerned.

"He's your brother. You ask him. I'll talk to you later, Marie. I have to go. Bye." She didn't want to take out the anger she felt toward Al on Marie. She thought it best if she didn't say anything else. Darlene picked up her purse and left. She arrived at her aunt's house at nine-thirty. Darryl was still asleep. She sat and talked with her aunt awhile. She told her aunt she had a lot of errands to run and her aunt offered to keep the baby while she did what she had to do. So she left.

Darlene realized she didn't know anything about buying locks. She had Vincent's card in her wallet, but she didn't want to bother him so early. She decided to pass by the shop where he worked. She would ask for his advice if he was there. If not, she would do it on her own. But she was in luck. The shop was open and she saw his truck. She asked for him and he came out a few minutes later. He smiled when he saw her.

"Hey," he greeted her.

"Hi, Vincent."

"How'd it go last night?" he asked, leaning against her car.

"That's why I'm here," she said. "Could you sit inside the car for a minute? You must be cold standing out there."

Vincent didn't know if she was saying what he thought she was saying. He was thinking that she was going to take him up on his offer. He slowly walked around the car and got in on the passenger side.

"About what I said last night, Darlene—"

"Relax, Vincent. I don't have my suitcases packed and in the trunk. I just thought you could help me find a good place to get some locks for my doors. But thanks for the offer anyway," she said.

"My offer still stands, Darlene," he said honestly.

"Thanks, but it won't be necessary. I'm not leaving my house." And it was her house. Al put it in her name. He was just paying the mortgage on it.

"I can get you some locks and install them for you," he offered.

"No. I don't think that would be a good idea. Just tell me where to go. I'll get my cousin to install them."

Darlene had been keeping her face slightly adverted from him. When Al slapped her, her lip was cut on her teeth in the corner of her mouth. Vincent had just noticed it.

"What happened to your mouth?" he asked, looking more closely.

"Nothing."

"He hit you, didn't he?" Vincent asked angrily. He hated men that beat up on women.

"Yeah. Once. I threw him out afterwards."

"Good. Come by here around noon and I'll take you to the hardware store."

"All right. I'll see you then." Vincent got out of the car and went back into the shop.

Darlene stopped and ate breakfast at a fast food restaurant. She felt numb that morning. She went back to her aunt's house and picked up her son. She wanted Darryl to come with her to get the locks and install them for her. She didn't offer any explanations and he didn't ask for any.

She put the baby's things in the car. And once she had him strapped securely in his car seat, she and Darryl left. Vincent was waiting when she arrived. He thought she would be alone, but it didn't matter to him. She followed him to the hardware store.

The baby started crying when the car stopped. She had intended on leaving him in the car with Darryl, but they all got out and went inside. She was holding the baby while they looked at locks. All shc needed were two locks, one for the front door and one for the door leading from the garage.

Vincent wanted to talk to her before she got back in the car. She walked over to his truck with him. "Are you sure you're going to be okay?"

"Yeah."

He bent over and kissed her on the corner of her mouth, right where the cut was. It was a very soft and gentle kiss. "Call me if you need me, okay?"

"I will. And thanks, Vincent," she said and walked back to her car.

Darryl had seen the kiss. And he didn't like it. He waited until she got in the car and asked about it. "What's going on between you and him?"

"Nothing."

"It didn't look like nothing to me," he said, looking at Vincent's truck as it drove away.

"He's just a friend. A really good friend. I'm not fooling around with him or anything."

"Oh," he said. She thought that was the end of discussion. Wrong. "What are the locks for?"

"I need to change the locks on my doors."

"Why, somebody tried to break in or something?"

"No. Just don't worry about it for now. You think you can install them?" she asked.

"Yeah."

When Darlene drove up, she saw Al's car in the driveway. She was hoping he would have stayed wherever he was. She went straight to the baby's room to change his diaper. Darryl came up soon afterwards with the baby's things. She took a bottle out and told him to put the others in the refrigerator. He started changing the locks after he did that.

Al had been sleeping in the bedroom. He heard Darlene talking, but he didn't know who with. He got up and went to look for her. He found her in the other bedroom feeding the baby. She was sitting in a rocking chair. She looked up at him and rolled her eyes.

"Who was that I heard you talking to?" he asked.

"Darryl."

"What brought him by?"

"I wanted him to do something for me."

"Do what?" he asked but she ignored him. He left the room. He went downstairs and saw Darryl at the front door. He couldn't make out what he was doing so he went to get a closer look. He saw that Darryl was in the process of removing the lock on the front door.

"What are you doin' Darryl?" he asked, looking at the new lock sitting on the floor.

"Putting on a new lock."

"For what?"

"Darlene said she wanted new locks on the doors," Darryl informed him. Al turned away from him and headed back upstairs.

Darlene had gotten the baby to go back to sleep. She was in her bedroom making the bed when the door was pushed opened.

"Why are you changing the locks?" Al demanded.

"So you can't come in my house," she said calmly.

"What?"

"You heard me. I don't want you here anymore. I thought I made myself clear last night," she said, continuing to make the bed.

"I'm not leaving, Darlene. So if you're changing the locks, I'll have a key also."

"Like hell you will. I'm sure you can find somewhere else to stay. You didn't have a problem last night," she said and walked to the other side of the bed, which was near him to finish making the bed.

"I stayed at a hotel last night."

"And I'm sure you weren't alone."

Al grabbed her by her arm and pulled her to him. That's when he saw the cut on her mouth. He raised his hand to her face to inspect it and she flinched. "I'm not going to hit you, Darlene," he said.

"I thought that at one time, but I see I was wrong."

"I'm sorry I hit you last night, baby. I didn't mean to. We can work things out. C'mon, baby," he said, hugging her stiff body.

"There's nothing to work out. It's over. Monday morning I'm filing for a divorce."

This was it, Al thought. She was definitely leaving him and he only had himself to blame. He had messed up bad. And twice in one night. He cheated on her then he hit her. How could he have been so stupid? But he still couldn't let her leave him.

"I'm not giving you a divorce," he said.

She didn't try to force her way out of his embrace. She just stood there. "I'm filing on grounds of adultery. I have a witness who saw you at the club with the woman then go into a motel with her. And by your own admission you had sex with her. So as far as I'm concerned, you can keep on having sex with her," she said and attempted to walk away from him, but he held her tighter.

"I'm still not divorcing you."

"If you're worried about me taking any of your money, don't. I don't want anything from you. Me and Jamal will be fine on our own."

"You ain't taking my son."

"Fine. You can keep the baby. That's just how bad I want to get away from you." This time she stepped out of his arms and went to the bathroom and slammed the door. She wasn't going to let him keep her baby. If she had to run away while he was at work she would.

Al stood there absorbing everything she had said. She actually hated him, he thought because she was willing to leave her own baby just to get away from him. He couldn't live with that. He had to make her stay with him. He walked in the bathroom where she was and saw her washing her face. She looked over at him and couldn't understand how he could have treated her so badly after all she had done for him. She had lied to the police for him many times. She gave him her love unconditionally. And she had given him a son.

"I won't let you leave me, Darlene. I want us to be together."

"You don't have any wants as far as I'm concerned."

He walked toward her with a menacing look that she refused to back away from. "I told you in the beginning that you will be my wife 'til death do us part."

"So what are you going to do? Kill me?" she asked with sarcasm. She was scared, but not showing it.

"I love you too much for that, Darlene. I just don't want to lose you," he said, trying to convince her.

"You lost me when you had sex with somebody else. I don't believe in sharing a man. No man with nobody. I don't care if it was a one-night stand."

"I keep telling you I'm sorry. What more do you want?"

"I want you to leave me alone." With that she walked out the bathroom.

Al didn't know what else to do. It seemed like all the wrong things he had done and had said to her in the past years came crashing down around him. He figured one more bad thing wasn't going to hurt. He was a desperate man. And desperate people make bad choices.

Darlene was sitting on the bed when Darryl came in the bedroom and told her he was finished. She told him she would bring him back home in a few minutes then he went back downstairs. That's it, Al thought. He went and kneeled down beside her and held her hands.

"Darlene, please stay with me. I promise I'll never cheat on you or hit you again." He paused. "I'm begging you, baby."

"No," she said, pulling her hands free from his grasp. She didn't care how sincere he was. She had had enough.

Al closed his eyes tight for a few seconds, as if he was contemplating a major decision. Then he opened them and said, "If you don't want your cousin to end up like Vaughn, you'll stay with me." She didn't take what he said seriously for a moment. Then she turned to look at him. "I mean it, Darlene. Don't leave me."

She stood up slowly and he let her. She walked over and stood by the window and stared out. "How could Darryl end up like Vaughn if I leave you?"

"I mean he'll turn up dead."

She turned to face him. He looked like a stranger to her. She couldn't figure out how her leaving him would have anything to do with her cousin ending up dead like Vaughn. "What are you talking about?"

"If you leave me, your cousin's dead body will turn up somewhere just like Vaughn's did."

"But you didn't have anything to do with that," she said.

"I never said that," he said and stood up and walked slowly toward her.

Darlene looked at him. The man approaching her was not the man she married. He was not the man she fell in love with. This was somebody entirely different. Suddenly realization hit her in the face. "You lied to me. You told me you didn't kill him."

"And I didn't. All I did was close the trunk of the car. I didn't put him in there and I didn't put any bullets in him."

"But you were involved. And he would have died anyway. You killed him!" she said the words accusingly.

"And now you know. That makes you an accessory after the fact. And if you divorce me, you will be able to testify against me on anything. And I'm not about to let that happen. I'm not going to jail, Darlene." Darlene's legs seemed to give away beneath her and she slumped down to the floor. Al went and gathered her in his arms. "Darlene, I love you," he said, holding her tight. "And I'm sorry for what happened, but I can't let you leave me." He kissed her on top of her head. "I'll go and bring your cousin home so we can talk and—"

She quickly scrambled out of his arms. "No! I-I-I'll b-bring him myself," she said, wiping at tears that wouldn't stop falling from her face. Al looked down and saw the same fear he had seen on her face before. It was when she had heard about Vaughn's death and was worried that he was involved. He hated himself for what he was doing to her, but he couldn't help it.

"I'm not gonna hurt him. I'll just bring him home. Are you going to be here when I get back?" She nodded. "I won't do anything to him as long as I have you," he said and leaned over to kiss her.

The tears came again. Darlene wished she could just die right then and there. She just sat and cried silently. Al tried to calm her down, but the more he touched her the more she cried. And when he left she was still crying.

Al came back as soon as he dropped Darryl off. He walked in the door and headed upstairs. He heard the baby crying. He went in the room and picked him up. He went in their bedroom to look for Darlene. She was still sitting on the floor in the spot where he had left her. She was just sitting there staring at nothing. No movement. Nothing. He tried to get her to move or say something, but she didn't respond. He called his sister and told her to hurry over. He was waiting at the door when she arrived. They hurried upstairs. They walked in and saw Darlene sitting on the floor.

"What's wrong with her?" Marie asked.

"I don't know. She's just sitting there." Marie went over to Darlene. She kneeled down and talked to her, but she didn't get a response either. She shook her and still didn't get a response.

"What happened? I talked to her this morning and she seemed all right. A little mad though." Al didn't say anything. "I saw you leave with that woman last night."

"You told Darlene about that?" he asked. He would have never thought his sister would do something like that to him.

"No, I didn't tell her."

"Then I wonder who told her," he said.

"You mean to tell me she found out."

"Yeah. And I messed up bad this time."

"Al, tell me you didn't sleep with the woman you left with," Marie almost begged him, but he couldn't say anything. "And you told Darlene?"

"She knew."

"I don't know what to do then," Marie said, looking at Darlene. "Call an ambulance or take her to the hospital. They might be able to help her."

"Take the baby," he said, handing his son to his sister. He sat on the floor next to Darlene and hugged her to him. She still didn't respond. He sat and rocked with her back and forth. Marie left them alone. Al kissed her near her ear. "It's gonna be all right, baby. Dee, I love you so much," he whispered in her ear. "I didn't mean it. I swear to God I didn't mean to have sex with that woman. I was just feeling so useless. I'll make it up to you, baby, I swear. Just don't leave me."

Darlene felt wetness on her hand. She realized it was tears. She knew it couldn't have been tears from her eyes because she was all cried out. She turned to look at Al and saw him crying. That was the first time she had ever seen him cry. She had heard it in his voice before, but this time she actually saw the tears falling from his eyes. He tried wiping them away. Any other time she would have thrown her arms around him and comforted him. But she didn't have anything in her to console him with. She slowly moved out of his embrace and stood up.

"Dee, you okay?"

"Yes, Alvin," she said and walked out the room. She decided that was the last time she would ever call him Alvin.

Marie looked up when Darlene walked into the living room. She walked over and retrieved her son from Marie then she went into the kitchen.

Al came downstairs a few minutes later. He went into the kitchen also. Marie was sitting at the table watching Darlene who was holding her son in one arm while she looked in the refrigerator for something to eat. She couldn't find what she wanted. She took the phone directory out of one of the kitchen drawers and ordered a large pizza. She was acting as if no one else was in the room.

"Darlene, are you okay?" Marie asked.

"Yes. You're welcome to stay and have some pizza," Darlene told her invitingly.

"No thanks. I have to get back home. I'll call you later, okay?" Marie said, rising from the table.

"Okay."

Once she left, Al tried to hug Darlene. And that was all he did. Tried. She pushed him away. "I'll stay married to you, but that's about as far as it goes. If you want to hug, kiss, or have sex, go somewhere else," she said and walked away from him. She sat in the living room and patiently waited for her pizza to arrive.

She laid the baby down on a blanket Marie had brought down from his room. She was playing with her son when the doorbell sounded. She got up and answered the door. Al was approaching with money to pay for the pizza. She paid the delivery guy with a twenty-dollar bill and closed the door, leaving him a nice tip.

"I was about to pay for the pizza, Dee," he said.

"I don't want you buying me anything," she said and carried the pizza to the kitchen where she put a couple of slices on a plate and returned to the living room.

"Don't be like this, Dee. I want us to be the way we used to be."

"That's not possible. You made your choice last night. Now you have to live with it because I have lived with mine and I will keep on living with mine."

He didn't say anything. He just left.

The next couple of weeks were hell for Al. It was like living in the house with a stranger. Darlene wouldn't talk to him unless he said something to her. She wouldn't even sit down and eat with him. At least she still cooked. He had food to eat. But that was only when she didn't eat out. And he also had clean clothes. She was acting like a live-in maid. She slept in the other bedroom or sometimes she'd drag the padding from her futon chair in the den and slept in the room with the baby.

Al couldn't take it one night. He went into the other bedroom where she was sleeping. He climbed in bed with her and started caressing her breasts and she moaned. Then he raised up her nightgown. That woke her up. "Get away from me," she said in a cold voice.

"No, Dee. I want some," he said.

"I don't care if you do. You could have AIDS or some other disease as far as I know."

Al knew she could be right so he just backed off the bed and left.

Darlene returned to work the following week. She was eager to get back to work. She was tired of sitting at home. She started rescheduling her usually meal appointments, except she only saw them for lunch. Any evening appointments were done from her home office. They were very eager to see her so it didn't matter. She also had a lot of calls about filing income taxes again.

Darlene had made a lot of changes since her confrontation with Al. She got a safe deposit box at the bank where she had her separate checking account. She took all of her important papers and put them in there. She even had a will made out. She put money and jewelry away in a different safe deposit box. She didn't want to wear anything Al had bought her, except her wedding rings, which he said she had to wear. She had offered to give the rest of the jewelry back to him, but he didn't want it. She stopped using the credit cards he had given her. If she bought something, it was bought with cash or a check from her personal accounts. She stopped depositing her checks from her job into their joint checking account. Al noticed how things were changing. He used to like paying the credit cards bills because he knew he was taking care of his wife. But now all he did was pay household bills. He was taking care of a house. He knew he should just let her go, but he couldn't. He decided to do something he hoped would make her happy. He had gotten another life insurance policy. This time it was for a million dollars with her and their son as beneficiaries. He even put it in an envelope with a ribbon around it. He was taking her out for Valentine's Day. He had sent a dozen roses to her at work and had offered to take her to lunch, but she was working through lunch so he suggested dinner.

Al had arranged for her aunt to watch the baby. He made reservations at a really nice restaurant for the evening. She had to work late and would meet him there. He didn't say anything. He just agreed.

Darlene had managed to come home late almost every night since she'd been back at work. Sometimes she was working. Usually she and the baby would stop by her aunt or stop and get something to eat. She really didn't want to have any contact with Al. And when she got home she would bathe the baby and then she would take a bath when she got him to sleep. And that hardly left any time for Al. She was glad he didn't come to her at night anymore.

Al was waiting patiently for Darlene to show up. She dropped the baby off at her aunt's house then headed for the restaurant. Al saw her walking toward him. It seemed to him that she was getting prettier by the day. Usually after a woman had a baby she got out of shape. But not Darlene. She was more beautiful and sexy than she was before. And he noticed a few heads turn when she walked past people. At one time he felt proud to know she could turn so many heads because she was all his. She was still all his, but not willingly. And that ate at him everyday.

Darlene didn't smile as she approached the table. Al helped her with her chair. A waiter came by and took their dinner order. Al ordered shrimp cocktails and steak and lobster for the both of them. Darlene didn't object. He reached into his coat pocket and handed her an envelope. She opened it and saw the policy. She read over it and then placed it back in the envelope and laid it on the table as if it was nothing important. She didn't give Al the reaction he was expecting so he didn't know what to do then. He made small talk and asked her about work. Their food came and they ate in virtual silence.

He took it upon himself to order dessert. It was strawberry cheesecake. This time he watched as she ate. Maybe it was because he hadn't made love to her in so long, but he was enjoying watching her lips. Darlene glanced at him and saw him looking at her. It was the same way her weekly lunch companions looked at her. She decided to try something out on Al. She deliberately ate sensual, letting her lips linger around the fork longer than necessary and removing the fork slowly then licking her lips slower. And she saw a change in the way Al was watching her. She figured if she could get that reaction out of her husband, she could get it out of the other men. And the more they wanted to see her, the more money she would make.

They left the restaurant in separate cars. Al suggested leaving her car and they ride together, but she didn't want to ride with him. She didn't tell him that though. She said she had work in her car she had to do that night. She walked off before he could give a rebuttal.

The baby was asleep when Darlene picked him up. She loaded all of his things in the car before she carried him out to the car. While she was strapping him in the car seat, she saw Al's car pull up beside hers. She walked around to the driver side of her car.

He rolled the passenger side window down and leaned over to talk to her. "I have to take care of some business tonight. I'll be home later," he told her.

"Sure."

"Darlene. It's business. I swear. Nothing else."

"Whatever you say," she said, opening the car door.

"I love you," he said. Darlene had gotten in the car and he didn't know if she heard him or not. He just drove off.

Darlene sat in the car a few minutes before she started it up. How could he tell her he loved her? He doesn't know the meaning of the word. And she was mad with herself because deep down, she still loved him. He had given her a son who was very precious to her. She knew she hadn't been ready to have a baby, but she was glad she did. And she knew she couldn't turn off her feelings for Al like a light switch. Although she wished she could.

When Darlene arrived at home, the baby was awake. She changed into a pair of jeans and a T-shirt. She feed him then brought him to the den with her and sat him in his swing while she did some work. The telephone rang and she went to answer it.

"Hello?"

"Hello, Darlene." The voice on the other end said.

"Who is this?" she asked not recognizing the voice.

"Vincent."

"Oh, hi. How did you get my number?"

"Somebody gave it to me. They told me they knew this fine lady who does income taxes," he said. He didn't tell her that the guy who told him about her said a lot of other guys went to her and tried to make a play for her.

"Oh. Well, I do it for a few people," she told him.

"I'd like to see you."

"Sure. When?"

"How about now?"

"Now?" she asked.

"Yeah. I can be over in twenty minutes," he told her. She looked at the clock and saw it wasn't quite nine o'clock yet.

"Okay, but I won't be able to start on them tonight," she told him.

"All right. I'll see you later," he said and hung up.

Darlene went into the living room and straightened up a little. When she went upstairs to put the baby in his crib, she brought down the cushion for the futon sofa. She got the monitor out of the bedroom and took it to the den so she could hear the baby if he cried.

She answered the door when the doorbell sounded. Vincent stood in her doorway looking as handsome as ever. She showed him in and led him to the den.

Once they entered the den, he closed the door behind them then followed her to where the computer was set up. She took a seat in the swivel chair and he sat in the folding chair.

Darlene took out different tax forms. She really didn't know that much about him. She had just assumed he wasn't married. She didn't know whether he was separated, divorced or if he had any children.

Well, she'd find all that out once she filed his taxes for him.

"Which tax form do you usually file?"

"I'm not here tonight for you to do my taxes," he said.

"Then why are you here?" she asked without a clue.

"I told you I wanted to see you. And since it's been a while since your husband left—" His words were cut off by the opening and closing of the front door. "Who's that?" Vincent asked.

"Al."

"You're still with him?" She nodded "After what he did to you?"

"A lot has happened since then. I can't go into it, but things are different between us now," she said, hoping he would understand since he always seemed to in the past.

"Different how?"

"I just can't leave him," she said and put her head down. Not in a stand-by-your-man sort of way, but in a trapped way. And Vincent picked up on it.

He leaned forward and looked at her closely. Their faces were only a few inches apart. He placed his hand under her chin and tilted her face up. "What did he do to you?" She looked up at him with tears in her eyes. And it would look like they were about to kiss or had just finished to anyone else. Just then the door to the den opened.

Al had been doing business with some new people. These were people Jeff didn't have any knowledge of. He had been working with them for months now. And he had just finished a deal. A big score. It wasn't fair, but life wasn't fair either. He wanted to surprise Darlene with what he had for her. He walked in the house looking for her. When he didn't find her anywhere upstairs, he checked the den. He was expecting to see her working. Alone. He didn't like it one bit that she was in the room with another man. The same man who always seemed to be with her when he should be with her. He just stood there looking at his wife. Then he walked away leaving the door opened.

"I think you should leave. I'll call you tomorrow and set up a time for you to come by," she said.

Vincent stood to leave. But before she walked off, he pulled her by her hand, tugging her toward him. In her ear he whispered, "You can call me whenever you need me." Then he kissed her softly near her ear.

She walked him to the door and he left. She went back to the den and retrieved the monitor and headed upstairs.

Al was in the bathroom getting ready for bed when he heard Darlene out in their bedroom. He walked out only wearing a towel. She was getting her nightgown and panties from her dresser.

"I guess what's good for the goose is good for the gander," he said sarcastically.

"Don't judge me by your standards. I'm not sleeping with him or anybody else unlike you," she said not looking at him. "But hey, I gave you permission to sleep around." Then she left the room.

As the months passed, things started getting worse. Al would come home late every night. That's if he came home at all. Darlene didn't know where he was and she didn't care. She would talk to Marie sometimes. Marie was very worried about her brother. He had been missing work a day or two a week. Darlene didn't know anything about it. She also told Darlene that Jeff wasn't doing too much of the other business anymore and he had tried to get Al to cut down.

Crystal called and invited Darlene and Al to a club one Friday night and she accepted. She had become a friend with her neighbors and she used their teenage daughter as a baby-sitter.

Darlene arrived at the club and immediately found her cousins. They asked about Al and she lied and told them that he had to work late. The truth of the matter was that she hadn't talked to him about them going out.

Darlene saw a few people she knew. Some were associates of Al's and the others were people she had met. They were all interested in seeing her and promised to call. A few of them were standing around talking to her when Al walked in the club. And he wasn't alone. Darlene tried to pretend like she didn't see him so she kept talking to the men around her. She glanced over in Al's direction and saw him looking directly at her. But when she saw a woman walk up and hug up on him, she left the men she was talking with. She told her cousin she was leaving. They asked why, but then she saw Al walking toward them.

"What are you doing here?" he asked, looking at her, but she didn't answer him. He pulled her toward him roughly. "What are you doing here?" he asked again.

Crystal stood up. "Darlene, what's wrong?" she asked concerned for her cousin.

"Nothing," she said.

Then the woman that was with Al walked up and said, "Come on, Al. Everybody's waiting."

Al leaned over and whispered in Darlene's ear, "It's only business. I'll see you at home." Then he left with the woman.

"What was that all about?" Crystal asked.

"I don't know. I'm going home." She walked away leaving her cousin.

Darlene had almost made it to her car when Al caught up to her and stopped her.

"What the hell were you doing here with those men?"

"They are associates of yours. It was business. And I wasn't here with them. I was here with Crystal and Carl. They invited the both of us," she said.

"I don't want you coming here again. I do a lot of business here."

"I didn't see Jeff," she said.

"This doesn't concern Jeff. So go home," he ordered.

"I'm not going home," she said, but she wasn't expecting him the grabbed her so forcefully.

He spun her around to face him and demanded, "Where are you going then?"

"Wherever I want to," she said and snatched her arm from him. A few people that were entering the club were watching.

"When will you be home?"

"I don't know," she said and walked off.

"How's Darryl these days?" he asked and Darlene stopped in her tracks. They mention of her cousin's name brought back everything. "Now, when will you be home?"

"Sunday. I need some time alone."

"Just as long as you be there Sunday," he said and turned and walked back to his business dealings.

Darlene went to her car. She was having trouble finding her keys in her purse because she was crying and couldn't see through her tears. Then she heard someone walk up behind her. She thought it was Al.

"Don't worry. I said I'll be home Sunday."

"I'm not worried about that," Vincent said. She turned to look at him. "What happened? I saw you and Al arguing as I was driving up."

"Nothing," she said and finally found her keys. "I just need to get away for a couple of days."

"Get away where?" he asked.

"A hotel I've stayed at before. I have to get my son and pack a few things."

"I'll follow you home," he said and headed back to his truck.

Darlene drove up in her driveway with Vincent seconds behind her. She got out of her car and he his truck. She paid the baby-sitter and thanked her. Vincent took a seat on the sofa while Darlene went upstairs and threw a few clothes in a bag. She packed diapers, cans of formula, and clothes in the duffel bag for the baby. She grabbed the baby's diaper bag and car seat. She put the baby in the car seat and walked out the door. Vincent carried the bags for her to the car. He followed her to a hotel that wasn't far away from her house. He watched as she went and checked in. He followed her to where the room was and helped her carry her things inside. He took a seat in a chair at the table while she laid the sleeping baby in the bed. He was wondering why would she stay with a man she had to get away from. Maybe she was leaving her husband, he thought. He had to know.

"Are you leaving him for good?" he asked after she moved from the bed.

"No."

"Why not?"

"Because I can't."

He stood up and went to her and said, "What do you mean you can't? Just leave him."

"I appreciate everything you've done, Vincent. It's just not that simple."

"Well, when it is that simple, give me a call," he said and turned to leave the room, but stopped. He turned back and pulled her into his arms and kissed her. She didn't stop him. She needed to be wanted and she melted in his arms and the kiss became heated. Her body was crying out for her to have sex with Vincent, but her mind was telling her not to risk it. And when his hand cupped her bottom and pressed her against his arousal she almost gave in to what her body wanted. But she couldn't let things go any further. She liked him too much as a friend so she ended the kiss.

"I really wish things could have been different," she told him with her head lying on his chest.

"Maybe if I would have wanted you more that first time we met it would have been," he said and released her. "Good-bye, Darlene," he said and walked out the room.

Darlene spent Saturday and almost all of Sunday in total peace. She was happy. But it only lasted until she got home. She stayed at the hotel until nine o'clock that night. Al greeted her as soon as she drove up. He helped her get the baby's things out the car and carried them into the house.

"Did you enjoy yourself?"

"Yes."

"Did you have any company?" he asked.

"No, Al. Just me and the baby stayed there."

"Why don't you go upstairs and go to bed," he suggested. She didn't argue. She just went up with the baby.

Al came up a few minutes later. He wanted to try and explain the things that had happened. He took a shower since she seemed to be interested in what was on TV. He came out wearing only a towel. He went and sat on the edge of the bed.

"About the other night. I'm sorry," he said to her. "Those guys don't know that I'm married and I would like to keep it that way. I don't want them anywhere near you and Jamal."

"Uh-huh," she said, getting ready for bed.

"I'm serious." Al walked up behind her and put his arms around her waist and pulled her against him.

Darlene slammed the drawer closed and saw his reflection in the mirror.

"Stop it, Al."

"How come you don't call me Alvin no more?" he asked and started kissing her on the nape of her neck.

"Because he's gone," she said.

Al turned her around to face him and that caused the towel to fall. He framed her face with his hands and said, “Baby, he’s right here.” Then he kissed her long and hard. “I want you so bad tonight. I’ve been thinking about making love to you for months,” he said. He slid his hands under her shirt and unclasped her bra and started massaged her breasts. Darlene couldn’t help responding. She had gone without sex for months. And Al knew how to arouse her. She forgot about everything for the moment. She wanted satisfaction. And he was there to give it to her.

Al led her to the bed. He took off her clothes and got in bed with her. He felt how wet she was. She had never been so wet for him. He joined them and things just stopped. He slipped in so easily. Too easy. Mentally he was seeing how wide she was and his erection went down and he rolled off her.

Darlene was so humiliated at that moment she started crying and ran to the bathroom. She hurriedly douched and took a shower. She tried to wash away the feel of him on her skin. How could she be so stupid? She didn’t even think to tell him to use protection. She could probably have some disease. She had to get away from him. If only for a few more days. She just had to leave.

Al was miserable. He couldn’t understand how he could stay hard for some other woman, but he couldn’t for his wife. After all that had happened between them in the past months, she was finally willing to make love to him. And what happened? He messed it up. There was only one way he knew that he could make her happy. He wrote a short note to her and left it on the bed with an envelope. Then he got dressed and left.

Chapter twenty three

Darlene came out of the bathroom a half an hour later and she didn't see Al. She put on her nightgown and panties and sat on the bed. That's when she noticed the letter and the envelope. She picked up the envelope first. It was filled with money, twenties, fifties, and hundreds. She couldn't begin to guess at how much was actually inside. But an off-hand guess put it somewhere in the thousands. She read the note.

> Dee,
>
> I'm sorry for what I did. You don't know how much it hurts me for things to be the way they are right now. I'll leave. I won't divorce you, but I'll leave the house. The money is for you and Jamal. It's ten thousand dollars. I'll get my things another time.
>
> I'll always love you,
>
> Alvin

Darlene cried after she read the letter. She really did love him. But too much had happened. She just got in bed and went to sleep.

Al checked into a hotel after he left home. He didn't know where else to go. His whole life was with his wife and son, but he didn't have them anymore. He felt he didn't have anything else to live for. He moved his clothes out of the house the following weekend. He didn't want to take anything else. He moved into a furnished one-bedroom apartment. He still wanted to come over to see his son and Darlene allowed him to come over whenever he wanted to. He also continued to pay the mortgage although she protested.

Marie called Darlene when Al told her he had moved out. She tried to get Darlene to talk about what happened, but she wouldn't. Marie had been seeing the way her brother was living. He had quit his job at the car dealership and she was worried about him.

Crystal had called Darlene a few times, because she had seen and people had told her that they had seen Al in clubs with other women. All Darlene told her cousin was that they were separated.

Darlene was at least glad to see Darryl. She really didn't want him anywhere near Al, but she couldn't tell him that. Darryl had seen Al at a club hugged up with some woman and confronted him. Al didn't like the way Darryl confronted him. Plus he was doing business at the time. And Darryl would have let it be known that he was married. They stepped outside and Darryl took a swing at Al, but he missed. Al told Darryl to go have a talk with Darlene.

That same night Darryl went to talk to her. He was angry. He knocked repeatedly on the door. Darlene was wondering who could be knocking on her door so late. She opened the door and found Darryl standing there looking like he'd just had a fight.

"What happened to you?" she asked, opening the door wider so he could come in.

"Don't you know Al is at some club with some woman?"

"So."

"So? Is that all you have to say?"

"Al can do what he wants to do."

"You don't care?"

"No."

"Then you should leave him. Divorce him. Something."

"I can't," she said and walked to the living room.

"Why can't you? I'll help you leave him, Darlene."

"I can't, Darryl."

"I don't understand you. You know he's messing around on you and you won't leave him. What happened to you? He got you strung-out on drugs or something?"

That remark hurt Darlene more than he would ever know. She was only staying with Al in order to spare his life and he was thinking she was a dope head.

"I don't take drugs, Darryl. And Al has never tried to give me any."

"Well, if you can't leave him, I'll make him leave you," he said and got up to leave. "I'll show him he can't treat you any kind of way."

That's when a new fear hit Darlene. She didn't want Darryl to provoke Al in any way. Darlene got up and ran after Darryl. She grabbed his arm just as he reached the door. "Darryl go back to school. I'll give you money to stay in a hotel until your classes start. Just leave."

"Come back with me, Darlene. You can get a job somewhere else."

"I can't."

"*Why?!*" he yelled.

She felt she didn't have any choice but to tell her cousin. "If I leave Al, he'll kill you," she said and started crying. It took a while for what Darlene said to sink in. Darryl stood there and looked down at her. "He told me he would kill you if I ever left him."

"And that's why you won't leave him?"

"Yes." Darryl paced and cursed at the same time. He felt responsible for his cousin's situation. "It's not that bad," Darlene said. "He's moved out. I just can't divorce him. I could live with the stares I get from people and the talking behind my back. I just couldn't live with him killing you. So please stay away from him."

"Okay, Darlene. I'll be going back to school in a week anyway. I'll keep in touch." He hugged his cousin and left.

When the summer was almost over, Darlene had hardly seen Al. She had been seeing him a few times a week, but that had stopped. He would call her often though. Then one Friday night he came by the house at about midnight.

Darlene was asleep and woke up when she heard the bedroom door open and close. She jumped up and grabbed the clock and threw it at the intruder.

"It's me, Darlene," Al said. "Al." She sat up and turned on the lamp sitting on her nightstand.

"What are you doing here?" she asked.

"I had to see you," he said and walked over to the bed. "Dee, I miss you so much, baby."

"What do you want, Al?" she asked.

"Can I stay here with you tonight?"

"Why?" she asked not liking what she was hearing.

"Please don't ask why because you don't wanna know. I'll give you a divorce if that's what you still want," he said. "I just can't go to my apartment tonight and I need a place to stay."

Darlene just looked at him and wondered what had he gotten himself into. It had to be serious, she thought, because he had been giving her money every time he visited her and the baby. Large amounts. Nothing under a thousand dollars each visit. She never asked any questions. But there was something different about him now.

"Okay. You can stay," she said and got out of bed.

"Where are you going?" he asked.

"To get something to drink," she said and walked out the door.

Darlene had an uneasy feeling. She didn't know if it had anything to do with her or Al. She went back to her bedroom after she had a drink of water. Al was lying in her bed.

"Why are you in my bed, Al?"

"Just this one night can you call me Alvin?"

"What difference would it make?" she said, walking around to her side of the bed.

"It would make a difference to me. I just want this one night to be like it used to be," he said.

"It can't."

"Just lay with me. Please, Dee. That's all I ask." She didn't see any harm in that request. When she got back in bed, she laid with her back to him. A lot of good that did. Al started talking about their past. Soon she was talking and laughing with him. Then he started talking about their wedding day. Darlene's eyes blurred with tears and she got silent. Al turned to her and said, "Baby, if I could take back what I did I would. You are the most important person in my life," he said and pulled her on top of him and hugged her. "I love you so much," he said then he started kissing her and she felt his erection. He rolled her over and pulled her gown up to expose her breasts. Her nipples harden instantly. He removed her panties and soon they were joined. Darlene started crying. "Shhh. It's all right, baby. I won't hurt you. I don't have anything. I'm clean. And I haven't been with anyone unprotected," he said and thrust within her. "I needed to make love to you one more time, Dee, to know that you love me," he said and kissed her again. Al didn't lose his erection this time. In fact, he stayed hard longer than he ever had. Darlene climaxed over and over before he finally did.

She woke up in Al's arms. Her movements woke him up. "Good morning," he said. She looked at him and turned to get out of bed. "Just lay here with me. Please, Dee," he said, holding on to her arm.

"Why did you have to come here?" she asked him. She had finally put her feelings for him away. And now she felt like she would have to start all over again.

"I had to give you something," he said. He got out of bed and retrieved his pants. He came back with two keys. "Listen to me, Dee. These are keys to lockers at the bus station. If something happens to me within the next few days, go and get what's in them."

"What?"

"Just do it, Dee. I'm gonna get dressed and leave. That's after I see Jamal." He got out of the bed and left. Darlene laid in bed in a daze. She couldn't have heard what she thought she heard. Was he trying to say that he was going to die soon? She jumped out of bed and ran to the other bedroom.

Al was standing over his son's bed looking down at him. He turned when he heard her enter the room. "He's handsome. And so big now," he said, looking at her in the doorway. He hadn't seen his son in a month. "He still looks just like you. I don't see anything of me in him," he said.

Darlene walked over and stood beside him. She pulled the thin blanket from over the baby. He was only wearing a T-shirt and diaper. "He has your bowlegs," she told Al and he smiled.

"I love you so much, Dee. Sometimes I think it was too much." He turned and looked at her. "I never would have hurt you cousin." She looked up at him. "I just thought that was the only way I could get you to stay with me. And it worked. I just messed up everything after that." He pulled her into his arms. "I love you, Darlene. You and Jamal were my life."

"I love you, too . . . Alvin," she said and felt him hold her tighter.

"I gotta go. Take care of our son." He walked away and soon left the house.

Darlene was relieved that after the next two days she heard from Al and she knew he was all right. He still wanted her to hold on to the keys with instructions that if a day went by and he didn't call her, she was to go to the lockers. Or if he called and told her to go to the lockers, she was to go there as soon as possible. Darlene didn't like what was going on. She wanted Al to explain, but he wouldn't. He told her everything would be explained when she retrieved the bags.

Darlene was scared for Al. She called Marie and told her what was going on. She didn't know what Al could have gotten involved in. Jeff had all together left that aspect of his business alone. He still knew some people and checked around to see what he could find out.

Weeks passed and no one had seen Al. He still called Darlene everyday. If he didn't talk to her he left a message on her answering machine. Then one time he called and wanted her to get the bags and meet him somewhere and to bring the baby. She was scared, but she did it. She was feeling paranoid while she walked through the bus station. She carried the baby in her arms because she didn't know how big the bags would be and she didn't want to have to struggle with the baby stroller. It wasn't long before she found the two lockers. She looked around to make sure no one was watching her. She retrieved the bags and went back to her car. They were two canvas gym bags. They weren't that heavy. Once she got in her car, she wanted to know what was in the bags, but she was too scared to open them.

Al was waiting for her at a run-down motel. He had been living in and out of motels for a month or so. He never stayed in one place for more than a few days. He was watching out the window for Darlene's car. As soon as she drove up, he opened the door and waved her in. She picked up the bags and the baby and went inside. Al closed the door quickly. He pulled her and the baby in his arms and said, "I'm so glad you're all right." And he was. He didn't want anything to happen to her. But the people he was dealing with now wouldn't hesitate to kill her or their son to get to him, especially after what he had done. He was desperate and that's why he involved her in the first place. And he was doing it for her and his son.

Darlene pulled out of his embrace. "What's going on, Alvin?" she asked, taking in his appearance for the first time. She hadn't seen him in months. He looked awful. He had lost weight and his clothes were wrinkled and he looked as if he hadn't had his hair cut in weeks. "What's happened to you?"

"I'll explain later," he said and went to the bags. He dumped out the contents of one bag on the bed. There was a lot of money in it in nice stacks held together with rubber bands and inside plastic bags. There must have been about one hundred bags. The other bag was filled with jewelry. There were watches, rings, bracelets, pendants, earrings and necklaces. All in gold, diamonds, rubies, and pearls. But mostly diamonds and gold. Darlene looked from the bed to Al. He saw the shocked expression on her face.

"You always wanted me to leave drugs alone. So I did," he said, attempting humor. Darlene didn't respond. All she did was stare at the jewelry. "Listen, Dee. And listen carefully. There's a half a million dollars in untraceable cash here. And this jewelry is worth three times as much. I want you to take it and put it somewhere safe. Check the back of the dresser I used at home. There are three keys for safe deposit boxes at your bank. I have important papers in them for you and Jamal." Darlene looked at him and started shaking her head. She was scared. "Baby, please. I want you and Jamal to move away from here. Take your cousin with you, too, if you want." He took the baby from her and she sat down on the bed. "The people I deal with don't know about you. And if they find out, tell them we were separated in the process of getting a divorce. Tell them how much you hated me and that you're glad I'm dead." At that remark, she looked at him. "Whenever that may happen," he said to avoid her from going into possible hysterics. "I know you're a smart woman. You'll know how to handle the money. You won't get hassled from the cops because you'll be getting a million and a half dollars from the insurance policies." She started crying and so did the baby. He pulled her to him. "Shhh, baby. Don't cry. I just went downhill after I messed up with you. I tried to leave drugs alone for you, but then I got involved with these other people and the money was so easy to get."

Al had gotten involved with guys that robbed banks and jewelry stores. It wasn't that risky because they were always working with someone on the inside so they had easy access.

"I got in over my head. But I want you and my son to never want for anything as long you live." Darlene sat there in his arms. She didn't know what to do or say. The man who came into her life three short years ago would in all probability be leaving her. She didn't realize how much she still loved him.

"Why can't you come with us?" she asked and he handed her the baby and stood up with his back to her. "You gave up drugs for me. Why can't you give this up and go away with me?"

"Because I can't. I won't risk you and Jamal. This is the only way I see that I can make up for what I put you through this past year. Now if you love me you'll do what I say. File for a divorce first thing in the morning. Put the money and jewelry somewhere safe. Not in the house because it might get searched. And once I'm dead and gone, you go and start a life somewhere else. You and Jamal." He turned to face her. "Don't ever get involved with somebody like me. And please keep my son away from drugs. Marie has a policy on me. Make sure she has it handy. Tell her I'll call her. Oh God, Dee, I love you so much."

"I love you, too, Alvin," Darlene said. She stood up with the baby and went to him.

"I'm so sorry to put you through this." The three of them stood there silently for a while. He held her in his arms and kissed her lovingly. Then he kissed his son on the forehead.

Weeks went by and Darlene only heard from Al by phone. She had done everything he had told her to. Al had all kinds of stock certificates and bonds in the safe deposit boxes mostly in her and Jamal's name. A few were in his sister and niece's name. One of the boxes had a cashier's check in it for one hundred thousand dollars with instructions for her to cash it the same day.

Marie was worried out of her mind about him. Jeff had called a few of his contacts, but he couldn't find out anything. All he knew was that Al had gotten involved with some new people he didn't know anything about. And the word on the street was that they were dangerous and had a contract out on Al's life.

Then it happened. A knock on the door one night. Two policemen came and told Darlene that Al was found dead. They found her address on his driver's license. They needed her to identify the body. She only stood there for a moment. She didn't move. The policeman offered to call someone for her and she gave him Marie and Jeff's home number. They were at her house in minutes.

Al had been found dead from a bullet wound to the head. The bullet entered through his forehead at point blank range. His mouth was taped and his wrists and ankles were tied. He wasn't found at the same motel she had met him at before. And although she knew this day would come, she still didn't believe Al was dead. She fainted after she saw his body. When she and Jeff got back to the house, the police was questioning Marie. Darlene answered all the questions they had. She really couldn't tell them anything because she hadn't seen Al in months.

Darlene had a one-day funeral service for Al. Her aunt kept her son. She sat on the front pew with Darryl, Marie, and Jeff. She saw a few familiar faces. She noticed two white men watching her closely. She even saw a few women practically throwing themselves at the casket crying for Al.

When it was time for them to say their last goodbye, Darlene let Marie and Jeff go first. Darryl was even a little teary eyed. She had explained to him that Al wouldn't have killed him. That he only said it to get her to stay with him. Darryl wasn't a hundred percent forgiving, but he did like the way Al had provided financially for Darlene and Jamal. She hadn't told Darryl about the other money. He only knew about the money from the insurance policies. Marie had a twenty-five thousand-dollar life insurance policy on her brother. She had offered to help Darlene with the funeral expenses, but Darlene told her to keep every cent. She paid for Al's funeral. She assured Marie and Jeff that Al had provided for her and Jamal's future.

A lot of people offered Darlene their condolences. She was pleased that so many people had showed up. She got up to say goodbye to Al before they went to the cemetery. Darryl led her to her husband. On their way outside to get in the limousine, the two men who had been watching her stopped them.

"Excuse us, Mrs. Williams. We were associates of your husband's and we would like to ask you a few questions."

"Can't you see she's grieving," Darryl spoke up.

"We can see that," one of them answered.

If these men were who she thought they were, she didn't want Darryl to provoke them.

"It's okay, Darryl. I'll hear what they have to say."

"In private," the other one said.

"Go on to the car, Darryl," she told him.

The men waited until they were practically alone before one said, "It appeared that your husband had some things that didn't belong to him. And we were wondering if you had any idea of where those things may be. You being his wife and all."

"We didn't know he was married," the other one said.

This was it she thought. She would do this last thing for her husband. Be his last alibi. "Al and I were separated for almost a year. We were in the process of getting a divorce, but as you can see I was widowed first. I haven't seen nor heard from him in almost a year. So if you need to know anything about him you can check out the apartment he was living in or the women he was with. But I can't help you with anything. I'm just glad he's out of my life for good. Anything else, gentlemen?" she asked, looking at the two men.

"No. I guess the location of what we're looking for is dead and buried with your husband."

"Sorry about that. If you'll excuse me, I'd like to get him in the ground as soon as possible."

"Sure. Sorry to have bothered you," they said and walked off.

Darryl had come back to see what was taking her so long. He overheard most of the conversation. "What was that all about? I didn't know you and Al were getting a divorce."

"It's a long story. I'll tell you about it later. Let's go to the cemetery."

Darlene wanted to move right away. She explained to Darryl about how things went with Al on her last time seeing him. He understood and was willing to do whatever she wanted to do. She had talked to her supervisor about getting a transfer to another branch. And it just so happened there was an opening in their home office branch in a neighboring state. She looked into buying a larger house where her and her son would live. She paid off her house and gave it to Crystal and Carl. Her aunt stayed there with them. Darryl didn't want to stay there. He was willing to move with Darlene.

Before she moved, Vincent came by and offered his condolences. She would always be grateful for his friendship. But she didn't want to get involved with anyone now. She had a new lease on life thanks to her husband.

In life there are choices made everyday. In three short years, Darlene's life had changed drastically due to the choices she made. She became a wife, a mother, and a widow. She had loved and she had lost. She was a little older and a lot wiser. And she owed it all to her late husband. But now she has a life of her own. And thanks to her late husband it is a life she will live extremely wealthy. She would have much preferred to live it with her husband, but the choices in life determine the outcomes of life. Ultimately those choices can lead to either life or death.

About the Author

Karen Jamison is a native of New Orleans, LA. She graduated from Booker T. Washington High School in 1984 and Dillard University in 1989. She is an Army wife with two children. She married her college sweetheart and has traveled with the Army since 1989 all over the United States and overseas.

She has been writing for eight years. Within those years she has received an Editor's Choice Award presented for outstanding achievement in poetry by The National Library of Poetry in which she has a poem published in their anthology title The Peace We Knew. She has had six articles published in the post newspaper Fort Leavenworth Lamp in Fort Leavenworth, KS.

Printed in the United States
99102LV00003B/137/A